"Robbins's dialogue is moving. . . . His people have the warmth of life."
—*The New York Times*

"Robbins has the ability to hold his readers absorbed."
—*Chicago Tribune*

"His characters are compelling, his dialogue is dramatic, and his style is simple and straightforward." —*Los Angeles Times*

"International settings . . . steamy sex scenes."
—*Romantic Times BOOKreviews* on *The Betrayers*

"Robbins's literary legacy remains very much alive, and his thousands of fans should experience a pleasant sense of déjà vu as they race through this latest installment."
—*Publishers Weekly* on *Heat of Passion*

"Robbins's sixth posthumous novel finds new cowriter Podrug outwriting the hormonal ghost. . . . Podrug's strong, crisp style excels." —*Kirkus Reviews* on *The Betrayers*

"Robbins fans will not be disappointed in this latest book."
—*Booklist* on *The Betrayers*

"Splendid pulp . . . stunningly well-written."
—*Kirkus Reviews* on *Heat of Passion*

HAROLD ROBBINS
AND JUNIUS PODRUG

The DEVIL TO Pay

FORGE®

A TOM DOHERTY ASSOCIATES BOOK
NEW YORK

This is a work of fiction. All of the characters, organizations, and events portrayed in this novel are either products of the authors' imagination or are used fictitiously.

THE DEVIL TO PAY

A Forge Book
Published by Tom Doherty Associates, LLC
175 Fifth Avenue
New York, NY 10010

www.tor-forge.com

Forge® is a registered trademark of Tom Doherty Associates, LLC.

ISBN-13: 978-0-7653-5008-4
ISBN-10: 0-7653-5008-4

First Edition: September 2006
First Mass Market Edition: September 2007

Printed in the United States of America

0 9 8 7 6 5 4 3 2 1

For

Jann Robbins,

keeper of the flame

Acknowledgments

The efforts of people who assisted in the preparation of this book are appreciated. They include Bob Gleason, Eric Raab, Elizabeth Winick, Hilda Krische, Robert Rees, and Barbara Wild. Also, Chuck Coffman and John Parks of Armeno Coffee Roasters, Ltd., were generous in explaining the techniques of roasting and cupping coffee. Any errors in describing the techniques are solely of my making.

Harold Robbins
left behind a rich heritage of novel ideas
and works in progress when he passed away in 1997.
Harold Robbins's estate and his editor worked with
a carefully selected writer to organize and complete
Harold Robbins's ideas to create this novel,
inspired by his storytelling brilliance,
in a manner faithful to
the Robbins style.

❖

Seattle, 1993

Coffee Capital of America

Coffee should be black as hell, strong as death, and sweet as love.

—TURKISH PROVERB

1

❖

Decaf Latte with Low-Fat Milk and Artificial Sweetener

"I've inherited what?"

I stared in disbelief at the man who had just told me I had
come into an inheritance. Behind me, my coffee and muffin
store—Café de Oro, an Urban Coffee Plantation—was in
ashes . . . literally.

An explosion had destroyed not only my business but my
financial vision for the future. Worse than the loss of my shop
and the damage to adjoining buildings, one of my employees
was dead. I hardly knew the victim, a Chinese emigrant
named Johnny Woo who had worked for me for a couple
weeks. Not a very agreeable type, but I'm sure someone
somewhere loved him.

A leaky gas line was the probable cause, a fireman told me.
I had gone into the smoldering rubble against the shouts of
firemen to find the cash box that held my weekend receipts and
a vitally important document. I came out empty-handed except
for a coating of gray-black ash, smoke in my eyes and lungs,
and a charcoal face streaked with tears that erupted when I
found out my business was gone and an employee dead.

As I came half-blind and stunned out of the debris, this suit with a Gucci briefcase and well-fed face was waiting to tell me I'd come into an inheritance. A bad joke on a day my dream went up in smoke and someone died.

"Screw off," I said. That wasn't the way I usually talked, although by today's standards of thirty-one-year-old women it was pretty mild. But with my business trashed, an employee dead, and the owners of adjoining businesses no doubt already calling their attorneys to crank out lawsuits, I was in no mood for some jerk to make a joke.

Fighting back tears, too devastated to pounce on him and his expensive gray suit with whatever force 125 pounds of angry female could muster, I brushed by him to find a taxi to get away from the smoldering ruin.

He spoke to my fleeing back. "I'm with the law firm of Kimball, Walters and Goldman. You're walking away from a substantial inheritance."

"He looks like a real lawyer to me," a fireman said. "I know; my wife's hauled me into court plenty of times."

I turned and sized up the man. The fireman was right—he had the smug look of someone who wins no matter what side loses. A business lawyer, not a clever street lawyer like Johnnie Cochran or a charismatic showman like Gerry Spence, but the type who had an office in an ivory tower, billed for every breath he took, and was a master at those quiddities, quillets, and tricks Hamlet complained about.

Tasseled cordovan loafers were the clincher. A female lawyer friend told me that along with their three-thousand-dollar Armani suits, male business lawyers wore tasseled loafers while criminal lawyers preferred cowboy boots.

He approached me, a little hesitant. My knees were wobbly, my heart pounding, I needed a bath, a good cry, and a plane ticket that would take me far away from the mess my life had suddenly become. From his point of view, I suppose I looked like a slightly scorched maniac.

"Miss Novak, we represent the Estate of Carlos Castillo. Mr. Castillo owned a coffee plantation."

"My shop—"

"Yes, you called your little coffee drink store a coffee plantation. But Mr. Castillo's business was an actual plantation."

"You mean a place with coffee plants—"

"I believe coffee grows on trees."

"Is this a joke?"

"I've tried to explain to you that—"

"Just tell me, is this a joke?"

"This is not a joke. Mr. Castillo passed away and left you his plantation."

"Left . . . me . . . his . . . plantation." I let the words swish around my brain, trying to make sense of them. I didn't know a Carlos Castillo. Or anyone who owned a coffee plantation. But I was desperate enough to clutch at what appeared to be a miracle. Or a mistake.

"Are you sure you have the right person? My name is Nash Novak, but I may not be the only Nash Novak in the world."

"I would hope that you are the only Nash Novak who owns a coffee store in Seattle named Café de Oro." He shook his head. "It's not a mistake; the only address we were given for you was your store." He glanced at the mess. "Former store."

"All right, tell me exactly what's going on; give me the bottom line."

He took a step closer but stayed out of arm's reach. "You have inherited a coffee plantation. I can understand why the news is such a surprise. We were advised that you had never met Mr. Castillo, your benefactor. My impression is that he was someone who knew of you and decided to benefit you."

"I inherited a coffee plantation. From a stranger." I could repeat the information, but my brain was having a difficult time processing it.

My store was in Pike Place Market, a cluster of quaint shops between First Avenue and the waterfront, overlooking Puget Sound. I stared out at the Sound, trying to get my feet under my brain. It was a gloom-and-doom morning; a haze of fog hadn't burned off the Sound yet. Neither had the fuddle in my mind.

I tried to deal with it logically: Someone—a stranger—died and left me a coffee plantation. A real coffee plantation, not just a name like I used on my shop. The "coffee plantation" extension of my store's name came from the interior decorations of green plastic plants and coffee bean sacks.

I struggled with the man's name—Carlos Castillo. It didn't

connect. The name conjured up nothing except for the fact it sounded Spanish or Portuguese. It wasn't possible a complete stranger would leave me an inheritance.

But that was exactly what this lawyer with tasseled shoes was telling me.

"This place . . . this plantation . . . what's it worth?"

"We haven't been given a valuation, but one can imagine that an actual coffee plantation would be worth a significant amount of money. Millions, for all we know."

I nearly swooned. I know, modern women don't swoon, but having your dreams and livelihood go up in smoke can ruin your whole day and send you back to basics. I gasped for air.

"Are you all right?"

I shook my head. "It's been a bad morning, the worst in my life. Tell me about the snake."

"The snake?"

"There's always a snake in paradise, a catch, someone or something that's going to throw cold water on winning the lottery, waiting for me to scratch the last number just to find out it's a loser."

"I honestly don't know that much about the situation. Like you, I've never met Mr. Castillo. We were hired through a law firm in Miami simply to notify you of the inheritance."

"Where's this plantation?"

"Colombia."

"Colombia? The country in South America?"

He smirked. "The last time I looked at a globe it was a country in South America. Just below Panama, I believe."

"Isn't that the place where there's so much violence? Civil war, murder, kidnappings, the government always on the verge of being overwhelmed by drug lords and commie guerrillas?"

"I believe there is a history of trouble in Colombia."

"How do I get my money?"

"Your money?"

"From my inheritance. Is this place going to be sold—"

"I really know little about the situation. The firm in Miami instructed us to give you the particulars on the lawyer in Colombia who handles the estate." He raised his eyebrows. "I understand the plantation is in the jungles of Colombia. My impression from the Miami firm is that they also know little about the situation. It appears that not all the information coming out of the country can be relied upon. They believe that you will have to go to Colombia to get the details and claim your inheritance."

I nodded, as if I was getting the big picture. "Okay, let me get this straight. You're saying that a stranger has left me a coffee plantation thousands of miles from here, and in order to claim it, I have to go to one of the most dangerous places in the world?"

He cleared his throat. "Naturally, the firm of Kimball, Walters and Goldman will expect a complete waiver, holding us harmless for any prospective detriment that might occur in claiming this inheritance."

"What makes you think I'd go to—"

"Nash! You bitch! I'm going to sue your ass!"

Vic Ferrara, the owner of the fish shop next to my coffee store, shouted and shook his fist at me. He was being restrained by two firemen. The smell of burnt cod was in the air.

The lawyer cleared his throat again as he handed me a manila envelope. "This is the contact information for the Colombian lawyer. I suppose that once you get this, uh, fire matter cleared up with your insurance company, you can decide what you want to do about your inheritance."

"Insurance company?" I began laughing, not with humor but the sort of hysterical laugh I'd give if my doctor told me that he had amputated the wrong leg.

That vitally important document in the cash box I couldn't find in the rubble was the overdue payment on my insurance policy.

2

❖

Still gripped by dread and confusion, I went up the street, away from irate fishmongers and my life's ruin. I needed a taxi, a bus, anything to get me off the street and to my apartment, where I could bar the door and shut out the world.

I headed for a taxicab parked up the street in front of a deli. As I hurried for it, I tore open the envelope the lawyer had given me. Nothing was in it but an expensive piece of stationery containing two pieces of information: the name, address, and phone number of an attorney in Medellín, Colombia, and an admonition that the firm of Kimball et al. did not represent me, take any responsibility for my well-being or the truth and veracity of the information they passed. Some other legalistic-sounding admonitions were on the paper, but my aching bloodshot eyes slid over them.

One thing I didn't skim over: *Medellín.*

From news reports I recognized the town as the site of the "Medellín cartel," a notorious drug-trafficking organization.

Wonderful. I inherit a coffee plantation—but it's in the midst of Colombia's drug war territory. Something like winning the lottery and being told you have terminal cancer on the same day.

After I had seen the rage in Vic Ferrara, a trip to the tropics until the dust—and soot—settled wasn't a bad idea. The "trop-ics," as in an idyllic island in the Caribbean, not the murder capital of the world.

As I opened the rear door to the cab, I heard a shout. A man with olive skin and a thin black mustache was trotting toward the taxi with a determined look. He waved at me.

I quickly slipped in and told the driver my cross streets. "Hurry, please."

Once we pulled away, I sighed and leaned my head back against the seat rest, taking in the smell of pastrami and mus-tard. My bad karma must still be working overtime when someone makes a dash to steal a taxi from me just as I'm get-ting into it. Seattle didn't have New York's mean-streets repu-tation for confrontations over taxis, not at least when it wasn't raining—which it did frequently in a city famous for rain, cof-fee, and Bill Gates.

It suddenly occurred to me that the man who had run for the taxi had a Hispanic look. I glanced out the back window, but no one was trotting behind the taxi.

I shook off the notion that just because the man looked as if his heritage was Latino he had something to do with my recent inheritance from the enigmatic "Carlos Castillo." Seattle was a multi-cultural city.

MY APARTMENT WAS in a four-story building sandwiched between retail stores. Lots of windows and a skylight in the bedroom and bathroom made the apartment appear bright and open.

On the top floor of a building with an angled roof, the apart-ment had a garret feel. No elevator made it cheaper because most people don't relish walking up four flights of stairs, but I didn't mind it at all; I liked the exercise—and the fact the apartment cost me less than what I'd been paying for a condo.

When I came across the apartment, I'd been looking for a smaller, less expensive place to live because I was going into business for myself and needed to cut expenses. Walking to meet a friend for dinner, I noticed a small handwritten note posted at the building entrance saying there was a small apart-ment for rent. I assumed there would be a stack of applications before me since downtown apartments with views were hard to find, but it didn't hurt to try, so I did. The landlord turned out to be a sweet elderly Filipino woman who liked me. She had just put up the notice that afternoon.

Some people would call me weird, but the minute I walked into the apartment, I felt good vibes—the place radiated positive feelings.

Bright and cheery, the pastel peach living room had floor-to-ceiling French doors that opened to a small balcony. Facing the living room was the kitchen with an open breakfast nook and butter-cream-colored cabinets. The bathroom had an old-fashioned claw-foot tub with a shower attachment, impractical but exactly what I always wanted. I loved to soak and take leisurely bubble baths. It was my one indulgence where I could totally relax and unwind. The bedroom, with its baby blue hue, was soothing and peaceful. The closet wasn't large, but adding shelves increased my storage space.

I also utilized the ceiling as storage space, hanging up baskets to hold various things, putting up bookshelves on the walls for my books and picture frames, and even hanging up my ironing board. A few small antique pieces placed here and there, mixed with some modern furniture and a couple of oil paintings, completed my eclectic apartment. Fresh flowers were everywhere. I would buy them at least once a week.

It wasn't just the serenity of the place but the view that I liked—scenic Elliott Bay in Puget Sound, the harbor, waterfront, green mountains, and beautiful sunsets.

MY HEAD WAS pounding by the time I got home. I needed a relaxing hot bath, and a pill to break the brutal stiffness tension had created in my back and neck.

Instead, I threw my purse on the coffee table and grabbed the phone. My first call was to my insurance agent. Naturally, he wasn't there. After navigating through the do-it-yourself phone system that repeatedly created hope that I would ultimately reach a human being, which never happened, I left a voice-mail message.

"Mike, I need to talk to you; there's been a fire; my store is gone; one of my employees is dead. You know my check bounced at my insurance company, they canceled me, and I had the cashier's check they demanded to get reinstated, but it was in the cash box and—shit, call me, please, right away, as soon as you can."

I banged the receiver down on the tabletop. *Stupid, stupid, stupid.* It was a twelve-hundred-dollar cashier's check and I had been stalling about sending it to the insurance company, thinking I might need to cash it to meet rent and payroll. Café de Oro, "coffee of gold," had started out well, but over the last couple of months it seemed to have developed a "business virus"—people got sick from something nasty in the counter milk, health department inspectors closed me for cockroaches that suddenly materialized as if they had been waiting for the inspectors to walk in, two employees were mugged in separate incidents, and I had to hire and train new help at a time when business had dropped in half.

Now the business blew up, taking that poor man with it. Facing disaster from every angle, I had shot myself in the foot by bouncing the renewal check on my insurance and sitting on the reinstatement fee.

I couldn't have done worse if I'd sat down and planned a business suicide.

The letter that had the Colombian lawyer's information in it gave the man's name as Francisco de Vega Gomez, with an address in Medellín, Colombia. I groaned again at the thought that my newfound inheritance was located there. "Cocaine cowboys," the news media called the cartel bosses challenging the Colombian government for power, billionaire criminals with well-equipped private armies.

After checking my phone book on how to place a call to Colombia, I dialed the number. Several bursts of tones and static later, a Spanish-language recording apologized that the call could not be completed but offered no clue as to why. I spoke pretty good Spanish, a heritage from my mother, who was a Peace Corps volunteer in Colombia during the early 1960s, but the linguistic ability didn't help in talking with a recording.

It had occurred to me that my benefactor, Senor Castillo, might be someone my mother had met when she was in the Peace Corps. A much more relevant thought buzzing in my head was could he be my father. You don't leave an inheritance to a stranger.

My mother had raised me in her role as a single parent. She had revealed little about who my father was.

For years I would lie awake at night and wonder about my father. I'd fantasize a scene in which I would meet my father and we would instantly bond as he explained where he'd been all my life. . . .

Naturally, an inheritance from a Colombian whom I had never met or heard of put Carlos Castillo at the head of the list. But I didn't have time to mull over the possible connection—I had a sudden, desperate need for money and the one place in the world where I would find it was south of the border, *way south.*

Unable to reach a human operator in Colombia even with the help of an American one, I put down the phone and rubbed my face. I couldn't understand how my life could change so fast and radically. My business was destroyed. I had no insurance. *My God, a man is dead.*

I staggered into the bathroom, washed my face, and scrubbed off the soot with a wet facecloth. My reflection in the mirror accurately reflected my mental state: a woman in despair. Besides being red and swollen, my eyes had a strange feral look I realized was shock and panic.

I stared at myself, wondering how so much of my life went by so fast in such a short time. Just about a year before, I'd left a successful career—burning my bridges as I was apt to do—and launched a business that I was sure would bring me success. At thirty-one, the good life seemed ripe for the picking. No man was in my life, but that was my fault, because I was too busy . . . and maybe because I'd been-there-done-that with casual sex and relationships and wanted something more meaningful and permanent.

Sex for the sake of sex wasn't satisfying, nor was dating guys who expected a blow job instead of a good-night kiss on the first date. I had had it with fallout from the sexual revolution my mother had fought in, and just wanted someone I loved and trusted to snuggle up to at night.

I had a firm, slender figure, not too muscular, page-boy-length chestnut hair that behaved unruly sometimes, and dark brown eyes. I had tried on a blond wig once to see what I would look like but decided it didn't agree with my tan shade of skin. And no one would expect to see me at a casting call for a movie, not unless the role was for the girl next door.

From the looks of my face in the mirror, right now I could be cast as the victim after that creep from the *Halloween* movies paid a visit.

I swallowed half a Valium. The woman next door had given me two of them after the health department closed my store for a week. Too bummed out to take a shower, I finished wiping soot off my face and arms and took a cold, damp washcloth to bed with me. Lying atop the blankets, I put the wet cloth over my eyes and forehead.

Migraines weren't new to me, but this was the worst I'd ever experienced. My eyes ached and I was sick to my stomach. I couldn't get an image of that poor man out of my head. Johnny Woo, a skinny guy who wasn't fresh off the boat but spoke English with a thick Cantonese accent.

A dour type who never smiled, in all honesty, I hadn't particularly cared for the man; he didn't have the personality or language skill for counter work. I hired him out of desperation when he showed up the morning I found out an employee had been hospitalized because of a mugging. But I couldn't help feeling terrible that he had been killed because of some freaky accident at my business.

Shoving Johnny Woo's face to the back of my mind, I thought about the strange twist of fate that would bring an inheritance from South America to me on the same day I suffered a disaster. I'd always felt a connection to Colombia because my mother had returned to the States pregnant at the end of her Peace Corps tour in that country. But that I would get an inheritance out of the blue thirty-one years later was completely dumbfounding. So were the circumstances that brought me to financial ruin.

Out of college, I had gone to work for a vineyard in Napa Valley that was out to make a name for itself. With an MBA in marketing, I wanted to work in the food and drink industry, having an ambition in the back of my head of someday running a chain of upscale restaurants. When I found out the winery needed a marketing director, I jumped to get an interview because it had a prestigious reputation despite the fact it was a small operation.

I ended up working there three years, learning how wine was made and marketed. I liked the job, but everything about wine was too slow for me—it took years to grow, make, and age the stuff. I moved on, in and out of several different business areas, before I discovered I had a talent for analyzing business operations.

From my last year in grad school through three years at the vineyard, I'd had a relationship with an up-and-coming San Francisco advertising exec. I liked him and thought in terms of marriage and kids, but I realized too late there was something missing in our relationship—he wasn't as committed as I was.

When an opportunity came for me to move to Seattle for a high-paying job with a business think tank, I found out that he wasn't ready for marriage, at least not with me. I told him I'd been offered the Seattle job but would turn it down to stay in the Bay Area with him; he stunned me by saying I should take it. "It's a good career move," he said.

"You fucking bastard," had been my reply. I don't usually talk like that, either, but sometimes these things leap off my tongue before I can stop them.

But he had been right—the offer was more money and opportunity—so it was time to burn my bridges in San Fran and head north.

The Seattle "think tank" was a firm that solved business problems and objectives of large corporations: increase sales, decrease overhead, expand or contract, open up a new territory, drop an old product line, develop a new one. The analytical process was the same regardless of the problem or objective, using a multi-disciplinary group to research and discuss the situation pretty much like military "think tanks" solved problems for the armed forces.

With an inquisitive mind, I was a natural for the job. Ambitious and a workaholic, I'd risen from team leader to vice president in charge of operational analysis, the core moneymaking aspect of the company, in two years. Along the way I'd acquired an engagement ring from a man whom I expected to spend the rest of my life with.

David was the chief financial officer, the guy who counted the firm's money. His loving, doting aunt was the widow of one of the founders. David and I hit it off immediately and became lovers after I'd gotten promoted to vice president—I didn't want anyone to claim I'd made it on anything but hard work. After I'd gotten the big promotion, there was office talk that when the other founder retired, I'd be a shoo-in for the job.

David popped the question and I said yes. Life looked like it had endless options, all good.

I shook my aching head, just thinking about it. Just a year ago, I'd had a secure career, a regular paycheck, a condo, and money in the bank—and a fiancé. But I'd been working too hard—and been too blind—to see the land mines.

Even though I was doing well working for a corporation, and saw myself running the think tank company, I'd always had a secret desire to work for myself. Not running a small business, but launching one that grew into a financial empire. My business models were Mrs. Fields of cookie fame and Martha Stewart of home and garden.

My mother had been taken away from me in a car accident when I was twenty, but before that she had often talked about the two of us starting a coffee business, a chain of stores specializing in coffee drinks like those in Europe. After she'd worked in the Colombian coffee region during her Peace Corps stint, she came back a coffee addict.

She passed beyond sorrow, as the Tibetans wisely describe death, about the time the Seattle retail coffee industry was on its way to go national with a chain called Starbucks.

With my business analysis background, I found it interesting that Starbucks's path to national prominence had an analogy to the planet's most successful food chain, McDonald's. In both cases, a smart businessman who was a stranger to the industry had discovered that somebody was doing something right—and taken the "something right" national.

McDonald's success started when Ray Kroc, a Chicago

milk-shake machine salesman, went out west to San Bernardino, a parched, dusty town an hour east of L.A., to find out why a single hamburger joint named McDonald's was using eight of his five-shakes-at-a-time machines. He discovered that the McDonald brothers had a talent for making popular fast food. And Kroc had the talent and ambition to build a retail food empire.

Starbucks was a small chain with five or six coffee stores in Seattle when it caught the eye of a plastics salesman named Howard Schultz. Schultz wondered why the little company ordered so many drip brewing thermoses from the Swedish manufacturer he represented. Like Ray Kroc's realization that the McDonald brothers had a winning formula he could pick up and run with, Schultz realized the world was waiting for the right cup of coffee. And the rest is retail history. . . .

But the opportunity to get my feet wet in my own business started more like a drowning.

I think David actually loved me, at least I hope he did, but he was one of those men who were too polygamous to stay faithful. Maybe if I'd been an understanding woman who realized that some men stray and come back, it would have been different. But not only did I lack understanding and compassion for a sonofabitch who cheated on me; he added insult to injury by sticking his dick in the wrong place—in this case, my cute new assistant who had everything I didn't have: melon boobs, cupid lips, firm tush, all the beauty marks of a modern woman who spends every spare cent on plastic surgery.

All right, I don't know that any of it was phony, but it didn't really matter; it really boiled down to a question of loyalty and common sense—you don't fuck your boss's fiancé.

The worst part was that because I was so busy working to make money for the company, I was the only one who didn't know the two were getting it on, often right in his office.

A work friend clued me in on what was going on while we were out Christmas shopping. When I returned to the office and saw the knowing looks the staff exchanged when the little slut headed toward David's office, love turned to hate. He had not only hurt me as a woman; he'd humiliated me at the office.

The bastard and the slut had to pay.

Planning revenge was a natural for a woman who specialized in analyzing problems the same way the military analyzed combat situations. I thought of it as just another problem to solve: How do I get even by cutting off David's dick so no other woman would have to suffer humiliation, and chop off the slut's knees and sew her mouth shut so she'd never be able to kneel down and give another man a blow job at the office?

Christmastime fit nicely into the scheme I envisioned. Because we had so many business clients, we threw two Christmas parties before we wrapped up the holidays with a third office party for the staff and their families.

Realizing that with all the booze and flirting that goes on at Christmas parties it would be inevitable that David and Slut would sneak to his office to knock off a quickie, I bought a video camera with a motion-detection feature that turned the camera on when movement came within its range. I hid it in his office during the first party and got nothing for my troubles except David coming and going. During the second party, I struck pay dirt—David came into the office; Slut came in; he locked the door.

The video caught it all—he bent her over his desk, pulled her dress up and piled it on top of her back, pulled down her panties—she had not worn panty nose, of course. When her panties were off, he bent down and kissed both cheeks of her tush.

Dear God . . . she wiggled and giggled as he bit at them.

She spun around and unzipped his pants. Calling his penis "my hero" (*oh God!*), she got onto her knees and swallowed it, sucking it like a lollipop, unclenching her mouth hold to ogle up at him with juices running down the corner of her mouth.

Short of time, he put her back over the desk, pulled back up the dress, stuck his cock in, and pumped, shooting in less time than it takes to say wham-bam-thank-you-ma'am.

Slut went into ecstasy, moaning and twisting as if she'd just been fucked by Don Juan.

The little bitch faked her orgasm.

When I watched the tape later, a drink in one hand, a handkerchief in the other to wipe away tears, I broke out laughing when I realized her moans of ecstasy were as phony as a whore's. Which she was.

And then she told him it was the best sex she'd ever had.

I howled with laughter, spilling wine on my dress and onto the rug, but I didn't care. She was so phony and he was so damn vain, he bought every false moan and bat of her extra-long, store-bought eyelashes.

God, men who think with their dicks are so stupid.

The video was priceless. I had only intended to leave it on his desk, along with a copy of my letter of resignation, then ride away into the sunset, sure that he would wither from love lost . . .

But after seeing how utterly stupid he was, and what a truly conniving bitch she was, I decided to share this piece of video art with the world.

When the office Christmas party came around, I had gift-wrapped copies of the video under the tree. I labeled it "Office Party."

I only wish I had been a fly on the wall in homes of our coworkers when they played the video to their family and friends. . . .

3

❖

Half a Valium was usually enough to let me drift into sleep, but my mind and body were too wound up. At least the feeling of nausea was gone and the pain had lessened around my eyes.

I got out of bed and went to the balcony and opened the door, keeping the blanket wrapped around me.

I loved the view of Puget Sound. The waters were metallic under the gray sky. The Sound was an inlet from the Pacific Ocean indenting into Washington State. Almost one hundred miles long, and navigable by large ships and pleasure boats, the Sound made Seattle a major port miles from the open sea. It was named after a British naval officer named Puget who accompanied the explorer George Vancouver to the Pacific Northwest in the late 1700s.

From another window I could also see the Space Needle located at the Seattle Center, the site of the 1962 world's fair. The Needle stood over six hundred feet high, had been built for the fair, and had a revolving restaurant on top. I'd heard that in a bizarre stunt during the "streaking" phase a naked man once dangled from a small plane as it circled the Needle's restaurant level. Fifteen minutes of fame by letting it all hang out.

I wanted to live in the downtown area because of the energy and excitement in the heart of the city. I was within walking distance or a short bus ride of historic landmarks, shopping, restaurants, and the waterfront.

My favorite place was the Pike Place Market. That's why I chose it for my store. The market had something for everyone, from junk jewelry to unique pieces of art. Tree-lined First Avenue had an assortment of clothing boutiques, restaurants, and cafés. The first Starbucks coffee store was even located nearby.

And not too far away was Pioneer Square when I wanted nightlife. The Square even had the city's most unusual tourist attraction: an underground "city" composed of a five-block area. Subterranean sidewalks and storefronts ended up underground when street levels were raised as much as thirty-five feet following a disastrous fire over a hundred years ago.

I did a lot of walking, even though I had a VW Bug that had once belonged to my mother. The Bug had transported me through college and now was kept running by a good mechanic that I was lucky to find.

I liked Seattle, as much as I had liked San Francisco when I lived there. The city is built across hills and ridges and surrounded by beautiful scenery—the jagged Olympic Mountains to the west and the volcanic peaks of the Cascade Range, which includes Mount Rainer, to the east.

They call Seattle the Emerald City because rain and mists keep the surroundings fresh and green, but the average temperature is not that cold because the city is warmed by the Japan current, shielded by the Olympic Mountains from excessive winter rains, and protected by the Cascades from winter blasts.

The city had an interesting, Old West history. The first settlement was made by white pioneers in 1851 following the California Gold Rush and later moved to what is now the Pioneer Square area of downtown. The pioneers named the city after a friendly Native American chief named Sealth. Its early claim to fame was as a sawmill center. In fact, the expression "skid row" came from lumbering—the road that the logs were skidded down was called "skid road," which later evolved into "skid row" as it became lined with the homes of poor logging families.

In those early days there were few women, so a brave soul went east and persuaded eleven proper young women from New England to sail with him around the Horn to Seattle to take husbands among the pioneers. He went back again and recruited one hundred Civil War widows. Many families today proudly trace their lineage to these women.

Built of wood, the city was destroyed in 1889 when a painter's glue pot boiled over and started the Great Fire. Along with fire, flood, and famine, the city survived Indian attacks, harddrinking lumberjacks, and anti-Chinese riots.

The town's development was slow until the transcontinental railroad reached Seattle. When a ship arrived from Alaska with a "ton of gold" in 1897, the great Klondike Gold Rush was on, converting Seattle into a boomtown. Seattle's harbor developed into one of the world's great seaports. Boeing and the aerospace industry stimulated its growth. By the 1980s, Microsoft and other computer companies arrived in the area and the town saw another economic boom.

I thought I was going to be part of the Great Seattle Coffee Boom, but my dream was now ashes.

After burning my bridges at the think tank, I sold my condo, emptied my bank account, and did the proverbial beg, borrow, and steal routine to open Café de Oro. To give it a little "coffee plantation" look, I had real-looking coffee trees with shiny green leaves and clusters of red coffee "cherries" and burlap coffee sacks of unroasted green coffee beans from growers around the world scattered around the café.

I also bought a small roaster that was modern but reminded me of those old train steam engines that the Indians called "iron horses." An exhaust fan blew the aromatic smell of roasting beans onto the sidewalk in front of the store.

An antique espresso machine came from Milan and I even had an old sock stained with coffee on display, along with a battered pot—in the Old West, to make coffee out on the range, cowboys put coffee grinds into a sock and put the sock in boiling water over a campfire.

Hopefully they used a clean sock.

I figured what Mrs. Fields did with cookies I could do with

coffee and muffins. I gave up eating out, going to movies, and male companionship, my three favorite pastimes—not necessarily in that order—to devote myself to the business. It took over a year to get the business plan down pat, open my flagship store, and watch people line up for lattes, cappuccinos, and muffins. Based on the success of the store, I was in negotiations with a venture capitalist to open six more stores over the next three years.

It took less than two months to bring it all crashing down. Nothing in my university training or experience advising big businesses prepared me for dealing with city health inspectors over bacteria-tainted milk, cockroaches that seemed to have materialized out of thin air, and mugged employees.

I had put everything I had into an interesting store layout and expensive heart-of-the-city location. When my customers fled, along with my venture capitalist, I suddenly found myself in a cash pinch. And bounced checks.

The most important one was my fire insurance payment.

What a piece of bad luck—and bad timing—that was.

Lamenting my losses and poor Johnny Woo, I went to the front door to answer a knock. The Valium had taken effect now, and I was a little groggy and out of sorts as I shuffled to the door in bare feet and opened it. And immediately regretted it as I stared at a tall man with a scar across his neck.

At my own height of five-seven, when I looked up at him the most prominent feature was the scar. His complexion was shaded, his hair and thin mustache black, I took him to be Hispanic, and the scar stood out, darker than his olive skin. It wasn't a jagged wound, but a thin scar, in my movie-polluted mind the result of being garroted by piano wire.

I immediately realized this was the man who had run for the cab. Only it must have been me he was running after.

"I have an offer for the plantation."

"The plantation? My store—you mean that other thing?"

"The coffee plantation, you are to sell it to me."

"I am?" It was the second time that day that I had been reduced to a dim-witted response.

"You have no use for it. You need the money."

His accent was thick and definitely Hispanic. His tone was not a statement, but a command. It raised my ire.

"Excuse me, but who do you think you are? What—"

He jabbed his index finger in my face and I took a step backward. "Ten thousand dollars. I will have the money for you tomorrow. *Comprende*?"

Voices and the sound of heavy feet came from the stairwell.

He glanced to the rear and back to me. His eyes were dark, the shade of mud. "*Mañana*." Tomorrow.

He turned on his heel and walked away, going down the steps as a man and woman came up. I had started to close the door when the man saw me and said, "Miss Novak?"

"Yes."

"Detective Evans." He flashed a badge as he approached. He was short, had a beer belly, pale skin, and dirty blond hair cut in a 1950s flattop style. His tie hung loose from the open collar of his shirt; his shiny gray suit was wrinkled polyester. He indicated the woman with him. "My partner, Detective Stacy."

Stacy was of African descent, also short, no belly.

I was relieved that Scar had left, but the body language of the two officers wasn't encouraging.

"Did you see that man that passed you?" I asked.

"It was kind of hard not to," Evans said. "We almost rubbed shoulders. Why? He bother you?"

"I . . ." What could I say? He didn't really do anything offensive; he just offered me money. But his tone scared me. "Nothing, I just didn't like him. Did you need to see me about the store?"

"Need to talk about the fire. Can we come in?"

It wasn't really a question. I backed up and they came in without waiting for an invite.

"Are you with the fire department?" I had been told a fire department investigator would be contacting me.

"Seattle PD. Where were you when your business went up?"

"At my accountant's. He's only a few minutes from the shop."

"Can I have his name, address, and phone number, please."

"Sure. I'll give you his card." Getting his card from my desk gave me a chance to gather my wits. I handed it to Evans and asked, "Is there something wrong?"

He raised his eyebrows. "Should there be?"

No, dummy, I have cops pushing their way into my apartment all the time. Jesus. I tried to control the irritation in my voice. "My business has burned down; an employee is dead; I'm being questioned by the police; I'm having the worst bad-hair day in my life. I just hope you're not here to add to it."

"Why do you think we'll be adding to your problems?"

I realized this was some sort of police questioning method, maybe to get a suspect angry enough to blurt out something, but I had no idea why the officer was playing games with me. "Why are you here? What do you want to know?" I couldn't keep the irritation out of my voice.

"How long did you know Ho Lung?"

"Ho Lung?"

"The man killed in the explosion at your shop."

"Johnny Woo—"

"His real name is Ho Lung. How long did you know him?"

"A couple weeks; he started on the twelfth. Why do you say 'his real name'? Why did he need an alias?"

"Why'd you hire him?"

"I needed help; he washed dishes, cleaned up the place," I shrugged, "that sort of thing."

"Was torching your business part of his duties?"

That from Detective Stacy.

I gaped at her. "Torching the place? There was a gas leak—"

"Created by Ho Lung when he set out to torch the place," Evans said. "Let's stop beating around the bush; this can go easy on you—or hard. Why don't you just tell us about it?"

The whole world is going nuts.

"Tell you about what? The firemen said there was a gas leak, an explosion—"

"Lung is a member of Vancouver, BC's toughest gang. He didn't come across the border to wash dishes and sweep your floor. They call him the Torch. His specialty is arson."

"Ar—arson? You mean setting fires? He's a firebug?"

"No, I don't mean he's a firebug; he's a professional arsonist. Sometimes he's hired out by the gang; sometimes he free-lances; in any case, he torches places for money."

"Torches places for money." I repeated the words because they were making no sense. The pounding started again in my head. "Why would he burn my place?"

"That's what we came to ask you." He grinned. "Obviously, we can't ask Ho Lung."

"Why are you asking me?" I realized the stupidity of the question as soon as the words left my mouth. "You think I had something to do with it? *That I hired this man to burn my own business?*"

The enormity of the question made me gasp.

"Why don't you just tell us about it?" Detective Stacy's voice was warm, comforting. "Let us help you; we know how difficult things have been, that you only did what you thought you had to. Your back was to the wall, wasn't it?"

If I'd had a guilty conscience, I would have sat down with her and emptied my soul.

"This is insane. Why would you think I hired an arsonist?"

Evans began counting off on his fingers. "You hired him; that's a given. He doesn't do dishes; he does fires. He's a pro from across the border—hard to track because he's here today, gone tomorrow. Looks like he started a gas leak in the base-ment, one that would blow after he blew.

"Something went wrong—dead wrong, for him. The place went up before he made it out of the building. We know from your Pike Place neighbors that your business is in deep shit; you've been operating off of a wing and a prayer. Your land-lord says you're behind in the rent and that your hope for fi-nancial backing flew the coop when the health department shut you down. The fire and explosion were no accident. Going out of business with a *fire* sale is a long tradition with failing busi-ness owners."

By the time he ran out of fingers, I ran out of strength. I sat down and stared up at them. "This is completely insane. You just made an ironclad case, but the problem is, none of it's true."

"We checked with your insurance agent. Three months ago you increased your insurance."

"It was a requirement of an investor who planned to come into the business." I kept my voice under control, but more of the thread of my sanity was unraveling. I wanted to scream. "You don't know what you're talking about. I don't even have insurance; the check went up with the building."

"Tough break, but if a gas pipe hadn't broken when Lung was rigging it, it would have taken a couple hours for the place to go up. And you would have had plenty of time to get the check to your agent."

"You think I tried to destroy my own business? This was my dream; everything I had was—"

"You know it's murder, don't you?"

That from Detective Stacy.

I stared at her. "Murder?"

"When a co-conspirator is killed committing a crime, the other conspirator is guilty of murder." The woman sat down on the couch next to me. "Detective Evans, why don't you go get a cup of coffee and a donut while Nash and I have a talk."

I leaped off the couch. "No, no, no, no good-cop, bad-cop. I'm not a criminal; I'm not talking about anything. I'm calling my lawyer. Thank you; you can leave now."

Stacy went out first and Evans paused to toss his card on a stand next to the door. He looked back at me, raising his eyebrows. "It appears Lung had accidentally created a big gas leak while trying to create a small leak. He was trying to get out of the place when the thermostat came on and sent a signal to the electric starter in the furnace, igniting the furnace. Looks like someone had tampered with the thermostat."

"The thermostat didn't work right; every morning I had to . . . to . . ."

He grinned at me. "Like I said, someone tampered with the thermostat. Lucky break for you, wasn't it." He threw his hands into the air. "*Boom!* All the evidence and an arsonist who can blackmail you go up when the thermostat suddenly goes on."

I slammed the door.

Evans's *boom!* echoed in my head as I staggered to my phone and dialed my friend Christen's number by memory. Christen was a lawyer, the friend who explained lawyers' shoes to me. Her boyfriend was my former fiancé's best friend and we had double-dated a number of times. She was something more than an acquaintance but not really a close friend, not the kind I'd share intimacies with. I was something of a loner and didn't have running-buddy-type friends. She worked for a business law firm and had checked out my lease when I rented the shop. For a fee of twenty-five hundred dollars.

I pressed buttons to navigate through her firm's "automated" telephone system. Her voice-mail recording said she was either on the phone or away from the office and would get back to me. I left her a long message, taking a deep breath and trying to keep my voice from shaking as I explained that my business had gone up in smoke and the police had accused me of hiring—and murdering—an arsonist.

That dirty little bastard. I'd been lamenting his death all morning. I hoped the little shit burned in the everlasting fires of hell.

I staggered to the bathroom and gulped down the other half of the Valium.

4

❖

Not even the Valium could relax me or put me to sleep. I lay atop the bed and vibrated, my right foot shaking, as I tried to piece together a day in which all Four Horsemen of the Apocalypse had ridden into my life.

The sedative made my mind wander, but it didn't go far. Each time it slipped out of my head, it would snap back like a rubber band as I made one revelation after another.

Contaminated milk. Health inspectors conveniently showing up as cockroaches did the Dance of the Troubadours across my shop floor. My store being destroyed by a professional.

Johnny Woo, Ho Lung, whatever his name was, had been a small, thin, taciturn man who claimed his age as thirty-five. He spoke with a thick Chinese accent. Neither a Chinese heritage nor accent was unusual in Seattle—the city had a large Chinese population, dating back to the last century. Added to that, immigrants who spoke little English were part of the norm.

But why he would come across the Canadian border to destroy my place was not part of the norm. Vancouver, British Columbia, Canada, wasn't far. It also had a large Chinese population. Someone had reached across the border to hire a Canadian because he could slip back across after the fire.

But who would want to destroy my business?

Add in a lawyer telling me I had inherited a coffee plantation, and a Colombian with a scar and a threatening attitude who wants to buy it . . . my mind tried to escape my head on a path greased by Valium. I pulled it back in, but my head pounded.

The phone rang and my jangled nerves almost sent me to the ceiling.

"Ms. Novak? This is Steve Berger; I'm an associate of Christen Levine. She referred your call to me because I do criminal defense work."

I started a blow-by-blow account of my discussion with the two police officers. He cut me short.

"I know Evans; I gave him a call after Christen called me. His theory is that you could be a poster girl for the going-out-of-business fire-sale racket. Insurance upped, professional arsonist on the payroll—"

"This is all insane; someone is doing this to me."

"Right, we'll talk about that, but right now you need to get prepared."

"Prepared for what?"

"To get arrested."

Oh my God!

"You have one lucky break; these arson things with a body are weighed heavy with evidence—police and fire department paperwork, coroner reports, and lab results. It'll take Evans several days to get his ducks in line, maybe even a week, but I don't think he'll wait that long. It's the kind of case he'd take to the grand jury for an indictment rather than a contested probable cause hearing before a judge."

"What does this mean for me?"

"It means you didn't get arrested today, but you're looking at cuffs in the near future. Today is Thursday; he'll probably get an indictment sometime next week."

Oh my God!

I was breathless. I couldn't breathe, couldn't speak.

"Don't worry; that's why you're hiring me: I do the worrying and the winning. Money is the salvation in these cases."

"How much?" I couldn't get the quiver out of my voice.

"My retainer is a hundred thousand; that's up to trial. If we go to trial, it's another five per court day, minimum of another hundred up front."

I tried to add up what he was talking about, but my brain wouldn't function.

"That's two hundred thousand dollars if it goes to trial, non-refundable. These cases are top-heavy with expensive expert testimony, too. We'll need an arson expert to show how you couldn't have been involved in setting it. I know a guy we can use, Bob Rees, an insurance arson expert, but he's not cheap. Also a CPA to counter the DA's expert who will claim your business was failing. Figure twenty-five for each of them. We'll use a psychiatrist to prove that Lung was crazy because he was under drugs at the time."

"Was he?"

"If we pay an expert, that's what he'll say. In this business, you get what you pay for. Most experts who testify regularly in court have the same ethics as the world's oldest profession. But that's to your advantage; the prosecution doesn't have the big bucks to hire top people."

Nor did I. "How much in total is this going to cost?"

"In round terms, you can figure about three hundred. You'll also have to set bail, probably in the half-million range. You can cover it with a bondsman for ten percent down, fifty thou, but the bondsman needs a security interest in more than a half mil in real property or certificates of deposit before they'd make bail for you. . . ."

He droned on with me only half-listening. Including the bail, which would have to be put up in its entirety because I didn't have assets to get a bondsman to take the risk of covering it for me for just 10 percent, the figures Berger threw out added up to the million-dollar range.

I had a few hundred dollars in the bank, $2,286 in the top drawer of my dresser I was saving to cover business expenses, and a credit card with a few thousand left on the credit line.

He asked me a question and I jerked back online with him. "I'm sorry; what did you say?"

"I said, the fees quoted don't include the federal case."

"Federal case?"

"Ho Lung was imported talent. Right now this is a local case, Evans is a Seattle cop, but the Feds can file on the basis Ho Lung came across the border to do the job."

"What does that mean?"

"It means you could end up with two cases, one in the state courts and one in federal. The Feds are bastards to deal with, much nastier than the locals; the judges are tougher and the sentences are longer. So costs go up if the case goes federal. What are your assets? Bank accounts, real estate?"

I took a deep breath. "I have an extensive holding in real estate, but it's out of state." Way out of state. Maybe several thousand miles south of the border with Mexico, down below the Panama Canal . . .

"Make sure it's not too far away; you won't be able to bail out without surrendering your passport."

"Surrendering my passport?"

"To make sure you can't leave the country. Even if you make bail, the judge will order you to give your passport to the prosecutor before letting you walk out of the courtroom."

I felt like someone had a pillow over my face and was pressing it down, smothering me.

I said, "I need to contact someone about my property; I'll get back to you." I hung up.

I lay quivering for a while, trying to keep my mind in my head. Finally, I dialed Colombia again. And got the same recorded voice apologizing for the fact my call could not be completed. I put the phone back into the cradle.

Standing up, a little unsteady from the pill, I said, "All right, you have to get it all together. You can tackle this just as you tackle a business problem. You've done this before; it's a piece of cake."

I sat back down and cried.

AN HOUR LATER, I stood at the balcony and stared down at the dark street below. I was too bummed out to even turn on my own apartment lights. Fog had dropped onto the city, turning the night gloomy, blurring lights. My eyes were red and swollen and my head buzzed from the sedative and some wine I'd added to the cure.

I wanted to call someone, share my misery, but no one was in my life I could reach out to. For the first time, I felt the upshot of always going it alone. Now I had nobody to turn to. They say women need other people more than men, that in an emotional crisis a woman needs to talk when most men are too uptight to express their feelings. It was true, because right now I needed someone.

On the dark street below, a man stepped into the light of the street lamp on the corner. He paused and flipped away a cigarette.

I had the impression he looked up at my window as he stepped off the curb.

I moved away from the window and pulled the curtain over the balcony door. For added measure, I stuck a wood chair under the handle of the front door. It probably wasn't Scar I had seen, he had said "mañana," but a disturbing thought had crept out of my wine and sedative haze.

The police officer said the thermostat had turned on the basement furnace after the arsonist had inadvertently created a big gas leak. I could picture what happened.

Not having a key to the place, he either broke in this morning or entered with a key stolen from the spares I kept in my office. Before going down to the basement, he would have first shut off the thermostat. The control was in the entryway at the back of the store.

What he didn't know was that I'd been having trouble with the thermostat, that the gadget had developed an annoying mind of its own. I'd been so broke I'd lived with the problem rather than getting someone in to fix it.

Suspecting that I had rigged the thermostat to kill the man after hiring him to torch the store was a natural conclusion for the police. But since I was innocent, the fact the thermostat would turn on the furnace and create an explosion raised an even grimmer prospect.

The arsonist's intent was to create a small leak, let gas accumulate in the basement. Heavier than air, the gas would accumulate on the concrete floor.

Each morning, I had the same routine as I entered. I turned on the lights and set the thermostat higher to get the furnace going. I dropped by my accountant's this morning, but I still would have made it to the store before opening time.

If Woo/Lung hadn't botched the job, I would have been the one to enter and turn up the thermostat, turning on the furnace—creating a flame with a basement full of gas under my feet.

Now that was an unnerving thought.

Could someone dislike me enough to kill me?

How did it happen that my store blew up on the same day that I was told I'd inherited a coffee plantation in Colombia?

Who was on third? Or was Who on first?

My mind was too blown to remember the punch line. Or see through the layers of deceit that I had become entangled in.

5

❖

Analyzing the situation and coming up with a solution for my problems wasn't difficult for me. "There are logical patterns to problems and one merely has to use an analytical approach, consider all options," was the mantra of the business think tank where I had worked.

A logical analysis led me to one conclusion: *Follow the money.*

I don't remember where I heard the phrase, whether it was something someone said when I worked at the think tank or if I had picked it up from a TV crime show. But it was the logical place to begin when my business had been trashed by a hired arsonist. Someone had paid good money to import the arsonist from Canada. Someone with a motive.

I had no personal enemies, at least no one who hated me enough to want to destroy my business. Well, maybe a couple people—my ex-fiancé and his costar in the Christmas video would have cheered if my business failed. And I'm sure it wouldn't hurt their feelings if I died soon, either. However, I eliminated them—they both had motive, but neither had the guts nor imagination to blow me up.

No, it wasn't personal; I was sure of that. Someone set out to drive me out of business—and perhaps even kill me. I couldn't be sure that I was meant to die in the explosion; maybe Woo/Lung would have set the gas leak to explode before I arrived, but I couldn't dismiss the idea, either.

Contacts in the criminal milieu would also be needed—one didn't put an ad in the local paper for an arsonist or ask the bartender at your favorite watering hole whether he knew someone who could blow up a business.

The bottom line was that there had to be a financial motivation behind the destruction of my business. And following the money, there was only one suspect I could come up with: my landlord.

Coincidentally, like Woo/Lung, he was Chinese. Unlike Woo/Lung, my landlord was not the emigrant variety but one whose family had settled in Seattle generations ago.

A further "coincidence" was that I knew my landlord had relatives in Vancouver, British Columbia, which also had a large Chinese population. That didn't mean much; Seattle was only a couple hours' drive from Vancouver, many people had friends and relatives there, but I didn't like my landlord, and he didn't like me. . . .

Worse than possible coincidences, he was also a greedy shit, a common character trait for most of the big-city commercial landlords I had dealt with during my business career. I had gotten a long-term lease at a good price because the last two tenants for the store space had failed, with one dragging my landlord into an expensive bankruptcy proceeding.

When he saw my specialty coffee business take off like a rocket, he had tried to buy in. I turned him down because, unlike a venture capitalist, he would have been a constant annoyance in running the business, tapping the cash register every day under the guise of keeping the money out of the hands of the tax man.

If you followed the money, the person who would have profited most from the insurance proceeds would have been my landlord. I didn't just insure my business; the lease had a standard clause insuring his building and loss of rental income if it was destroyed.

If I hadn't dropped the ball with the insurance company, he would be looking forward to a fat check from the claim.

I shuddered. He probably didn't know my insurance policy had lapsed. If he didn't want to kill me before, he'd certainly want to once he found out I was fresh out of money and insurance.

The fact my landlord could have rigged the arson raised my ire and the hair on the back of my neck.

The weirdest coincidence was the news of the inheritance and the ominous offer to buy the coffee plantation. I couldn't make a connection between what happened here with a Chinese arsonist from Vancouver and a Colombian—which I assumed the man with the scar was—wanting to buy my inheritance.

It was a strange coincidence, for sure, that I learned of the inheritance the same day my business was destroyed, but I couldn't conjure up a motive for someone connected to the plantation to destroy my business or kill me. It would make more sense if I had a prosperous business in Seattle that I didn't want to leave.

Killing me didn't make much sense, either. Scar, or whoever hired him, wanted to buy the plantation. If I was dead, they'd still have to deal with my heir. I didn't have a will and Christen once told me that if I died, my estate would go to my closest relative, a cousin in Cleveland I'd only met once.

If I followed the money, the trail went back to my landlord, not Scar—as ominous as he seemed, he wanted to give me money, not take it.

The ten-thousand-dollar offer caused me to draw another conclusion: The plantation was worth much more. Scar probably believed since the plantation was thousands of miles away in a country more dangerous than the FBI's Most Wanted List that I would sell cheap.

With my mind working clearer, another grim scenario was too obvious to avoid. I was going to be arrested. If I couldn't raise bail—and I couldn't—I would sit in jail for months until trial. And if I didn't have the money for a good legal defense—which I didn't—I would spend the rest of my life in jail.

I couldn't remember if they had a death penalty in the state, but even if they didn't, I'd kill myself before I'd spend the rest of my life in closed spaces rubbing shoulders with crazy women who had killed their babies, while I satisfied the lusts of diesel dikes and earned extra privileges by giving blow jobs to prison guards.

"Follow the money," I told myself.

This time I meant money for my defense.

And there was only one place to get it.

JUST BEFORE THE crack of dawn, I left my apartment. My car was parked on the street in front, but I went out the building's back door, down the alley, and up the street to a bus stop. I was wearing a bandana for a disguise and had on a long coat that was designed for severe storms, but I figured it provided some camouflage for me to hide behind. I carried a small carpetbag valise that looked as much like something I could be taking to work as it did a travel bag. Under my coat, I wore a double set of clothes so the bag stayed thin. I'd put the extra clothes into the bag later.

I took the bus downtown to within walking distance of the Hilton Hotel and climbed into a taxi lined up in front of the hotel.

"SeaTac," I told the driver.

I settled back in the seat for the ride to the Seattle-Tacoma airport.

Years ago in college, I learned in Psychology 1A that children commonly either followed their parents' footsteps or went in the opposite direction. "The preacher's daughter syndrome," my politically incorrect instructor had called it—the preacher's daughter would turn out to be either a slut or a prude.

My mother had been a rolling stone. We moved continually as her restless spirit took her to a different job and different city almost annually like a migrating bird. As her only child, I suppose I could have ended up as someone with her feet permanently cemented or the proverbial rolling stone that never grew moss.

Luckily I didn't go from one extreme to the other but had landed somewhere in between, not quite the migrant my mother was but always ready to cut my losses and burn bridges when the need arose. I was not like some people who never wanted to move because they feared change or who felt content to stay in the same place and had no urge for adventure. I enjoyed traveling to new places, meeting new people. And I wasn't afraid to pack up and head out if the situation warranted. I was used to moving.

Besides, change was good for you. It brought you whole new experiences and adventures. My mother used to say, "Don't be afraid to reach out and experience new things, embrace life, try new adventures, take chances. What's the worst that could happen to you? You'll be a stronger person for it."

She was right, of course—up to a point. It took time to build relationships and careers. My mother had a career that permitted her to migrate and she avoided permanent relationships, so having a bag packed worked out well for her. I had the ability to grab a bag and run but only opted for burning bridges when everything was going to hell—like now.

I thought about my mother as the taxi carried me to the airport.

My mother, Sonja Marie Novak, was born in Cleveland. Her own parents both had a Slavic background, second-generation from Yugoslavia. Her father had been a machinist for the railroad and had died when my mother was a young teen. She left home at eighteen and never looked back or went back to visit.

I never really understood what the situation was between her and her mother. My mother didn't really talk much about those times. I never met my grandmother; she died when I was five. I knew my mother was down on organized religion and radical in her politics, and I got the impression both attitudes might have played a role in the estrangement with her mother.

In the late fifties my mother moved west to California and enrolled at Berkeley, a time before the riots caused by the Vietnam War and burning bras of the war between the sexes. She was a free spirit, hip and cool way before the hippies came on the scene. She joined the Peace Corps as soon as it opened its doors and was sent to Colombia to help educate the rural poor.

There she worked on a coffee plantation to be closer to the people she was sent to help.

Which, of course, was why I had concluded that Carlos Castillo, my mysterious Colombian benefactor, could be my father.

The notion that my father was a coffee plantation owner worked out perfectly for the father model I had mentally constructed: He was a charming and handsome son of a proud old family, a man who rode his horse across his great estate, looking much like a Latin movie star. Naturally, he had to give up my mother despite the fact that he loved her to marry a rich, stupid girl to save his family from financial ruin.

I'm sure I missed something from not having a father figure, but because of my mother, I didn't think of it as a void in my life.

If nothing else, there was no time to dwell on not having a father in your life when you were always traveling and getting used to new surroundings. If there was a time that I wanted the merry-go-round to stop, I certainly don't remember it. The hardest part was making new friends and leaving them, walking into another school, and having to start all over again. But my mother would always say that I would meet them again.

"Life is a journey," she would say, and there were always going to be ups and downs. "Everything happens for a reason."

After I had lost my mother, I began to think more about the fact I might have a living father somewhere, with Colombia topping the list. But I did nothing about looking into it because I was busy and Colombia was a long ways away.

I remember questioning my mother about him when I was little. I was curious about my father because when I went to school all the other kids would always talk about their fathers. It was probably in the third or fourth grade that I came home from school and asked my mother why I didn't have a father. I recall I would even go up to strangers and ask if they had a father. It must have always been in the back of my mind. Maybe it bothered me more than I realized—or wanted to admit. Every couple of years the question would come up, casually, not in arguments.

Sometimes she would get exasperated with my questions and get impatient and she would blurt out whatever was in her head at the time. One time she'd say he'd been a revolutionary who faced a firing squad because he fought for social change; another time he would be a big-time drug dealer who died in a shoot-out with the police. Another time she claimed she had been raped by guerrilla fighters in the jungle.

In other words, my mother had been totally evasive about who my father was. I never understood why.

"Don't ask any more questions; we'll never see him," she finally said to me. "I got knocked up by a South American prince. He got deposed by a revolution and was hanged by the little people he'd lorded over."

Knowing I would never get a straight answer from her, I finally gave up asking. But there were a few clues I picked up. She would talk about what she did in the Peace Corps and how she worked on a coffee plantation in Colombia to really get close to the people, how she worked the same hours as other workers, ate the same food, and slept in a worker's hut.

Her eyes lit up when she talked about those times, but she never spoke of a relationship with a man that resulted in her coming back to the States pregnant with me.

Looking back, I think she was only trying to protect me. What would I have done had she given me the name? Gone knocking on his door, of course. And what reaction would I have gotten as he stood there with his wife and family staring at me? A look of horror, no doubt. Before he slammed the door in my face.

As my mother told me more than once, "We can survive fine, just the two of us," and she would then proceed to give me a lecture on how a woman was just as capable as a man. Now, of course, women my age expect to have the same rights as a man—but she had had to fight for them.

Anyway, back in California after the Peace Corps, my mother strapped me on her back and took me with her when she returned to school to get a master's. By then it was the age of Vietnam riots, the sexual revolution, the war between the sexes over women's rights, and the battle by minorities for equal rights. Like the era that Dickens wrote about, it was the best of times and the worst of times . . . but one hell of a time; even I bore a scar from the era.

My favorite show-stopper comment at parties was to tell people that I was wounded during the Vietnam War. And it was true. My mother would take time out from classes at Berkeley to participate in slogan-shouting, rock-throwing anti-war demonstrations. Once, while she was running from a police barrage of water cannons and tear gas with me strapped to her back, I got hit in the shoulder by a flying tear gas canister. I still have the scar.

My mother received her master's degree in something called public administration, which, as she explained, enabled you to become a bureaucrat, a word that summed up everything she hated about politics. But there was a method to her madness—in her mind, her degree gave her the right to infiltrate politics and bring some honesty and hard work to the game.

She had a wonderful sparkling, effervescent personality and a sincere and uncontrollable impulse to help the underdog. Frankly, she was also one part flimflam artist and one part dramatic actress. The combination made her a terrific fund-raiser for social causes, and that became her forte.

Fund-raising was a pastime that kept us on the move as the number of worthy causes increased and their distance apart became more widespread. The dynamics of moving and change also suited my mother's personality perfectly. As for me, I learned to live out of a suitcase, changing schools and making and losing friends on a regular basis.

When I complained, my mother made me read the experiences of Nellie Bly, America's first female investigative reporter, who, in 1889, raced alone around the world by ship, train, and carriage to beat the eighty days of Jules Verne's fictional character Phineas Fogg. "And that was before planes, ATMs, and tampons," my mother would remind me.

If keeping up with my gypsy-soul mother had imbued me with any distinctive character, it was the ability to cut and run. I was now using that ability to escape the police before they put me away where I'd be helpless and took my passport so I couldn't leave the country even if I escaped.

I needed money for my defense and Colombia was the only place where I would get it. The fact that the country had changed since my mother's Peace Corps days did put a small damper on my enthusiasm.

As the newspapers put it, Colombia was the most dangerous place in the world.

And Medellín was the murder capital of Colombia.

SHANGHAI

Whore of the Orient

One never asked why someone had come to Shanghai. It was assumed everybody had something to hide.

—LADY JELLICOE

6

❖

Shanghai, three months earlier

"Golden Goddess." That was what the foreigner had called her. She stood in front of a full-length mirror in her room in a house of pleasure and wondered what she looked like through the eyes of "the foreigner" and the other men who benefited from the pleasure she gave. She was naked except for long clusters of diamonds dangling from each ear.

Her name was Lily Soong, but neither was her birth name. Her sign was the tiger. She had beauty and was cunning, both marks of the animal sign she was born under.

Skin of golden ivory, it was like the lush blond-fawn of a newborn gazelle. Her hair, pulled to the top of her head, exposing her long, slender gazelle neck, had the fine sheen of black velvet. The raven hair contrasted with red lips and perfect white teeth, so perfect they were called "diamond teeth."

Her eyes were almond and partly concealed by the taper of her eyelids, her eyebrows thin, little more than pencil marks.

She knew there were women in Hong Kong and Tokyo who had plastic surgery to open their "slanted" eyes, but she considered them fools—the tapered lids of women of the Far East spoke of mystery and the exotic, temple doors guarding secrets.

She touched her breasts, putting her hands under the small

mounds, pushing them up. The daughter of a poor farmer, when she was twelve and the blood had come she had been sold to a "fishball stall" in the Nanshi, the Old City district of Shanghai. The small booths specialized in providing young girls for quick sex to busy men, a kind of fast-food fucking. The shops were called fishballs because the breasts of the girls were small, pale, and soft like the dumplings in fish soup.

The foreigner was fond of touching her breasts, of kissing and sucking on her taut nipples. Chinese men were not as intently interested in a woman's mammary appendages as Western men, though some had their own unique fetish: For centuries, Chinese men had their prurient interests aroused not by breasts, buns, or legs but by the horrible deformity of bound feet. Baby girls' feet were tightly wrapped to keep the feet from growing normally, causing them to bunch up until the feet, when full grown, were only a few inches long.

A euphemism for the ugly stumps that fit into tiny, child-sized silk slippers was "lily-feet," so named when an emperor's concubine bound her feet with her toes down so she walked like a lily swaying in a breeze. The practice was gone, but many men still prized tiny feet. Even a younger generation of men, to whom the practice was nostalgic.

Lily Soong's most erotic feature, the one that most stimulated men, was her baby-smooth pubic mound. Her stomach was flat and firm, her skin warm and silky. The curves of her abdomen ended at her naked mons pubis. But unlike other women in the house of pleasure who shaved pubic hair, Lily Soong had been born without the ability to grow the hair in that area.

For eons, the great sculptors of history had re-created the female body in marble without hair in the private area. To the ancients and the artists of the Renaissance, hair was too lower animal to put on a stone goddess. Lily's naked mound made her a goddess, too, a golden one. It had been one of the reasons she had been lifted from fishball stalls to a pleasure palace to practice the most ancient of all professions.

Her door opened without a sound and a small bent but ageless woman dressed in black entered. She moved silently, fluidly, like a shadow.

Lily Soong waited until the woman was beside her before she acknowledged her presence.

"Great Mother."

"Are you fresh?" she asked. The old woman called Great Mother had spent almost her entire life in the House of the Celestial Gate, entering as a servant during the remarkable days when Shanghai vibrated with excitement and adventure, a feast for the senses of warring gangsters and beautiful women of the night, where spies and warlords rubbed shoulders, secrets were sold dearly, and life was cheap.

Over the decades, the old woman had learned the craft of whores without ever becoming one, becoming a master at training young girls to lose their innocence and permit their bodies to be violated, often by men old enough to be their grandfathers. Yet she had never lain with a man. She found no pleasure in matters of the flesh, and approached the conversion of girls into whores with little philosophical difference from a nun introducing girls to God.

"Yes, I am ready."

No part of a woman's body was sacred from a man's lust. Every part of the body, every inch of her flesh, had to be ready for a man's pleasure. Men particularly found Lily Soong's private area stimulating. When women shaved the area, or removed the hair with wax, there was always residue in feel or appearance that reminded the man that hair had been there. But Lily Soong's pubic area was as smooth and bare as a baby's.

"You understand what you have to do? You have been instructed about the foreigner?" She used the Mandarin word for foreigner, *waiguoren*. Mandarin was the official language of the country, the "common language" used nationally, but a Shanghaiese dialect was still generally used in the city. The madam, who had the bureaucratic heart and soul of the old officious Imperial eunuch class that dominated centuries of Chinese emperors, spoke only the official language, refusing to use the local dialect or even the Cantonese tongue of her birth. The Imperial eunuchs had passed into history, but there would always be people with their passion for bureaucratic red tape and steel-trap mentality.

When she spoke of the foreigner, her tone conveyed the contempt the Imperial eunuchs had had for Westerners, a people they considered to be devils and barbarians. Lily would not have been surprised if the woman had used an even older word for foreigners, one that conveyed the inference that foreigners were truly devils and barbarians—*fan kuei.*

Lily Soong dipped her finger in a jar of cream and rubbed the lotion on her breasts. Oil from the seeds of the opium poppy was in the cream. It was said to act as an aphrodisiac for men who smelled and licked it.

"Yes, I know what I must do."

THE WILD, WILD East. Wild and crazy, he thought. As a man from the West, the foreigner was a head taller than most of the crowd, but that didn't make it any easier for him to fight his way along the densely crowded, almost impassable streets.

The Chinese were probably the most polite and courteous people on planet Earth, especially to strangers. Under normal circumstances, when people saw the foreigner approaching, a man of a different skin color and a head taller than most others on the sidewalk, they would veer away, making space for him. Most Chinese were too polite, and their cities too crowded, to play the rude, king-of-the-sidewalk games of New York and Chicago.

But it was the New Year under the old Chinese calendar and a *billion* people were celebrating—and he was sure most of them were on the street he was trying to make his way down.

He had been in Shanghai for a week and had come down these same streets of the Old City almost daily from his hotel on the Bund. Even when the city was not celebrating, the back streets and narrow lanes of the Old City were a pandemonium of people, smells, and sounds that assaulted the senses—*ri nao* was what the Chinese called it. Hot noise. Food stalls, with their pungent smells of fish heads, pork rumps, and the city's succulent hairy crabs, along with endless chatter, offered a significant portion of the din.

The importance of food was characterized by a common greeting: *"Ni chi fan le mei yo?"* Have you eaten your rice yet? Some cities evoke images of foreign intrigue, of dangerous streets and shadowy figures in trench coats—Istanbul, Cairo, Tangiers, Casablanca, Macao. Shanghai was another city that carried a reputation as a place of mystery and intrigue. But unlike cities that could only boast of their intrigues, Shanghai also had a reputation for being rapacious and licentious. If there was a Sodom and Gomorrah of the East, it was this city where pleasure and sin had always been synonymous.

It was like no other city he had ever experienced or even imagined.

China was an ironfisted communist country and Shanghai its largest city. Those facts inferred that the city would be boring and sterile, its spirit of individualism smothered by communist red tape—communists rivaled the notorious Imperial eunuchs for their ability to drown humans under a bureaucratic morass.

But Shanghai was anything but a stereotype paradigm for urban socialism. Seeing the economic failure of communism from North Korea to the Soviet Union and Eastern Europe, and embarrassed by the economic "miracles" in South Korea, Japan, Taiwan, Singapore, and Hong Kong, by the mid-eighties Red China loosened its bureaucratic leash on Shanghai so the city could achieve its old standing as a world-class financial empire with a swinging, stunning social scene—aping Western disco culture.

In its Sodom days of decadence before the Second World War and the people's victory of Mao, the city called itself the Paris of the Orient, but it was a bastard child, part Oriental, part Occidental, a mixture that gave the city its own provocative persona. Now, the communist overlords of the modern city advertised it as the Pearl of the Orient. But old China hands, the businessmen and diplomats who had experienced the city when the yellow demon, opium, was king, when murder and sex, gangsters and sing-song girls, rubbed shoulders with warlords and revolutionaries in the city's nightclubs, called it the Whore of the Orient.

In the 1800s, the Western powers, led by the British, invaded and brought Chinese governments to their knees to force them to permit the sale of opium to their people, creating tens of millions of addicts. But in the true fashion of proverbial Eastern revenge, a slow strangle rather than a bullet to the head, the day would come when China would export opium's most potent by-product, heroin, to millions of addicts in Europe and America.

THE FOREIGNER HAD to leave his taxi blocks away and push his way through the press of people on the streets. Stepping into the gutter, he walked a block alongside a long red dragon that slithered down the center of the street, moving its head from side to side and blowing fire that brought shrieks from children.

Distracted by an endless sea of excited people, fantastic costumes, and the monsters of Chinese mythology, he never realized he was being followed by a killer.

THE SMALL, SLENDER man moved like a wraith behind the foreigner. His real name had long been extinguished by nonuse and he went now by his number, 186, and the name his fellow gang members gave him—Snake, a tribute to his ability to slither along behind a victim without being noticed.

Had the foreigner he was following known about Snake, he would have called him a "triad" gangster. But "triad," which was meant to imply a Chinese criminal organization like the Mafia, was a word used by Westerners for the secret organization, not by Far Easterners.

Secret societies have flourished in China almost during its entire recorded history. With their rituals, oath taking, and harsh penalties for violations of rules, societies were formed to give strength in numbers, beneficial clubs to aid business or workers. They were usually kept secret to keep oppressive governments from destroying them. But many secret societies found their tao, their heavenly path or way, with crime. These were called black societies.

The triad name arose from the obsession the black societies had with things associated with the number 3. Thus a triangle representing the tripartite of existence—heaven, earth, and man—became a banner and things in triple became used in ceremonies and even membership standing. Snake's gang number of 186, like all gang numbers, was divisible by 3. Perhaps the fact that 9 is considered a lucky number to many Chinese also fits into the equation of 3s.

Snake's gang was called the 24 Karat Society. It was well established in both Shanghai and Hong Kong. Not surprisingly, the communists were never able to stamp out gangs, in either China or other Red countries.

In the British Hong Kong colony, which was due to be turned back over to Red China in 1997, the gang had sometimes been used by China's KGB-type intelligence agency for "wet work," i.e., assassinations. Other times the gang was used to kidnap and bring back dissidents and scientists who had fled to foreign soil.

Snake was not an international gangster flush with a luxury car, palatial villa, and beautiful women, nor was he a simple triad "soldier" who ran drugs or hijacked trucks of computers. His specialty was quiet, efficient murder. Like his namesake, he slithered up behind his victims and struck without warning. He took neither pleasure nor regret from his work—it was simply the path his life took.

Like Lily Soong, the pleasure girl, his own path had been established when he came into the world as another mouth to feed in a family that had a less nutritious diet and less medical attention than most cats and dogs in America.

7

❖

When he was a hundred feet from the House of the Celestial Gate, the foreigner pushed his way through the crowd to reach the front door. The bottom floor of the five-floor building was a karaoke bar. He went into the bar.

The bar looked typical for karaoke, a man and woman singing along to the canned instrumental accompaniment, people drinking, laughing. But this was Shanghai, and nothing was what it appeared to be. The women were the tip-off—their eyes were too savvy from having seen too much; they were much too worldly to be wives or girlfriends; their clothes covered too little and cost too much. They wore traditional feminine dress—the *chi-pao*, a long tunic with a slit on the side—but instead of the modesty of long pants underneath, bare flesh was exposed by slits that came up to naked thighs. Their shoes were the "spike heels" that went in and out of vogue.

"China Dolls" was how Westerners thought of the bar girls—petite figures in bright red and yellow satin dresses, balanced on high heels. The girls looked as fragile as ceramic dolls but made men shake with sex.

The karaoke bar was an updated version of the nightclubs and "teahouses" where dime-a-dance and sing-song girls drank fuck-wine—dark, cold tea paid for as high-priced whiskey by male customers—and offered more than small talk to sailors and businessmen.

There were other bars and party rooms, places where any perversion or appetite could be satisfied, but his destination was a private room on the fifth floor where Lily Soong was waiting.

LILY SOONG ANSWERED a discreet tap on her door. She opened the door to Snake.

He looked at her with a question on his face.

"He's down in the karaoke bar," she said. "They'll call me when he leaves."

Snake slipped in, closing the door behind him.

"Did anyone see you come up?"

He shook his head. "You think I would let Celestial Gate see me?"

"Not if you expect to live."

"If I am to die in the war, many will go with me."

The "war" Snake mentioned was a turf battle. Triad gangs operated openly in Hong Kong, and had existed since time immemorial in Shanghai, but kept a low profile in the city because of the tight communist controls over the past decades. As Shanghai moved into the free market and controls loosened, Hong Kong's notorious 24 Karat black society pushed into the city from the British colony, igniting conflict with the long-established Shanghai triad, the Protectors of the Celestial Gate.

"Give me my money," Lily Soong said.

"When the job is done."

She held out her hand. "Give it to me."

He hesitated but pulled out a wad of bills and gave them to her. "Have patience; maybe you will get even more."

She smiled coyly at him. "How do I know that the foreigner won't kill you instead?"

Snake grinned and scoffed. "The Master of the Mountain knows who he sends. I am the best."

The Master of the Mountain was the head of a triad organization, a position akin to a "don" who headed a mafia family. The triad title came from the days when the black societies gathered on hilltops for their secret meetings.

"Do you plan to tell the foreigner why he's being killed?"

He snickered. "I will tell his ghost that he did business with the wrong people."

She wore an almost sheer nightgown. Her nude form was visible beneath the silk.

"You're the one with the bald eagle," he said. "When the job is done, will you let me see it?"

"Maybe. You have money?"

"Plenty of money."

"Why not now? They will call me when he starts up."

She went to a stuffed couch next to draped windows. The heavy drapes were pulled shut. She sat on an arm of the couch and pulled the gown up to her knees.

"Get down, here." She indicated the floor in front of her.

He knelt down on the floor. She slowly pulled up the gown. He watched, his eyes widening, his lips parting, as she exposed her naked thighs. She let him linger for a moment before she inched the silk up until he could see the V between her legs. He stared, unmoving, as she slowly lifted the gown and spread her legs.

His breathing stilled. He had seen a bare pubis before, but only on prepubescent girls. On a grown woman, it was not natural nakedness, but mesmerizing and erotic. She was a woman of legend, not one of the street whores he was used to paying for false cries of ecstasy and wonderment at his manhood.

Her jasmine scent filled his nostrils and clouded his thinking.

She put her hands behind his head and brought his head forward, lifting her legs up and spreading them wider. She pulled his head hard against her.

His lips opened and his tongue came out and slipped between the pink lips of her vulva.

The curtain behind him parted and a man stepped out and used two hands to plunge a long knife into the base of Snake's neck, severing his spinal cord.

The triad killer flopped over and rolled for a moment, gasping and jerking. His eyes went up in his head and he twitched convulsively.

The foreigner stared at Lily Soong, the bloody knife in his hand.

His hand was shaking. He wasn't used to killing.

Colombia

TRAVEL WARNING
United States Department of State

This travel warning is being issued to remind American citizens of ongoing security concerns in Colombia, continues to warn against travel to Colombia, and notes a continuing threat.

Violence by narco-terrorist groups and other elements continues to affect all parts of the country.

American kidnap or murder victims have included journalists, missionaries, scientists, human rights workers, businesspeople, as well as persons on tourism or family visits.

No one can be considered immune.

Since it is U.S. policy not to make concessions to, or strike deals with, terrorists and criminals, the U.S. government's ability to assist kidnapped U.S. citizens is severely limited.

8

❖

I got off the plane in San Francisco and looked at the monitors for the first flight scheduled for anywhere south of the border. It was a chartered flight to Cancun, Mexico's Caribbean coast party town.

A big map on a wall told me that Cancun was a hop, skip, and a jump to Colombia, with Central America and some water in between. The best thing about a flight to Cancun was that the plane was taking off shortly and the destination was out of the country and in the same general direction as Colombia.

The flight was already boarding as I hurried up to the ticket counter.

"Mr. Sully, that gentleman in the blue blazer, is the charter's flight manager," the counter clerk said. "You have to get his permission to buy a ticket if you don't already have a reservation."

Mr. Sully was a middle-aged man with gray slacks and white tasseled loafers to go with his blue blazer. I wondered if he was a lawyer in real life.

I introduced myself and asked if I could buy a ticket on the flight.

"Another last-minute friend?" he asked.

I didn't know whose friend I could be, but I tried to look apologetic. "I'm sorry, it was a last-minute decision."

"All right, but you understand, you have to abide by our society's rules or we'll have to enforce sanctions."

I murmured my assent and hurried to get a ticket. I didn't know what the rules were, some sort of religious thing, probably, but at the moment, I'd make a deal with the devil herself to get on the plane.

As I surrendered my boarding pass at the gate, I saw a sign for the flight: *Mimesis Society, The Oneness of Us and Nature.*

I thought I'd heard of the group before. An organization for smart people, as I recalled. I had a friend in college that joined it.

The plane was mid-sized, with three seats on one side and two on the side I was on. I had the window seat next to a man in his early thirties. Attractive, with an ebony complexion and short-cropped hair revealing an African-American heritage, he looked more athletic and outdoorsy than cerebral. He smiled and got up to let me slip into my seat.

I sighed with relief and closed my eyes as soon as we rolled away from the gate. *Adios, Seattle police! Mexico, here I come!*

"I was told we won't be able to start until we've leveled off and the seat-belt sign goes off," my companion said. "This is my first time. Have you attended many of the events?"

"Uh, no, my first, too."

"Apparently we have to use some discretion in Cancun; the Mexicans aren't as open about these things as other places in the Caribbean."

"Hmmm." An inane listening response was the best I could muster. I couldn't imagine what Mexicans could have against a group of visiting geniuses. You'd think as a spring break Mecca, Cancun would tolerate anything, with the rather conservative-looking thirty-to-fifty crowd in the plane topping the list of visitors the city would love to attract.

Rushing from one plane and onto another, I hadn't had a chance to visit the restroom before we took off. As soon as the plane was leveling off, I got up and went to the rear. I smiled at the cute blond flight attendant who stood to the side to let me pass. He had dimples that made him look younger than the early twenties I guessed his age to be. I automatically wondered if he was gay. At my age, I had a fatalistic attitude that anyone that good-looking was probably gay. Or married. Or both.

I did my business in the restroom. I heard the seat-belt sign signal go off as I was washing up. I wondered what my seat companion had meant when he said they couldn't start until the seat-belt sign went off. I hoped they weren't going to engage in some kind of intellectual game that took a rocket scientist to play. It was hard enough for me to look intelligent without trying to act like it.

I stepped out of the cubbyhole restroom and almost into the arms of a naked man. Involuntarily, my eyes immediately went to his male part.

I had just enough composure to freeze in place and not scream, but I couldn't keep my jaw from dropping.

"Excuse me." He stepped around me to get into the restroom.

My feet stayed rooted in place as I rotated my head and stared down the aisle.

People were shedding their clothes—or had shed their clothes. They were in the aisles or kneeling on their seats, pulling off tops and bottoms. All layers. Men and women. Old and young. Fat and skinny. Black, white, yellow, brown, and shades in between.

The world was full of all types and all types were on the plane—in the flesh.

I thought about retreating to another toilet stall, but I'd look suspicious if I stayed there for the next few hours.

Taking a deep breath, keeping chin up and eyes straight ahead—as much as I could—I forced one foot in front of the other and proceeded down the plane aisle. It was impossible not to brush by bare flesh, some pumped, some sagging, as I went. I automatically murmured apologies.

My seat was halfway down the plane and it was the longest walk I'd ever taken.

Panic was rising in me. I had to make a decision. What the hell was I to do? These people were all insane nudist sex fiends; I didn't know yet what exactly they were, but I wanted no part of whatever game they were playing. We were at thirty-eight thousand feet. Dashing out the nearest exit was not an option, nor ignoring the fact that I was going to be the only person on the plane wearing clothes.

What had the charter manager said back at the airport? Something about *sanctions* if I didn't abide by the society's rules; I didn't know what he meant by that, but the last thing I needed was to draw attention to myself. And this was one time I couldn't hide behind my quick wits—or my clothes.

I paused by my seat neighbor. He was naked but was reading a magazine that covered his lap.

"Did you want to get undressed before you sat down?" he asked.

Not in front of a couple hundred people.

"I prefer being seated. Might get turbulence."

He got up and let me pass. I tried to keep my eyes straight, but they involuntarily glanced down as I went to my seat.

He was an adequate male. Thank God he wasn't aroused. I would have turned purple with embarrassment.

I started to put on my seat belt and he said, "You must really be afraid of turbulence."

I gave him a blank look.

"I've never heard of anyone taking off their clothes with their seat belt on."

Shit. I was drawing attention to myself. "Sorry, I'm not thinking; I've got a migraine."

I slowly unbuttoned my blouse and slipped it off. I folded it and left it in my lap. Next was a little cotton pullover. That came off. I folded it and put it on the pile I was starting on my lap. I glanced sideways at him. I was now exposing my pink bra, but he was still intent upon his magazine.

It was time to take off my pants. I had on blue jeans, the type you paid $150 for at a boutique when you can get them for $30 at a discount store. I slipped off my shoes and slowly pulled off my pants. I added the pants to the stack in my lap.

In pink panties and bra, I glanced sideways at him.

He had put away the magazine but didn't seem the least bit interested in the fact there was an attractive woman—me!—almost naked beside him.

I looked up as the cute blond flight attendant went by. He

smiled at me. "Better hurry; Mr. Sully wants everyone ready when we start our breathing and flex exercises."

Oh great, breathing and flex. Breathing I knew, but what the hell was flex? I hoped the hell we weren't going to take turns standing up in the aisle and flexing the muscles in our tushes.

It was time to give up the ghost. Smothering a little groan of modesty, or more accurately a lack of confidence that my naked form would compare favorably when stacked up—literally—against women who were buffed in more places than I could afford to augment surgically, I took off my bra.

I snuck a sideways glance at the attractive male beside me. Not a peek, sneaking or otherwise, from the stud.

What the hell? How could this man just sit there with his head in a magazine when I was letting it all hang out?

I was now down to basics. Bare boobs and dangling male parts were parading up and down the aisle as people walked and talked little differently than if they were at a cocktail party or barbecue after church. But I still dreaded the idea of being completely naked. It wasn't so much that I was a prude; I was just modest . . . embarrassed . . . not happy with my figure. All those things any woman who didn't spend every day at the gym and on the current diet rage would feel. And I'd feel the same way if I had the body of a supermodel.

But there was nothing I could do; whining wouldn't help. Get on with it or draw attention—and sanctions—to myself.

Besides, when in Rome . . .

I took off my panties.

Mr. Stud looked up from his magazine.

"Want me to put those in the overhead?" he asked. He was talking about the pile of clothes I was hiding behind.

Wow! What willpower—or lack of interest? He met me eye-to-eye, not straying to check out my naked breasts or pubic mound.

Every time I looked at him, my eyes went out of control and involuntarily dipped down to his midsection, but his eyes never strayed.

I'd heard that people at nudist colonies didn't walk around aroused—the men, I mean. That made sense. It would be awfully impolite if a man was talking to another man's wife and his thing suddenly started erupting. That wouldn't do, would it?

Maybe to this guy next to me having a naked woman beside him was like handling money in a bank. After a while, the millions of dollars bank tellers handle had to be just so much green paper, right? If they thought of it as *money,* as a new car, a nicer home, a Caribbean cruise . . . most bank robberies would be inside jobs.

That helped assuage my fragile ego. I was actually enjoying the freedom of no clothes, sipping a glass of wine, and talking to my companion—whose eyes never strayed to my breasts—when a question popped into my head. His name was Will and he turned out to be a computer executive from Phoenix.

"I forget—what do you call that organization of people who think they're smart?"

"Mensa?"

Yes, that was it; I just had the spelling a little wrong. At least the anxiety was over—I now knew what the people were up to on the plane and it was just some innocent nudism. No daisy chains or other group sex was parading up and down the aisle. People had a glass of wine or a beer and were into talking about the last nudist beach they'd hung out at.

I leaned back and closed my eyes. I was relaxed from the wine and from being a thousand miles and thirty-eight thousand feet from U.S. jurisdiction when my eyes involuntarily strayed open and I noticed that Will's male organ had suddenly come alive.

It was going up . . . up . . . up. . . . Swollen. Engorged. Raising like the Graf Zeppelin. Inflated like a condom blown up with a party store helium tank. Pulsating—angry, eager, anxious.

Oh my God. He had finally noticed me.

Pleased with myself, a little giddy from wine and my escape from the police, I started to lean a little closer to let him know I was interested when I realized he was staring intently down the aisle.

The cute flight attendant had dropped something. He was bending over, his tush pointed back at us.

He even had dimples on his buns.

9

I was feeling very drowsy and tired, probably because I had gotten little sleep the night before and then caught an early flight out of Seattle that morning.

Or maybe it was drinking a glass of red wine with little food in my stomach. I normally didn't care for red wine. Everyone was saying it was healthy, but sometimes the stuff gave me a headache. I also found it too heavy for me. I preferred a dry white wine, like a pinot grigio or sauvignon blanc, even when I was eating a meal that called for red wine.

For some reason today I had a craving for red wine. Lots of people on the plane were drinking it and Will was working on his second glass. I wasn't much of a wine connoisseur. Having worked in the business, I knew a lot about wines, but I drank what I liked rather than what a sommelier said I was supposed to drink. And sometimes I was guilty of buying a brand just because I liked the label. But watching Will enjoy the red wine, I suddenly had a strong desire to have a glass. Maybe it was a sexual thing. When I looked at the dark red color, it reminded me of passion . . . love . . . romance. . . .

I could barely keep my eyelids open.

I looked over to Will. "I'm taking a little nap. Don't wake me up for the food."

Like anyone with taste buds, I didn't care for airline food. I usually passed it up whenever I flew, because more often than not the food was terrible. Once in a while I had their egg omelet and sometimes even that was uneatable. Normally I ate something before the flight. This morning I barely had time to throw some protein bars in my purse.

The flight attendant had come by again and Will's lascivious gaze locked back on the guy's rear dimples. Will didn't even bother looking at me when he said, "Okay."

"Would you grab me a pillow from overhead?" I asked, breaking his concentration. "And a blanket," I added. "I feel a bit chilly."

"Sure."

Even though I was getting used to sitting next to Will with both of us naked, I still didn't feel comfortable with exposing my naked body to total strangers. Shedding my clothes for a guy was one thing, but parading around for the whole world to see was something else. Plus, in the back of my mind, I kept having this recurring thought of how many germs were lurking on the airline seat. When he stood up and faced me, his penis stood straight up.

His erections had killed my theory about nudists never getting aroused. This time I barely glanced at it. Like handling money in a bank—once a guy lets me know that I'm the wrong gender, I lose interest.

Before he sat down, I asked for a second blanket so I could sit on it.

After wrapping up, the last thing I remember before I dozed off was Will talking to the cute flight attendant and following him down the aisle with a glass of red wine.

10

❖

I drifted into a peaceful sleep. An image of rows and rows of leafy green grapevines on trellises with clumps of plump purple grapes swirled in my drowsy head. . . .

I walked in the warmth of the afternoon sun among the endless sloping hills of vineyards, not really sure where I was. In the far distance atop a hill was a whitewashed house with a red tiled roof.

I picked a cluster of sun-kissed grapes, savoring their sweetness as I bit into the ripe fruit.

The sun felt good as I walked down toward a winery I saw in the distance. The annual harvesting celebration had already begun. I heard people singing, music, laughter. In the heart of the celebration was a large vat, with sides several feet high, looking much like an oversized wooden barrel. Three women were in it, laughing and singing as they stomped grapes, their clothes and faces splashed with the juice.

I suddenly wanted to submerge myself in the deep purple and ruby red juices and soak in their intense aroma and flavor. I wanted to squish the grapes with my feet.

I eagerly joined the three women in the oversized barrel as

they crushed the succulent grapes with their washed feet. Suddenly instead of having stained clothes, they were naked, their bodies covered with the juices and skins of the grapes. I unashamedly tore off my own clothing.

People around us were singing and clapping as we danced in the grapes, mashing them down with our feet.

I stomped and stomped, trying to keep myself balanced in the dense volume of grapes. A splash of crushed grapes hit my back. I swirled around. One of the women had a handful of smashed grapes in her hand. She had a playful look in her eyes, ready to throw another round. Her body was supple and shapely, full round breasts jutting forward, her hands resting on her hips now, which swayed suggestively back and forth.

I picked up a good handful of the mushy grapes and threw them on her breasts, almost knocking her off balance. She boldly hit me back harder, knocking me off my feet, and I fell backward up to my chest in the mushy fruit.

All at once she lunged at me and we wrestled with each other, our whole bodies now covered from head to foot in grape juice.

We finally broke apart, exhausted, leaning against the back of the barrel, choking out a mouthful of grapes. Both of us broke out laughing.

It was only when we stopped that I noticed we were all alone. Everyone else had disappeared.

We were sitting next to each other, still trying to catch our breath. The laughter was now replaced with desire as her eyes lingered on my nipples, taut with excitement. Her fingers circled around each of them, down my abdomen, and moved around my inner thighs and paused. I was beginning to feel a tingling sensation creep into my lower abdomen. I didn't want her to stop . . . I wanted her to continue . . . I wanted her to probe me deeper with her finger. . . .

I felt the hand on my shoulder. "Don't stop," I said.

"Don't stop what? Hey, wake up."

"No. . . ." I opened my eyes.

It was Will. "Sorry to wake you."

"No, that's okay."

"We're going to land in a few minutes."

"What? You mean I slept all this time?"

"Yeah. I thought I'd better wake you before the final announcement comes on. To get dressed. You can't get off the plane without clothes on."

"Thanks. I guess I really conked out."

It was only then that I realized he had all his clothes on and so did most of the other passengers. A few stragglers were waiting until the last minute. I suddenly felt very naked even though I had a blanket covering me.

"You must have had one hell of a dream."

A wave of embarrassment suddenly hit me. I noticed my hand was between my legs. And I felt flushed. Had I just had an orgasm? I wondered how long Will had been sitting there. Had he been watching me?

"I did? Why do you say that?"

"You're sweating. And you kept saying, 'Don't stop; don't stop.' Maybe I shouldn't have awakened you."

"Yeah . . . I mean no, nothing happened," I lied. "Well, I'd better get dressed. Thanks for waking me."

"Sure. I'm going to the galley to get some water. Do you want any?"

"No, thanks." I kept the blanket wrapped around me as I headed toward the toilets in the back of the plane. I went into one and locked the door. I gave myself a quick bath under the arms with paper towels and got dressed. A hot bath would have been better, but this would have to do.

Will hadn't returned yet when I got back to my seat. No doubt he wasn't just getting water from the galley, but whatever else the cute flight attendant was dishing out.

11

❖

The next flight in the general direction of Colombia out of Cancun was to Panama City, Panama. I took it.

As soon as I arrived at the airport in Panama City, I boarded a plane that was going to Bogotá, the capital of Colombia. A direct flight to Medellín left Panama City three hours later, but I decided not to hang around. Panama was the site of the all-important canal and there was a heavy American influence in the little country. About three years ago American troops invaded the country, arrested the dictator, Manuel Noriega, and took him to Miami for a trial on drug-trafficking charges.

I didn't think my Seattle problem would be worth an invasion, but the whole scenario showed more U.S. influence in the country than I liked at the moment.

Besides, with Medellín's evil reputation as a center for drugs and violence, a stopover in Bogotá to orientate myself and learn the ropes for Colombia sounded like a good idea.

Since I only had one carry-on bag, I didn't have to hassle with any check-in luggage. I bought my ticket and got boarded almost immediately, sure I could have made the *Guinness Book of Records* for least time in airports on an international flight.

I had just enough time to pick up a South American tour book in the airport bookstore before I boarded the plane. Once I settled in my seat, I began reading the guidebook, putting it aside to lean back and close my eyes as the plane began its takeoff. The sensation of the plane accelerating and surging upward into the air always thrilled me. That and when the plane came in for its landing were the best two times of flying—I'd read that they were also the only times people were likely to survive a plane crash.

I thought about the countless times my mother and I took off to a new place, how excited we were at the prospect of seeing new territory. My mother always made it sound like a fun adventure. Now I was going on another adventure, running off to a whole different country. Only this time I was a little apprehensive of what to expect when I arrived. I always remind myself that the "adventure" part only comes later when the tale is told—adventures are usually pure misery when they're happening.

I suddenly wished my mother was here with me. She'd figure some way to make running from the police and a murder charge fun. There were times when I really missed her, and this was one of them. She'd always been there when I needed a shoulder to cry on, giving me good advice, but hiding her wisdom behind a little humor to make it sound less like a lecture.

I stared out the window, her image in my mind, trying to imagine what she would tell me if she were here, but I couldn't concentrate.

I went back to the guidebook and starting reading about Colombia. I hadn't gotten very far when a perfectly handsome man came up and gestured at the empty aisle seat next to me.

"Buenos dias," he said with a big smile. He was a Latin type, the kind of South American in a 1930s movie who wore white linen suits when he wasn't in his gaucho cowboy outfit. His gleaming teeth were amazingly white. "Is this seat available?"

Several other empty seats were readily available—why had he chosen the one next to mine? I didn't consider myself a knockout beauty—not even pretty. I've been told my most prominent asset was my generous smile, that it was infectious. My mother always said I had a personality that made people gravitate toward me, but I knew I wasn't a showstopper when it came to men—more like someone to talk to during intermission.

"Yes, it is." For sure it was for him. It isn't every day that a good-looking man sits down next to you.

"Then, with your permission . . ."

"Of course." I moved my handbag off the empty seat.

His English had just a hint of foreign intrigue to it. He was tall and slender, with light brown hair, his Coppertone complexion a shade darker than mine. With long eyelashes and emerald green eyes, he was sexy and stank of being filthy rich, definitely old money, the kind who knew how to spend it but never got his hands dirty earning any of it. He had an air of confidence about him that was much more appealing to a woman than what the beer and macho types displayed.

What is it an anonymous—but very perceptive—woman said? Coffee, chocolate, and men are better when they're rich?

After he settled in, he said, "I hope you don't mind the companionship. The person I was sitting next to in first class has a cold."

"No, I understand perfectly. All they do on planes is circulate dirty air from the cabin back into the plane. Sometimes I think we should all wear surgery masks on a plane."

"An excellent idea. I've seen people in Japan wear such face masks, both as a courtesy not to spread a cold and not to get one. Ramon Alavar," he said, offering me his hand.

"Nash Novak." His hand was cool, not as firm as I was expecting, but smooth and polished. For sure, the only things the man had handled were money and women. I felt a little shiver of excitement as I let go of his hand. He was a man who radiated sex. If he'd been on the nudist flight, I'd have ripped off my clothes eagerly.

"Are you certain I'm not intruding? I have to confess, I chose you because you are the most attractive woman on the plane."

Oh my God. "And there was an empty seat," I stammered, unable to take the compliment.

He smiled. "That helped, too."

My cheeks suddenly felt warm. Was I blushing or did it suddenly get warmer in the plane?

His vibrant green eyes appraised me. "You have a very pretty smile."

I mumbled a thank-you and started thumbing through the pages of my guidebook. Wow, this guy oozed sex appeal at a higher octane than I was used to. I usually don't get flustered and start mumbling like a dork when a man tries to put the make on me.

My guidebook stated that about 60 percent of the people of Colombia were "mestizo," a mixture created by intermarriages of Europeans, mostly Spanish, with Native Americans. The rest were either pure European or pure indigenous. Ramon's handsome looks struck me as the best of everything Colombia had to offer.

The flight attendant came by and smiled at my companion. "Senor, you were just on my flight from Bogotá. Returning so soon? You could hardly have left the airport."

"A business emergency," he said.

After the flight attendant moved on, Ramon turned to me. "I see you've been reading about my country. No doubt the book tells you many negative things about my beautiful country. Let me offer a word of advice: Do not believe everything you read. *Norteamericanos* don't understand the culture of Latin America. You expect everything to be orderly, time and statements to have precise meaning, but so much precision takes much of the mystery and magic out of life, doesn't it?"

I cleared my throat and read from a summary in the travel book. The book didn't pull any punches about traveling in the country. It repeated facts and information it claimed came from U.S. State Department statistics.

" 'The number one cause of death in Colombia is not from heart attacks or cancer, but homicide. There is open warfare between the government, the cocaine cartels, and politically extreme rebel groups. In the past few years, four presidential candidates, several dozen judges, the minister of justice, and hundreds of police officers, along with a couple dozen journalists, have been murdered. In one incident, a passenger plane with over a hundred people aboard was blown up because it was thought a presidential candidate was on board.' "

He shrugged and raised his eyebrows. *"Plata o plomo."*

I knew what the words meant—silver or lead—but I didn't comprehend the reference to them. "I don't follow you."

"Don Pablo Escobar and his Medellín cartel *compañeros* made the government an offer: Don't attempt to extradite them to the United States, give them amnesty for their crimes, and they will pour billions into the Colombian economy, money that is badly needed. Their offer was refused. Now Escobar offers judges, police officials, and politicians silver or lead— take his bribe or hot lead from his *sicarios.*"

"Sicarios?"

"Gunmen. A biblical expression. The political assassins of the Holy Land during Roman times were called *sicarii.* It's the surname that history gave Judas. There is a rumor that Escobar has a school for his *sicarii* gunmen, that he has the assassins learn how to kill and not be caught and what to do if they are caught. Like the Old Man of the Mountain."

"Old Man of the Mountain?"

"The word 'assassin' comes from an Arabic name for hashish. The Old Man of the Mountain was the name given to the leader of an Islamic sect of terrorists that existed hundreds of years ago. They would get high on the drug before they went out and committed murder. They also got a promise of having a harem in heaven with twenty beautiful women if they were killed."

He leaned closer and spoke in a lower voice. "A presidential candidate Don Pablo didn't like was scheduled to be a passenger on the plane that was blown up. Don Pablo told one of his underlings to board the plane and carry a suitcase with a listening device on it. Do you know what was in the suitcase?"

"Let me guess . . . a bomb?"

"Exactly, much to the surprise of the don's man. And, of course, the candidate had canceled the trip, so a planeload of innocents died for nothing."

I gave him a bright smile. "It's nice that modern Colombia fits in so well with ancient and modern violence. Sounds like a wonderful country. I can't wait to get off the plane and be murdered."

His laugh was genuine. "You have to understand, of course, that the people who are being murdered are the ones who are either involved in drug trafficking or who oppose it. Ordinary people aren't killed unless they are in the wrong place at the wrong time."

"That's comforting to know—unless I happen to get caught in the cross fire."

"Don't worry; cocaine cowboys and revolutionaries are no different than the other men of Colombia—we don't shoot beautiful women; we worship them and smother them with jewels."

Does he think I am beautiful? Or was it just a line?

Who cared? It sounded good.

He had the good manners to pat my arm and not my knee as so many men would do. "Don't worry; criminals will not spoil your visit. Are you going to Colombia on business?"

I started to say yes but then caught myself. I knew zero about business in Colombia. I decided to tell him a version of the truth.

"I'm visiting my uncle. He owns a coffee plantation."

"Excellent. Coffee is the heart of my country. Where is your uncle's plantation?"

I didn't want to give him the location. Anyway, I wasn't sure myself if I really knew where it was. I knew the lawyer was in Medellín. And I didn't want to mention that city because it was my ultimate destination.

"Bogotá." The capital was the only name that popped into my head.

His beautiful groomed eyebrows lifted upward. "How interesting. The capital is not a major growing region. It's at a rather high altitude for growing coffee."

Shit. Now he knows I'm lying.

"What's your uncle's name?"

"Juan Valdez," escaped past my lips. It was the first name that came to mind.

"A very common name." He smiled. "Something like your John Smith, I imagine. I thought perhaps I might know him, the name is familiar, but I don't recall a Juan Valdez growing coffee in the capital."

I gave him a feeble smile. "Wouldn't that be pretty unlikely? I mean, your country isn't that small. Aren't there over thirty million people?"

"True, but in a way, I'm in the same business as your uncle."

"You have a coffee plantation?"

Was I digging a deeper hole for myself? I had no idea of how many coffee plantations were in the country. Maybe there were only a few and everyone in the business knew everyone else.

"No, but I am intimately connected to the business. I'm with the department of agriculture. I'm honored to be their deputy director. My division deals directly with the coffee-growing industry."

Damn damn damn. I smiled bravely. "How interesting."

"Of course, you have to understand that most of the coffee farms are very small and number in the hundreds of thousands. If your uncle has one of the larger plantations, I would probably know him."

"No, he has a small farm. A part-time thing, I believe."

"Ah, yes, there are many of those. Some *cafeteros* run coffee operations similar to the winemakers of the Napa Valley in your country and Europe. They can spend years developing their own premium strains of coffee plants. Are you familiar with the production of coffee?"

"I'm afraid my experience with coffee has been limited to drinking it."

I didn't dare volunteer that I'd owned a coffee store and once worked with a wine producer in the Napa Valley. Everything I said seemed to come back to bite me.

"Then you have a treat coming. There is much more to coffee than scooping coffee into a pot. You know, of course, that Colombia produces the finest coffee in the world. Brazil produces more coffee in general, but we are the largest producers of mild Arabica, the only coffee worth brewing, which I'm sure you will learn from your uncle."

I knew that there were two main strains of coffee beans, Arabica and Robusta, and that the Arabica bean was considered the milder and better tasting of the two. It was the only coffee I sold in my store. The Robusta was a cheaper variety with a heavier taste and more caffeine. But I pretended complete ignorance—which wasn't difficult. I knew plenty about *selling* coffee to consumers, but nothing about growing it.

"Are you going directly to your uncle's plantation from the airport?"

"No, he won't be there. I'm going to spend a few days in Bogotá before seeing my uncle." That seemed like a good bet; otherwise it would be an invitation for Ramon to hang around with me at the airport to meet my uncle "the *cafetero*."

"Where will you be staying in Bogotá?"

I hadn't picked a place yet. "I'm playing it by ear. Sometimes you can get the best deal by talking to a taxi driver."

He shook his head. "You are truly an innocent abroad. You are arriving in what you call the most dangerous city in the world and you don't even have a hotel reservation." He raised those beautiful eyebrows. "Senorita, I must take you under my wing and protect you. You cannot trust taxi drivers—or hotel staff. While most murders arise from drug trafficking, it is considered open season on tourists at all times. My car and driver will meet the plane. I will take you to a safe hotel and see to it that they understand you are under my protection. Then I will escort you to the finest restaurant in the city and introduce you to the wines and foods of the greatest city in the world."

He leaned closer to me. The scent of his masculine cologne filled my nostrils.

I admit that I have always had a weakness for hot-blooded men. I hated men whose first love was their car, their muscles, or their sports team. Give me a man anytime who wants to make mad, passionate love.

"I have a hacienda in the Llanos. Perhaps when you tire of coffee trees, you will honor me with a visit to my home. I will show you the charming culture of Old Colombia."

"That sounds interesting." I gave the standard cocktail-party inane reply to almost anything, but I had to keep from drooling at the idea of having this beautiful man sweep me off my feet and onto his white charger, taking me to his hacienda as we rode off into the sunset. God, I'd never met anyone who had a hacienda.

His knee brushed against mine ever so slightly and excitement again raced through my body. I suddenly found myself wishing he would make mad, passionate love to me.

I pulled my blanket up to my neck and closed my eyes, and wondered if I had hit the jackpot or what. I needed a guide and protector and Ramon Alavar was a godsend.

Maybe he was so filthy rich, he could buy me out of my problems in Seattle.

Now that was a pleasant thought, meeting a sexy guy who falls madly in love with me and has all my problems go away with a wave of his checkbook. It's happened to other women. Like winning the lottery—

Damn, I immediately wondered what the snake was, that serpent who always shows up in paradise to take away all the fun. I gave him a sideways glance—Ramon had to be for real; he was too perfect to come with a snake attached.

A LITTLE LATER, as I was flying miles high over Colombia, it suddenly dawned on me why he had given me an odd look after I told him my uncle's name was Juan Valdez. I realized with horror and embarrassment why the name had leaped off my tongue so easily.

"Juan Valdez" was the name of the fictional coffee grower used in Colombian coffee TV and print advertising. His face, poncho, wide-brimmed hat, and donkey with sacks of coffee beans aboard was beamed all over the world by the Colombian coffee industry.

It was about as clever as telling someone in Virginia that my uncle was the Marlboro Man.

Shit.

12

❖

I woke up when the pilot announced we would be landing in thirty minutes. I suddenly realized my head had been leaning against Ramon's shoulder.

"Sorry, I didn't mean to impose on you," I told him as I straightened myself back in my seat. "I guess I slept most of the way."

"I didn't mind at all. I'm glad my shoulder was available."

His locked his dreamy green eyes into mine and I felt like a lovesick teenager. For some reason, this guy sent shivers up my body whenever he gave me a lingering look. I looked down and pretended to check my seat belt. It was fastened tight.

Maybe I was just horny. I hadn't had any sexual relations with a guy for weeks now; no, when I thought about it, it was actually more like months. Was I that preoccupied with my café? The days seemed to quickly turn into weeks and then into months. Some days were so exhausting that I just fell straight into bed.

"If I may give you another word of advice. Bogotá is over a mile and a half high, over eight thousand feet. Don't exert yourself too much until you get used to the altitude. My driver will take care of your luggage."

"Actually, I don't have any luggage, just a small carry-on."

He raised his eyebrows. "You are the first woman I've met that travels so light."

"Well, it, uh, gives me an excuse to shop; you know, I've nothing to wear so I have to buy something."

"Excellent. Bogotá is a world-class city. If you don't mind, I will be happy to escort you to the best shops."

I couldn't afford to buy anything at the best shops, but I had a suspicion that Senor Alavar was the kind of man who wouldn't let a woman pay for anything. At least that was the image I had conjured up.

I looked out the plane and could see the green and sometimes snow-covered Andes mountains below, with the ranges divided by deep, narrow depressions. The scenery was beautiful.

"Most of our people live in cities," he said, "and most of the large cities are found in the valleys and along the sides of our great Andes mountain ranges. We also have jungles and great plains."

Bogotá was stunning from the air, sprawling between mountains and neatly laid out in grid patterns.

"Despite the fact we are near the equator, we have three climates," Ramon said. "The weather depends on how high one lives. At the lower altitudes, it's very hot and wet, a torrid zone that includes rain forests. When you get higher, what we call *tierra del café,* the moderate mid-region of the mountainsides where coffee is grown, the weather is very mild year-round and has moderate rain. The upper region below the snow line is the *tierra fria,* the cold zone. That's where Bogotá is, at an elevation of almost nine thousand feet, nearly twice as high as your Denver, but not so cold. You should find the temperature pleasant, cool, but milder than Seattle."

I leaned back and looked out the window, a disturbing question suddenly buzzing in my head.

Had I told him I was from Seattle?

I couldn't remember. I didn't think I had, but I had been cozying up to him—who knows what I said. I also had to wonder whether Seattle, like Denver, was just an offhanded remark.

I shook off the suspicion, certain I had gotten out of Seattle too fast and clever for anyone to have followed me. I'd met this man in an airport—how would anyone know that I'd bought a ticket in Cancun for Panama City and the next one for Bogotá?

Besides, there was no chance this rich, sexy man who stroked my feminine fires—and ego—could possibly be involved in the insanity that had gripped my life.

I had left all that back in Seattle. It was a new day, a new country, new friends. Ramon was going to be a lifesaver.

I'd bet my life on it.

RAMON FLASHED HIS official identification at the customs official. My passport was stamped without formality, not even a question or a peek into my bag. We were escorted the rest of the way through customs and into the baggage claims area.

He grinned when he saw the surprised expression on my face.

"Yes, my position provides some privileges, but in truth, the customs people are not worried about someone smuggling something *into* the country," he said.

When we came out into the crowded baggage area, his driver was waiting to get Ramon's luggage.

Ramon pointed out his black Mercedes limo at the curb, visible through the large plate glass window. "As soon as my luggage arrives, we can be on our way. Why don't you give Rafael your bag so he can put it in the limo?"

"I'll need it for a moment; I need to visit the ladies' room."

I used the excuse because the tiny mirror in the airplane didn't give me a chance to get a good look at the condition of my makeup and hair. After I brushed my hair and added a little blush to my cheeks, I went back to the baggage claims area.

Rafael, the driver, was still there, his back to me as he waited for Ramon's luggage to come down the rotating carousel. Through the big window, I spotted Ramon standing by the limo talking to a man.

I stopped in my tracks and froze.

The man was Scar, the menacing character who had insisted I sell him my coffee plantation.

I spun on my heel and went the opposite direction, back into the terminal. I walked fast and aimlessly, just getting distance between myself and whatever plots or conspiracies were being hatched at the limousine back at the curb.

Fortunately my feet knew exactly what to do, because my brain had frozen. When my senses snapped back to life, panic set in.

How in God's name could I have been tracked from Seattle to San Fran, from Cancun to Panama City, and have that ominous bastard waiting for me like a vulture ready to rip out my liver? Only governments had the authority to get information from airlines. How could—

Stupid me—this was Colombia. As Ramon said, the country didn't operate exactly like the States. A little money passed hands and someone at an airport tracked my itinerary.

I had come thousands of miles to get away from my troubles in Seattle and one of them was waiting for me.

So much for Ramon being my knight in shining armor. The fact that a high official with the Colombian coffee ministry sat down next to me on the plane was too much of a coincidence; he was just too perfect and sexy for me to see it. What had that flight attendant said to him? He'd just flown in from Bogotá—and had gotten on a return flight without having even left the airport.

I should have known he was too good to be true. And that I wasn't beautiful enough for a rich, handsome man to fall for me at first sight. Female flight attendants probably papered him with their phone numbers as he left planes.

But what Ramon and Scar were up to was beyond me. There was one possibility that screamed at me: They wanted to steal my inheritance for a pittance. It was the obvious motive for Scar's offer of ten thousand dollars in Seattle. Ramon's connection with the coffee industry meant he probably knew exactly what Carlos Castillo's plantation was worth. For the trouble Ramon and Scar were going through to put one over on me, the plantation had to be worth plenty.

What did they plan to do with me once they had me in the limo or wherever they planned to take me? Have me sign a purchase and sale agreement in blood? I caught myself looking over my shoulder for Ramon or Scar. I didn't see them.

I went up an escalator and kept walking, aimlessly putting distance between me and the men waiting for me outside. No more than a minute had passed; they probably weren't hunting for me—yet. The pleasant glow I had been experiencing at the thought of a passionate evening with a good-looking man had been replaced by an icy chill of fear and a frosting of red-hot anger. I was getting tired of being a punching bag.

Christ, what had I done to deserve all the hell and damnation that had suddenly exploded under my feet? I shook my head and kept my wobbly knees under me and my frantic feet moving. I just didn't understand it—my business gets blown up, the police think I'm a murderer, a strange inheritance turns into an international intrigue . . . my karma seemed to have gotten infected by something akin to those computer viruses that I've read about.

I passed a flight monitor displaying the current flights that were arriving and departing. A flight was leaving for Medellín in thirty minutes. Without a moment's hesitation, I hurriedly purchased a ticket and boarded the plane. I was the last person on board—my modus operandi, as they say in crime movies.

As we took off, Ramon was probably wondering whether I had been flushed down the toilet. Or worse, whether I had been kidnapped—*by someone else.*

Coco
Loco Land

Colombia is currently the most dangerous place in the Western Hemisphere, and perhaps the world. . . .

If you travel to Colombia, you will be the target of thieves, kidnappers and murderers. . . . Civilians and soldiers are routinely stopped at roadblocks, dragged out of their cars and summarily executed. . . .

Tourists are drugged in bars and discos, then robbed and murdered. . . .

—*FIELDING'S THE WORLD'S
MOST DANGEROUS PLACES*

13

❖

Medellín

A little over an hour later, I stepped out of the Medellín airport, located at nearby Rionegro. A line of taxis waited at the curb. I wondered if Ramon and his scar-faced pal had tracked me here already and arranged a reception committee.

I did what came natural to me—burned a bridge. Refusing the first taxi, I climbed into the second one. That got raised eyebrows, but I didn't care. I could have explained that a friend had once told me that Sherlock Holmes often refused to take the first taxi in line, but I feared no one would know what I was talking about.

Just being clever about a taxi didn't mean I was safe. Ramon said the country's extravagant murder rate was reserved for the proponents and opponents of the drug trade. How about white-collar bandidos who stole coffee plantations? Did they add to the murder rate? Were Ramon and Scar making me an offer I couldn't refuse, Colombian style—silver or lead?

I got a hotel recommendation from one of the flight attendants who assured me that it was a safe place to stay. "Hotel Vista Verde," I told the cabbie.

A few minutes' drive from the airport we veered off the main road, taking a detour. We passed by something that made my jaw drop: Lying on the side of the road was the body of a man. His white shirt was bloodstained.

I twisted around and stared out the back window, my mouth agape. A dead body. A violent death. Murder? A hit-and-run? Out in plain sight, no police cars, no yellow plastic stay-away tape, no cops holding back crowds, no forensic experts preserving evidence. Just a dead man lying on the highway. Raising eyebrows from passing motorists—but was that all?

"What happened to that man?"

He shrugged. "Someone killed him."

He made it sound like it was an ordinary occurrence. I wondered about his shrug—was it a sign of ignorance as to the reason for the man's demise, or indifference?

"I can see that. But what—what did they do to him? It looked like something was shoved into his neck."

"No, senorita, not shoved in, *pulled out.*"

"Pulled out?"

"His tongue. It is called a Medellín necktie. . . ." He gave me another enigmatic shrug.

It was indifference, I saw that; the cabbie didn't care about the man with his . . . *his tongue pulled out.*

I spoke as calmly as I could. "What do you mean, his tongue was pulled out?"

"A Medellín necktie. Or a Cali one." He twisted in the seat and glanced back at me. "It depends on where you are, you know, senorita, Medellín or Cali, where you are when the tongue is pulled out."

Stay calm. I'm in a different country. This isn't the States. I reminded myself again what Ramon had said—things were different down here. The travel guide and everything I'd ever heard or read said it was a dangerous place. But seeing horror was different from just hearing about it.

"What—"

"His throat is cut, you understand?" The driver slit his own throat with his forefinger. "They cut his throat and then they pull it out, the tongue."

"The tongue?"

"*Sí, sí,* the tongue, his tongue is pulled out his throat, out the hole they made in his throat. The tongue is longer than we think, no?"

I cleared my throat. It was all becoming as clear as mud to me. Again, I spoke clearly, concisely, and slowly so my textbook Spanish would not be misinterpreted.

"Why would anyone do that?"

I wanted to grab him and shake. *Good God*—a dead man lying on the side of the road, his throat cut open, his tongue pulled out the hole. That meant someone, the killer, had to reach in the opening to the throat, grab the back of the tongue, and pull it—

Aaaakkkk! I screamed silently, but I wanted to let out one that was heard from here to Bogotá. What kind of country was this? Weren't the people civilized? Why would they let something so gross happen—and ignore it?

"Why?" I repeated.

Another shrug from him. Shrugs seemed to be the national body language of Colombian taxi drivers to explain why dead bodies were out on public display along roadsides. I could see the wheels turning in his head as he tried to explain local murder customs to an ignorant foreigner.

"Who knows? The police from the capital storm into the Los Olivos district of the city and kill people who they think are supporters of Don Pablo. Don Pablo's men storm and kill people who they think talk too freely to the police." He made the sign of the cross. "That one back there, only God knows who he offended. Did he speak too freely to the police so the don's *sicarii* punished him . . . or did he refuse to tell the police what they wanted to hear so they . . ." He made another slicing motion across his throat. "It is not a pretty sight to see, senorita, but it is not an uncommon sight in our city." He glanced sideways at me. "It was left there as a warning."

"A warning to who?"

Shrug. "To whoever the man was loyal to. A warning to his *compañeros* that when they are asked the questions, they give the right answers. Perhaps the man offended Don Pablo—it's said the don has men killed just for looking at him the wrong way."

"Don Pablo . . . you mean Pablo Escobar, the—" I started to

say "drug lord" and caught myself. I didn't know which side the cabbie was on.

"Sí, the doctor himself."

From my Spanish-language classes, I knew "doctor" was a title of honor and respect conferred upon people of education and knowledge. "Don" was an even older title of honor and respect, more than simply "senor." In the old days it was used somewhat the same way "sir" was used in addressing a British knight.

"Does Don Pablo still live in Medellín? Someone told me he had, uh, a disagreement with the government."

A "shooting war" with the government would have been more accurate, but the grotesque mutilation to the body back on the roadside made me keep a civil tongue in my own mouth. The man's tone when he spoke of Pablo Escobar was one of genuine respect.

"Don Pablo *is* Medellín. He's the king of our city and our benefactor. They say he sells cocaine to the *norteamericanos,* but . . ."

He looked back at me in the rearview mirror, raising his eyebrows at the same time he gave me a shrug that said, *Who cares about those rich bastards who sit up north and leer down at us poor people?*

He said, "I could drive you through the city and show you many things that he built, office buildings, apartment buildings, soccer fields, ice-skating rinks, parks and playgrounds, hospitals, many things, even restaurants and discos where people dance. Out where the city's garbage is dumped and whole families spend their days wading in it to find something to eat or sell, he has built places for the poor to live."

Another raise of his eyebrows in the rearview mirror. "I ask you, who else builds for the poor? The government? The rich?"

The cabbie shook his index finger in the air. "You understand, senorita, they say he makes his money selling cocaine. But I ask you, does it matter how he makes his money—or how he spends it? He takes from the rich and gives to the poor. The fat cats in Bogotá who own most of the land in our country, they take from the poor and keep it all for themselves."

I looked out the window and tried to enjoy the scenery as he went on about how the rich got richer. I wondered why people were so stupid—not him; he was just a taxi driver, probably working his butt off to feed a family. No, I wondered about the rich—didn't it occur to them that they might be a lot better off if they put some of that money back into the people rather than one-thousand-dollar bottles of champagne and ten-thousand-dollar-a-night hotel rooms?

A few minutes later he pulled up to a modern but hospitable-looking hotel. It looked clean and well kept on the outside, with several clay pots of colorful flowers all around the entrance. Most of all, it looked safe from whatever craziness was going on between "Don Pablo," the police, and the peculiar kind of necktie party practiced in Colombia.

I gave him a big tip, hoping he'd like me for it, hoping he'd go home and have dinner and forget he drove a *norteamericana* to the hotel.

After registering and walking up to my room on the second floor, I ordered room service for dinner and looked up the Medellín lawyer in the phone book while I waited for my food.

The number that was listed in the book was the same one I had tried to call from Seattle. I dialed it from my room and got a similar apologetic message that said the call could not be completed. I found out why from the front desk. A telephone equipment office had been damaged in a battle between police and a group of "others."

It looked like I would have to make a cold call on the lawyer tomorrow, which was what I planned to do anyway. I was already imagining that police with an extradition warrant would be waiting for me.

Weary from worrying and traveling, after I ate I took a hot shower and went to bed.

My eyes were burning from too much anxiety and too many catnaps on planes. I needed a good sleep, but most of all I needed to be left alone. Hounds from hell seemed to be dogging my heels.

Ramon, you handsome bastard, I hope you rot in hell.

I should never have trusted a man that good-looking. Handsome men are like beautiful women: They're shallow because they always get everything they want without having to be real or honest.

I was truly disappointed that the man had obviously been more interested in my coffee plantation than my feminine charms.

I was angry at myself for falling for his lines. *"I chose you because you are the most attractive woman on the plane."*

I pulled my hair. *Idiot.* Dumb, dumb, dumb.

Did I really fall for that line?

I had to admit that the man had me hooked. But that really didn't matter in the final analysis. What did matter came down to one thing.

Not getting murdered.

14

❖

I awoke in the middle of the night with thoughts of my mother floating through my head, pondering the possible connection between Carlos Castillo and my mother.

It had been inexcusable for her not to tell me about my father, but growing up with my mother was growing up with a woman who never really grew up herself. In some ways, it was more like being raised by an older sister—a wild and crazy one.

We were always doing something fun during those times when life got too mundane or we were bored and needed some excitement. Whether it was going to movies, window-shopping, driving to some new place, or eating out, my mother was never satisfied with the ordinary. I'll never forget the countless times she would say, "You only live once," or, "You can't take it with you," which is why we never had a lot of money saved.

So we lived one day at a time, never planning for anything long-term because there would usually be disappointment when things didn't turn out the way they were planned. Spontaneity was the spice of life. I think it went back to my mother's upbringing in a religious family in the Midwest where life was structured and built around church and neighbors—my mother was definitely not the type to sing hymns at church every Sunday.

"Change" and "spontaneity" were also the catchwords for her relationships with men. Fanatically independent, she never had a long-term relationship with a man, at least no one that I knew about.

That didn't stop her from having sex—she had very liberal ideas about lovemaking and every few months another man would start coming around, but she moved on with lovers as the gypsy she was about everything else.

She once told me that she took a "lease on love" and shacked up rather than tying herself down permanently.

Now that I look back on it, I think she was probably afraid of getting hurt or disappointed. The moment she started to get serious, she got scared and moved on to someone else. Of course, I had no clue at the time. I was just a kid; I thought everything was fine in our lives. There was never any yelling or angry words between her and men she dated, at least not in front of me.

I realize now that although my mother was a strong person, when it came to commitment with a man she was afraid to give it a chance. The fear of failure in a relationship was always there, never expressed, but a latent disease that would ultimately spell disaster for the relationship.

The men in her life were mostly decent guys, too. She didn't date any weirdos or crazies. I actually felt sorry for some of them, and I always knew when their time was up. It was the same routine, every time. She would have excuses not to see them, not return their phone calls, or pretend she wasn't home if they showed up. Pretty soon they'd get the picture and give up.

She never wanted to simply come out and say it was over. I suppose she thought it was more gracious to avoid them until they took the hint. It worked for her, but never for me—when it was over between me and a man, I usually let him know up front exactly what his sins were, at least with the two men I'd had a relationship with.

I'm not quite the love gypsy, but I do know a woman has to think of herself as sensuous and it was pointed out that I seemed to have less confidence in my appeal to the opposite sex than I should have. And that I seemed to have more than an average number of short-term relationships. Not that I was into one-night stands. I had to get to know a man and like him before sex entered the picture.

My mother was very much the lady when it came to dealing with men and it was only by accident that my first real awareness of sex, other than giggling with other girls about male anatomy, came about by seeing her with one of her male friends.

I was twelve at the time and I still hadn't received the lecture about the birds and the bees yet, which wasn't unusual in those days. It was the mid-seventies and most mothers still didn't talk frankly about sex with their daughters, not unless something happened, and even then they tried to avoid it and act like it didn't exist.

That was hypocritical for a mother like mine, who had been something of a Berkeley burn-your-bra type who rebelled against her own parents' sexual attitudes, but I'm sure her only motivation was to protect me. She taught me to value my body and what I shared with a man.

Maybe she was waiting for the right time to talk to me. Some of the other mothers had waited until their girls got their period before they talked to them. I hadn't started menstruating yet, and she might have been putting it off until then.

The night I got the full works of Intercourse 101 in one big dose happened when I was supposed to have stayed at a girlfriend's house for the night, but we had gotten into one of those dumb spats kids get into and I didn't want to hang out with her anymore, so I had walked home.

When I got there, a car I didn't recognize was in our driveway. I figured it was someone new my mom was seeing. She didn't bring men home for the night, not unless I was staying over somewhere else. I never really thought of the reason why; sex wasn't something on my mind in those days.

I was just going to sneak up to my room and turn on the stereo so they knew I was home when I thought I heard voices coming from the living room. I stopped and waited a few seconds. They were in the living room, which was a little unusual because my mother always went in her bedroom when she wanted some privacy with a man. Then again, she wasn't expecting me to be home until later, so I guess she wasn't worried.

I don't know why, but I walked toward the living room door. It wasn't completely closed, but about an inch ajar. I walked up to the door quietly and looked through the crack. We had a large mirror on the wall and I could just barely see them in it. I very carefully pushed the door open a tiny bit wider.

They were too engrossed in each other to notice me. Both of them were naked. When I looked down, my mother's blouse lay on the floor by my feet. They obviously couldn't wait to get upstairs to the bedroom. I put my hand over my mouth to smother a laugh. I had seen my mother with no clothes lots of times, but this was the first time I had seen a full naked man. Well, I only saw his behind. He was facing the opposite wall, so I only had a back view. I remember thinking at the time how cute his behind was, tight and firm like the guys on the high school football team.

I knew it was wrong for me to watch them, but there was a naughty part of me that couldn't resist. I was almost about to leave but then changed my mind. *One more peek,* I told myself. *Then I'll leave.*

When I looked back at the mirror, I could see he had my mother pressed against the wall. His hands were roaming everywhere on her body as they kissed each other. Now his body was slowly moving up and down, back and forth. I couldn't see her face, but she seemed to like what he was doing. Her hands were all over his body, too.

My mother would've killed me if she had known I was spying on her. I looked at my feet thinking I should leave, but I stood riveted in the doorway.

In the mirror I could see his behind now moving more frantically, pumping her back and forth. My mother let out a moan. They were definitely doing it. I suddenly felt guilty watching my mother have sex with a man. I couldn't watch anymore. Sex was a private thing between two people and I felt ashamed for watching them. I closed the door to where it was before.

I wanted to let her know I was back, so I slammed the front door shut and shouted out loud, "Hi, Mom, I'm home early," and ran up to my room and turned on the stereo.

15

❖

THE ONLY WITNESS

let them get away from here. I tried to open my eyes, but they were closed.

I was so tired now. I could barely stay awake. My head was hurting so bad, and I had this ringing in my ears. Everything was getting dark. Now I could not even open my eyes.

Nothing was ever said about that night. However, a few days later she finally decided to talk to me about the birds and bees. I basically already knew everything there was to know. What we didn't learn from other girls we found out from the mandatory sexuality and reproduction class that was supposed to teach you where babies came from. And there was always some creep who made stupid jokes about a girl's anatomy.

Of course, you were told not to have sex until you got married. If you did, you got pregnant. But there was the condom if a girl really wanted to.

I would let guys kiss me, even French-kiss me if I really liked the guy, but if they got out of line and started to put their hands under my blouse or skirt, I would just punch them in the stomach. I usually would never be asked out again, but I didn't care. There were plenty of other guys around who just wanted to have fun and did not want to go all the way. I wasn't a prude, but I wasn't easy, either. When I was ready, I'd share myself with a man, but I wasn't going to do it to be popular or get dates.

As I lay in bed in a strange hotel in a strange country, the image of my mother and her naked friend made me think about my own first sexual experience at age sixteen.

My boyish figure had finally gotten some curves in the right places and I was proud of showing it off. I guess I showed it off once too often.

My mother was dating a jock kind of guy, not her usual type. He had bigger muscles than intellect, but he was a nice guy and I think his good nature, along with his pumped physique, was what attracted my mother to him. His name was Guy and I called him Sir Guy after a knight in a story I'd read.

We were living in San Diego that year. My mother was raising money for a mayoral candidate, a radical one, doomed to lose in a yuppie town, and we were lucky to get a house with a pool.

The weather had finally heated up and I was taking advantage of it. The warm sun felt good on my skin. I had been on my back to tan the front of my body. The strap to my top was undone, my breasts barely covered. Blaring out from my radio was Yvonne Elliman singing "If I Can't Have You" from the *Saturday Night Fever* soundtrack.

When I turned over on my stomach, my top slipped off. I just let it drop to the side. I was alone and the fence was tall enough to discourage Peeping Toms.

A few minutes went by and then a shadow fell over me.

Sir Guy was standing there, wearing his trademark gaudy Hawaiian shirt and shorts. He looked like a movie star, his skin bronzed, his blond hair bleached golden by the sun.

I suppose if I had screamed and moved away, it might have come down differently. Instead, I just lay there for a second. Then I reached down and got my top and put it loosely on my breasts.

I was innocent enough to believe he wouldn't do anything to me since he was dating my mother. Or to be honest, maybe because he was such a nice guy and dating my mother. I wasn't as concerned about what might happen between him and me. Or . . . okay, to be more honest, I was young; my body was stretching and filling in certain places; my hormones were getting a workout, Sir Guy was a nice guy and a sexy stud, a nice combination to just have fun with. So maybe I wasn't as innocent as I pretended. . . .

The few times I had seen him around, I noticed how his eyes

scanned my body. I usually wore a T-shirt and jeans, so there wasn't much to see. But I knew I had a pretty decent figure from the looks the guys at school gave me and chitchat with my girlfriends.

I wasn't sure if my mother was aware of it. I don't think she was; she had zero tolerance for men whose eyes strayed anywhere but onto her.

"How'd you get in?"

"The side gate. It wasn't latched."

"Oh." Damn, I had forgotten to check the latch. I usually made sure it was locked when I was home alone. "My mom didn't tell me you were coming."

"I didn't tell her. I was in the neighborhood so I thought I'd drop by. Is she here?"

"Uh-huh, she should be home soon," I lied. I didn't know when she would be home.

He sat down next to me and picked up the bottle of suntan lotion I had lying on the ground.

"Let me put some lotion on you. You're getting red." He squirted the lotion into his hand and began rubbing it on my back. "You know, you can get away with this much sun at your age right now, but you'll need to stay out of it when you get older. Look at me. I get a lot of sun, but I grease up at night like a roasted pig to keep my skin from getting wrinkled and old looking."

As he talked, his hand ran over my bare back in a lazy manner, working the lotion into my skin. I kept my head down and my arms near my sides as he rambled on. There were no coherent thoughts going on in my head; things were just flying in and around in a mad scramble. I probably should have gotten up, but I lay frozen in place, afraid to move, hoping he would go away.

He kept up the chatter about the sun being bad for you as he rubbed the lotion on my thighs and legs. I didn't like the way his hand traveled over my body in that slow, deliberate manner as if he had a right to it. My blood started to pound.

"You know, you really have a nice body."

"Thanks," I murmured.

"Just like your mom's."

I didn't answer him. I had never encouraged him in any way.

In fact, the few times he came around, I really had little conversation with him, always rushing out the door to meet my friends.

His hands skimmed up the insides of my legs and thighs and over my bikini bottom. A throbbing sensation was starting to build between my legs. The more he rubbed, the more I felt the urgency in my body. His fingers worked to push down the material until he had it completely lowered. My behind was completely exposed as his hands started massaging the lotion on my white skin, lightly touching my pubic hair when his fingers reached that area.

My mind told me to stop him before he went any further, but I was carried away by the sensuous way his hands felt on my body. I didn't want him to stop. I couldn't control the sexual desire that was going through my body. I wanted to give in to the pleasure, to experience it.

A lot of my friends had already had sex and kidded me for not going all the way yet. I wouldn't give in to their pressure. I was holding out for marriage and the right man. I would let guys feel me up a little, but I was able to stop them when things started to get out of control.

His hand deliberately moved down between my legs and he began to massage the sensuous spot between my legs and I swayed with his touch as the sensation of pleasure grew stronger and stronger.

I couldn't fight the ache rising inside my body any longer. I tried to control it, but it got away from me and I found myself suddenly jerking back and forth, until the pleasure became unbearable and I pushed his hand away.

After a moment, my eyes tightly closed, my legs locked tightly together, the pounding of blood starting to subside. I turned around and sat up, not worried about my exposed breasts. I kissed him hard on the lips. All my inhibitions left me. He stuck his tongue deep in my mouth.

He took my hand and wrapped it around the hard bulge inside his pants. It was the first time I had ever felt, really felt, a man's penis.

"Go ahead, squeeze it," he whispered.

The stiff organ felt moist in my hand, and a few seconds

later the throbbing stopped and wet liquid filled my hand. I pulled my sticky hand away and wiped it on my towel.

We both turned as the screen door to the patio opened. I didn't know how long my mother had been standing in the doorway. Or how much she had seen. I was expecting anger, outrage, but she calmly walked up to Guy and just said, "I'm giving you three seconds to get out of here before I call the police and accuse you of raping my daughter." He was gone in two.

I felt ashamed of what had just happened, ashamed of what my mother had seen. She had every right to be angry at me, but she wasn't.

"Are you okay?"

"Yes."

"Good riddance," she said after he had left. Instead of getting angry, she was relieved.

"You're not upset?"

"No. It wasn't your fault. I knew it was coming. I'm just glad he's gone. I should have gotten rid of him sooner. I don't know why I was attracted to him."

"His body?" I grinned.

"Yeah, I guess so," she said, smiling.

I listened as she reminded me that women were really the ones who gave the permission when it came to sex. "If a man really loves you, he shouldn't force you to do anything you don't want to do," she emphasized again. I already knew that. I was the one who controlled the necking and kissing with the guys I went out with. I knew what would happen if I gave in to their persuasion, and I wasn't ready for that.

There was plenty of time for love, marriage, and children later, she told me. Right now the important thing was to finish school, get a college degree, and see the world.

"Men will come and go in your life, and when the right man comes along you may not even know it, but the magic will be there and you won't be able to live without him," she said.

I guess my mother hadn't found the right man yet.

16

❖

The law office of Francisco de Vega Gomez was walking distance from the hotel. Medellín seemed like a normal city with a normal business district as I stepped out of the hotel and went down the street. Coming in to the city from the airport, I had seen a great deal of manufacturing and other commercial buildings. One of the flight attendants told me that the city had so much heavy industry, people called it the "Manchester" of Colombia, named after the British city.

I walked down a pleasant street lined with flowers and populated by people who all appeared normal.

None of it jived with the fact that a body had been laid out for public view yesterday. But Medellín was a big city, and I guess people got killed in big cities everywhere. It just happened more frequently here. And openly.

At the lawyer's office, the secretary showed no surprise that I had walked in without an appointment. I knew from employing people who were raised in Latin America that they often had a different idea about time than me—they would show up without calling ahead or appear for an appointment two hours late.

Perhaps she would have been more surprised if she knew that yesterday I had been in Seattle—and suspected of murder.

Her boss had a different attitude. He came out of his office and stared at me as if I'd been beamed down by Scotty. He just stood in the reception area and looked at me. I had the impression he was wishing I would disappear as quickly as I had materialized.

I smiled. "I'm real."

"What are you doing here?"

"I dropped by to get information about the estate I've inherited."

That managed to return him to a state of speechlessness. He stared at me some more, kind of gawking—not unlike the way I'd gaped at the man whose tongue was hanging out his throat.

A moment later we were seated in his office and I was offered bottled water, coffee, or soda pop. At least he had not forgotten his manners.

I shook my head and smiled my thanks.

Senor Vega Gomez was in his sixties, with almost white hair but eyebrows and mustache so black it looked like he colored them with shoe polish. Like the Seattle lawyer, he appeared smugly well fed, a man who had money chase him. I hadn't looked to see whether he wore tasseled loafers.

He leaned back in his chair behind his desk and shook his head. "Senorita Novak, have you been to Colombia before?"

"No, I haven't."

"Are you a student of Colombia? Someone who has spent years studying the customs, the political and social—"

"No, not at all, none of that. And if you want to know whether I am suicidal, the answer is also no."

He shook his head some more. "You are a very impetuous young woman. There are people in Bogotá who would not come to Medellín under the present circumstances." He leaned forward. "I must tell you, there are people in Medellín who wouldn't live here if it was not demanded by family and economics, including myself." He lifted his hands in resignation. "But . . . senorita, you are here. What may I do for you?"

"I came to claim my inheritance. I don't know Colombian law, but I suspect that's my right."

"Of course. There is a will; there is property; you are the heir of Carlos Castillo; it is your right to claim the estate."

"Can you tell me about it? The estate? And Senor Castillo?"

"Carlos Castillo was a longtime client of our firm, but I regret that I was not well acquainted with him. He was advised by my partner, who has since also passed away."

"From natural causes?"

"Perdón?"

"Sorry, I saw a body on the side of the road yesterday, a man's, whose tongue was pulled out of a hole in his throat."

He cleared his own throat. He looked both embarrassed and grieved. "I regret that you saw such savagery, but please don't judge my city or my country by the acts of a few evil men. Colombia is a good country, nowhere are people more friendly and hospitable, but as you know, the coca bandidos have brought violence to our country. As to the cause of my partner's death," he tapped his chest, "he was ill for many years."

"And Senor Castillo? Can you tell me how he died? Was it from natural causes?"

"That is my understanding. I heard he had a heart attack, but I wasn't personally familiar with the state of his health, mentally or physically, prior to his death. As I said, my partner was his personal attorney, not me."

He sounded like those three monkeys who didn't see anything, didn't hear anything or say anything. Only he also didn't know anything.

He frowned at the look of cynicism on my face. "He was a client of my deceased partner. He last visited the office a few months ago when he changed his will. My partner prepared the paperwork. I didn't see Senor Castillo at that time. My best recollection is that I cast eyes on him several years ago when he was in to see my partner about a business matter. He appeared in good health at that time."

"You say he changed his will?"

"The change made you the sole heir, but I am not at liberty to discuss the contents of his prior will with you."

"Can you just tell me if I was mentioned in the prior will?"

"Yes, you were."

So he had disinherited someone to make me sole heir. I really wanted to know who, but it was useless to try to pry the name out of the lawyer. It occurred to me that if someone was disinherited, they might be behind the attempt to purchase the property.

"What exactly have I inherited?"

"Café de Oro."

The name caught me by surprise.

"That's the name of his coffee *finca,* his coffee farm, or as you might call it, his plantation. I have been informed that you had a store with the same name that sold coffee."

"Yes, it's a name I'd heard my mother use in the past." I deliberately mentioned my mother in the hopes that it would strike a chord with him and he'd volunteer what I suspected—that Carlos was my father. But he didn't pick up the idea and run with it.

"How big is it?"

"In terms of coffee farms, I understand it's a significant holding, some hundreds of hecates. Most farms are very small, a hecate or two, so that would make it much larger than the sort of holding run by a single *cafetero* and his family."

I couldn't remember exactly what a hecate was but thought it was equivalent to two or three acres.

"How much is it worth?"

"That is not a question I can answer. I know nothing about the coffee trade except that it is subject to ups and downs in the world market, and I don't know what the production is at the plantation. But just based on the size, I would expect that in a booming coffee market and without significant debt, the inheritance would make you a millionaire."

"Is there anything else? Money?" I tried to keep the hope and desperation out of my voice.

He shook his head. "Nothing significant. I've heard that the plantation has considerable debt and its cash receipts are controlled by the bank that made the loans, but I don't know the details. I'll look into the matter at greater length if you desire."

"Yes, I would appreciate that. How far is the plantation?"

"More than four hours, slow-going by car. It is in the mountains of course. Coffee is grown at about a mile high, the same altitude as Medellín, but once you leave the city and the main highway, the roads are narrow, most often unpaved, no doubt impassable during part of the rainy season.

"The majordomo is Cesar Montez, a young man about your

own age. I understand he's spent his entire life on the plantation. He will be your best source of information. There is also a housekeeper, Juana, who has been there for many decades, I believe."

"How do I get there?"

He sighed and looked up at the ceiling for a moment, perhaps to get an opinion from heaven concerning my sanity. "You are truly an impetuous young woman. You are an intelligent human being, you know that it is dangerous to come here, more dangerous to leave the city, especially for a foreigner, but I can see that there is no way to reason with you."

He lifted his hands in resignation. "There's a train that can get you to within an hour of the plantation. That would be your safest way. I will call and have Cesar meet the train. God willing, he will get you safely to the plantation. When do you plan to go?"

"Is there a train leaving later today?"

"I should have guessed your schedule."

A phone call confirmed that the last train had already left for the day.

"Then I'll go tomorrow."

I stood up and thanked the lawyer and agreed to return in a few days to sign papers that would complete the transfer. I asked, "Do you know a man named Ramon Alavar?"

"No."

The slightest hesitation revealed that I had caught him by surprise again. And I caught something else . . . alarm?

The interview had left a million questions dangling, but I could see I had reached my limit with the lawyer. But not being one to go away quietly, I turned back when I reached the door.

"You know that I never met Carlos Castillo?"

"That's my understanding."

"Do you know why he left me his property?"

"No."

"Have you ever heard of my mother—Sonja Marie Novak?"

"No."

"Do you know if he was my father?"

"No."

I left the office, recalling a joke my lawyer friend in Seattle once told me:

How can you tell when a lawyer's lying?
When his lips are moving.

Out on the street, my head buzzed. Attorney Vega Gomez could have told me a lot more but wouldn't. Some of it was because of the sealed lips that attorneys are forced to have. But my instinct told me that there was some skullduggery in the air, too. I didn't know if the attorney was part of it . . . or just a citizen of Medellín trying to keep out of the cross fire.

At least one thing was clear: I had little chance of immediately getting my hands on a large amount of cash. I had inherited physical property, not cash. The property would have to be sold to turn it into legal fees and bail money for my Seattle woes.

I had to get out to the plantation and evaluate the situation, see if it could be sold quickly. I also wanted to get out of Medellín as soon as possible. I didn't want to add to the death rate.

Medellín was in the tropic zone of the planet, but with a temperate climate because it was a mile high. Not only was my clothing intended for Seattle's much cooler climate, but the clothes made me look like a foreigner.

In a country famous for kidnapping—and killing—Americans, it wasn't a good idea to leave the impression I was one. Walking back to the hotel from the lawyer's office, I decided to buy some clothes that would make me look like a native. Or at least less conspicuous.

By mid-afternoon I made up my mind about the trip to the plantation. The lawyer was right about one thing: The safest bet was to go by train and have the majordomo pick me up. Unfortunately, that also meant that the lawyer and the people at the plantation would know my plans. Plus the people at the hotel who made the train reservation for me, the taxi driver who took me to the station, the ticket clerk at the station . . . in other words, if someone wanted to know the when-and-where about me tomorrow, or the whereabouts of a "rich American," it would be easy to find out because a long list of people were involved in getting me into a train seat.

Before I reached the hotel, on impulse, I walked into a rental car agency. After assuring them that I had no intention of traveling except to drive around the city to look at churches for a book I was doing, and paying a king's ransom in insurance, I was able to rent a car, a small subcompact Honda with a standard transmission. Fortunately, I owned a Bug and knew how to use a clutch.

I parked the car at an indoor garage with twenty-four-hour security a block from my hotel.

At the hotel, I conspicuously inquired about the train and had the clerk reserve a seat for the next day. I got a map and went over it with the clerk as if I were interested in the route that the train took when I was actually planning out a car trip.

Very pleased at having fooled all the murderers and kidnappers in the city, I retired to my room and stayed there, relying on room service again rather than showing my *norteamericana* face in the restaurant.

The telephone rang.

"You should have taken my offer," the voice on the other end said.

It took only a split second and the hair rising on the back of my neck for me to identify my caller as Scar. *Sonofabitch.* I didn't need to leave bread crumbs; these Colombians must have had spy cameras in satellites keeping track of me.

I took a deep breath and tried to keep my voice steady. "I'm still open to offers . . . but ten thousand dollars isn't going to do it. I know what the plantation is worth; I'm not going to let you steal it."

"You don't know what you have gotten yourself into."

I gripped the phone tighter. Wasn't that the truth? Every time I turned around, there was some new hurdle to jump. Trying to keep the jitters out of my voice, I said, "Why don't you tell me what I've gotten myself into."

There was a long pause on the other end, enough to get my nerves vibrating. I gripped the phone even tighter, trying to keep a lid on my fears. *It's just about the price,* I told myself. *Stay tough; don't show weakness; don't let him know you're scared or anxious.*

"I am authorized to offer you three things." His voice came across as ominous as the scars on his neck that were remnants of his violent past. "Fifty thousand dollars cash. And I will not inform the police in your country that you are in Colombia."

No one had to tell the Seattle cops where I had fled—I had left a trail a blind man could follow. If Scar, Ramon, and whoever else were able to easily track me, the police certainly wouldn't be stymied.

"What's the third thing?" I asked.

Another long pause. Scar was an expert at psychological warfare—the kind that made prisoners scream confessions. He managed to say more with silence than a mugger with a knife. I took a deep breath to calm the tremors in my voice. *Steady, girl. He's just trying to scare you.*

And doing a damn fine job at it.

"I want more money, but I'm willing to discuss it. Can you meet me here at the hotel tomorrow morning?"

"We meet now."

"No, I can't. I'm sick; I've had a bad day, stomach problems, Montezuma's revenge, *turista*." I didn't know if either expression would be understood by a Colombian, but they were the only expressions I knew for the infliction that sent travelers to the toilet and bed in misery. "I'll meet you *mañana*. I have to catch a train tomorrow at eleven. If you come by at ten, we can talk."

"I'll be there at nine. In the lobby. Be ready to sign papers."

He didn't say "or else," but the phrase resounded in my ears, anyway.

"Fine, nine. But remember, I know what the plantation is worth. I want more money." My voice shook with that last bit and I hastily slammed down the phone, hoping he would think it was my stomach problems that were causing the duress and not good old-fashioned fear.

My hands were shaking when I hung up the phone. Of course, I had no intention of meeting with him. I was deathly afraid of him. The man was trying to intimidate me and was doing a good job. My only hope was to get out of Medellín and to what I hoped was the safety of the plantation. It was a large holding; there would be people there, besides the majordomo and housekeeper, workers, foremen, I suppose their families, too. At the very least, I wouldn't be alone like I was now.

The phone conversation had one point I found interesting: He had raised the offer to *five times* what it had been in Seattle. But fifty thousand wouldn't help me any more than ten would. I needed to get into the hundreds of thousands before I set foot back in Seattle. But a 500 percent increase by me showing my face in Colombia gave me hope that we would get to a price that I could live with—and I do mean *live*.

I mulled it over some more, but more questions than answers kept popping up. I didn't know who Scar was or his connection to Ramon—or the connection, if any, the two of them had to my Seattle problems, but it was pretty obvious he or they were trying to extort my inheritance from me. And I didn't see someone as affluent as Ramon appear in this for chump change—they were after a killing.

Again, that told me the plantation had to be worth much more than they were offering. Enough to kill me for? Was Colombia such a lawless country that a person could actually be killed for her property?

I refused to believe that. It had to be a country full of good, law-abiding people who were being victimized by sudden wealth brought to the criminal faction by the cocaine trade. It couldn't be a country where everything was so violent, where innocents got murdered.

Could it . . . ?

That line of thinking brought my thoughts back to the third thing Scar said he would give me, the one he didn't verbalize.

It was a no-brainer.

The third thing was my life.

17

❖

I left the hotel in the wee hours, a half an hour before the break of dawn. The clerk was not in sight behind the counter. I smiled at the front door guard as I went by him and to the street. "Getting some air."

No comprende was the silent message on his incredulous features. Who would go out while it was still dark? I could have told him that I learned the tactic from my mother.

My cut-and-run, burn-your-bridges mother was very streetwise. She'd traveled extensively before and after I came about. Most of her traveling was as a woman alone and as a woman alone with a child. And she had her own theories about how to get safely to where she was going.

When we lived in Southern California and needed to get to Las Vegas or San Francisco, two trips we made frequently, we had to cover hundreds of miles of desert and the like. Her theory was to start out very early in the morning, just before the break of dawn. She said, "The drunks have all been arrested or have passed out, and the killers and rapists are asleep. If anything happens to the car, we'll have hours of daylight to deal with it."

It made sense—whoever heard of someone getting mugged on the way *to* work?

That was my game plan when I left the hotel with the streets still asleep. All the perverts and murderers would still be asleep—including Scar. And I'd be safely at the plantation before Scar realized I'd ditched him.

Last night I assumed the plantation meant safety—the whole country couldn't be kill crazy? But the country's state of mind was a question, not a fact. I just didn't think it was possible people in the coffee country would be as murderously insane as the cocaine gangs.

I hurried to the garage, looking over my shoulder all the way. The security guard for the guaranteed 24-hour security was either asleep or AWOL, because the guard booth was dark. I checked the backseat to make sure there were no murderers hiding there, then slipped behind the wheel, locked the door, and drove out of the garage. I had paid the night before, so short of my being murdered getting the car out, it didn't matter if the guard was there when I left.

I white-knuckled the steering wheel in very light traffic, cognizant of the reality that I was driving through a dangerous city on my way to a highway full of danger.

I had had a bad night, tossing and turning as I struggled with my options. The situation really came down to two decisions: go to the airport and take the first plane out that would get me en route to the States or bite the bullet and head for the plantation to see exactly what I had inherited.

Meeting with Scar was too scary to even be an option. I suspected that his idea of negotiating would be a give-and-take process in which I did all the giving.

The problem with going back was that it could only mean instant confinement in jail, especially now that I had made myself an obvious flight risk. Locked up and with no money to hire a good lawyer wasn't a good option, I decided.

Nearing the highway that would lead me out of town, a convoy of unmarked trucks passed me from the opposite direction. I got a glimpse of men holding guns as the trucks rumbled by. The uniforms were the olive drab that was typical of governments' military units—and of the guerrilla armies fighting them. I didn't know what color uniforms the narco-armies wore.

I hoped my mother was right about nothing happening at the break of dawn.

EMBASSY OF THE UNITED STATES
Calle 22D Bis, No. 47-51
Bogotá, Colombia
Tele. (571) 315-0811
Fax: (571) 315-2197

TRAVEL BULLETIN

Safety of Public Transportation:	Poor
Urban Road Conditions/Maintenance:	Poor
Rural Road Conditions/Maintenance:	Poor
Availability of Roadside Assistance:	Poor

Traffic laws are sporadically followed and rarely enforced, a chaotic and dangerous reality for travelers.

For security reasons, the Embassy strongly recommends against most rural road travel by American citizens. The strong presence of guerrilla and paramilitary groups and common criminals makes travel dangerous.

Roadblocks are frequently established to rob and/or kidnap travelers.

Travel by road outside major cities is dangerous.

18

❖

Stupid, stupid, stupid. It didn't occur to this city girl that the
road signs were going to be fewer and farther between than
paved roads. I stopped after two hours to get something to eat
and drink at a roadside shack, a Colombian version of a rural
truck stop. I bought arepas, a cornmeal concoction that looked
like a pancake. Arepas, eaten plain or sliced for butter, cheeses,
or meats, were a national food, not unlike hamburgers and tor-
tillas. I bought bottled water, *agua puro,* rather than juice from
the *jugos* stand. I wasn't sure what the sanitary conditions were
for a roadside juice stand.

In the rural area, I saw more people wearing ruanas, woolen
cloaks with an opening in the middle for a person's head. It
was a similar concept to the poncho but usually only fell to
about the waist. People kept them folded over one shoulder;
schoolchildren had them pinned around their necks. When it
got cold or wet, they slipped the ruanas on. I guess it was a
south of the border version of what we'd call a windbreaker.

Earlier I had stopped at a gas station and asked about instructions to El Miro, the nearest village of any size to the
plantation. I reviewed the instructions again at the food stand.

As at the gas station, I wasn't a hundred percent sure about what I was told. Either they weren't exactly certain as to where the village was or my Spanish just wasn't good enough to pick up all the nuances of their speech and arm waving, but I finally decided after hearing several different versions that people were too polite not to tell me something, even if it was wrong.

I finally got smart and got behind a bus whose driver told me he would pass near the village. The bus was a charmer—called a *chiva*, it looked like an old-fashioned American school bus with a longer front end and one major modification: Rather than allowing people to enter a door and proceed down a central aisle, each side of the bus was open enough for people to slip directly from the ground onto benches. The entire top was a cargo area and passenger area—people climbed up two ladders at the back and grabbed onto crisscrossed cords to pull themselves onto the roof. The bus was about as safe as driving blindfolded around dangerous curves.

Everything had changed once out of the metro area and off main highways. I went from a modern city to a third-world country. Clothing, vehicles, even the language had differences. I now understood what they meant by Colombia being a land of rich and poor. It wasn't just barrios and mansions in cities— all big cities are places of haves and have-nots—it was two different worlds, a place of Gucci versus raw cowhide.

It was nearly noon before I arrived at the village of El Miro. The trip was a six-hour ordeal that I thought from looking at a map would take a fraction of that time. I stopped at the village, bought purified water and fruit I could peel, again knowing about rural sanitary conditions and Montezuma's revenge.

Once again, I went through the explanations and sign language of getting instructions to the plantation on roads that had never seen pavement or signs. Up to now, I'd found that the most accurate instructions were ones scratched into dirt with a stick. After the water seller made some dirt scratches that resembled a complicated maze, I left the village on a rut that passed for a road.

I was hot, tired, and irritable by the time I met a Jeep coming down the same dirt road I was traveling. The Jeep had an open top and looked like something from army surplus. It was going too fast on the narrow road.

I slowed and pulled to the right as much as I could, because there wasn't room for two cars to pass. I could see through the Jeep's bug-encrusted windshield that the only occupant was a man. Mostly what I saw was a big straw hat, a light-colored beard, and a hand waving me out of his way.

He hit his horn, but there was no place for me to go.

Rude bastard!

In the States, I would have stood my ground and called his bluff, hoping he wasn't high on crank, but I was in a country where road rage was more likely to be acted out with rounds from an Uzi or AK-47 than flipping the bird. But there still wasn't anywhere for me to go but into bushes and trees.

I slammed on the brakes and gawked as the Jeep came at me, sliding as he hit his brakes. The Jeep stopped almost bumper-to-bumper with me.

I took a deep breath as the dust settled. *Jesus.*

"Get the fuck out of the way!" he shouted, and laid on his horn.

I gritted my teeth and put the rental car in reverse and started backing up, but the rear end of the car didn't want to go exactly where I wanted it to go. I tried to stay on the road but veered off, into a gully.

Shit. I put it into forward and let out the clutch. My tires spun. I was stuck.

Angry, I got out of the car, slamming the door behind me. "Excuse me, would you—"

The Jeep came at me and I jumped back against my car.

"Fuck off," he said, as he passed. He steered around my car and hit the gas, kicking dirt and rocks back at me and my car.

"You sonofabitch!"

He was too far away to hear me, but I had gotten a better look at him as he went by—shaggy blond hair under the dark hat, and a ruddy complexion that had been burned deep brown by the sun. He needed a shave, a bath, and an attitude adjustment.

All in all, he looked like a degenerate American college type who had given up his surfboard and education a decade ago to come down to South America and stay stoned while he smuggled drugs. His nationality was confirmed when he dropped the *F* word on me—he'd spoken in English, without an accent. And I had cursed at him in English.

Come to think of it, the entire conversation had taken place in English, from the moment he ordered me out of the way. That gave me pause. I stared down the road, at the curve he'd disappeared around.

Why would a complete stranger have spoken to me in English?

The Medellín lawyer couldn't call ahead to tell the people at the plantation I was coming because the phone lines were down or inoperable, which was often the same thing in the country. He said it was likely the majordomo at the plantation had a mobile phone, and probably even a ham radio, but that he didn't know how to contact either. However, he would get a message through to the nearest police station via radio and ask the officer to let the majordomo, Cesar Montez, know I was coming so he could meet my train.

Okay, it was possible that the lawyer called the local police and word got around that an American was coming. But that theory did nothing to reduce my state of paranoia.

I cursed the rude bastard as I walked a mile to a cluster of three small shacks on a farm where two nice men with a shovel and a donkey returned to help pull my car out of the rut.

The two men, farmworkers who made a few dollars a day and supported families on that little, refused to take the twenty dollars in Colombian pesos I offered. I didn't push it for fear of embarrassing them, but I insisted upon getting their names. I would find out at the plantation how I could thank them properly.

An hour later I found Plantacíon Café de Oro.

"Coffee country" was lush and beautiful. Not dense jungle, but temperate, thick with green trees, shrubs, bushes. Coffee trees, with their big shiny green leaves and clusters of red, cherry-looking berries, were growing in the shade of a variety of taller trees—banana trees, prehistoric ferns, hardwoods, fig trees, and flowering fruit trees.

It was warm, but the mile-high elevation of the temperate zone took the edge off the heat, making it comfortable.

As I came into view of the plantation's *grande casa,* the sight took my breath away. I stopped the car and stared. I had never seen anything so captivating in my life.

The house was a large two-story on the top of a hill, square shaped, with a slanted roof of redbrick half rounds I called Spanish tile. A pillared veranda ran the entire length of the front and, from what I could see, continued around both sides and maybe even the back of the house.

The entire veranda was ablaze in brilliant flowers: bright red, white, and purple bougainvilleas and many other colorful varieties that I couldn't name. The entire hillside leading up to the house was draped in luxurious flowers that flourished in the warm, temperate environment.

On a green-vine-covered hill to the right of the house, a stream of water cascaded a hundred feet or more down to a glittering emerald pool.

I just stared at the scenery. It was nothing I had ever personally experienced before. I fell in love with it immediately. For some strange reason, I felt like I had come home. My first thought was that I had been conceived here.

I knew it was strange, the idea that I could have some memory of this place imprinted while I was in my mother's womb, but that was how I felt, a sense of déjà vu.

No one was around, no workers. I understood a six-day workweek was common, so even though it was Saturday, people probably weren't working because it was siesta time.

I followed the dirt road down a grade and then up to the yard. I pulled up on the side of the house where a three-car garage was located. The garage doors were closed.

A woman came out of a doorway on the side where I'd parked as I was getting out of the car. She stood at the top of the steps leading to the veranda and stared at me.

She was in her fifties, a "handsome" older woman, a word more commonly used with men. She wore a black dress, simple but with a quiet elegance, and had a white, laced half apron over the dress.

Like the Medellín lawyer, she stared at me as if I had been beamed down.

"Senorita, you are not supposed to be here."

"I'm not?"

"Cesar went to the train station to get you. How—?" She gestured at the car. "All the way from Medellín? *Alone?*"

"I'm afraid so. I thought I'd see some of the country. I didn't realize how much of the country I'd end up seeing because of wrong turns." I laughed.

She came down the steps, shaking her head. There seemed to be a growing number of people who shook their head in disbelief at me.

"I am Juana Montez. I was Senor Castillo's housekeeper."

"Nash Novak."

I made the connection with the names immediately—Cesar the majordomo was also a Montez, probably her son.

I offered my hand. I had a firm handshake, but she had come from a generation and culture in which women didn't shake hands, so her grip was not as strong. But it was warm and comforting, as were her eyes. I liked her immediately.

She said, "I apologize for my surprise. We expected you, of course; we got the message that you were coming by train. It's just that—"

"I understand. It's my fault."

"No matter, it is done. The train will have arrived by now, so Cesar is probably on his way home."

"How far is the station?"

"Not far as birds fly, but you have seen our roads. Over an hour. Come in, please, have something cold to drink and a snack. As soon as Cesar gets back, we will have our meal."

"Just something to drink, thanks."

With a glass of ice-cold lemonade, I followed Juana around the house. Despite its large size, it had the feel of a bungalow, with its shady veranda, high ceilings, large double doors, and tall windows to promote the circulation of air.

The most incredible surprise was in the center of the house—an atrium with plants and a waterfall. The atrium had glass walls to all the adjoining rooms. It was a marvelous effect—the house surrounded by lush vegetation outside, and a rain forest in its heart.

"I love it," I told her.

"It was Senor Castillo's design. He said the Romans had open patios in their homes."

When Juana used Castillo's name, I heard the sentimentality in her voice despite the appearance of formality inferred by calling him "senor." In fact, her tone struck me as unusually tender for a mere housekeeper. Despite her age and conservative dress and manner, Juana appeared to be a sensuous woman whom most men would find desirable and not irresistible for very long if they lived in the same house. And from what the lawyer told me, she had lived with Castillo for decades.

We went into the tall living room and paused at the foot of the stairway that led up to the second floor. A series of paintings were on the wall.

"Carlos, his father, and his grandfather," she said.

Was this my father and his family? Carlos had strong features, masculine, even patrician. His hair was long, falling over his ears; his eyes were large and full of expression. He reminded me of pictures I'd seen of caballeros of the era when most Latin America countries were Spanish colonies. Caballeros, wealthy horsemen and hacienda owners, were the "knights" of the age. Carlos had that proud look of a Spanish aristocrat, not arrogant but intelligent, confident, and courageous.

Ramon, my bastard plane companion, also had those handsome Latin looks, but he was just sexy. Carlos looked distinguished and had a commanding presence.

I saw something else, too.

"A poet," I said.

"A poet?"

"That's what he reminds me of. I see an artistic side to him. Did he write or paint?"

"His life was the coffee. He believed you had to live it, breathe it, even love it, to understand it. So yes, he was an artist—and his canvas was the plantation. He had a reputation for growing the finest coffee beans in the country. Of course, that means the finest in the world, because Colombia has the best coffee anywhere. The only recreation that he took was sometimes he would go into the mountains by himself."

"To hunt?"

"No, he didn't hunt. He loved finding exotic plants, ones he had never seen before. He would sometimes bring them back to the plantation and plant them or send them to a friend, a botany professor at a university in Bogotá. Several times the plants were types no one had brought forward before."

I stared at the portraits again, looking for myself in them. It was probably only my imagination, but I was certain that I saw my eyes and lips in Carlos's face.

Like the house, I felt an immediate connection with him. Maybe it was just my imagination again—my wish to have a father—but I felt like I knew him. No, not knew him, but understood him.

Juana said, "I'll show you the second level, but we need to be quiet because—"

"No necessity to be quiet," a voice from the top of the steps said. "I am awake."

The woman at the top of the stairs would not have been a surprise to me in Seattle, but it was a shock here in Colombia's coffee plantation country.

19

❖

The woman staring down at us from the top of the stairs was Chinese, but not *just* Chinese—she was a China Doll, one of those exotic and provocative women who infatuate Western men.

She had spoken in Spanish, heavily accented with foreign intrigue.

She had nothing on under her sheer silk nightgown, which was obvious even from the bottom of the steps. Her small breasts jutted up against the transparent silk in a way mine hadn't done since I left young womanhood behind.

I was petty enough to immediately wonder if her breasts had some artificial help in standing at attention but immediately realized that my thoughts were wishful thinking. Her breasts were too small and delicate to have been surgically enhanced. Anything beyond a mouthful for a man was a waste, a friend once told me.

She looked as if she had stepped out of a James Bond movie—in which she played the role of the sexy villain.

As a woman who has had her own moments of playing the slut, I recognized one when I saw one.

She stared down at us, her face impassive. The only clue to her feelings was that they couldn't be read.

"Senoritas, Nash Novak, Lily Soong."

"How do you do?" I smiled up at her.

She nodded down at me, a queen acknowledging the salutation of a subject. Then she turned and walked away.

Seeing Juana's embarrassment, I grabbed her arm. "We can see the upstairs later. Tell me about the marvelous plants that are shading the veranda. They're gorgeous and I don't recognize them."

When we were on the veranda, I asked, "Is she Cesar's wife?"

"His girlfriend, the daughter of a man who is doing coffee experiments." Juana scowled. "When I was young, a woman would not have thought of ending an evening with her boyfriend by staying overnight."

I didn't point out that that was before the Pill and the sexual revolution, and probably wasn't completely true, anyway. To my generation, Juana's attitude was typical of the sexual hypocrisy that had a different standard for female sexual behavior than male.

"Senorita Soong's father is a scientist visiting here from China, a chemist. He is working with a Colombian chemist to develop a coffee tree that will produce decaffeinated coffee beans."

"Decaffeinated coffee right off the tree? That's a wonderful idea."

"An idea only. I don't believe they have succeeded, nor will they during my lifetime. Carlos had worked with a chemist, too, for many years, trying to develop such a plant, but nothing came of it. Now Cesar has permitted these two men to set up shop in workers' huts about a mile from here. You will meet them tonight. Now that Senorita Soong has seen you, it will only be polite to invite them to dinner tonight." Juana took my arm. "I want to show you something."

She led me to the garage and lifted one of the doors. A green car faced me. It was old, 1950s, I thought, and rather elegant. The front grille was broad and its headlights double. A wide V with an 8 in the middle indicated the car was a V-8. Despite the fact the car was built before the space age, the futuristic hood ornament, two rockets looped together, could have been used for a spaceship in the *Star Wars* movie.

"An old Rolls?" I asked.

"A 1957 Nash Ambassador."

"Really? A Nash? You know, someone told me there was a car by that name, but I thought it was a small car, some sort of early compact. This car is elegant; it's fabulous."

"Carlos told me that the Nash changed when it was merged with another type of car, but this was his favorite model. He would not have traded it for the Rolls you mentioned. It was his baby, as he called it; he kept it in perfect condition. As you can see, it looks new."

I realized that my name had come from this car.

"Where's he buried?" I asked.

Juana nodded at the top of the hill where the falls began.

"Up there, so he can look down at the plantation he loved."

I wanted to see it, but not now, maybe later when I could go up alone.

"Did you know my mother?" I asked.

She looked away from me. "No."

I sensed she wasn't telling me the truth but was interrupted from asking her why she had lied by the sound of a car coming up the hill.

"Cesar has returned," she said.

20

❖

He hated me on first sight. But that was probably an understatement—more likely, he hated the idea of my existence long before he saw me in the flesh.

A couple of things were pretty obvious to me the moment I saw him step out of the SUV, slamming the door behind him.

He was probably Carlos's son—I noticed some similarities.

And the person who had been disinherited.

He had not bothered being polite but started in on me, demanding to know who the hell I was to drive to the plantation when he was told to pick me up at the train station.

I locked eyes with him. "Last time I looked I'm an adult who isn't answerable to you. And if you had some way for people to communicate with you, there wouldn't be a problem."

"Please, Cesar, she just arrived. . . ."

He walked past me and into the house. I soothed Juana's distress and let her show me to my room. I lay on the bed for a while, trying to sleep, but gave it up. I was still upset by Cesar's rude behavior toward me. I took a shower and got ready for dinner.

Cesar was close to my age. I learned from Juana that he was twenty-nine, which made him two years younger than me, but he seemed older. He was average height, a couple inches over my five-seven, and had dark hair with a little curl, and long, thick sideburns. Machismo sideburns was how I thought of them. He wore a Panama hat and open shirt with a heavy gold chain.

I hate gold chains on men—why does it always seem to be the most masculine men who wear them, and men who leave the tops of their shirts unbuttoned so their chest hair puffs out?

Cesar had something of the grandee aristocrat about him. Giving commands appeared to come naturally to him. Having supervised my own employees, with an iron fist when it was needed, I had no doubt Cesar let his underlings know who was in charge.

Something else struck me about him almost immediately. The fact that he was Carlos's son would make him my half brother. That Carlos was my father was no longer a question, at least to me.

Why he had disinherited his son and left me a plantation in the most dangerous country in the world still puzzled me.

Soon after Cesar arrived, preparations for dinner had started at the plantation. My plantation. But by dinnertime, I knew little about the plantation, except that the main casa was more stunning than I had imagined it would be.

I sort of expected that someone—Cesar, the majordomo— would have shown me around a little before dinner, but I suppose I was lucky he didn't throttle me.

My first thought about my dinner companions was, *Wow, what strange bedfellows.* We had gathered for drinks in the living room before dinner. It was all very casual. The night air and the house had a tropical ambiance despite the fact we were too high in the Andes to be in the tropics.

China Doll was there with her father. Dr. Soong, I was told, was a chemist from Hong Kong. They were an odd couple. The two had about as much family relationship as a Siamese cat and a mutt. Dr. Soong said almost nothing, and when he did, it was in barely recognizable shattered Spanish. His sole interest in social affairs was to loudly slurp his soup and chew his food with his mouth open. In other words, he had zero social decorum.

His daughter, on the other hand, was ravishingly beautiful, sexy, and I hated the fact that every man in the room, including her father, stared at her with unrequited lust, which made me wonder about what kind of father–daughter relationship they had.

Dr. Soong's partner, Julio Sanchez, was a university professor from Medellín. Sanchez was top-heavy, rotund, with a short, fat Hitler mustache. He suffered from sinus problems of a type I'd seen with an employee who helped himself to money in my cash register to support his habit—an inflamed, dripping nose from a cocaine habit.

The two chemists had taken over a group of huts for living and working quarters at the far end of the plantation. Juana told me the buildings were used by migrant workers during harvests and Cesar had loaned them to the scientists to pursue their idea of developing a coffee tree that grew decaffeinated beans. The terms were not explained to me, but I was left with the impression that the plantation would be rewarded with an interest in the process if it was successfully developed.

Lily lived in a hut with her father. I was tempted to ask if that was when she wasn't at the main house fucking Cesar.

I admit I was probably jealous that she made me feel like an old padded bra in an age of surgically enhanced breasts, but there was a look in her eyes, an amusement almost, as if she knew something that I didn't know—something about me.

Which wasn't hard, since I was operating almost completely in the dark about everything.

Dr. Sanchez stared lasciviously at Lily. As he looked at her while he chewed on a piece of beef, I had this image of the plump scientist chewing on China Doll.

Cesar had taken the commanding position at the head of the table, and Juana, being diplomatic, had steered me toward the other "head" of the table at the far end. It was a place of respect that I thought the older woman full of grace should take. I took a different seat and insisted she sit at the head of the table. Two women served us.

We no sooner sat down when we had surprise visitors—a man and woman. My eyes widened and my temper rose the moment I saw the man. It was the bastard who had made me back up into a gully that left my rental car stuck.

My blood boiled when he walked in.

He grinned as he was introduced. "Nice to meet you."

"I wish I could say the same."

It took him a moment to realize who I was—maybe it was the fact that I glared at him the moment he walked in.

Juana, a little surprised, asked, "You two have met?"

"This is the person who ran me off the road."

"Sorry, I was putting out a fire; I needed to get down the road."

Cesar howled. "The fire was probably from the police. He was running from them; that's why he had to run you off the road. That's the life of a smuggler; one day you are buying champagne and the next you're one step ahead of the police."

His name was Josh Morris. He had no class. His hair was too long; he didn't shave often enough, and lacked the courtesy to sit down to dinner without removing a ragged Boston Red Sox baseball cap.

I knew the type—losers who have dropped out of the mainstream to make a run at success, taking shortcuts and avoiding hard work. Not uncommonly getting involved in get-rich-quick schemes that included a dishonest buck.

He hadn't stopped for dinner but came to talk to Cesar. It didn't surprise me that they would be friends. It appeared the only way either one of them knew how to talk was with a beer in hand.

The worst thing about Josh that annoyed me was the woman who was with him. Fleshy, big-busted, she couldn't have been a day older than a very mature, very well developed sixteen-year-old—and she was young enough to carry off being a saucy girl that aroused the prurient interests of the men in the room.

Caught between the elegant butterfly from China and the Colombian Lolita, I felt uglier and dumpier than usual.

What strange bedfellows, I thought again. While Cesar and Josh chatted about soccer and poker, and Juana went out of her way to make me comfortable, the rest of the group had absolutely nothing in common. The two chemists didn't seem to relate to each other any better than they did with anyone else. China Doll and Lolita didn't speak to each other or anyone else, but I'm sure neither of them could have carried any heavier subject matter than the colors of nail polish.

When the chemists announced they were retiring, Juana signaled Cesar to offer a toast to me.

He stood up, glass in hand, and the others stood up.

"To our *norteamericana* visitor, may her days in our beautiful country be profitable and her problems at home disappear."

Juana gave him a look that said she wasn't pleased with the toast. I smiled my thanks and, for Juana's sake, smothered my annoyance. I would have rather told Cesar I wasn't a "visitor" but the new owner and asked him how he knew about my "problems at home."

It did occur to me that the Seattle attorney told the Medellín attorney who told Cesar, but that was doubtful, since he couldn't even phone him about the train. I was more inclined to see conspiracies than easy explanations. And an easy conspiracy theory connected Cesar with Scar and Ramon. The thought struck me that Cesar might be the one behind the offers, perhaps bringing in the other two for a piece of the action for helping him.

Another thought also jumped out at me. A Chinese connection in Colombia . . . a Chinese gangster in Seattle blows up my business . . .

I had so many conspiracy theories swirling in my head, I was sure the dark thoughts would be obvious to everyone around the table.

I got up and excused myself to get some fresh air.

A full moon and delightful scents greeted me. It was paradise. But every paradise has its proverbial snakes.

I was leaning against a tree, staring up at the waterfall that glistened in the moonlight, when I realized I wasn't alone.

Josh was suddenly beside me.

I grimaced and ignored him, folding my arms, looking back up at the falls.

"Is there something you'd like to say to me?" he asked.

"Good-bye? Good riddance?"

"I know down deep that you really like me—"

"You're delusional."

"Why—"

"I don't like people who run me off the road because they are rude and stupid. How did you know I was an American? You cussed at me in English."

"Cesar told me you were coming. Is there anything else you'd like to get off your chest?"

"I don't like drug smugglers. You're a slime, a sick criminal who spreads poison. I suppose you hang around school grounds to sell your stuff. Which is probably where you met your little friend. What are you paying her to be with you— cocaine in her baby bottle?"

"You're jealous; I saw it immediately. You fell for me the moment I ran you off the road. You're the kind of woman who gets excited when a real man pushes her around."

I hated his cocky attitude. I wanted to punch him in the face.

"*Josh!* Did you forget me?"

Lolita had followed him out. Good thing, because he had left me completely speechless. I had absolutely no comeback for his ridiculous statement. I swept by Lolita and hurried back to the house.

That night I lay awake in bed and listened to the passions of Cesar and Lily in the room above me until I couldn't stand it anymore. I grabbed a blanket and went out to a swinging wicker couch on the veranda.

I didn't know what to make of the plantation and the people on it. I did know I was alone. And scared. My instincts told me I could trust Juana, there wasn't any malice or deception in her . . . but the rest of them, what an ugly rogues' gallery.

I wondered what the relationship was between Josh and Cesar exactly. Were they just friends . . . or did Cesar grow cocaine somewhere on the plantation for Josh to smuggle?

Thinking about Josh's remark that I was attracted to him gave me tight jaws. What really antagonized me about the man was that I did have an immediate sexual attraction to him. And not because he ran me off the road. There was a certain wildness and magnetism about him that attracted me.

Why is it that so many of us good women make bad decisions about men? This jerk literally ran me off the road, used foul language on me, robbed the cradle, and here I was, an intelligent, successful businesswoman instantly attracted to him.

21

❖

I was having coffee and toast with Juana in the kitchen the following morning when Cesar came in and asked if I was ready
to see the plantation. He seemed to be in a better mood than
last night, at least to the extent that he didn't come across as a
smoldering volcano.

Petty on my part, but I had to wonder whether he had simply
resolved to deal with me . . . or his anger level had been lowered by last night's passions with the China Doll.

Before we left the kitchen, Cesar gave Juana a breakfast-in-
bed order for Lily. Juana raised her eyebrows and muttered
something I didn't make out, but I'm sure it wasn't compli-
mentary toward the guest upstairs.

"We'll start with the nursery," Cesar said. "It's Sunday, but
there'll be a few workers around."

The nursery was a garden area where coffee trees were
started from seeds. He said it took about eight weeks for the
seeds to germinate.

"Not just any seeds are planted; we choose the best. And we
keep weeding out poorer plants. Our beans are very large; I
know of no plantation growing bigger or better beans in all of
Colombia."

"Larger beans from Central America are called elephant beans." I knew the name from buying beans to roast and grind in my store. The theory was that the larger the bean, the better the coffee.

"The secret of why Café de Oro grows the finest coffee beans is the care that is taken every step of the way. Carlos was a genius at selecting the best plants. For decades, he personally chose every bean that went into the nursery from trees he believed would produce the best coffee. Many people can tell you how beans are to be selected, but few have the talent to be able to actually pick the best."

"What was he like, personally?"

"A fool," Cesar snapped.

Despite the harsh characterization, there was no question that he had spoken with pride about Carlos. I didn't ask why Carlos was a fool—I thought it best to get a tour of the plantation before starting any conversations that could go to hell.

I followed Cesar to the area where the plants were growing over knee-high.

"When the plants are about two feet tall, we use them to replace trees that are no longer good producers."

"How long before plants produce usable coffee?"

"It takes several years before we get blooms and cherries, but we are working them long before they bloom and continuously afterwards. If left unattended, the trees can grow over thirty feet high. We keep them trimmed down so the cherries can be hand-picked. Picking is another labor-intensive process. We pick the cherries only when they're a deep red, but they don't ripen all at the same time. That means workers have to return to a tree seven or eight times during the harvesting season."

"How much coffee does each tree produce?"

"On the average, you can think of it as about a pound per tree. We have about two hundred and fifty thousand trees spread over the five hundred acres of the plantation."

I quickly figured the plantation produced about a quarter of a million pounds of coffee each year. I didn't know how much plantation coffee sold for or what the profit margin was, but I knew enough to realize that that much coffee did not put me into the class of a superrich heir.

"You understand, of course, we grow only Arabica coffee."

"Yes, I sold only Arabica in my store. I've been told that you don't grow Robusta in Colombia."

"We grow many things in our country, some of which gets sold on the streets of your country in white powder form. So it wouldn't surprise me if there are plantations in the lowlands growing Robusta and selling it as Arabica. Do you know the difference between the two strains?"

"A little. Robustas are grown mostly in Africa and Asia, Arabicas in the Western Hemisphere, mostly Colombia, Central America, Brazil, and southern Mexico, some in Africa. Robusta has a heavier and harsher taste and twice the caffeine."

"Robusta is junk coffee. The reason French and Italian roasts are so dark is because they originally got their coffee from Turkey and it was Robusta. They have to burn in the roasting process to make it palatable. But it can be grown cheaper than Arabica and in enormous quantities. It's easier to grow and harvest. Even the Vietnamese have entered the coffee market, mostly with Robusta, but they are also producing Arabica. The last few years they've flooded the world market with Robusta."

I knew that Arabica was sold through a New York commodities market and Robusta was sold through London. Coffee was the second most traded commodity in the world, outranked only by petroleum. Regardless of where the central commodities market was, both Robusta and Arabica make it into the can in Britain and the States.

He said, "With Robusta selling for half the price of Arabica, most of your supermarket brands mix it with Arabica. People in America and Europe don't realize that unless the label says it's pure Arabica, they are getting inferior coffee mixed in."

He pulled a cherry off a tree and broke it open. "Each coffee cherry contains two beans in it. The beans are covered with layers of outer material that have to be removed before they're shipped to roasters in the United States and Europe. The outer skin of the cherry and the wet pulp surrounding the beans is removed in our de-pulping machine. We de-pulp quickly after picking, usually within twenty-four hours."

The de-pulping machine looked like a big, iron meat

grinder. Cherries were poured into a vat on top. Beans and the mucilaginous pulp poured out the bottom.

"The pulp is a sticky, gelatinous substance. You can see some of it still clings to the beans after the de-pulping. To remove it, we wash the beans. But washing is also an important step in creating aromatic coffee. We put the beans into tanks for several days where the rest of the pulp is naturally removed by fermentation."

He took me to where beans were being dried on concrete terraces. Barefoot workers walked on the beans while raking. "The beans are raked and turned over several times a day to aid in the drying. Depending on the weather, it can take up to a couple weeks for them to dry. We don't have hot-air dryers; we rely on sunshine. We cover the beans at night and when it rains. We lose part of the crop to moisture. If we had dryers, we wouldn't lose so much."

"Why no dryers?"

"Too much money to buy and to run." He picked up dried beans. "At this point we call this parchment coffee because it still has skin on it. After the beans are dried, we do our own milling to remove the parchment with a polishing process."

After milling, the beans were packed in burlap bags. Each bag weighed 132 pounds.

"Most growers simply truck the bags of green coffee to the port as soon as the sacks are full. Carlos always insisted on leaving the beans on the plantation for two more months after they were processed. He said it permitted the beans to get conditioned to their nakedness while still breathing the plantation air that they were grown in."

"Like aging a fine wine."

"Exactly. He believed that the composition of the soil even affected the taste. He refused to use commercial fertilizers."

"That's good, isn't it? Organic is healthier."

"It costs less to use commercial fertilizers than natural ones. And we've had a war with *la broca,* a coffee worm, *bastardos* that bore into the cherry. You can't get rid of them with cow manure and the pulp from the de-pulping machine we use for fertilizer. It takes chemicals."

"How many workers does the plantation employ?"

"During harvesting we have over a hundred, but most of those are *colonos* working off their rent."

Colonos. The word meant something like "farmers."

"What do you mean, working off their rent?"

"We have three hundred *colonos* paying rent, some of them pay in labor."

"Are they paying rent for houses?"

He gave me an odd look. "You don't understand the system, do you?"

I shrugged. "I'm learning it now."

"The *colonos* are tenant farmers. They work their farms for a share of the profits."

"They work the plantation—"

"Not the plantation. The other fifteen hundred acres Carlos owned."

"There's fifteen hundred more acres?"

"You inherited two thousand acres. Five hundred in the main part of the plantation we run directly; the rest is rented to three hundred tenant farmers, averaging about five acres each. The farmers work the land allotted to them and get part of the crop in payment. And some help with the harvest on the plantation."

Sharecroppers, immediately came to my mind.

I had inherited two thousand acres. At five hundred trees per acre, that was a million trees. A million pounds of coffee each year.

I was rich!

Cesar caught my thoughts and laughed without humor. "Don't start spending it yet. Carlos was broke."

"Broke? But you said—"

"A million pounds of green coffee can be produced each year, but coffee is selling for ninety cents a pound and it costs us nearly a dollar to produce it, so we lose a little on each pound. And it's been down to seventy cents a pound. That's for coffee you sold for six or eight dollars a pound in your Seattle store."

"The plantation, with its tenant farmers, is losing money?"

"It's a hole in the ground that Carlos threw money into. The debacle started about five years ago. Up to then, an international agreement set the price paid to coffee bean growers. The restrictions were dropped so the marketplace could set its own price. Everyone was already overproducing and on top of that, cheap Robusta and sun-grown Arabica flooded the market. The price of coffee dropped more than in half, and the small farmer's cash crop became a starvation crop. The only people making money are the big, mechanized corporate farms growing sun coffee."

"Why is there such a big difference between the price of coffee grown in the sun and shade-grown?"

"Shade coffee is labor-intensive and has fewer trees per acre because it requires a canopy of trees that takes up space. You can get two or three times as many trees per acre if you clear the land of the canopy. And the canopy keeps us from using mechanical equipment for harvesting. Most coffee in this country is now being sun grown, the same way Brazil does their coffee. Shade-grown is the past, one we can't afford."

"But aren't shade-grown plants less damaging to the environment, what they call bird friendly, and healthier for us because they don't require as much agrochemicals, the pesticides, fertilizers—"

"Shade coffee is good for feeding birds—if you can afford it. If you want to make money, you knock down the forests, plant more trees, and bring in a few pieces of equipment that do the work of a hundred laborers. This plantation would be worth millions if the canopy was cleared, the tenant farmers evicted, and trees planted densely."

"But that would change the entire environment. Don't they call sun coffee an environmental desert? And the coffee would not be the high quality that Café de Oro produces—"

His features darkened with annoyance. "You sound like Carlos. I told you he was a fool; he could have been rich, but he was too soft to evict the tenant farmers and too full of pride at growing fine coffee. What good is it to grow the best coffee if someone in Africa or Asia or even your next-door neighbor is producing inferior beans and doing it cheaper?

"You think the restaurant and fast-food chains, the supermarkets and discount stores, care about what's in the can? All they care about is making a blend that disguises the chemicals used to grow and process it and the fact it's loaded with cheap Robusta."

"There has to be some pride in what we do. Just because other growers have a mentality—"

"You don't understand, it's hard work, backbreaking, day and night, year after year, for what? To have our fine coffee dumped into cans and mixed with sun-grown or Robustas? The big wholesale coffee buyers only want to talk about price, not the environment. When a commodity trader in New York is setting the price for coffee, he doesn't give a damn where or how it was grown; it's just so many pounds, figures on a piece of paper, to him."

"But what about the little farmers, the *colonos,* what would they do? They have families—"

"These people have been poor their entire lives; it would be an act of mercy to turn them out. They can go to work for the cartels producing the most profitable cash crop in the country."

"That's cruel."

"That's life." He stalked away, only to suddenly turn back to face me. "Your inheritance is owned by the bank and the note is due in a few months. When they take over the plantation, they'll do exactly what I tried to get Carlos to do—turn the operation into a sun farm. He was too proud and inflexible; he died broke. You should have taken the offer to sell—stick around and you'll just get evicted by the bank along with the *colonos.*"

22

❖

Like I've always said, there's a snake in every paradise. I was rich—for about two seconds. Now it looked like all I'd inherited was trouble.

I walked through the shade canopy, listening to the chatter of birds, soaking in the wonder of it all while my mind buzzed with questions.

Cesar knew an awful lot about my affairs. Last night he mentioned my Seattle problems. Today he revealed he knew about the attempt to buy the plantation. What else did he know? Was the plan to get the plantation for peanuts and turn it into a profitable sun farm—or did Cesar, Scar, and whoever else was involved plan to use it to grow that most profitable of all Colombian crops: cocaine?

I didn't know anything about cocaine except that I had read in the South American travel book that the stuff was processed from the coca plant. I had no idea what the plant looked like except that I assumed it was green and leafy. The stuff could be growing all around me and I wouldn't know it. Someone told me it used to be an ingredient in Coca-Cola, but they took it out eons ago.

I hummed "I get no kick from cocaine" as I walked alone, trying to remember what song the words came from.

The weird twists my life was taking were mind-boggling. I seemed to race from one puddle of trouble to another. Puddle? Troubles were coming at me like tsunamis.

The source of my Seattle problems was here on the plantation; that was a no-brainer. My landlord was innocent—at least of blowing up my business. An attempt was made to create financial havoc for me in Seattle, so I'd jump when a lowball offer to buy the plantation was made. That was it in a nutshell. It was Cesar, Ramon, Scar, and probably wild man Josh, all in it together.

The attempt nearly got me killed, but I hoped that wasn't part of the plan.

Pieces falling together into a nice pattern, at least in my mind, was a relief. I also knew the solution—cut and run. But I was fresh out of places to run. I'd be out of here in a New York minute if I had anywhere to go. I was stuck here. But I was getting tired of being used as a punching bag. My ire was up. The bastards had ruined my life.

The only way I was going to be able to recover what I had had, clear my name, and get what I had coming out of the plantation was to be smarter than them. And stay alive along the way.

I couldn't confront Cesar and Company because I couldn't call the cops. I somehow doubted he could kill me deliberately—I mean, blow up my business, yes, but I couldn't believe that Cesar and the rest of them would deliberately try to kill me, except maybe Scar. And even that was only a possibility, because they wanted to buy the plantation, not complicate things.

Something else had also gotten under my craw. The *colonos*. Three hundred tenant farmers and their families. I met some of them today and saw the hard work they performed and the honor in their eyes and on their faces.

I'm not a world saver, not like my mother, who was ready to put up her dukes and fight for any good cause that came along. But I wasn't Simon Legree, either. I couldn't stomach the idea of ripping out all the lush vegetation any more than I could of evicting hundreds of families.

Cesar was wrong when he said it would do them a favor to cut their ties with the plantation. I knew enough about the economy of a country like Colombia to know there's a small cadre of elite rich at the top and an enormous mass of poor at their feet—with almost no opportunity for the poor to improve their lot. There was no place for them to go. That's why there were so many guerrilla movements in the country—millions of Colombians were at the bottom and had no hope or future.

Selling the tenant farms out from under the *colonos* would be cruel. It wasn't something I could do, no matter how desperate I was.

The notion of losing the plantation to a bank—a bloodless, heartless stone entity—was just as repulsive. The bank would send a liquidator to the plantation to rip out the families and the canopy of trees and sell the place to a big sun farm concern.

Jesus, what a load of problems I'd inherited. It sounded like a miracle was needed to keep the place in business. And to clear my name in Seattle.

So far there had been little heavenly intervention in my affairs. Mostly it had been the work of the devil.

Deep in thought, I walked along until I came across a hut with only three walls. Seeing it was furnished with a small roaster, a coffee grinder, bottled water, cups, a coffeemaker, and filters, it didn't take me long to figure out what it was—a cupping station.

Cupping was the process by which experts and connoisseurs tasted coffees and appraised their qualities. It was also used to find defects or to perfect blends of coffee.

A worker in a straw hat came along, a man who looked to be in his forties. "*Buenos días,*" he said.

"I'm Nash Novak."

"Tomas Nunez."

We shook hands. I didn't tell him I was the new owner—I'm sure everyone around knew.

"You're working on Sunday?"

"I'm a foreman; it is not work to me, but pleasure."

"How long have you worked here?"

He gave me a shy smile. "That is the same as asking me how old I am. I first came into the fields on my mother's back."

"Then you can tell me about Carlos Castillo. I never met him."

He took off his straw hat and wiped sweat from his forehead. "It is unfortunate that you never met Senor Castillo. He was not just the owner of the *finca* but a *patrón,* perhaps an old-fashioned word now. Do *norteamericanos* use this word?"

"Not the same way it's used here. It refers to the owner?"

"Yes, but in the old days it meant more than an owner. When I was younger, the owners and the workers were all part of a big family and the *patrón* was the head of the family. He was not just an employer, but the protector of the family. Today, most large farms are run as businesses and the owner is a businessman or even a corporation. Workers are treated as strangers, to be hired and fired at will."

"But Carlos was not that way?"

"To him, growing coffee was not a business; it was the work of a family. It is hard for me to put into words, but Senor Castillo didn't treat the land as a stranger, either. The trees themselves were part of the family. He didn't walk onto a field and see a thousand trees; he knew every tree, just as he knew every worker and every tenant farmer."

He went on to tell me that Carlos was respected not just on the plantation but throughout the region for his knowledge of coffee growing and his generosity. He let small farmers use the mill to process the beans even when they couldn't pay.

"When things started getting bad because the price of beans fell, many families would have starved if it was not for him."

"Are they afraid now because I've inherited the place?"

"We hear many stories, sometimes that machines used for sun coffee destroy the canopy and we would no longer be needed; sometimes a rumor starts that nothing will change. We don't know what to think. Most of us were born on Café de Oro." He smiled shyly. "And we would like to be able to die on the soil when God takes us."

He left, with me depressed. Hundreds of people depended on this place and they were all standing on my shoulders. It made my knees feel weak. I couldn't even handle my own problems, much less worry about a host of others. But the foreman's description of the people and land as a family—damn, what would happen to these poor people if I sold out to Scar and Company?

I looked over the cupping station, trying to put horror stories out of my mind.

Juana had told me many farmers sent out beans without cupping them first, but that Carlos had the cupping station set up near the mill so he could taste beans and discard batches that didn't meet his high standard.

I knew a little about cupping. I held cupping "juries" at my store to draw people in and get them interested in coffees instead of just scooping the stuff into a filter and pouring in water. Like holding wine tastings, the cupping sessions got customers more interested in the selection of coffee, rather than just drinking it.

Taking a supply of green beans I found in a can on the cupping table, I put them in the small roaster. Coffee came "green" to my Seattle store and I roasted it to create different flavors. Temperatures for roasting ranged from the high three hundreds to low four hundred degrees. If you didn't roast the beans enough, they had a green, almost grassy taste, and if you roasted them too long, you got something darker and more bitter than hell.

The roaster wasn't just an oven but a rotating drum that provided a tumbling action, turning the beans over and over to create even roasting.

A master roaster worked with a clock for timing a roast and a glass window in the roaster that showed the color of the beans as they roasted. When the beans reached the desired color, they were poured out of the roaster and into a pan with airholes that allowed them to cool evenly.

As the beans were heated, they went from pale green, to yellow, to tan, to light brown and eventually "popped" like popcorn. Called the "first crack," the coffee beans doubled in size.

The analogy to cooking popcorn wasn't strained—home countertop roasters resembled popcorn makers.

While I roasted the beans, I heated water in a pot.

Once the beans had reached the desired color—I preferred a

medium brown—I stopped the roasting process. Roasting creates the characteristic aroma and taste of coffee that appeals to our senses. If the beans continued to cook, they went through a "second crack" and even beyond, to the oily, dark finish known as French roast and the even darker Italian roast. I liked to finish my roast close to, but not beyond, the second crack.

I ground the roasted coffee beans, using a medium setting. Water filters the fastest through coarse coffee, leaving behind much less taste than finely ground coffee. I preferred mine in between.

I smelled the grounds, noting the fragrance. Aroma, or fragrance, was one of the factors used in judging a coffee's flavor. The other criteria were taste, or flavor, and its acidity—which, in judging coffee, was not a bad thing because it referred to how much zest the coffee had and its feel in the mouth.

I spooned the grounds into a cup and poured hot water over them. The technique created a "float" or crust of coffee at the top of the cup. I smelled the float, judging its aroma. After it cooled enough for me to drink, I used a spoon and scooped up some of the float and noisily slurped it. The idea was to mix the coffee with air, so it sprayed across the palate.

The coffee was mellow but with a tangy zest. The most outstanding feature was its uniqueness. No blending was needed; it had a full-bodied taste that easily stood alone.

"How is it?"

I nearly jumped out of my pants. I had a visitor. Josh Morris. And the Latina Lolita wasn't with him.

"Did you leave your friend at a day-care center?" I asked.

Oh God, that sounded like a jealous woman.

He ignored my catty remark. "How's the coffee?"

I cleared my throat. "Very distinctive, full-bodied with deep-toned flavors. In layman's terms, it's damn good. Better than what I sold in my store as premium stand-alones and blends."

"Drinkable, huh."

"That, too. Am I keeping you from something?"

"Are you trying to get rid of me?"

"Yes. I don't like drug runners."

"Oh, so that's it; that's why you don't like me. I thought there were a lot of other reasons, but I'm glad it's just that. Well, you have no reason to dislike me; I don't run drugs."

"But Cesar said—"

"I was a smuggler, I know. But I don't smuggle drugs. Do you have anything against an emerald smuggler?"

"Emerald smuggler?"

"Yeah, you know, those sparkling green gems they dig out of the mountains here. The flawless ones are rare and more valuable than diamonds." He took a small, green piece out of his pocket. "Here, for you."

I looked it over. "What's it worth?"

"It's flawed, but still it's worth a few hundred dollars. Keep it as a souvenir of your *short* stay in Colombia."

"Smuggling emeralds still makes you a crook."

"But not a corrupter of children and destroyer of lives. I'm only taking emeralds that have been stolen from rich mine owners by poor, slaving mine workers and smuggling them out of the country. It's a win-win scenario for me and the miner, as long as we don't get caught."

"I see. You imagine yourself as a Robin Hood. What exactly do you give back to the poor?"

He tried to look sincere. "I'm saving up to build a children's hospital."

"You're a liar."

"Of course. It goes with the territory."

"Why were you running from the police yesterday?"

"Not from, I was running *to* the police. They'd busted one of my couriers carrying gems. I had to get to the cops and buy them back before someone offered more money."

"What a country. Is there anyone honest in it?"

"About ninety-nine percent of the people. The problem is, the country has being bad down to an art. When someone is bad, they're really bad."

"Why don't you go back to the States and stop adding to the misery of a poor third-world country."

"Now tell me the truth; you can be brutally honest. You don't like me, do you?"

"Frankly . . . I find you repulsive and offensive."

"But you'd like to have sex with me; I could tell that from the moment I saw you."

"My God, your delusions are getting worse." I got up. "You'll have to excuse me; I have an urgent appointment."

"If you leave, you'll never get answers to your questions. I imagine that you must have more questions than answers, right?"

I gave him a once-over. "And you have answers?"

"To some things. Com'on, there's a fig tree a ways down; I love fresh figs. There's something sexy about fig leaves, don't you think? Biblical and all that. And speaking of biblical sex, how were Lily and Cesar last night? Knowing your room was below, Cesar probably banged her harder, or at least louder than necessary, bed banging against the wall as he humped, that sort of thing."

"You are disgusting, you know that. Worse, you are juvenile. Is that how you get it off? Listening to other people having sex? Look, next time I'm attracted to a man, I'll give you a call. You can watch. And even join in—not with me, but maybe the guy will want you."

"Hey, you have claws and teeth."

"Only to people who deserve it. You've been down here living a fairy-tale existence as a macho bandido for too long. You need to go back home and put your nose to the grindstone like the rest of us."

"Sounds like a prison sentence."

As we walked, he said, "Did that worker tell you about the dark side of coffee farming, about planting a little coca in the rear fields to feed his starving kids?"

I shot him a look. "How long have you been watching me?"

"I dropped by to roast and grind beans for my own coffee. You looked so devastated after talking to him, I thought I'd let you cool off before I approached."

"He told me about hopes and dreams for a better life."

"And you had instant guilt, because you plan to sell and run."

"I don't know what I plan—and from the sounds of it, no one is going to throw a lot of money at me."

"Hasn't Cesar offered to buy the place?"

"What do you know about that?"

"Nothing. I just assumed he'd want to buy the place, tear it down, put in a parking lot, as the old song goes."

"I thought you were going to give me information."

"Okay, here's some information. You're no longer in Kansas, Dorothy; this is Colombia, where the wicked witch of the east runs a drug cartel and murders for business and pleasure. Based upon that, you should take the next plane home, no matter what you're facing."

I stopped and locked eyes with him. "What exactly do you know about what I'm facing back home?"

"I hear you had a coffee store in Seattle that blew up."

"What exactly did you hear?"

"What exactly am I supposed to have heard?"

"I see you're bubbling with information."

"I need to get to know you better to find out what you need to know."

"Why don't we start with the truth."

"You're old enough to know that there are many different species of truth. Here's one of them—people who rig buildings to blow up when you walk in have an even easier time rigging your car to explode when you turn the key. You remember that old saying about jumping out of the frying pan and into the fire? Colombia's a country on fire."

"You keep talking in generalities."

"Maybe I don't know as much as you think. What was your game plan in Seattle?"

He was trying to change the subject. So far, he'd told me nothing except rumor and innuendo.

I said, "Do with coffee and muffins what Mrs. Fields does with cookies. Most coffee sellers don't have good bread items to go with their coffee. They don't bake their own muffins, cookies, or cakes themselves but buy mostly generic stuff. I concentrated just on coffee and homemade muffins, nothing else, to keep it simple and the quality high."

"There any money in coffee and muffins?"

"If you go national, there is. I was on my way, but my dream got cut short by someone sabotaging my business and then blowing it up, almost with me inside. It's caused a mess back home that I need a lot of money to fix. We both know who's behind it; I just need confirmation. Now, what are your answers?"

"Take the money and run."

We stopped and faced each other again. I put my hands on my hips. He was the most frustrating man I'd ever met. He said just enough to keep me from stamping away in a huff but told me exactly nothing.

"Why don't you stop playing games and tell me what's going on?"

"Okay. Let's see, you've walked into a dangerous game, someone tried to kill you in Seattle, someone wants your share of the plantation—"

"My share *is* the plantation. Yesterday, I wasn't offered enough money for it. Today, the plantation isn't for sale."

"You don't understand what you've got yourself into."

"You keep saying that, but all your answers are just hot air. I don't have to be told that I've lost my business to a criminal act, that I nearly got blown to pieces, that I've fled my country one step ahead of the police. Everyone in Colombia seems to know it, too. Someone's set out to trash my life and I'm pretty sure I know who's doing it. Could I get a little help on this? Maybe we could play charades or twenty questions."

He stopped smiling. "Listen to me carefully; your life depends on it. You are a brave and resourceful woman, amazingly resourceful, but you have too much confidence in a situation you know nothing about and are completely unable to handle. No matter what's happened around you, to you, what you've seen and heard about Colombia, you still think in *civilized* terms because that's how you've done it all your life.

"You grew up in a country where it's safe to get in your car and drive three thousand miles across the country without having to worry about guerrilla armies, kidnap gangs, drug wars, or crooked police. But you're not home now, so stop thinking like an American. Colombia deserves its reputation as the most dangerous place in the world. Here, if someone wants to get rid of you, they'll hire someone to walk up to you on the street and shoot you between the eyes—in broad daylight."

"Cesar wants the plantation bad enough to murder me?"

He scoffed. "Cesar has his own problems."

That stopped me in my tracks. I stared at Josh, puzzled. "Are you telling me Cesar isn't behind blowing up my business?"

"I'm not telling you anything; I don't know who tried to blow up your store. But don't assume that just because Cesar would like to have the plantation, he'd murder for it. Don't even assume he's the only one in the world interested in the plantation."

"I don't get it; who else would want the plantation?"

We heard the sound of vehicles.

"You have visitors."

A line of oversized black SUVs were on the dirt road that crisscrossed the mountain. They were heading for the main house of the plantation.

"Who are they?"

"You're about to meet Pablo Escobar. The most wanted criminal on the planet. Also the richest and most dangerous. I suggest you don't remind him of the lives he's destroyed with drugs or the people he's had murdered."

MURDER AS A WAY OF LIFE

Relying on paid assassins, locally known as *sicarios,* Colombia's drug lords not only fought among themselves but also launched a systematic campaign of murder and intimidation against Colombia's government . . . In the process, they effectively paralyzed the country's system of justice . . .

They also contributed significantly to the "devaluation" of life throughout Colombia and converted murder and brutality into a regular source of income for some sectors of society . . .

—*Colombia: A Country Study*
Federal Research Division, Library of Congress
Edited by Dennis M. Hanratty and Sandra W. Meditz

COLOMBIA HAD A SHOCKING HISTORY
OF VIOLENCE "B.C."
(BEFORE COCAINE)

"La Violencia" was an eighteen-year period (1948–1966) of political violence during which over 200,000 Colombians were murdered.

In a bizarre twist, *women were murdered to keep them from having children that could grow up and fight:*

"The massacres perpetrated by *bandoleros* against entire peasant families involved women, although not simply as just other victims, but rather in representation of the enemy's whole collectivity. Their violent death and, frequently, their rape, torture, and mutilation when pregnant exacerbated this symbolism, as summarized in a single expression coined during the period: 'leave not even the seed.'

"Rape was frequent and expressed not only the male desire to dominate the opposite gender, but also, as in many other wars, the supreme humiliation of and scorn for enemies . . .

"The *sons and daughters of La Violencia* made violence an inevitable evil, a way of life."

—*Bandits, Peasants, and Politics,*
by Gonzalo Sanchez and Donny Meertens
(Trans. by Alan Hynds)

23

❖

Meeting the most dangerous man in the most dangerous country in the world was not high on my list of wants. I asked Josh as we walked slowly back toward the house, "Why's he come? What's he want?"

"I think that's something you're going to find out."

"How do you know it's Pablo Escobar?"

"The modus operandi. An unannounced visit, roaring up in oversized SUVs with pumped-up motors and a small army of guards. If it's not the president of the country, it's King Pablo."

"Uh . . . how do I avoid meeting this man?"

The SUVs making their way to the house had disappeared out of sight. They would get there before we would.

"You can jump off the planet. But since he's already here, I suggest we put a happy face on his visit."

"How can he be wanted by the police and still run around loose? Why don't they arrest him?"

Josh laughed without humor. "That's a question asked daily in Washington and Bogotá. Brigades of Colombian federal police and army, U.S. drug agents, and now U.S. commandos would like to do just that, but they have to operate in his territory. They get no help from the locals. The local police leave him entirely alone and are almost always on his payroll. Several hundred Medellín cops who didn't take his silver ate his lead."

"That's insane; a criminal can't just take over an area where a couple million people live."

"Tell that to the people of Chicago during Al Capone's heyday. The big problem is that there is less respect in Medellín for the Bogotá crowd that runs the country than there is for Pablo, at least among the have-nots. He's the local boy who's made good and feeds back his success with public building projects that are easy to see."

"And people let him get away with murder."

"Literally. In Medellín and the surrounding towns, you can always tell when there's going to be another murder committed. The police disappear off the streets. They don't come back until it's time to remove the body. And there's no effort to find the killer."

"Jesus."

"I don't think you're going to find him around here. Colombia is a wild country; all of Latin America has a history of civil wars and political violence, but Colombia takes to violence more than any of them. Are you familiar with Colombian history?"

"I know they speak Spanish and grow coffee."

"Another Ugly American proud of her ignorance."

"Very funny. I know very little."

"Here's your instant lesson in Colombian History 101. Start with the fact the place breeds outlaws, revolutionaries, and blood vendettas. It's a land of a few very rich and an enormous number of very poor, with almost everyone having a different political opinion. Currently, there isn't just one revolt against the government, but *half a dozen*. Revolutionaries have never been too good at overthrowing the government because they can't get together and agree on anything. Including who they're supposed to be killing.

"The country has had a history of bloody conflict from the time it separated from Spain a couple hundred years ago, and the worst period of violence isn't ancient history, but started following the Second World War and continued right into the mid-to-late sixties.

"It's called La Violencia, the violent times. It began as fighting between political parties in the forties and didn't stop for almost twenty years, ending up with the deaths of hundreds of thousands of people. Escobar wasn't even born when it started, but he was in his mid-teens by the time it ended. To understand Pablo you have to realize he was a child of La Violencia, that much of his character was molded by the spectacular era."

"What made it so spectacular?"

"Savage, brutal, vindictive, uncontrolled violence—in a country where the people involved were mostly educated and affluent. Unimaginable cruelty was the name of the game—torture, mutilation, even rape and murder of innocent family members."

"All this by civilized people."

"All this in the world's most beautiful country, populated by the nicest people I've ever met. And Pablo Escobar is a good example. He's known for being polite, courteous, even charming. He wasn't brought up in poverty. His mother's a schoolteacher and his father owns a small piece of land, making them sort of lower-middle-class types.

"But he's still a product of La Violencia. I suppose when you grow up in a country where the leaders who are sworn to uphold the law in turn practice brutality that would have made some of Hitler's and Stalin's henchmen shudder, you get immune to it. Violence becomes another way of life, a negotiating point in making a deal."

"When did he turn bad?"

"He started in crime as a teenager, with petty thefts and street hustling. He graduated into robbing banks and running a chop shop for a large-scale car theft ring. There's no honor among thieves, and Pablo got an early start in violence by dealing swiftly and lethally with anyone who screwed him. He has nerves of steel and is completely without a conscience. Early on, he ventured into kidnapping, sometimes murdering the victim even when the ransom was paid if he didn't like the person or the money was paid too slowly. Sometimes the victim's enemy put up more to have him killed than the ransom."

"Pablo sounds charming, a real Robin Hood type."

"It gets worse. He entered the cocaine business as a small-timer. But he quickly went right to the top—he promoted himself in narco-business by murdering the guy who ran much of the stuff in the Medellín area. Simply killed him and announced he was the new boss. He was under thirty at the time. Hell, he's only in his early forties now."

"He simply took over a crime empire that easily?"

"It wasn't an empire ten or fifteen years ago. Annual narco-trafficking in those days was in the hundreds of kilos—today, it's in the *hundreds of tons*. He was a prime mover turning it into a billion-dollar industry. And spending it, too. He has a preference for palatial estates, expensive cars, beautiful women—preferably young teens. . . ." He grinned at the look I gave him.

"He also plays the grandee. He's built housing for the poor, a park and soccer field, things that are highly visible. He tosses bones to the poor and they think he really *is* Robin Hood. I've heard him called El Padrino, the Godfather, and El Benefici-ador, the Benefactor. *Forbes* lists him as one of the ten richest people in the world."

"And he does it by just being brutal."

"At his level, it goes beyond simply being a thug. Stalin, Hitler, Mafia crime bosses, they all share a common trait—a complete lack of conscience and the willingness to spill the blood of anyone, any time they believe they are threatened or even opposed. They act quickly and savagely to protect their power.

"Pablo has that same ruthless mentality. If he wasn't rich and successful, we would call him a serial killer in the sense that he kills a certain type of person—people who oppose him. And he'll kill your wife, children, and parents, too, if he can't find you or if that's the best kind of method of persuasion. Hell, *he'd kill his own wife and kids* if they got in his way. You have to comprehend the most important thing about him—*he strikes terror in violent criminals who strike terror in the rest of us.*"

"*Plata o plomo,*" I added.

"Yeah, that's what he offers judges and the police—take his money or his bullets. And he absolutely means it. He kills judges and police officers like we squash bugs. He's killed some of the country's top policemen and judges, not to mention the minister of justice and presidential candidates. He arranged to have a passenger airliner blown out of the sky because he thought a candidate adverse to his interests was on it."

I had mentioned that fact to my handsome friend on the plane from Panama City to Bogotá. I decided to see if Josh knew the man. "Do you know Ramon Alavar?"

"Alavar?" He shrugged. "I've heard the name."

"You're lying."

"Of course. He has something to do with coffee."

"And Pablo Escobar?"

"I don't know, Pablo has something to do with everything in the region, including coffee, so he and Alavar could have a connection. Anyway, Pablo learned the extended family routine from La Violencia—when bribes or threats don't work with a judge or police official, you send a murder squad to burn down his house, murder his kids, and rape his wife. If the official's been real tough, you rape and murder them with the guy watching."

"Jesus."

"I told you, he's not in Colombia, though there's divine intervention of a sort. An outfit called Los Pepes claims to be composed of surviving victims and families of victims of Pablo's crimes. It's a murder squad, probably with unofficial-official support. They've gone after Pablo with the same sort of savage violence he made famous as a narco-terrorist. They've killed members of his family, friends, bankers, business associates, and lawyers. While this was going on, in the States millions of dollars of his assets in real estate are being confiscated. The idea is to follow the money, tie up his billions, and isolate him from the support of his followers."

"Sounds like an old-fashioned Argentine-type death squad."

"That and a Charles Bronson *Death Wish* vigilante group. They've offered a big reward for Pablo's hide, over six million, but it's a dead man's gambit, because Pablo never goes anywhere without a small army of bodyguards. And he changes those constantly."

I took a deep breath.

We were in sight of the house. A group of men had exited the cars and were in front of the house talking to Cesar and Lily.

The thought occurred to me that Josh seemed to know a lot about Pablo Escobar, but it could have just been the fascination of the macabre.

"Anything else I should know?"

"Yeah, don't piss him off. His favorite method of killing people is to hang them upside down and burn them—slowly."

My heart starting racing, not because of what Josh had just said but because I saw the familiar face.

Scar, my friend from Seattle.

24

❖

It was easy to pick out which of the visitors was Pablo Escobar—he was the only one who looked calm and relaxed. Everyone else around him, from his bodyguards to Cesar, had a nervous edge. Only Lily managed to maintain her sphinxlike inscrutability.

Even though I had been told that the man orders murders with the sort of ease most of us order pizzas, he was not a guy that stood out, at least not in his appearance. With a thick bushy black mustache, short curly black hair, jowls starting to sag, and his belly drooping over his belt—from carrying too much weight—he reminded me a little bit of Stalin. I suspect the image had been planted in my mind by Josh's comments about bloody dictators.

If I were a contestant on a TV game show and had to guess Escobar's occupation, I'd have answered "dentist." Dentists tend to be the middle-of-the-road types—they lack the predatory look of trial lawyers, the smug satisfaction of CPAs that they control your money, and the arrogance of medical doctors that let you know that your life is in their hands.

Scar gave me an angry glare as I came up to the group. He

looked like an annoyed crow that couldn't quite get its beak on a piece of roadkill.

Pablo laughed. "I do not need to be introduced to this lovely senorita. Obviously, she is the one who has left Jorge eating her dust as she roared out of Seattle and Medellín."

Escobar was a charming bastard. And Scar had a name, Jorge—George in English. *J*s sounded like *h*s in Spanish, so his name was pronounced something like "whore-hey." I preferred "Scar."

I smiled and offered my hand. "And you must be Don Pablo. I've heard so much about you."

He shook hands and gave me a polite little bow of his head. "And how did you know who I am, senorita?"

"You're the only one who isn't wetting his pants."

He tried to smother a laugher but gave up the ghost, throwing back his head with a good guffaw.

"Jorge, I can see why this one was too tricky for you." He shook his finger at me like a schoolteacher gently reprimanding a student. "But you must not be tricky with me, eh, senorita?"

I gave him a generous smile. I almost popped out with, *What will you do? Have me murdered?* but put a brake on my tongue before it slipped out.

Josh answered before I was able to say anything. "Don Pablo, I have a small, trivial gift for you." He pulled the small black-velvet pouch out of his coat pocket that had contained the stone he'd given me earlier and shook out a brilliant green gem.

"A rare and beautiful flawless emerald," he told Escobar. "To be worn by one who is also flawless."

Josh was certainly silver-tongued when he wanted to be. I was only worth a little chip of flawed emerald, but the world's most dangerous killer got nothing but the best.

"Gracias, amigo," Escobar said. "But my friend, I have told you before, you are wasting your time smuggling these stones. You can make more money on cocaine than emeralds. When you are ready, I will finance your first shipment."

"Cocaine is too dangerous a game for me. No one gets too excited about emeralds, not even the customs people."

"I hope you have made a fine gift of a priceless gem for this beautiful woman." Escobar grinned at me. "I admire a woman who is fast on her feet, who travels light and changes planes on a whim. I am a man who also has to be fast. Maybe I should hire you to keep me one step ahead of the death squads that want my blood, eh?"

I smiled. And wondered what the pay would be. . . .

He shook his finger again. "They have brought in a *norteamericano* death squad to kill me, something called Delta Force." He looked around at his entourage. They all seemed to snap to attention. "Amigos, I ask you, do I look like a man who deserves to die?"

There was a universal disclaimer and sympathetic murmurings of, "No, Don Pablo."

I just smiled again, remembering the taxi driver's comment that Escobar had men killed if they looked at him the wrong way.

He sighed. "I could go live on the French Riviera in great comfort, but here I am, looking after the poor people, the people of the ghettos and the poor farmers. It is for them that I risk my life."

I was too scared to laugh.

"Now that Don Carlos is no longer with us, it is up to me to ensure that his *colonos* still have a *patrón,* no?"

I guess that was his way of telling me that he had staked a claim on my plantation.

LUNCH WAS SERVED in the atrium around a large table. Everyone except Escobar and Scar seemed about as cheerful as immediate family at a wake.

Cesar was obviously worried and uneasy with Escobar's presence. His nervousness drove up my fear level because he was the one who'd been worrying me up to now. What he was up to with Escobar certainly wasn't making him a happy camper at the moment. It made me suddenly realize that I might be giving Cesar too much credit for being the lynchpin behind blowing up my business with me in it. Maybe he was just a whipping boy for the man who frightened the murderers who scared the rest of us. Josh had intimated that.

Oh, what tangled webs we get ourselves into just by living and breathing. Like a genetic defect passed on by my parents, it seemed like I was paying for their prides and passions. Why couldn't my mother have gotten pregnant by a rich old man in Boston who left her beaucoup bucks instead of a coffee grower in coco loco land?

Lily's face was still unreadable, but her eyes weren't. She was meeting Escobar's blunt stare with bedroom eyes. I wondered if she was calculating how much a billion dollars was in Chinese yuan.

Dr. Soong and Dr. Sanchez joined us for lunch. Soong buried his head in food and drink and paid no attention to any of us. Sanchez treated Escobar with the cautious respect and toadiness a mass murderer deserves.

It was obvious that everyone at the table knew something that I didn't know. There was a connection between everyone at the table and Escobar. I was reasonably certain that even Josh fitted somewhere into the scenario, too. The boyish emerald smuggler routine was too innocuous to be true.

Small talk about the weather, coffee prices, politics, and other mindless subjects went on for about an hour. As the dishes were being cleared by women at Juana's direction, Josh gave me a nod. "Com'on, let me show you the pond on top of the falls."

When we were out of their earshot I asked him, "You were told to take me away, weren't you?"

"No, I wasn't."

"Why is it every time you move your lips a lie slips out?"

"I wasn't *told*. Pablo gave me a meaningful look and jerked his head in your direction."

"In other words, it was time for me to leave so the others could talk business. What are they going to talk about? How they're going to steal the plantation from me? Or maybe how they'll murder me to get it?"

He rubbed his forehead. "I doubt they're talking about that."

"Which? The stealing or the murder?"

He didn't answer.

Halfway up the hill I stopped and glared at Josh. "This is insane. That man's a criminal, we should call the police. You said everyone's looking for him; we just tell them that he's here."

"Shhh, don't say anything like that out loud, don't even think it. He'd disappear long before they got here and leave behind a couple dozen bodies, with ours in pieces."

"It doesn't sound to me like the Colombian authorities really want to find him."

"There have been accusations from the State Department that the Colombians don't try hard enough. Deliberately. But the truth is, he's just been more clever and vicious than them. He has more authority in this region than the government does."

"I don't get it; why does he need this plantation for his cocaine crop? There must be a thousand places like it."

He shrugged. "I don't know what Pablo's up to; he may have just dropped by because he was in the area."

"In a pig's eye. That bastard is after the plantation—over my dead body, if necessary. He wants to grow cocaine on it."

"No, for sure, he doesn't. Pablo's not in the business of growing the coca plant. You don't understand cocaine trafficking. There's a million people in this country and the rest of South America growing it, mostly small farmers. There isn't a lot of money in growing the stuff. The big money, the cartel billions, comes from processing and smuggling it.

"To turn coca leaves into cocaine, you need chemicals and a processing plant. In fact, the stuff gets processed several times from the time it's picked to the time it's shipped to Europe and the States. The cartels buy the chemicals and smuggle them into Colombia; they process the drug in jungle factories, and ship it out to the States and Europe. They don't need your plantation for growing the stuff; they have thousands of small farmers. And it's too open and obvious for a processing plant; they hide those in jungles."

"If he doesn't want the plantation to grow cocaine, what does he want? Why is he here?"

Josh grinned without humor. "I'm sure that's a question a hell of a lot of drug enforcement cops would like an answer to."

"Well, here's another question. What are you doing here? This region produces coffee, not emeralds." I found that out from Juana.

"I used to hang around the mining region, but I nearly got lead poisoning when a mine owner sent around a hit man to rid the world of me."

He was lying again. But I was beginning to see the picture. "You smuggle your gems out in bags of coffee, don't you. It would be a perfect place to hide them. You pay Cesar to let you do it. And if the country runs true to form like the rest of the world, you're paying Pablo protection money to operate in his territory."

He gave me a sharp glance.

I shrugged, modestly. "I used to analyze business operations. A lot of businesspeople today think pretty much like you—how to get rich without really working at it. They usually fail in the end."

The pond atop the hill overlooking the plantation house was a narrow lagoon crowded with large, leafy green plants and white flowers. It was a serene spot.

I noticed a wooden chair and a small table a few feet from the water.

"Juana told me Don Carlos used to come up here to read," I said.

Then I saw the cross. A simple white wooden cross. It was the only evidence of a grave. I walked slowly to it. I knew it was Carlos's grave. And it had great emotional meaning to me. There was no longer any question in my mind, Carlos was my mother's lover.

This was the grave of my father.

I knelt by the cross. A fine ground cover with tiny red flowers flowed out from the cross. I'd seen the same tiny flowers in the atrium. Juana had surely planted them up here.

Life is so unfair. For a moment I was angry at my mother. What right did she have to deny me a father? I could understand that for whatever reason they were not meant for each other, that perhaps all that was between them was a moment of unbridled passion. My mother was both a free spirit and a woman who feared relationships. I suspected that was the reason she fled Carlos, as she would go on to flee other men over the years.

I didn't know that for sure, Carlos could have instigated the separation, he could have been a bastard to live with, could have beat his women or even just bored them to death, but as I had seen my mother cut and run from other men, my instinct was that she wasn't ready to give up her freedom and settle down with Carlos.

That was her decision to make, her right; no woman had to stay with a man she didn't want to be with. But I had two parents and I deserved to have had a relationship with both of them.

Perhaps I wouldn't have liked my father. Whatever drove my mother away might have kept me from wanting to be around him, too. But I should have had the right to make that decision myself.

"Did you know him?" I asked Josh.

"No, he died about the time I met Cesar. But I've heard a lot about him. He was a genius at growing coffee."

I sat in the chair. Josh sprawled out on his side on the green mat of vegetation, staring up at me, his head propped up by his hand with his elbow on the ground.

"What happened between Carlos and Cesar?" I asked. "What did Cesar tell you?"

"Not much; mostly I picked up stuff from the workers. The bottom line was that Carlos had an old-fashioned attitude about the plantation that Cesar didn't share."

"Carlos treated it as a family."

"I suppose so, and that worked when the market for coffee was rigged so that all producers were paid enough to cover their expenses and generate a profit. But the market changed; the bottom fell out. Cesar began to see Carlos as a dinosaur. The future was in knocking down the shade trees and growing sun coffee. Cesar's a realist. If that meant replacing a hundred workers with one machine in order to compete, that was how it had to be."

He chewed on a piece of grass and stared at me. "But that's not you, is it? With all that business training you have, you still think like Carlos."

I shrugged. "I'm not sure I think like either one of them. I can understand both their viewpoints. Carlos couldn't ignore the changing marketplace in a blind hope to keep the status quo, but I would look for something besides Cesar's solution.

I'd look for one that didn't mean throwing the baby out with the wash. If it's not too late. What exactly are your pals Cesar and Pablo up to if it isn't growing cocaine?"

"You keep putting me in with the lions, when I'm just a pussycat."

"What happened to you?" I asked him. "How did you end up in Colombia, with a career in smuggling gems?"

"The luck of the draw, I guess. My father was an engineer from Nebraska. He came down here to work in the oil industry. He met my mother here, in Cartagena, which is where I was born, but they eventually moved back to the States. I grew up in Los Angeles. I ran into a little trouble in college because of a cheating scheme, but got a degree in engineering with bad grades and then eventually got married. I ended up getting a divorce after I got into a little trouble for messing around.

"I got a job at my old man's company, they sent me down here, I got into a little trouble after U.S. Customs found some emeralds in a company packet I sent back to the States—"

"So that's the story of your life? A little trouble here, a little trouble there?"

He stood up and walked toward me. "No, occasionally I get myself into big trouble."

Without any hesitation he pulled me up to him and kissed me on the lips, tenderly at first and then with more fiery ardor. My knees turned to jelly. I experienced a longing inside me that I hadn't felt in a very long time. My legs suddenly went weak and I was glad he was holding me. With all the troubles in the world bearing down on me, it was comforting to be in his arms. I relaxed and enjoyed his strong arms around me, feeling safe and protected.

"I've been wanting to do that ever since I first saw you," he said, still holding me in his arms. He looked in my eyes for some response from me, but I was still trying to recover from his impulsive move.

I hadn't made any move to resist him, or rather my body hadn't resisted. Mentally I was saying, *No, this guy is no good for you, don't start anything,* yet my body was saying something totally different. I had melted in his arms when he kissed me. But then an image of my mother suddenly came inside my head and wiped away my indecision.

He pressed closer to me.

"Wait; stop."

"Why? You want it as much as me."

"Yes . . . no . . . I mean, I don't know you." That was an understatement. So far all I knew was that he lied almost every time he opened his mouth.

"Yes, you do; I just told you everything about me. You know everything there is to know."

I didn't totally trust him. There were too many unanswered questions. I was certainly attracted to him; that was a given. But if he was into smuggling jewels, what other bad stuff was he involved with? My woman's intuition was telling me to hold back.

"No, you never answered any of my questions; there are too many things about you that don't add up."

"Nobody's perfect."

"You're not even in the running on that score."

25

❖

Pablo followed Lily up the stairs to the bedroom wing. He paused at the top of the stairs and let Lily continue into the bedroom. Pablo looked back down at two men standing at the foot of the stairs.

Cesar was rooted at the bottom, staring up, his feet unable to move, his features turning dark as he struggled to keep from exposing his anger. He could read nothing in the expression on Pablo's face, just his usual amiable countenance, but Cesar knew that opening his mouth was a death sentence. Jorge was behind him. A nod from Pablo, and Cesar knew the thug would put a bullet in the back of his head.

Cesar turned and walked out of the room.

"Watch him." Pablo spoke quietly to Jorge. "A man can do foolish things when another man is fucking his woman."

LILY WAS SITTING on a chair facing the vanity mirror when Pablo came up behind her. The Oriental red satin robe she had on was open, revealing the sheer red nightie underneath, prominently exposing her nipples. She wore red silk nylons, a garter, and a sheer G-string thong.

She had done her research—red was Pablo's favorite color.

"You look good in red," he said, resting his hands on her shoulders. He let the robe slide off her shoulders. Looking at her in the mirror, he said, "I want to see all of you."

She felt the bulge in his pants press against her back. She stood up. Taking her time, she removed the nightie, exposing her milky white breasts. Her nipples were already hard. Her arousal was real, even though Escobar was not a sexy man. His reputation was exciting to her. The idea of making love with the most feared man in the country was tantalizing.

He bent down and licked a circle around each nipple, before taking each one in his mouth and sucking it.

She took off the rest of her undergarments as he watched her in the mirror. For several minutes he just stared at her body, especially at the bare mound between her legs.

He had taken out his rigid phallus and was now rubbing it against her buttocks. He turned her around and suddenly his open hand caught her cheek. "Suck my cock, you whore."

She felt the slight sting as he forced his organ in her mouth. A moment later orgasm racked his body. She almost choked as the thick, white liquid flowed into her mouth.

PABLO LAY ON the bed and blew smoke rings from his cigar up at the ceiling. "I want you to return to Shanghai to make the final arrangements. I don't like the way things are going. Everyone is dragging their feet."

She shrugged off his concern. "It's something new; no one knows how to deal with it."

His hand flew at her throat like a lunging snake. He grabbed her and pulled her close to his face and blew cigar smoke in her eyes.

"They better learn quickly. I don't like delays. I'm being hounded on all sides. I need the money."

He let her go and she collapsed back, clutching her throat. "You must be patient; we're close to being finished. You'll get the money."

"I know that. People pay me . . . if they want to stay alive." He looked at her. "How are you getting along with the American girl?" Pablo asked.

"We need to get rid of her."

Pablo sighed. "Not today. I filled my quota this morning."

26

❖

I spent the next two days learning all the fine details of how coffee was grown, using the foremen and workers as teachers, from how they selected the finished beans right down to how they selected the seedlings that would grow into a coffee tree.

But I didn't fool myself in thinking that I would pick up the art of coffee growing by talking to the workers. Something I'd learned in the business market was that there is both art and science in any field of endeavor.

The technical part, the science, was the easier to learn; you got it out of books and learning by doing—lawyers with their law books, doctors with their medical manuals, stockbrokers with their graphs and historical analyses. But great lawyers, doctors, and Indian chiefs went beyond books and what they saw around them—they had a talent for their work, developed partly from experience and partly from their own innate abilities.

When I first went into business analysis, my boss complimented me, telling me that I had a knack for it. He's the one who pointed out that the best in any field go beyond what they were taught: "Anyone can learn from books the science of investing in the stock market. All stockbrokers know the rules of prudent investing. But few stockbrokers know the *art of making money* on the stock market. And it's not something that can be taught at business school."

The plantation workers all knew how to grow good coffee, but as more than one admitted, none of them had Carlos's knack for selecting just the right seedling, just the right beans—that was the art of coffee growing.

I didn't know if I'd ever have the talent my father had—that was how I now always thought of him, as my father—but at least he had left the plantation in good shape in terms of the quality of its products. And I carried his genes.

There probably isn't any scientific evidence to prove that you can genetically inherit a talent, or at least the ability to develop a talent, from your parents, but I think what we are has more to do with what we get physically from our parents than science gives credit for.

Thinking about whether I could inherit a talent for growing coffee from my father, I pulled on my right earlobe and got a memory flash from when I was a little girl. My mother had seen me pulling on my ear and told me that my father had had the same habit. Since I had never met the man, I certainly didn't pick up the habit from seeing him do it.

To learn more about how coffee was grown, I asked a reluctant Cesar to guide me through the process of what happened once the coffee left the plantation. He wasn't happy about it, but he drove me to the port, introducing me to people who warehoused, bought, and shipped the coffee.

He had been moody since Pablo had come—and gone, with no dead bodies left behind, at least none I knew about.

I noticed Cesar had also been irritable toward Lily. From the way Lily had been looking at Pablo, my analytical brain, which invariably saw the dark side of human nature, concluded that Cesar was jealous of Pablo—for good cause, of course.

What Cesar, Lily, the two chemists, and Josh had going in the huts, or wherever there was other skullduggery on the plantation, was still a mystery to me. From Cesar's body language around Pablo and Josh's comments, I did realize that Cesar was not in control. I no longer thought of him as the person who almost got me killed in Seattle, deliberately or inadvertently, but that didn't mean he was innocent of scheming to steal the plantation from me.

We spoke very little on the trip. Cesar didn't fear traveling the roads and highways. As Josh explained it to me, the locals were not much bothered unless they were involved in catching criminals or competing with them, because killing locals made for bad press—and few people had enough money to make good kidnap victims.

Juana decided to come along, to do some shopping. Maybe she really did want to get off the plantation, but I suspected that she wanted to make sure I made it safely back.

I still hadn't been able to figure out Cesar. At times he seemed like a decent guy—and other times he was abrupt and downright rude to me. The *bastardo* in him came out more when he drank too much.

Besides Carlos being my father, I had also accepted Cesar as my half brother. But having the same father wasn't a subject that came up between us. I didn't know how to approach it; the relationship came with too much baggage. Plots against me aside, it had to eat at him that he had been disinherited in favor of a stranger.

Even though I kept quiet about it, the fact I had a sibling was a significant event in my life. At the age of thirty-one, I suddenly had "family" beyond my mother and what she'd told me about her parents.

Under ordinary circumstances, offering to make him a partner in the plantation would have occurred to me. Growing coffee was not only in his blood; he'd had three decades of training from a master. But these weren't ordinary circumstances—I sensed plots and conspiracies whirling around me.

Whatever was coming down, the "decaffeinated coffee tree" project of chemists Soong and Sanchez was part of it. It didn't take a rocket scientist to see from the faces of the workers I talked to that something besides experiments with coffee was taking place. The workers immediately got cautious when I subtly brought up the subject. The place was off-limits to them.

Tomas, the foreman, intimated to me that a worker had been badly beaten by Sanchez for getting too nosy about the project.

I'd been by the huts where the two chemists lived and worked. Each time, I was with a foreman or worker who veered me away from actually going over and sticking my nose into the huts.

I owned the property, I had every right to check out what was going on, but I wasn't foolish enough to think I could just waltz over to the huts and see what the two chemists were up to.

At least not when there was a chance I'd get caught.

When I returned from the visit to the port, I waited until Cesar was away from the plantation and the chemists went into town for drinking, and whatever else they did, before I snuck over to check out the place. It was siesta time, which reduced my chances of running into anyone.

There were four huts, all with unpainted wood walls and tin roofs. They were built to house itinerant workers during peak harvesttime. The huts all had wood doors and large, uncovered windows all the way around—except for one.

It was late in the afternoon but still daylight when I scurried over to take a quick look. The first two huts were easy to figure out—through the windows, I could see clothes that I recognized as belonging to Soong in one, Sanchez in the other. A third hut was a no-brainer also—it was set up for cooking and eating. The wife of one of the foremen came in every day to prepare meals for the two men.

It didn't take a great deal of imagination on my part to see that the fourth hut, what I took to be the lab, was shrouded in mystery and intrigue. The thin, bare wood door that the other huts had had been replaced by a metal door. All the windows were covered by louvered shutters made of metal and fastened on the inside.

It was a regular Fort Knox.

At the back was a large generator, the type used for running electrical equipment at large construction sites. The other huts didn't have lights, but I could see from the setup that the generator provided lights, heat and air-conditioning, and whatever other uses in the lab that required electricity. A water tank had been set up next to the hut, with a pipe leading inside.

A truck with a cargo area was next to the generator. The cargo doors were locked.

So far I had learned exactly nothing. Water and electricity would be expected if the interior of the hut was being used to grow experimental coffee plants.

I tried peering between slats of a louvered shutter. I could see light inside but couldn't make out anything. The louvers were not heavy metal but felt like aluminum. I wondered if I could bend back one enough to see inside—and rebend it back into its original shape good enough so it wouldn't be noticed.

I stepped away from the window, shaking my head. *I must be nuts!* It would be pure insanity to do that. Whatever was going on inside involved Pablo Escobar . . . and the one thing Josh told me that I had complete faith in was that Escobar was a poisonous snake that struck if you crossed him.

I started to walk away but swung back around. *This is my property.* I should be able to do what I damn well pleased. I didn't have any choice—I was certain that whatever was going on in that hut was connected to Escobar nearly having me killed in Seattle; who else could reach that far?

I might as well go back to Seattle and turn myself in if I was going to let fear of criminals keep me from getting to the truth.

The hut next door, the one being used as a kitchen, was unlocked. I found a large kitchen knife I thought would do the job. Clutching the knife, I went back to the louvered shutter.

Courage, girl. As I looked over the louvers, they didn't appear to be difficult to bend. I could put the knife blade in, twist it to bend the slat up a little, peek in, and then tap the metal back down with the wooden handle. It would be a piece of cake.

I stuck the knife in and twisted. The metal was harder than I thought. I couldn't bend it. I stopped and picked up a rock about the size of my fist. Putting the knife blade back in, I banged on the handle to force it up against the louver.

I was going to bang a second time when I heard the door to the hut being opened.

Shit.

I dropped the rock and the knife and flew into the bushes. I kept running, in pure mindless panic.

Christ! Somebody had been in the building.

I tripped and went down and got back up to my knees, my breath coming hard, my heart beating wildly.

I heard someone in the bushes—it had to be a man by the way he was crashing through, heavy, violent, not the progress a woman would make.

The foliage was thick. My only chance was to hide. It was easier not to be seen if I went down and lay perfectly still.

That's what I did, at the spot where I was, going flat on the dirt, barely breathing, listening to the person stomping and pushing through the growth.

Then I heard nothing. He was probably standing still. Listening for me as I listened for him, not moving a muscle except to breathe, and doing little of that.

I lay motionless, sure that my pounding heart could be heard beating like a jungle drum.

I don't know how much time passed, probably seconds, but it seemed like an eternity until I heard him moving again. Then I heard something else—the hack of a machete. Everybody on the plantation seemed to have one—whoever he was, he must have come out of the hut with one of those long, swordlike jungle tamers.

That thought scared the hell out of me—he hadn't even yelled when he came out the door to scare me off. He wanted to catch me. What did he intend to do? Chop my head off? My arms and legs so I could be questioned before I died? And who was he?

I didn't dare move my head up to get a look. I lay flat on the ground, trembling, terrified the blade being used to hack about the brush was going to slice into me.

I had to wait it out—*shit, something's crawling up my leg.*

I was wearing long pants, but it had gotten inside a pant leg and onto my bare flesh. I could feel the creature on my skin, crawling up my leg, toward the inside of my thigh.

I imagined a giant centipede, a big hairy spider, a scorpion; it could be any of those.

The hacking grew closer. The thing in my pants reached my

knee. I pressed my knees together, trying to crush it. I felt it backtrack and move about the blockage. It slipped by and onto my inner thigh.

I smothered a scream.

I couldn't take it any longer—I leaned up a little so I could reach down and grabbed the thing in my pants, crushing it with my hand. I still didn't know what it was.

Before I could lie back down, the blade of the machete whacked the foliage next to me, inches from me.

I screamed.

First I saw the blade, raised above my head.

Then the man.

"You!"

27

❖

Ramon Alavar stared down on me, his green eyes full of fire, the machete raised. My left arm instinctively went up in a defensive gesture, a useless one against a machete, but mostly I just froze, paralyzed, gaping up at him.

The machete trembled, as if he was fighting an urge to use it—or not. His features also wrestled with emotions.

"Hello," I squeaked.

He slowly unwound, the tension visibly draining out of him, the machete slowly lowering, until it was at his side.

I got off the ground, shaking my leg to get the dead creature out—a big bug, hard-shelled, like a giant cockroach. I brushed off my clothes as Ramon stared at me, machete still at the ready.

"If you're not going to murder me, why don't you relax? You look like you're going to chop off my head." My voice came out much calmer than I felt.

He smiled. A beautiful smile, the perfect white teeth you see on movie stars. Damn, why did he have to be so handsome.

"What were you doing?" he asked.

"I own this place. I was trying to see what you were doing."

He seemed to reflect on my comment as we walked slowly back toward the hut. We were nearly there when he said, "You're lying. You didn't know anyone was inside; you wouldn't have made all that noise if you had." He stopped and faced me, appraisingly. "You were breaking into the hut."

"True, but what exactly were you doing in the hut?"

He smiled, beautifully again. "I asked you first."

"I own this property." I kept repeating the claim of ownership in the hopes that would impress him.

"But I have the machete. I'm afraid in my country, that beats mere legal title."

I stopped and faced him. "All right, the truth. Everyone's pretty vague about how the chemists are coming along with their work developing a decaffeinated coffee tree. I was told that if they're successful, it would be worth a lot of money.

"I don't want to go into it, but I have some very pressing problems back home that require money to resolve. I'd like to know more about how far they've gotten in developing the plant . . . and no one will tell me anything."

I was certain he knew exactly what my problems back home were. No doubt he was on the long list of conspirators that had created them, but this wasn't a time to sound like I knew too much—which of course, I didn't anyway.

He pursed his lips and slowly shook his head. "You're probably only telling me half the truth, but I am easily fooled by beautiful women."

Now that I knew his attraction to me on the plane was planned, I wasn't ready to swoon when he called me beautiful. But it did make my heart skip a beat.

"It's your turn," I said.

"My reasons are different, but like you, I have a pressing need for money. Sadly, I was more familiar with raising polo ponies than managing my properties and investments. As an official with the coffee administration, I'm well aware that attempts are being made to produce a decaffeinated bean, not just here, but in several places. If I had some, uh, shall we say, insider information, about a successful process, my financial problems would go away and I could go back to petting my ponies and women."

We walked again, as he talked. There was a certain amount of callous sincerity in his version. He was the type who probably did squander a fortune, polo ponies were unquestionably more up his line than investments, and he appeared shallow enough to steal someone else's hard work.

Plus he had the machete.

He said, "As you might imagine, a coffee bean grown naturally without caffeine would have an instant market. Are you familiar with how coffee is decaffeinated?"

"A little."

Coffee was decaffeinated before it was roasted to preserve flavors—but even at that, decaffeination resulted in some loss of flavor. Even after processing, decaf still had caffeine in it because it was considered decaffeinated if 97 percent of the caffeine was removed.

I avoided decaf coffee because I never knew how it was being processed—even if told, I wasn't sure if I could trust the information.

The traditional way coffee had been decaffeinated was by the use of a solvent, usually methylene chloride or ethyl acetate—basically *paint removers*. The beans were steamed to raise their moisture level, bringing the caffeine to the surface, and then were washed in the solvent and then resteamed to remove the solvent.

Methylene chloride was flat-out toxic. Incredibly, decaffeination with ethyl acetate, which is volatile and flammable, was considered a "natural" process because the substance is found in some fruits. The FDA permits the use of the chemicals because it claims little residue of the toxins is left in the process. Of course, that's the same FDA that had approved numerous drugs that sometimes kill when swallowed.

Some American roasters had stopped using the solvents and were using carbon dioxide or a water process, both of which were considered natural processes. But I preferred my coffee with caffeine, anyway.

I also knew that besides the Soong-Sanchez project there were frantic efforts being made to produce a decaffeinated bean in other parts of the world. In the coffee business, producing a bean that didn't have caffeine in it was like the fabled dream of untold riches that medieval alchemists had about making gold.

Deep down, I had hoped that the two scientists were producing a caffeine-free bean and that even after being robbed by Escobar there would be enough money left over to save the plantation and fight my Seattle problems.

Ramon said, "As you know, regardless of how it's done, it involves an expensive process. Discovery of a bean decaffeinated right off the tree would be worth tens of millions of dollars. Coffee is my country's biggest crop, so naturally, our government is very interested in the process."

He gave me another brilliant smile.

I gave him a sour grin. "A moment ago you said you were interested because you needed the money."

"Like you, there are many levels and lies to my actions. But as you *norteamericanas* would say, let's get down to the bottom line. Like you, I was doing a bit of spying."

We had walked to where a man was waiting in a Jeep Cherokee.

We paused before we reached the vehicle and Ramon said, "I must ask two favors of you. Don't tell anyone that you found me in the hut. People interested in the process might take offense—Colombian style."

"I really can't tell without exposing myself, can I?"

"Very true," he said, flashing his smile. "The other favor is that you have dinner with me."

I nodded. "On one condition. That you tell me why you went through all the trouble of trying to lure me into a car with Sca—Pablo's friend, Jorge."

I knew better than to ask the stupid question. I might as well have come right out and asked why he was trying to kidnap me in Bogotá. So I did.

"Was I to be just kidnapped? Murdered?"

"Isn't it obvious? *Plata o plomo.*"

"You're on Pablo Escobar's payroll?" That was a no-brainer.

"Oh, nothing so crude. I'm from a prominent old family, with many social and financial connections. We do not take money from nouveau riche like Escobar. Not at least in so crass a manner as an open bribe. What happens, instead, is we do a favor . . . and a discreet package arrives at our back door. If you have been helpful, it is full of pesos. And if you haven't, you find your firstborn's head—"

He laughed at my expression of disgust.

"Just joking; the point is, I'm not on his payroll. However, I've been using my authority as an official with the coffee ministry to make sure the plantation is not bothered by inspectors so the work in the huts can go on in secret."

Some secret; everyone on the plantation knew experimenting was being done to develop the plant.

"Also, because of my connections in the government and society, I hear things. And sometimes I pass on to Pablo what I hear. In your case, I was going to Panama City on government business. I had spoken to Pablo earlier because he wanted to carry a message to an official in the Canal Zone. To be crass, it was a customs official turning his head so he wouldn't see tons of cocaine going through.

"I was about to board in Bogotá when Pablo called and asked me to take the same return flight you were on. My understanding is that Jorge had never gotten the opportunity to sit down and negotiate a selling price for the plantation."

"I don't think his idea of negotiations is taught in business school."

Ramon laughed. "No, you're right, but you would have been safe with me. Bogotá is not Medellín. But now you must let me make it up to you. Please, come to my *casa* for dinner."

I didn't realize he lived in the area. How could I refuse? He was lying to me; I was lying to him; maybe if we talked enough, I'd learn something that slipped out of the cracks. Besides, he was a perfectly gorgeous man.

"I need to stop by the house, grab a wrap, and let Juana know I won't be home for dinner."

"I'll have the driver take you while I wait here. It's better that I am not seen at the plantation."

A half an hour later, the SUV carrying us to Ramon's *casa* pulled up to a small airplane parked off a dirt road.

"What's this?"

"A golden carriage with wings to take you to my casa."

"How did you land here?"

"At this point, the road is straight and reasonably smooth. It only takes a moment to get into the air."

"This is insane."

"No, this is Colombia. I can cover in two hours by air what would take two days by car." He took my arm. "When you get above the Andes, the sight is amazing. These are great mountains, some several miles high, and lush valleys. You will think you died and went to heaven."

I let him pull me to the plane, but I didn't fool myself—the pearly gates weren't going to be my destination when I gave up the ghost. I had been paving a road to hell for a long time.

28

❖

Soaring over mountains miles high in a small plane gave me thrills I hadn't experienced since riding on very large roller coasters when I was a little girl. There was no comparison with flying encased in a commercial airliner. The small plane gave stunning bird's-eye views. It gave me the sensation of being able to step out and walk on the clouds.

A little over an hour in flight we went beyond mountains and soared over a vast savannah.

"Los Llanos," Ramon said.

Like the cattle country in Texas, pampas in Argentina, the Llanos was a grassland that stretched forever. I saw rivers and scattered trees, but its most prominent feature was its very lack of physical attributes.

"My country has jungles, mountains, lush valleys—now you see our other prominent landscape, our great plains. Little is down there; it can be very hot and treeless; it lacks large populations, industry, and farmlands. What it doesn't lack is cattle. My family has been raising cattle on our hacienda for over two centuries, since before your Declaration of Independence was signed."

The ranch's grand casa topped a small hill. More than a

house, the dun-covered grand casa was a complex. From the air I could see the square-shaped main house, surrounded by high walls, occupied less than half of the space within the walls.

"There are stables for our horses, a blacksmith shop, storage bins for food and water," he said.

"It looks like a fortress."

"For good reason. The Llanos is sparsely populated. It's long been the rule that a family could own only as much land as they could defend. It is no longer the Wild West, but in my country, one must still show strength or the vultures will tear out your liver."

Below it was a small village, set next to a river, for the vaqueros who worked the cattle.

"How big is your hacienda?"

"It extends for six miles up the river and three to four in width."

As the plane was coming in for a landing on a narrow strip that didn't look much different from the dirt road we'd taken off from, I thought about how much different my own country was from much of the rest of the world. Most of the "class" differences in the States were based upon money—in other places, social differences often had as much to do with heritage, with ancestors weighing in more than bank accounts.

Just as Carlos had been the *patrón* of Casa de Oro, spoken of by the workers and *colonos* with greater respect than just a landowner would get, Ramon was the hacienda's *patrón*. From the moment we stepped off the plane, I could see from the attitude of the driver of a station wagon waiting for us that "Don Ramon" was not just the owner of the hacienda but the master of it.

Like the workers on the coffee plantation, those on the cattle ranch didn't so much count their seniority by years as by generations.

I assumed that despite the huge size, like the coffee plantation, the hacienda provided more reward from pride of ownership and maintaining traditions than financial rewards. Unless one struck oil, these places usually made one "land rich" rather than rich in spending money. And Ramon struck me as a man who needed more than pocket change.

He had had a limo waiting for him the day I ditched him in Bogotá, and had mentioned on the plane that he owned a large house in the capital. I imagined that a private plane, a Rolex, and polo ponies were just a small part of the extravagant lifestyle he was accustomed to. I didn't get any more information out of him about his connection to the drug cartel king, but I managed to keep my own mouth shut, too.

The inside of the *casa* was pretty much what I expected from its appearance on the outside: Colombian rustic, lots of cowhide and wood furniture, big stone fireplaces, a stove in the kitchen you could almost cook a cow on, and one outside in the patio you *could* cook a cow on—not that it was necessary; an entire cow was already roasting on a spit.

Ramon introduced a pretty young girl about sixteen as his niece, Elena. She had Ramon's tanned complexion and soft brown hair. He had already explained to me that Elena's parents, his sister and brother-in-law, had been killed in a car accident. "My own parents are gone and I haven't married, so that leaves Elena and me as our total family."

Elena was eager to ask me questions about America and even about what was happening in Medellín. She squealed when I told her I had met Pablo Escobar.

Ramon shot me a look and I pretended to Elena that the meeting had been purely by accident.

She gave me a tour of the *casa* as Ramon attended to some business matters. I soon found out that she had cabin fever.

"Ramon insists that I stay here, in the Llanos. I am so bored; there are few girls my age and most of them work all day on the ranch. None of them have even been to Bogotá. I would love to live in the capital, to go to school there. As it is, a teacher comes here twice a week to tutor me. The rest of the time, I am left on my own to study. I am so tired of books! I have no friends, nothing to do except read."

"Why do you have to stay here?"

"Ramon says it is to protect me."

"Is the capital so dangerous? I understand it's dangerous for people like judges and reporters who fight the cartels, but isn't it just another big city otherwise?"

"That's what I say, but Ramon says I must stay here. He says I will remain pure here, but would be polluted if I go to Bogotá." She suddenly smiled and her eyes got a warm glow. "But I don't mind, as long as Ramon is here at least a couple days a week."

Of course she did mind. I wondered why, if he thought Bogotá was not the right place, he didn't send her off to Europe or the States to go to school. But it was none of my business, so I didn't volunteer the idea.

That night we had dinner in a delightful garden, with subdued lighting, a frolicking fountain, and music. Men and women from the village entertained us with music and dancing. Some of the music was called *vallenata* and had developed in the cattle ranches along the Atlantic coast. There was a gyrating, vibrating African rhythm to the sounds.

Later, Ramon took me for a walk down to the river. He suddenly put his arms around me. I turned my head and pulled away as he tried to kiss me.

"Have I offended you?" he asked.

I smiled. "I don't trust you. You're still allied with the man trying to steal my plantation."

"Perhaps you should try to be a little nicer so you'd have allies of your own."

"What I've seen so far brings to mind an old American expression: With friends like you, I don't need enemies. Do you mind if we go back to the house? I'm tired and I'd like to get an early start in the morning back to the plantation."

He was puzzled and so was I. I don't know what came over me. One minute I was intrigued about making love to the gorgeous stud, even though I knew he was a villain—sort of how James Bond feels when he makes love to the temptress who has a knife under the pillow—and the next minute I rebuffed him.

But I had a bad feeling in my gut. Sort of free-floating anxiety and paranoia. Something wasn't right about Ramon, the situation; something I'd seen or heard had affected me and I didn't know what it was yet. I just suddenly had bad feelings and wished the hell I had never come.

At the casa, I said good night to Elena. The bedrooms were on the second floor, with balconies that overlooked the garden. I barred the door, propping a chair up under the handle, then opened the balcony doors and turned off my lights. I really wasn't tired; I just wanted to be alone.

I leaned against the door frame and looked around me. A bright moon sailed overhead. A light, warm breeze stirred the night. I sighed. It was a night for passionate love, and I had turned off, kicked out of bed, one of the handsomest men I'd ever met.

Good work, girl!

I was ready to go inside when I saw them in the garden. Ramon and Elena. They paused by the fountain and he took her in his arms. He gave her the kiss I had rejected.

His hands went down her back, to her tush, and he pulled her hard against him. His hands came back up, onto her shoulders, and pushed her down to her knees. As he unzipped his pants, I shut the balcony doors.

Fucking bastard.

Now I knew why he kept his niece a prisoner at an isolated ranch in the Llanos.

And I knew what had been bothering me all night.

It was Elena's smile and eyes, how she came alive when she said it was all right as long as Ramon was there.

What I saw was the young girl expressing her love—her desire—for him.

And he was a disgusting bastard. He could have gotten any woman, but incest must have given him that extra thrill he needed.

I also knew one other thing.

He had staged the blow job so I would see it from my room. Revenge for my rebuff? Or more of a turn-on for him?

I hope one day someone bites off his prick.

29

❖

The plane ride back the next morning was cold and silent. Ramon was in a dark mood and I was ready to tell him he was a bastard and a pervert. Only the fact that he might throw me out at twenty thousand feet kept my mouth shut.

He never spoke to me all the way back, until we had stopped taxiing on the dirt road. The Jeep Cherokee that had chauffeured us before was waiting.

When the plane had stopped and I opened the door to get out, he said, "Keep your mouth shut about me. If I hear anything, you'll wish you were safely in a Seattle jail."

"You really make that old expression true."

"What old expression?"

"About beauty being skin-deep. You're slime underneath that pretty face."

He turned several shades darker and I got quickly out of the plane and hurried to the SUV. We made it a couple hundred yards when a familiar Jeep blocked our way. Josh waved for me to get in.

I got out of the SUV and climbed into the Jeep. He popped the clutch and we took off with tires kicking dirt and rock. He was in a grim mood.

"So . . . what kind of fuck was he?"

The roof blew off my temper. "That's none of your damn business! I am so sick and tired of being accountable to all you crazy people in this crazy country, to have everyone walking on my heels, threatening me and telling me how to lead my life. You're all a bunch of fucking lunatics and losers. Why don't you go home and get an honest job?"

I was irritable and his sarcastic remark infuriated me even more.

He kept driving but gave me a sideways glance. "Well, at least I'm happy to see that you didn't have a good time."

It suddenly hit me. "You're jealous."

"Naw, I was curious."

"Jealous," I repeated. God, I loved the word. "Jealous." It was delicious. A man I was attracted to was honestly jealous over me.

"Okay, I was jealous. So what happened? How did you suddenly link up with Ramon Alavar?"

I gave him the whole nine yards, me trying to pry the louver, Ramon with the machete. When I got to the part about the niece, Josh got mad, too.

"Fuckin' predator."

"More than that, it's a power trip," I said. "He keeps her prisoner and gets an extra kick out of fucking her. Before I leave this country, I swear, Ramon will pay for what he's doing to her, even if I have to take out ads in newspapers because the authorities won't do anything." I turned to Josh and couldn't resist making a catty remark. "Of course, he's not the only one robbing the cradle."

"She's not my niece and she's pushing thirty."

"She's not more than sixteen or seventeen."

"I wasn't talking about her chronological age. Besides, now that we've met and clicked, I've given her up."

"Clicked? *Clicked?* I don't even like you."

"I don't like me much myself, but I'm trying to change." He stopped the Jeep and locked eyes with me. "Ramon the Perv gave you one good piece of advice."

"Keep my mouth shut."

He nodded. "To everyone—and I mean everyone. You can probably trust Juana, but don't tell her anything. What she doesn't know won't hurt you, her—or me. Like he told you, don't even let anyone know he was here. If anyone gets too nosy, say you were with me . . . and please, don't scowl when you say it like I wasn't a good fuck."

I ignored his last comment. My mind was spinning with questions.

"What's going on, Josh? There's a Chinese connection, a cartel connection; now Ramon's part of it. What's going on in that laboratory? Are they close to developing the decaffeinated bean?"

He shrugged. "How would I know?"

"You seem to know everything else that goes on around here—like even the schedule of Ramon's plane. How did you know we'd be landing? Or even that I left? And don't tell me you were on your way to bribe more cops."

"I pay to know some things; everyone knows that; they come to me whenever a stranger shows up. It's insurance on my part. It could be a killer hired by a mine owner."

"I think you know more than you're letting on. Why don't you tell me what's going on?"

"What did I just say? Talk kills. Whatever's going on in that laboratory, Pablo Escobar's a major player. That's reason enough for you to keep your mouth shut. And run as fast as you can away from here."

"How can I keep my mouth shut? I inherited this place. And I need the damn money it can give me, bad. I need to get to the bottom of the cesspool my life has been dropped into."

"Sell the plantation."

"Not enough money's offered. I wouldn't do that anyway, not unless I knew the people who rely on the plantation would be taken care of."

"Jesus, now that's a load for you to carry: You're not just going to help yourself; you're going to save hundreds of workers and their families. I hope you walk on water, because you're going to need to perform miracles. You better be bullet-proof, too."

He pulled over and faced me. "I care for you, Nash. I don't want anything to happen to you. If I could arrange for you to go someplace else, maybe farther south, Uruguay's a nice country, they call it the Switzerland of South America, you could just wait and ride out—"

"Ride out what? Are you going to tell me what's going on?"

He reached over and kissed me on the lips. I shut my eyes and didn't resist, then opened them and stared at him. He wasn't as handsome as Ramon; he still needed a shave and a haircut. But I was inexorably drawn to him.

Before I found out the man was a pervert, Ramon had excited me sexually. But I think it was more titillation, the idea of making love to a man that other women drooled over.

Josh had a more profound effect on me. I felt secure and comfortable with him. A feeling that I had finally found the man I'd spent the last dozen years yearning for. But we were still on two different paths.

"Get this through your thick head—I will not sell the plantation to anyone who will screw the workers and the sharecroppers."

"Then what do you plan to do?"

I snapped at him, "I don't know, damn it . . . I don't know." I was irritable and suddenly tired.

For a moment he just looked at me, but then he broke out in an amused grin. "You know, you're cute when you get angry," he said in a calm and soothing voice.

"I'm glad you find this amusing."

He was still smiling and I couldn't help but return his smile.

Damn it, he had a way of breaking my resistance. I couldn't ignore the sexual tension in the air. It was there and I know he felt it, too. I had an overwhelming desire to be in his arms, to have him hold me, comfort me, tell me everything was going to be all right. I wanted him to make love to me, really make love to me, something I hadn't had for so long.

"Let's go somewhere where we can be alone," I said.

"I know just the place."

We arrived at his place a few minutes later. It was surprisingly neater than I expected, small but cozy.

He led me to the bedroom and began to take off my clothes, not in a hurried manner but in a deliberate and sensuous manner. There was no need for any words between us. It was plain that the sexual hunger in our bodies had to be satisfied. I felt no shame in standing there naked in front of him as I waited for him to take off his own clothes.

He took my hand and guided me to the bed. I was already wet with desire and he was already hard as he entered me easily and quickly. I kissed him with a fire I hadn't known before. My heartbeat raced and my blood pounded. I swayed to the ecstasy of pleasure throbbing through my body. It came quickly and I cried out as I felt the explosion inside me. I pulled him deeper inside me and he shuddered against me as he rode the same wave of ecstasy.

For a few minutes our bodies clung together until the tremors of pleasure began to calm down. He released the weight of his body and pulled me to him. I felt warm and comfortable as I snuggled up against him, a feeling of completeness inside me. We fell asleep in each other's arms.

30

❖

When I returned to the plantation, nothing had changed: Juana was warm as usual toward me, Cesar cold, as if he could barely tolerate me—that wasn't news—and Lily Soong was still more interested in the shade of her fingernail polish than me. But there was another presence, an uninvited guest: an aura of doom and gloom that had hovered over the plantation house ever since Pablo Escobar's visit.

Everyone seemed to be affected by it, their nerves on edge, as well as looking a little depressed. Even Lily seemed a bit gloomy as she polished her nails on the veranda.

I tried to probe Juana about why everyone had the blues, but she immediately started to tear up. My bottom-line conclusion was that she really didn't understand what was going on and wasn't the type to dig for answers.

The day after I got back, a man drove up in a black SUV and left an envelope with a single notation inside: *$100,000.*

I found it curious that Escobar didn't simply send some of his *sicarii* assassins to give me an attitude adjustment until I signed over the plantation. But from table talk, newspapers, and the radio I got the impression that Don Pablo was busy with his war against U.S. and Colombian military and paramilitary units. I also had to wonder whether his real interest in the plantation was the place as a whole or just whatever was going on in the laboratory.

Josh said that they didn't need the plantation to grow coca and it was too open and obvious for a processing plant. That boiled down to the laboratory. Which led me to wonder whether Escobar was not that interested in acquiring the coffee plantation and Scar was teaming up with someone else—Cesar, of course—to steal it from me at a fire-sale price, after making sure I badly needed the money by trashing my Seattle dream.

I had a lot of thinking to do. And needed someone to talk to, someone who wasn't going to skew everything.

So I went back to the hill, to my father's grave.

I spent hours there, just *listening* to the earth, hearing and reading the plantation from the bird's-eye view.

Like a kid wondering whether she should be a police officer, firefighter, or computer hacker, I finally reached a conclusion as to what I would do when I grew up.

Three days after I returned from the Llanos, Juana prepared a dinner for Cesar on his birthday. Josh joined us for dinner. Juana said Drs. Soong and Sanchez were too busy to attend.

"Still working day and night on their black magic?" I didn't bother to leave the sarcasm out of my tone. I constantly vacillated on what I thought was going on in the laboratory hut, sometimes sure they were working on something for a drug cartel, other times that they really were developing a decaf plant and there would be enough money to make all my dreams come true.

"They went to town to get the velvet rubbed off their cocks," Cesar said.

"Cesar!" Juana stood at the table. "How dare you talk that way at the table."

He shrugged. He had had a couple drinks and was in a sour, arrogant mood. "Okay, is this better? They went to the local whorehouse."

Juana looked miserable but managed to keep her emotions

tightly drawn. I felt sorry for her. *She has no way out,* I thought. She had spent her entire life on the plantation, a place of peace and serenity, and now the ugly world was invading it.

I made an announcement.

"I received a message from Jorge, the gentleman who has been trying to buy the plantation."

Cesar sneered. "Don Pablo's investment counselor."

"The offer on the plantation has gone to a hundred thousand dollars."

No one seemed surprised. Cesar looked smug.

"You should take it and return home," Juana said. Her voice quivered as she spoke. Selling the plantation to Escobar—if he was actually the buyer—would mean the end of the only life she had known.

Josh said, "You should take it."

I looked around the table, meeting the eyes of each of them. The amount of money involved meant nothing to me; it wasn't enough for me to set bail on the Seattle case, much less hire a lawyer. But at the moment, I wouldn't have sold the plantation if the offer had been a million dollars.

I couldn't explain it to them, but I knew why Carlos had made me his sole heir. He had checked me out and I think he knew that I would fight to keep the plantation alive. And he had been right.

"I'm not selling the plantation."

Juana clasped her hands together. "Nash, you must; you don't understand—"

"Don't worry about her," Cesar said. "If she's that stupid, let her dig her own grave."

"I went to town this afternoon; I sent a wire to a friend in the States, describing everything that's going on around here, including Escobar's unhealthy interest in my property. I also sent her a list of government agencies in the U.S. and Colombia to forward it to if anything happens to me."

My statement made a silent implosion in the room. No one moved; no one said a word. Finally, Josh said, very quietly, "What do you think that will accomplish?"

"If something happens to me, it'll put the plantation on the DEA's watch list. And it's a clue that it wasn't an accident."

I didn't know what good it would do, either, but my back was to the wall and it was a shot in the dark.

Cesar shook his head at Josh. "If you have any influence with this crazy woman, you had better get her out of here now; get her on a plane back to your country. She has signed her own death sentence."

"I'm going to save this plantation," I said.

Cesar exploded. "You're insane!"

Juana put a hand on his arm. "Please, don't shout at her. She means well."

He struggled to regain his composure. "You know nothing about growing coffee. A walk in the fields doesn't make you a *cafetero*."

"Let her speak," Juana said. "She knows more than you think."

I said, "This place doesn't need an expert coffee grower. Carlos was the world's greatest *cafetero;* Cesar knows how to grow great coffee; that's not the plantation's weakness. What's missing is a *businessperson*. I ran a coffee store in Seattle, but before that I was an executive with—"

Cesar shook his head. "Listen to me; even if you didn't get yourself killed, the plantation will go to the bank. Your experience running a little store thousands of miles away doesn't qualify you to run a plantation in our outlaw country. We don't do business like the rest of the world."

"My *little* store was designed to be a successful flagship of a national chain. Agreements were already being drawn up when people here reached out and brought the roof down on my head."

"Even if you know how to retail coffee, you don't know how to grow and sell it on the national market. It's not a job for a woman."

"Excuse me, but you've been living in a male-dominated society for too long. Maybe if you got off this plantation for a while, you'd realize there is a whole different world out there, one in which women are included. Before I decided to develop a chain of retail stores, I was a business executive, a highly paid problem solver dealing with billion-dollar situations. Wealthy, successful executives paid enormous amounts of money to have me tell them how to run their businesses."

Cesar raised his eyebrows. "All right, why don't you enlighten us with your vast business knowledge? How are you going to save the plantation?" His tone was that of addressing a child.

"If you stop interrupting me, I'll tell you." I glared at him. "Let's start out with the fact that you don't understand the phenomenon—or the arithmetic—of the coffee boom in America. Carlos didn't, either, because it happened so fast. During the last few years, while you were struggling with the crash in the world price of coffee, coffee boutiques have been opening up everywhere in the States, thousands of them. People have gone from having a simple cup of coffee at breakfast to having designer coffees at any time of the day and night. Words like 'latte,' 'cappuccino,' and 'mocha' that had hardly been used in the last thousand years suddenly are on everyone's lips.

"And it's a phenomenon that is spreading around the world—coffee shops are opening up in places like Moscow and Tokyo. They take to designer coffee like they took to American soda pop."

I looked at Cesar. "When you quoted me the financial end of coffee farming, that it costs nearly a dollar a pound to produce and that you only get ninety cents a pound from wholesalers, you're talking about selling coffee on the *open market*. I didn't buy coffee on the open market, and neither do the better coffee boutiques in America, the ones that survive and grow into national chains.

"I bought *specialty* coffees because no one is going to come into my store and slap down eight or ten dollars for a pound of coffee they can get for three or four dollars at the supermarket across the street. And the customer isn't going to pay two or three dollars for a coffee drink that isn't brewed from premium beans.

"I bought direct from a farm in Costa Rica and I paid three dollars a pound. That's three times what you're getting for the plantation's coffee. It's a different market than the one you're selling to. Carlos was an artist at growing coffee, but he didn't know how to sell it. *He was producing specialty beans and selling them as ordinary ones.*"

"Is this true?" Juana asked Cesar. "We grow the best coffee in the world. Why can't we get more for it than other growers?"

"Because she has left out the fact that we would need an office in America and salespeople. And it would take years to build up a reputation, a brand name, that is recognized so these coffee stores she's talking about will know about us."

"That's all true, but not the whole truth," I said. "A single large retail specialty chain, or a wholesaler supplying specialty coffee stores, could take the entire output of all the acres under cultivation and then some. We only need one sale to one significant retail chain or wholesaler of better coffees. And if we get a signed contract, money can be advanced to keep us in business."

No one spoke. They sat there and chewed on my words as if they had just been served from the kitchen.

Of course, what I described was a house of cards. In truth, buying lottery tickets and hoping all your dreams will come through with a single scratch would be about as good a business plan for the plantation. The theory was good, but there were two problems: The first was that it would take time and money for me to return to the States with a marketing plan and storm the offices of coffee buyers with samples from the plantation. I might get lucky right away and hit a big sale, but the reality was that it would take months and then years buying up the reputation of the brand. In other words, Cesar was right.

The second problem was that I might get arrested getting off the plane on my first business trip.

I hadn't lied about one thing: A single chain adopting our coffee as its specialty brand would put the plantation—and my Seattle problems—on easy street. But as I said, so would winning the lottery, which had about the same odds. . . .

Besides a desperate gamble, I had decided someone wanted

me dead. Maybe even everyone at the table, except Juana, would have liked to hasten my demise. I couldn't be completely sure about Josh, even with my feelings for him. With no place to run to, and no money to get there, I needed a business plan to keep me alive. I wanted to give them a reason to keep me alive. The foreman said the people felt hope about my arrival. Now I wanted to give Cesar hope. Until something else came along that I could use as a life raft.

"Shanghai," Lily said, breaking the silence.

It was a showstopper. All of us stared at her. She rarely said a word at dinner or any time when she was around us. I didn't know what she said when she was alone with Cesar, but I suspected it was all body language.

"What about Shanghai?" I asked.

"It's the biggest city in China, perhaps in the world. You said Tokyo and Moscow are new markets for coffee. Shanghai is bigger than either of them. Sell your coffee in Shanghai."

"China's a communist country," Josh said.

"Communists are no problem; the government has opened Shanghai to the West, just as it did in the past."

"She's right," Cesar said. "It's a brand-new, untapped market."

They were both right. I started trembling as pieces fell from the sky, falling down all around me. I had an epiphany. A revelation.

The pieces fell together perfectly. Competition would be fierce in the States and Europe, where selling coffee was a well-established business. It would take a long time and fantastic luck to crack a market in which everybody was trying for the same brass ring.

But Shanghai. China. It was only a couple years ago that China was a completely closed nation. Now there was constant news about China opening up this and that for trade.

I recalled business articles I'd read about Shanghai. It had only been open to the West for a couple years. Coffee would be a natural there.

I started trembling. *My God, it's virgin territory.* But what if . . .

I asked Lily, "What if coffee's already big there?"

"It isn't. I'm from Shanghai. Everyone drinks tea. Coffee is available, it has always been, but I don't know of any businesses that sell coffee as their main product, as you describe happening in America."

"It might take years to get permission—"

She cut me off with a shake of her head. "No, the government is very lenient about business in Shanghai. They want Western business dollars to come there. Besides, my uncle in the city has great influence. He can get permission with a wave of his hand."

Lily Soong smiled sweetly at me. It was the first time she'd shown any positive emotion in my direction.

"We go to Shanghai, sell your coffee, save the plantation."

I felt like I was walking on water. For about three seconds.

Something about the smug look Lily and Cesar exchanged caused some of my elation to deflate.

I didn't like the way Josh refused to meet my eye, and I saw fear on Juana's face.

None of it was doing anything for my confidence.

And, of course, there had been that "we" part of going to Shanghai. I would have a traveling companion.

I leaned back and let out a little sigh. I needed a miracle and it had appeared. But like I keep saying about a snake in every paradise . . .

I didn't have any other choices. I needed virgin territory, and from the sounds of it, Shanghai was waiting to be exploited. And the city itself was big enough to be an enormous market.

In a way, I saw it as another change of planes.

I could jump on a plane to Shanghai and duck the trouble in Colombia.

What's the worse that could happen if I ran to the Far East?

Hong Kong

Capitalism Gone Gonzo

31

❖

Flying halfway around the world with the China Doll was ego busting. It was hard on a woman's self-image to walk through an airport terminal and have every man in the place turn and look—at the woman next to her.

I discovered during our time together that besides oozing with sex appeal, Lily Soong had a good mind—but she was deviously clever at keeping it concealed. She pretended with men that she was a sex object and with women that she was more interested in the color of her fingernails than reading a book. I don't know if she read, but I could almost see the wheels in her head moving as she analyzed situations, all the while pretending to concentrate on her fingernails or to stare blankly past me.

I suspected that men who were drawn into her web by her exotic sexuality soon discovered that she was more of a lioness than a house cat. When they crossed her women would soon discover those fingernails became claws.

We would arrive in Hong Kong before noon and the itinerary she set up had us staying overnight there before catching a flight to Shanghai. That wasn't surprising; even though a flight was available later that afternoon to Shanghai, we would both be tired after an agonizingly long flight and changing planes. But in my suspicious mind, everything Lily did had an ulterior motive.

"I have an uncle in Hong Kong," she told me. "It would be rude if I didn't see him while I was in the city."

She gave me information about the "New China" during the flight, stepping for a moment out of her China Doll persona and exposing her knowledge of world events.

"The Chinese leadership has had more intelligence than the rest of the communist world. It looked around and saw the failure of a communist economy. The Soviet Union has crumbled because the communist system was so bad, they manufactured products that didn't work and couldn't grow enough grains to feed their own people. North Korea is such a failure that we hear stories that people are turning to cannibalism."

On the other hand, South Korea, Japan, Taiwan, Hong Kong, and Singapore were booming.

"That's why our leaders opened Shanghai to the West. It was once the financial center of the Far East. They opened it up so China would have a door to the Western financial centers."

I said, "I've read that the city is famous not only for having been a financial center, but in the old days it was notorious for its corrupt, depraved lifestyles. Gangsters, dens of iniquity where drugs and sex were sold . . ."

She shrugged. "Is there anywhere in the world where there are no drugs, prostitution, and crime?"

"True . . . but most places don't have them in the abundance that Shanghai has been famous for." Medellín had the world's leading drug king in residence, but the Colombian city lacked Shanghai's reputation for the exotic and kinkier kinds of pleasure.

She kept a blank face, but I saw she was smothering a laugh.

"Is Hong Kong like Shanghai? I mean, I know Hong Kong is famous for its merchandise, but it's also kind of a Sin City, too, isn't it?"

"Hong Kong has house cats; Shanghai has jungle cats." She met my eye, a small, secret smile on her lips. "The Chinese in Hong Kong have been governed by the British. If you do wrong, you go to court. In Shanghai, the government is not so lenient. If you do wrong, sometimes they just shoot you. It makes for criminals who will do *anything* not to get caught."

It made sense. The stories coming out of Russia about its "mafiya" left the impression that Russian criminals were much more brutal than organized crime in the States—because when Russian cops gave an "attitude adjustment," the recipient didn't always survive.

I said, "I've heard that with the British turning Hong Kong over to Red China in a few years, businesspeople are desperate to establish a financial base in other countries, especially in the U.S. and Europe."

She shrugged and examined her fingernails, signaling that she was getting bored with thinking—or educating me.

I read in the guidebook I'd bought in the airport that some Hong Kong money was also being directed to Shanghai as a place of opportunity as the town turned to a boomtown, Wild West economy. I decided to let her off the hook about Far East economies, but I had one more question.

"What does your uncle do in Hong Kong?" I asked.

"Business."

"What kind of business?"

"Big business. Like my uncle in Shanghai."

"Anything that can use our coffee?"

"No."

Okay. That was all very enlightening. When she wanted to be evasive, Lily was a master at it. But *c'est la vie;* I didn't care what Lily did as long as it didn't affect my plans to break into—or create—a Shanghai coffee market.

Along with my basic carry-on, for a change I had a checked piece of luggage. It contained sealed one-pound bags of roasted beans from the plantation. Rather than grinding the beans ahead of time, to ensure I was able to provide potential distributors with the freshest taste I also brought along a small, hand-cranked grinder, the type used for nuts, and filters. In addition, I threw in three small coffee brewers, the two-cup varieties found in hotel rooms, along with paper filters.

Add hot water, and I was set up to make fresh-brewed coffee on the spot for buyers.

I needed a "famous" brand look for the coffee packages. I

took a picture of the plantation and waterfall, with the surrounding lush greenery and plants in colorful bloom. A friend of Juana's was an artist. The artist turned the picture into a painting and I had a print shop in Medellín do labels that we stuck on the one-pound bags.

Cesar thought the time and expense of making the packages attractive was a waste, but he knew zero about marketing. However, he took surprisingly well to Lily and me heading to China with a suitcase full of coffee. Which made me suspicious. Raising my paranoia even further was Josh's attitude. He seemed genuinely worried. Knowing that he was more worried about me going to Shanghai than he had been about me staying in Colombia, where he thought I would be murdered, did make me wonder what might be waiting for me in the biggest city in the most populated country on the planet—where I didn't speak the language, didn't know the customs, and could be arrested as a foreign spy for spitting on the sidewalk.

"How did your father end up experimenting in growing a naturally decaf coffee plant?" I asked.

"Would it be strange to you if an American scientist came to Colombia to experiment on coffee plants? Do you only find it strange because my father is a Chinese?"

I found it strange that the man was even her father, but I didn't volunteer that. "I wouldn't find it strange for an American scientist because the person would have been raised in a coffee culture. China is a tea culture. Your father drinks tea. I haven't seen him drink a single cup of coffee at the plantation. I've never seen you drink coffee. I was just curious what directed your father toward experimenting with coffee, rather than tea or some other product linked to China."

She avoided my eyes and looked toward the front of the plane, a sure sign she was thinking up a lie.

"My father's work is in modifying plants. He doesn't care if it's to take the caffeine out of coffee or make bananas glow in the dark."

Good reply. Evasive and vague because she spoke in nothing but generalities, but it was at least plausible and showed that she was a better liar than me. Perhaps she'd had more practice at it. I just couldn't place her as the daughter of a scientist—or the niece of a businessman in Hong Kong and Shanghai. Lily was a sensuous woman, with an air of the exotic and the erotic. When it came to older men in her life, the quaint old phrase "Sugar Daddy" came to mind.

I still had my doubts about the familial relationship between Dr. Soong and her. It wasn't just the lack of resemblance, but the body language didn't connect, either. She not only didn't ever touch him or speak to him, but she didn't really even look at him. She paid no more attention to Dr. Soong than she did to his partner, Dr. Sanchez. And the only looks she got from "her father" weren't the type of looks fathers usually gave their daughters, not unless they wanted to sleep with them.

I couldn't help but wonder what Lily's game was. I couldn't buy the idea that she was so supportive of my dream of saving the plantation that she was willing to accompany me to China. I was being steered to China for reasons other than opening a coffee market; that was a no-brainer.

Lily—along with Cesar and maybe even Josh—had her own agenda. That was okay with me, since the trip suited my purposes, too. But I felt uncomfortable with her. I had the feeling that she knew something I didn't—something that could hurt me. Sometimes it seemed like it amused her, that she was secretly laughing at me, but I had to admit, she seemed that way around Cesar, too, as if she knew something funny that he didn't know.

Not that Cesar was showing his cards. Juana had made one slip about Cesar: She said he had met Lily in Shanghai. I tried to follow up on the comment, but by the time I got the chance, she clammed up. She seemed to only give me so much and then caution set in.

I asked Cesar later if he had ever been to China and all I got for an answer was that it was none of my business.

I was reasonably sure I was being used as an excuse for a trip to Shanghai. But what Lily's—or their—plans were escaped me. I certainly wasn't being lured into white slavery—I wasn't sexy enough for the trade.

Not that Lily's motives were all that important to me at the moment. Life is all about options—and at the moment the only alternative I had was to play along in the hopes that whatever she was up to would work to my advantage in the long run.

I turned back to reading the guide books on Hong Kong and Shanghai I'd bought at the airport. They pretty much read like the conversation I had with Lily—business, sex, and crime were the three big commodities of Hong Kong and Shanghai. I hadn't been that interested in world politics when I was a struggling businesswoman in Seattle, but I figured I'd better know a little of how the game was played in the Far East, even if that meant digesting a little history. I didn't expose my ignorance of Asian history to Lily by telling her how aghast I was at reading how shabbily the Western powers had treated the Chinese.

I learned that in the nineteenth century the Chinese were forced to turn over concessions to Britain and other countries as a result of the Opium Wars. The wars were "trade wars" that began when the British insisted that the Chinese government permit its merchants to market opium to the people of China. The drug trade had turned millions of Chinese into opium addicts. It was a time in the world during which imperialistic greed was a stronger driving force than human kindness. Trade and other concessions in Hong Kong, Shanghai, and other places were forced on the Chinese when they lost the wars.

The British initially obtained Hong Kong Island, and increased the size of the colony over the years. In 1898 the British leased for ninety-nine years a large area adjoining the colony. That lease was due to expire in 1997, four years from now. The British agreed that when the lease was up, all of the area that now comprised Hong Kong would revert to Red China.

Opium smoking didn't get substantially eradicated until after World War II when the Red Chinese attacked it. They managed to reduce it but were unable to completely stamp it out.

When the communists took over mainland China in 1949, many of Shanghai's moneyed elite—which included triad gangster bosses—packed up their money and moved to Hong Kong but kept their fingers in the Shanghai pie. As communist attitudes about Shanghai's contacts with the Free World softened, many of these wealthy business and criminal expatriates began once again to take large slices of the pie.

Nowhere in my reading did it say that the Chinese were chomping at the bit for a chance to drink coffee.

I sighed and laid the book down in my lap. Like Lily, I could handle only so much knowledge at a time. "Coffee or tea?" I asked. Lily had gone to the bathroom, so my comment was thrown to the wind.

A white-haired gentleman of Chinese ancestry on the aisle seat across from me gave me a quizzical look.

"I'm a coffee grower," I told him. "I'm going to try to open the Shanghai market."

We started talking and he told me he was a history professor from Hong Kong.

"You will find selling coffee to China a difficult proposition, what you Americans call a tough row to hoe. Tea has long been part of the culture of the Far East. That's not as true in the West. In Britain and many other European countries, tea was the preferred drink not because of taste, but because it was available.

"The British were once coffee drinkers, but when they began to grow tea in India, the government forced the British public to buy it instead of coffee by making coffee too expensive to import. It was simple economics—the government and business made more money from tea than coffee. As you know, the rebellion of the Americans against the British arose partly from the monopoly and tax on tea."

"Boston Tea Party," I quipped, "taxation without representation. So it would have been the Boston Coffee Party if the British had cultivated coffee in India instead of tea?"

"Yes. Tea was drunk because it could be grown in British colonial possessions. After your revolution, another drink was needed because tea was grown so far away. Had the temperate zones of Latin America cultivated tea instead of coffee, Americans today would be tea drinkers."

"But have the Chinese always stayed with tea?"

"Always. In the days when China had a near monopoly on the cultivation of tea, it was such an important product that the Chinese government attempted to keep the secret of cultivating the best blends under heavy guard. The monopoly was broken when a Dutch tea taster named Jacobson risked his life to infiltrate forbidden Chinese tea gardens and smuggled out tea seeds.

"The most important thing you must realize about tea versus coffee is that tea is not drunk in China just because it is grown there, but because it has become part of the culture. We Chinese have been drinking tea for at least five thousand years, perhaps even longer, though we don't have records going back further. We became tea drinkers initially because it was available, and now it not only suits our taste buds, but over the centuries tea has also come to have medicinal and ceremonial roles in our culture."

"Coffee is being introduced successfully in Hong Kong."

"Hong Kong has long been exposed to Western culture. Perhaps coffee has made inroads there, but Shanghai has had its doors closed for almost half a century. That means it has not been exposed to the coffee revolution that has been taking place in Europe and America.

"You must understand our Chinese culture to get us to drink your coffee. That is the secret you must learn to be successful. Show how coffee fits into our culture and you will succeed."

He shook a bony finger at me. "Remember this, young woman. Tea is East; coffee is West."

32

❖

The Hong Kong Mandarin Empress was a small, superluxurious hotel. It was all three-room suites and all overlooked Victoria Harbor. The moment I saw the tropical hardwood floors, Italian marble, and brass railing, I knew it was designed for the Rich and Famous and we couldn't afford the tariff.

"Don't worry," Lily said. "My uncle is paying."

Uncle was also treating us to dinner at a restaurant she said he owned. Somehow, Lily having an uncle with big money didn't fit my mental image of her scheming with Cesar for the plantation.

I dressed for dinner in my only outfit for going someplace respectable, a two-piece business suit. I waited an hour on the couch in the living room, surfing TV channels that appeared to come in enough languages to accommodate the United Nations General Assembly, while Lily dressed.

When she came out, she had on a lot less clothes than I did and looked a whole lot better in them. She wore a traditional Chinese tunic dress over silk pants—but the dress was golden silk that left the impression it might be transparent, which the pants certainly were. She wore shoes with heels so high I would have appeared to be on stilts if I'd worn them.

Jewelry, makeup, attitude, made her dynamite sexy. And I looked like her old-maid aunt.

I stood up and smiled. "Any chance I can just stay at the hotel and do room service?"

"My uncle wants to meet you. Maybe he will invest in your coffee business."

Yeah, and maybe hell will freeze over.

A pleasant surprise was waiting out front for us—a black Rolls-Royce limo. Outrageously elegant and ostentatious, unlike the stretch limos that kids rode around in on graduation night.

"Your uncle must be really rich," I said.

She smiled and said nothing.

The second surprise came when we pulled up at our destination. It wasn't a restaurant but a nightclub in the Lan Kwai Fong district. My travel book called it the colony's nightlife district. As we walked in, my eyes started popping. It began with the picture gallery of past acts along both walls of the long, narrow entryway. The pictures weren't of a smiling restaurant manager shoulder-to-shoulder with a celebrity. As I hurried along beside her, I saw pictures of mud wrestling, erotic striptease, and physical sporting competitions, some of which were performed naked.

We entered the nightclub proper and I almost gasped. It was built in amphitheater style, a circular interior, with a large center stage at the bottom that could be used for dancing or show acts. Tiers rose from the bottom, each crowded with tables and chairs.

The nightclub was interesting enough, but the act on the stage was a showstopper—Chinese acrobats performing on bars, wiggling down and around the bars with the fluid, tree animal movements of Cirque du Soleil performers. Only these performers were women—and their "costumes" were painted on, leaving not much guesswork about their anatomy.

I looked up at the people sitting at the tables on the tiers. A couple hundred Lily Soongs were in the room, one or two at each table, enough sex appeal to fuel a NASA rocket.

Shit. I really did look stupid in my business suit. I felt like crawling under a table.

Most of the women were East Asian, but like on the TV channels back at the hotel, the whole spectrum of nationalities was represented, feminine beauty covering the whole spectrum of planet Earth, from ebony goddesses and olive-skinned Mediterraneans to blond Norse beauties.

The men at the tables also represented the world's spectrum, businessmen and tourists of all nationalities. And none of them were there for the circus act.

"What is this place? A high-class whorehouse?" I asked.

"A hostess club."

I recognized the phrase. My guidebook described a hostess club as a nightclub where women with night heat acted as companions to "lonely" businessmen. The women kept time cards and the men paid for their companionship by the minute. It also mentioned that besides the girl's time and the cost of the booze, a man could order "extras."

As I followed Lily to an elevator, I heard an American, a middle-aged business type holding a nightclub bill in his hand, complaining that the bottle of champagne he'd ordered had cost the equivalent of two thousand dollars—U.S.

"Two thousand dollars for a bottle of champagne," I said to Lily. "Wait till he finds out what sex will cost."

"Sex is cheap; it's included in the cost of the drinks. A man can get a fuck anywhere in Hong Kong, but it can't go on his expense account. Champagne can."

A large, dangerous-looking bouncer type guarding the elevator nodded at Lily as we came up. He indicated we could enter.

The elevator took us to the highest tier, four levels above the main floor, where Lily's uncle was holding court at a large, round table. I never did get his name; Lily merely said, "This is my uncle," to me in English and he gave me a half nod.

He looked a little like the white-haired historian I met on the plane, same modest business suit and conservative tie, but there was something aloof about him. Like Escobar, he had the impersonal persona of a stone killer. I had the impression he was sizing me up and analyzing how he might make use of me someday—or get rid of the body.

His tastes also ran toward very young women. The China

Doll at his side didn't look much older than Josh's Colombian Lolita. And he liked jewelry. The diamond on a middle-finger ring was smaller than a golf ball but definitely in the category of gems you find in the queen's crown jewels.

Three other men were at the table. Like Uncle, each had a pretty hostess at his side—sex toys for old men who had snow on top, a fire still going in the furnace, and money to burn.

I was ignored. All attention went to Lily. The table conversation was entirely in Chinese and rapid-fire to my ears, which weren't tuned into the language.

After sitting down, I picked out a spot on the wall across the way and stared at it, resisting the impulse to leave—or at the very least, to stand up and ask why everyone was pretending they didn't know enough English to at least say, "Hi." I know that I have that ridiculous Anglo-American misconception that everyone in the world is supposed to speak English, but I also found it hard to believe that not a single person at a table full of adults in a place that had been a British colony for nearly a hundred and fifty years didn't know enough English to say hello—or have enough courtesy to acknowledge my presence with a smile.

While the Chinese words may not have been intelligible to my untrained ear, the body language wasn't. Lily was being grilled by Uncle, and she had to defend herself. And once again, there was that complete lack of familial warmth that one would expect from close relatives who met after being apart for some time.

I hadn't asked her which side of the family this uncle was on, but he looked nothing like Dr. Soong.

The act on the stage below ended and a couple skinny kids came out and began kickboxing. No one seemed to pay them much attention and I took them to be the intermission act.

My mind was floating around the room, taking in the intense discussions between horny men and sexy women who made a profession of ratcheting up male testosterone, when my eye caught three men coming into the club from the same public entryway that Lily and I had used. They were young, Chinese, and dressed in black.

And each of them had a gun that looked like those modern machine guns they call Uzis.

I stared stupidly at the men as they raised their weapons toward us and sent a blaze of lead up. I'm not sure whether I dove off the chair or just fell off it, but I was soon on the floor with everyone else at the table as the shocking-explosive sound of rapid gunfire filled the air.

Chips and chunks of ceiling rained down.

And then it was over. Just a couple of seconds of gunfire that seemed to last an eternity. The roar of the guns had stopped, leaving behind the silence of the grave. Then the club was filled with screams, tears, shouts, and the scrabble of feet. The people around me got up, chattering to one another. I was the last one on my feet.

I stared around. No one at the table was bleeding. I looked down the tiers—many people had headed for the exits while others were standing around or hiding under tables, but I didn't see any evidence that anyone was killed or even wounded.

My ears were ringing; my nostrils were filled with the acrid smell of gunfire.

I met Uncle's eye. "What happened?"

He pointed up at the ceiling over their table and grinned. "Warning shots."

His English was perfect.

33

❖

The Rolls limo took us back to the hotel. This time the driver had someone riding shotgun.

Lily said, "They will drop us off in back. It's been arranged for us to go through the kitchen and use the room service elevator to get to our suite."

I said nothing. I had stopped shaking before we left the nightclub, but I hadn't stopped being angry. One of the things that made my blood boil was the way everyone at the table simply sat down and began talking again as if nothing had happened. I'm sure that if I hadn't told Lily I was leaving, we'd still be back there—waiting for the next volley.

Lily said absolutely nothing about the fact we were part of a group sprayed with bullets. That added to my blood temperature.

I kept my mouth shut in the limo because I didn't know if the driver spoke English. It was obvious that Lily's "uncle" was a gangster, and I didn't want to say anything that would offend him. But the moment we got back to the suite, I wanted answers.

"What happened back there? I want the truth."

Lily stared at me as if she was calculating how much of the

truth to tell me. "They were warning shots. No one was killed. This time."

"What do you mean, warning shots? Warning about what? Who's your uncle? If he is your uncle."

"He's triad. Some other gangs want something he has, maybe a piece of the action."

Triads were Asiatic gangs, like mafias were gangs in the States and Europe.

"This whole planet has gone crazy. How can there be so many criminals in the world?"

Lily shrugged. "Maybe if you went hungry, you'd—"

"I'd work at an honest job before I'd harm other people."

"That depends. Maybe the only job available is to kill or be killed."

I went to my room and slammed the door behind me. I threw my hands up to the ceiling. "Jesus. I can't believe this is happening."

My knees were still weak. For a brief moment at the nightclub, I had stared at what appeared to be my own sudden, violent death.

I was now reasonably certain that whatever Lily, Cesar, and Uncle were involved in, it had to be about drugs. Cocaine was Colombia's cash crop, cash cow, whatever they called it. Pablo was a drug cartel boss, Lily's so-called uncle was a criminal gang boss, so it all added up to a drug connection.

I took off my clothes and took a hot shower, thawing my jangled nerves. I had flown halfway around the world, leaving the "most dangerous place in the world," only to nearly be murdered in a civilized British colony.

When I came out of the bathroom, wrapped in a hotel robe, Lily was sitting on my bed, her back against pillows propped up against the headboard. She wore a sheer nightgown. I was beginning to wonder if she owned any clothes that weren't see-through. She had a bottle of champagne and two glasses.

"We must celebrate."

"What are we celebrating?"

"Being alive." Lily patted the pillows beside her.

I hesitated.

Lily said, "Please, don't be angry at me. I did not know we were going to be shot at."

"I think there is a whole list of things that *I* don't know."

"Yes, but you must also understand that there are things that you should not know. You have come to China for your reasons; I have come for mine. I will not interfere with yours. You should not interfere with mine." She patted the bed again. "There may be more bad moments ahead of us. I came in to make friends because we may need each other."

That made sense. I sat on the bed. She poured me champagne. I sipped it and shut my eyes. After a moment I said, "That man, he's not your uncle, is he?"

"I call him Uncle; many people do."

"Do you actually have family in Hong Kong, blood-relative types?"

"No."

"So all your family is in Shanghai, except for your father?"

"Yes."

She said "yes," but my ears heard "no."

"And Dr. Soong's not your father, is he?"

She didn't answer and I drank more champagne. I had my head back, my eyes closed, when she said, "I do what I have to do to survive. I used to have to do things just to get enough food to eat. Now I want more than my stomach full."

I didn't know how to respond to what she said or even if she expected a response. Finally, I said, "I had a strange upbringing, but it was not a terrible life; I never had to worry about food, for sure. My mother was wonderfully crazy. If she had been Irish, people probably would have said she thought like a pixie. She fought for causes, social change, but never stuck to anything, anyplace, not even any cause. We moved from town to town, I went to a different school almost every year, lived in a different house, but I think in most ways that sort of gypsy life just made me more pliable, better able to deal with change, emergencies, anything out of the norm."

I droned on about how gypsies didn't have their feet stuck in cement and more about life with my mother, as I sipped champagne. The alcohol was relaxing my mind and body. I only talked to make up for the silence. I felt like I had to keep conversation going so Lily wouldn't have to reveal things about her life that she was ashamed of—or that would make me sad.

After a while, Lily opened another bottle of champagne. I was feeling warm and snug when I heard her voice.

"My mother worked like a farm animal."

I said nothing. My instincts told me I was going to hear things that made me feel like a Rich—and Ugly—American in a world of need.

"Girls were not wanted because they could not do as much physical labor as a boy. The government forbade the killing of girl babies, but there are millions of peasants in China who hardly know the government exists. I was lucky that I was the first girl-child in the family—none of my sisters lived more than a day. They had to be killed before my parents bonded with them."

Jesus.

"My mother was a wrinkled old woman by the time she was thirty. She sent me away at twelve. It was not to a finishing school in Switzerland. It was not even to a life someone like you can imagine. She did not think she was doing a terrible thing to her daughter; she sacrificed by sending me away at a time when I finally reached the age where I could do the job of a grown woman in the fields. She did it to help me."

"What does she think of your life now?"

"I don't know; I've never been back."

"You never went back to see your parents?"

"No. It would shame them."

"How about some music?" I turned on the radio and selected soft listening music to tune out the horrors of life.

Lily had not revealed what kind of life her mother had sent her to, but it didn't take a rocket scientist to realize there weren't that many options open for a poor, uneducated girl in China. I didn't want to hear any more. I felt compassion for her. I leaned over and kissed her on the cheek.

"You did fine; so did your mother. You did what you had to do."

I finished my champagne and set the glass on the end table. My eyes were closing on me. That's how liquor affected me;

wine, beer, champagne, too much made me sleepy. But it also relaxed me and gave me a glowing feeling inside.

I was fading when she kissed me.

I don't know if I was expecting it; maybe I had even invited it. I don't find myself attracted sexually to other women, but sometimes an intimacy arises between women that goes beyond the usual hug and kiss friends give each other as a greeting.

When I felt her lips brush mine, I got an image of another time a woman's lips had been on mine. It was in high school; a girlfriend had stayed the night, sharing my bed. We had laughed and talked and giggled about boys and sex, comparing the male anatomy each of us had seen—and felt. We were huddled together, getting hot from our imaginations, when my friend leaned closer to me and kissed me. She said, "I'm horny."

I didn't react much at all. I lay there thinking about it, then said, "I'm sleepy," and turned over.

I felt Lily's lips again. The first time she had just brushed mine, hardly touching them. Now her lips parted and pressed against mine. The kiss lasted only a moment. She cuddled up against me, her forehead against my cheek, her warm breath against my neck. I felt something against the side of my face and I realized she was crying, softly.

My heart bled for her. I could only imagine what had happened to her on the streets of Shanghai.

I shut my eyes, letting the champagne close down my mind. She stirred beside me and her lips found mine again. This time she licked my lips with her tongue, first outlining the shape of my lips, then slipped her tongue in my mouth.

She parted my robe. I was warm, too hot, and having the robe pushed back felt good. Her fingers teased my abdomen, tracing the circle around my belly button, and worked her way down as far as the mound of my pubic hair. Her hand came back to cuddle my breast. She squeezed gently. Her head started to go down to my breast and I slid my hand in between.

"Thank you," I said. "Let's go to sleep now." I pulled the robe back over me and rolled over onto my side, away from her.

She didn't say anything and just draped her arm over my side.

———

I AWOKE IN the middle of the night with the tip of her finger stroking my nipple. I lay still, as I first recognized the pleasant sensation, then felt the desire begin to stir in my body. My nipple was hard and her finger was as gentle as a feather.

She leaned over me and her wet mouth found the nipple. She rolled her tongue around it, then tickled it with the tip of her tongue. The touch sent a shiver through my body.

Her hand went over the mound of my pubic area and split the lips of my vulva. As her finger started to massage my swollen clit, she kissed me on the lips. Her mouth felt soft and warm.

"Lily—," I whispered.

"Shhh."

The ache inside me was building the more she touched me. She teased one nipple and then another, moving back and forth, sending waves of sensuous pleasure through my body. I didn't stop her but gave in to the ecstasy.

She worked her way down my abdomen. I couldn't control the explosion that coursed its way through my body. She grasped my clit with her lips and teeth and I moaned out loud as the climax racked inside me.

As the orgasm subsided, she straddled me, a knee on each side above my chest.

This was the first time I had seen a woman with no pubic hair.

$\mathcal{S}$HANGHAI

Everywhere one jostled adventurers and rubbed shoulders with people who had no inkling how extraordinary they were; the extraordinary had become ordinary; the freakish commonplace.

—*SIR HAROLD ACTON,*
MEMOIRS OF AN AESTHETE

Tea is East;
Coffee is West.

34

❖

We were met at the airport with a Mercedes limo driven by a gangster type with another riding shotgun.

"Another uncle in the triad business?" I asked.

Lily said nothing. The China Doll had again retreated into herself. We had hardly spoken since we got up this morning and dressed. No mention was made about the intimacy we had shared. But there had been a subtle change in her. I didn't get vibes that she was being deceitful every moment. She seemed a shade more relaxed, but definitely introspective. I wasn't sure exactly what was waiting for her in Shanghai—hopefully, nothing worse than three guys with machine guns shooting up a nightclub.

We were driving for ten minutes before she spoke. When she did, she held a magazine up in front of her mouth and whispered.

"I'm not going to be seeing you once we reach the hotel. Be careful. You are in no danger as long as you stay away from me."

"That explains a lot," I murmured back.

We were to have separate rooms at the hotel, but I had expected her not only to help me book meetings but to attend them with me. Lily already knew the basics about coffee—it would be much harder with a translator. But I was actually glad I would be running alone. I didn't want to share any more intimacies with her. I already had enough complications in my life; I didn't need a sexual one.

Shanghai appeared to me to be very much like all cities with enormous metropolitan areas, endless apartment and business buildings. I told Lily what I'd read in the guidebook.

"Shanghai's the biggest city in China, but if you count all the millions of people who live here but aren't registered with the government, it's probably the biggest city in the world."

Along the Bund, skyscrapers faced the river.

"The Bund was called million-dollar row back in the thirties," Lily said. "The price tag is back on it, but now they call it billion-dollar row."

Small talk. It was the first time we had engaged in it. She told me more about the city, again surprising me with her knowledge. I knew she was from Shanghai, but until recently, I hadn't realized what a smart lady she was.

On the East China Sea coast, it was both a river port and a seaport and was the most significant transportation center in the country. The Huangpu River winds through the city before dumping into the Yangtze, the longest and most important river in China.

"We were the first major Chinese port to be opened to trade with Europe," she said. Defeat in the Opium Wars resulted in China not only permitting the opium trade but making concessions to Britain and later other powers. Those concessions permitted the Western countries to take over and put their imprint on designated areas of the city. Explaining how the Europeans created millions of Chinese opium addicts out of greed, she said, "That's why old Chinese still refer to Western foreigners as devils."

The Chinese communists made a great physical impact on the city, but their focus was on the suburban areas. There was little development in the downtown area; so many of the pre–World War II buildings that once housed diplomatic missions and foreign corporations were still standing, giving some parts of the city a 1930s retro look, a little Oriental art deco.

She made a comment in Chinese to the driver and said to me, "I told him to take us by the Old City. It's Old China, with narrow alleys. I have been there a hundred times and still can get lost."

It was near the river, half-surrounded in the old days by the French Concession. "There used to be a wall around it. The foreigners thought the wall was there to protect them, but the Chinese believed it was there to keep out the devils." She smothered a giggle.

I found Shanghai fascinating. I had never been in a city with so many clashes of history and cultures. The ambiance had been tempered by Chinese emperors and Chinese gangsters, by Imperialistic Westerners—the British, French, Americans—by "White Russians" fleeing communist revolutions, communists and capitalistic Chinese armies and warlords, over decades of communist austerity and Brave New Worldism, and now was being recast as the Queen of the Far East.

THE PEACE HOTEL was a remnant from the days of grand hotels of yesteryear's Shanghai. It was known as the Cathay Hotel in the days when Shanghai was decadent, but the Red Chinese had changed the name, probably in an attempt to wipe away the hotel's stigma as one of the hot spots when the city was called the Whore of the Orient.

Unlike the five-star modern hotel we stayed at in Hong Kong, the Peace Hotel had old-world charm. It was art deco, a relic of the golden era before World War II. I liked it immediately. The hotel was elegant and had aged gracefully. Long and narrow, twelve stories high, it had a peaked structure mounted like a crown on the front. On the Bund, facing the Huangpu River, it was centrally located in the city's business heart.

Our rooms were on the same floor. When we stepped out of the elevator with the bellman, a man came out of a room at the end of the hall and leaned against the wall next to the door he had exited.

He was a handsome Chinese, perhaps on the sunny side of thirty years old. I had by now become familiar with the black suits and expensive, colorful shirts preferred by the young men I'd come to identify as triad gangsters—and he fitted the mode perfectly.

I glanced at Lily. She had a wide smile at seeing him—and bedroom eyes. Old acquaintances, for sure.

I was relieved. I didn't care if she fucked gangsters; sex was preferable over having them shoot up the hotel with me in it.

While the bellman was depositing my luggage inside, I paused by my open door as Lily spoke in a sotto voce undertone to me.

"Be careful. Shanghai is more dangerous than Colombia. Pablo is a mad-dog killer, but in my country we are thousands of years ahead in intrigue and violence."

"Okay."

"You may be called to meet him. If you do, take care in what you say. And be pleasant and submissive. Don't ask any questions. Answer truthfully; he will know if you are lying."

"Meet who?" I asked.

"The Master of the Mountain."

As I shut the door behind me, three things struck me. The first was that there was actual concern in her voice for me. I knew it wasn't from the intimacy we had shared—she was a woman whose profession catered to intimacies, no doubt with both sexes. But something else had transpired between us when we exposed a little about our backgrounds to each other—perhaps mutual understanding and respect.

The second was confirmation of what she had implied earlier when she said we wouldn't be seeing each other—whatever need she had for me had evaporated. She was now back in Shanghai and I was excess baggage. She had cut me loose.

That was fine with me, even if it would've been easier having her along—though the thought did occur to me more than once that she might have been more of a distraction than a help, a distraction because I probably would be dealing with male buyers who would be ogling her while I tried to hold their attention with a cup of coffee.

I threw my luggage on the bed and stepped to the window.

"I've come to Shanghai to sell coffee and I have a plan!" I announced.

None of the people on the street ten stories below seemed to take notice of my proclamation.

Before I left Colombia, I contacted a business research firm that I had used frequently during my tenure analyzing business operations for the Seattle think tank. I had them do research on fast-food-type chain store operations in Shanghai. Best of all, because they didn't know I had left my old firm and the country, I had them send the bill to my cheatin' heart former fiancé.

By "fast-food" I didn't mean hamburger or finger-lickin' chicken places. Those were not yet in great supply in the city that was still under communist rule. I was looking for business firms that had experience selling directly to the public from multiple locations. I was surprised that there were few such operations. Maybe it was too capitalistic for the communist leadership that had opened the door to Shanghai to the West. But the research firm had come up with several names, including a tea merchant with business contacts in Hong Kong and Honolulu.

Best of all, the tea man, Feng Teh, spoke English. Mr. Feng—last names were first in Chinese—was on the top of my list. There were other tea merchants who ran stands, but none of them had the size and type of operation Feng had.

And none spoke English.

Of course, there was a third thing that bothered me: Lily's last comment. Who—or what—was she talking about when she warned me about meeting the Master of the Mountain?

I recalled Ramon's comment on the plane that the word "assassin" came from "hashish" and that the leader of terrorists was called the Old Man of the Mountain.

I just hoped the Master of the Mountain wasn't China's version of a master of assassins.

35

❖

I needed to soak up the atmosphere of Shanghai, to understand the culture of the city. The Hong Kong history professor that I had met on the plane was right. If I was going to sell coffee to tea drinkers, I had to know how to fit it into their lifestyle.

The best place to start was in the nightlife.

I was too wound up to sleep or even take a nap. The sun had gone down as I set out to walk as much of the strange city as I could.

I learned from the concierge that most of Shanghai's new wave restaurants and bars were run by foreigners or by Chinese who had studied or worked abroad. Many of the Chinese were the children of people who had decades before fled to Hong Kong and Taiwan.

What I immediately discovered walking down the street was that the younger Chinese generation had adopted Western culture in a big way but added a big dose of Shanghai-ness to it.

I stepped inside a disco just down the street from the hotel. The dancers dressed pretty much like they did in Seattle or New York discos, the music was similar, but the atmosphere was different. It wasn't just the color of skin; there were plenty of people of Chinese ancestry in San Francisco and Seattle, even some just off the boat, but a disco in Chinatown there was just like a disco in other parts of town. A disco in Shanghai was an East Asian experience, because the music, drinks, clothes, hairstyles, and of course the verbal noise had a slightly exotic flavor.

What wasn't different was blaring music that could knock down ordinary walls, and the tariff wasn't cheap. The place catered to the city's middle-management yuppies, which told me that there was some real money in the city, besides whatever the old commies hid in their mattresses.

There were also high-priced sex joints popular with male yuppies and the foreign crowd. The most popular were "bathhouses" in which a man could have a spa, a meal, maybe some karaoke or billiards, and a "date" with a pretty woman. That was traditional Shanghai, with a few modern amenities.

As I wandered down the street and popped my head in bars and restaurants, shaking my head at inquiring glances from doormen and come-ons from men, the secret of selling coffee to Shanghai suddenly struck me.

36

❖

After a restful twelve hours of sleep, the next morning I called
the telephone number I had been given for Mr. Feng's office.
The report I had commissioned on Mr. Feng said he spoke English, but I fell into the Anglo-American mental trap of believ-
ing that *everyone* speaks English. What I soon discovered was
that the person who answered the phone at Mr. Feng's office
didn't understand a word I said.

Through a series of phone calls between the hotel concierge,
who was a woman, and Mr. Feng's office, I managed to get an
appointment. Mr. Feng's intermediary had demanded to know
the exact nature of the business I wanted to discuss with her
boss. I had the concierge tell her the simple truth—I had come
to show him a product that would increase sales at his tea
shops.

From the concierge, I learned that the tea shops were in high-
end areas—major skyscrapers and expensive shopping areas.

She offered to hire a car with driver and an interpreter to accompany me and I requested them for the next day. Today I
wanted to pick up the flavor and tempo of the city—and Mr.
Feng's tea shops.

She gave me directions to the nearest one, a shop in a high-rise that I could visit on my way to Feng's office.

My contact in Seattle had said that Mr. Feng was known to be associated with a tong with branches in San Francisco and Honolulu. I wasn't exactly sure what a tong was. I asked the concierge.

She shook her head. "I believe tongs are beneficial organizations of Chinese businessmen mostly. They occur in America, but they may have members in China, too. I really don't know much about them. They are old-fashioned, something that was around before our People's Republic. I don't believe they are legal now, at least not in China."

"I seem to recall that in the past some tongs were associated with crime, importing opium into the States, stuff like that. Isn't that kind of what triads do?"

"I'm sorry, I'm not familiar with that term, either."

I didn't know if she was being evasive or if "triad" was an English word and the Chinese had a different word for the gangs.

"We call them triads," I said, "but you may call them something else. Gangs, organizations of criminals to run rackets, drugs, prostitution, smuggling, mafia, that sort of thing."

"Yes, we did have such gangs in the past, but our leaders have rid society of such social evils."

I didn't want to mention that she had a couple of those social evils upstairs in a room just down the hall from me, not to mention the gang members who drove us in from the airport. I thanked and tipped the concierge, and was about to walk away but thought I'd try another question on her.

"Who is the Master of the Mountain?"

The concierge reacted as if I had slapped her. She looked around anxiously to see if anyone had heard my comment.

"Where did you hear that expression?"

"From a friend. What does it mean?"

"It's from the old days; the big boss of each triad was called the Master of the Mountain. He was given that name because meetings were held outside of town, usually on a hillside where they were able to keep watch for police or attacks from other gangs."

"Do they still have triads in Shanghai?"

"Of course not. I told you, the government has forbidden them."

Sure, just like the American, Italian, and Russian governments have forbidden the mafia. And the Colombians have outlawed the cartels.

Just as she had first claimed ignorance of the word "triad."

Before I left the hotel, I took my one large piece of luggage down to the bellman on duty and checked it in. It contained my coffee samples and grinder. It was too big to haul with me and I wanted it on the bottom floor readily available in case I had to rush back to grab more samples.

I had already ground several pounds, including one I took with me in my shoulder bag. Also inside the bag was a two-cup coffeemaker. I figured water and cups would be found on all business premises, considering how much tea got consumed in the country.

I STEPPED OUTSIDE the hotel and paused for a cab. As I waited for a VW Bug taxi to pull up to the curb, I noticed a man about fifty feet away reading a newspaper. I pretended not to look at him but was struck by the fact that he bore a superficial resemblance to a guy I had dated a few times in Seattle.

Joey Chin was his name, and he was a stud. I met him at a disco. He was a great dancer, and had even greater moves in bed—the only problem with him was that after he gained carnal knowledge of me, I found out he had a wife and two kids, a small detail he forgot to mention.

The building where Mr. Feng had one of his tea shops was located a few blocks down the street. With sign language, I got the taxi driver to understand that he was to wait for me when I went in to check the shop.

Located on the first floor, it had a counter where tea was served, a little standup counter space along two sidewalls for people to stand and drink their tea, and some small round merchandise display tables. It reminded me of a coffee bar in Italy. The shop was wedged between a shop that sold newspapers and one that sold bowls of noodles.

Mr. Feng owned eighty of these tea shops, all located in business and tourist locations.

It wouldn't take much to add coffee to the menus. Better yet, to stop selling tea and start selling coffee.

Like tea, making and serving coffee did not take up a great deal of space. Basically little more was needed than a back counter where coffee drinks and add-ons were prepared and a small front counter to pass purchases to the customers.

When I came back out and got into the taxi, a man came out of the same building and jumped into a car a few feet back from the taxi.

I forced myself not to do a double take but keep looking straight ahead.

Okay, I could buy the fact that the man who looked like Joey Chin was staying at or near the same hotel as me. And that he had a very brief appointment, the same amount of time it took me to check out the tea bar, at the same building I did.

Coincidences happen.

But chance stopped and design became apparent when he followed me to another destination down the street.

I didn't know who was behind me or what to do. *Stay calm; you're being followed.* That much I knew. Was it someone sent by the Master of the Mountain? I doubted it. After seeing triad gangsters in Hong Kong and Shanghai, I knew that the man didn't fit the mode—the gangsters went for black suits, colored shirts, slick hair, and carried arrogant mannerisms.

This guy faded into the woodwork, an office type more likely to pull out a pen than a machine gun. I wouldn't have even noticed him if he didn't look a little like Joey the Rat. His white shirt, black tie, conservative brown business suit which looked plain and inexpensive, reminded me of the wrinkled polyester suit worn by the Seattle cop who wanted to lock me away.

That was it. A police officer. That's what he had to be. The only other possibility was that he was hired by the tea-growing industry of China to keep out a coffee invasion from Colombia—and that theory didn't fly.

Why would I be followed by the police?

Why not? I came to the city with a woman who had organized crime contacts from Asia to South America.

What had she gotten me into?

I reminded myself that I had brought nothing into the country except a couple changes of clothes, and a suitcase full of coffee. Whatever was going on, it had to be that I was the subject of police surveillance just because I had traveled with Lily.

I hoped.

We stopped at another building and I popped in to look over the tea shop. It was a duplicate of the last one. My shadow in the car to the rear didn't follow me inside. He must have figured that I was only doing a quick look-see like the last place. But he did follow me to my ultimate destination.

Mr. Feng's office was located in a warehouse at a dock along the river. The car shadowing me went by slowly as I got out and walked into the warehouse, resisting the temptation to challenge them with a look.

Even though the tea shops I'd seen were modern, the warehouse had the look of something from the last century. Sacks of tea had that Chinese logogram script that looks so mysterious—and incomprehensible—to Western eyes painted on the bags. Sweet and pungent tea aromas filled the air.

I loved the elegant enigmatic look of Chinese writing. European-based languages were based upon the "sound" of words, using the letters of the alphabet to create words. Words with similar sounds usually shared some similarity in spelling. My guidebooks said Chinese writing was based upon how a "character" is drawn, a character being a combination of what appeared to my untrained eye as slash marks. Each character represented a word or thought, and because the characters were not based upon sound, two words sounding exactly the same did not have a similarity in spelling. That meant you had to do a lot of memorizing. Lily told me that to be literate, one had to learn the meaning of at least two thousand characters, and to be considered educated, you needed to know about four thousand. Westerners only had to learn their ABCs and a bunch of rules for using the twenty-six or so letters.

Inside the warehouse, I introduced myself in English to a clerical worker at a front desk, who replied in Chinese—but she got the idea. There couldn't be that many American women visiting each day. She disappeared for a moment and came back to indicate I was to follow her.

As I came into his office, Mr. Feng stood up before an old-fashioned rolltop desk. He was short, pudgy, had a round face with several moles, and a large, unruly mop of hair that was pure black, with not a strand of gray in it. He wore a gray three-piece suit of good wool made many years before.

He struck me immediately as not just a conservative businessman but a traditional one. He and his cluttered office would not have looked out of place in Victorian times. I could see him as the head of the traditional tea company but had a hard time envisioning him as the head of modern tea shops, much less a place that I anticipated would soon be selling sugar-free decaf lattes with low-fat milk and an extra shot of espresso.

The report I'd obtained about the potential coffee marketeers recommended I have business cards made up, English on one side, the reverse side incorporating as much Chinese script as possible. Lily had done the translating for the Colombian printer. The report also suggested bringing a small gift to the meeting, nothing ostentatious—unless a bribe was needed.

I brought a coffeemaker to brew a sample of the coffee. When I left, I would leave the coffeemaker and two pounds of coffee with Mr. Feng.

He stood up and bowed. I handed him my business card, extending it with both hands, Chinese script up, as the report advised.

He extended his card the same way, except with the English-language side up. He indicated a wood chair that faced his.

"Please be seated, Miss Novak." His English was excellent, with just a slight accent. He did not offer to shake hands. He did offer tea.

"Actually, I was going to offer you coffee," I said.

He raised his eyebrows. "Doesn't it need to be brewed?"

I pulled the coffeemaker out of the bag. "If you can provide a little water and two cups, plus an electrical outlet, I would be happy to quickly brew a pot."

In the States, I might have been shown the door, but the Chinese are much more tolerant and civilized. I had coffee brewing in no time.

As it gurgled—with modern coffeemakers, coffee no longer perks—we exchanged pleasantries. I decided to be perfectly honest—stopping short of telling him I was a fugitive from American justice, rubbing shoulders with triad gangsters, and had lately been associating with the world's most notorious drug trafficker, all the while having a murder charge hanging over my own head.

I didn't know all the rules and etiquette for doing business in the city, but with the police on my tail, I decided to jump right in, because on my way over I had already decided after I left Mr. Feng I'd stop just long enough at the hotel to collect my carry-on bag and passport and my next stop was going to be the airport.

The fact that I knew I was being followed had spooked me. Combined with Lily's remark about meeting the Master of the Mountain, being followed by the police was exceptionally ominous, especially in a country where I suspected the justice system had yet to adopt the theory and practice of "due process."

I was certain the police were following me, but I was puzzled. I could understand triad gangsters following me. Whatever Lily, her "father," Cesar, Don Pablo, and the rest of the cartel were up to, it probably involved profits of crime, and as was sharply pointed out by three gunmen in Hong Kong, the gangs were competitive. But the police were a different matter—I personally hadn't done anything criminal. At least not that I knew.

It was time to cut and run, another retreat burning bridges behind me, making sure there were no bread crumbs to follow.

We kept up the pleasantries, without discussing business, until I poured coffee for each of us. As we sipped the fresh brew, I said, "I have come here to persuade you to sell coffee."

He raised his eyebrows. "You Americans are so impulsive. And move so quickly. I'm afraid that I am a product of an ancient culture that moves at a more leisurely pace."

"I know, I'm here out of the blue, but I have an urgent need. It's inevitable that a great deal of money is going to be made off of coffee in Shanghai in the near future, and throughout China in the long term, and I want to be a part of it."

"I wish you good luck in obtaining your fortune. Many foreigners are coming to Shanghai to get rich. It reminds me of what I have read about gold rushes and oil booms. This week I have been contacted by a German company that wants to sell me a computer, an American company that wants to sell me a program to use in the computer, a Swiss company that says they can make my inventory control work a thousand times better . . ." He raised his hands. "I bought none of their products. I am in the tea business, a business that my father and his father were in before me. As you Americans say, it would take much for this old dog to learn a new trick."

"Not as much as you might suspect. Your warehouse is already set up to handle and store coffee, because it's packed and handled the same as tea. Your shops just need to devote a little counter space to coffee and some training to learn to brew coffee drinks. Until the operation is going well, we can roast the beans before shipping them. It is not a complex operation, because it fits comfortably in the business organization you already have. Coffee and tea are not adverse; they complement each other."

"You are not the first person to come here and offer me coffee products. A man recently offered weasel coffee from Vietnam. He says that it is made from coffee excreted from weasels. They also offer a variety processed through cats. These exotic drinks sell for a great deal of money."

I knew the process, disgusting as it was. Feed the animals coffee beans and sell the excrement as coffee. People would pay a fortune for the stuff. Especially traditional Chinese who believed in a wide range of herbal remedies. I'd heard of people paying ten thousand dollars for a bite of tiger liver.

"Coffee made from cat and rat shit?" I asked. "That may work with old people who believe a tiger's liver is an aphrodisiac, but they're not the ones who will pay several dollars for a cup of designer coffee."

"I have been offered coffee from Vietnam that sells for half of what your Colombian coffee sells for—and with a fraction of the transportation costs."

"People in Shanghai aren't going to pay good money for coffee from Vietnam. Besides the fact your country and the Vietnamese have been enemies for a couple thousand years, the upward, financially mobile people in Shanghai want products from the West, not Vietnam. And they want the best. If you are going to use inferior Robusta beans, you might as well just save the money and put dirt in the coffee cups; it would be even cheaper and tastes about the same. Coffee *means Colombian.* Our shade-grown, organic, mild Colombian Arabica is the finest coffee on the planet."

"But does it fit the taste buds of a nation of tea drinkers is a more serious question."

"People keep saying that tea is East and coffee is West," I said.

He nodded. "Exactly. We are a nation of tea drinkers. Coffee is foreign to our palate. And that is why you will not find doors opening for your product. It is not just a matter of marketing, but getting people to adopt something new. As I told you, China is a very old country. We do not race to change."

"Mr. Feng, I will not insult your business acumen by claiming I know more than you do. You are a successful businessman with a long-established business, selling a product that has been around probably since humans conquered fire. But I identify with a different group of people than you. You are right; people of tradition will not rush to coffee. But with the greatest respect, I am going to point out that there is a race to change, and you are one of the leaders of it in this city. You may not be ready to start drinking coffee, but the people who are your customers, people we would call yuppies in my country, do not need their arms twisted to buy coffee drinks."

He raised his eyebrows. "If that is true, it is a revelation to me. And quite a conclusion to be raised by a young woman who has been in China for little more than twenty-four hours."

"The fact that I stepped off a plane yesterday is exactly why I was able to reach the conclusion. I wasn't born and raised here; I haven't been in business for years here; my ancestors can't be traced back to the Three Kingdoms. So I see the city with completely fresh eyes."

"And what do those fresh eyes see?"

"Change. Radical, racing, revolutionary change. Led by an invasion of Western culture." I took a sip of coffee and let him digest that a bit. He kept his features blank. "Over the centuries, China has exported and imported culture, often in the form of food. Chinese food is common in America and Europe and so is tea drinking. Right now the Euro-American business sector isn't just invading the city and the country with business technology; it's changing the way the youthful, upwardly mobile people dress, dance, listen to music, drink liquor, soda pop, and . . . tea."

He smiled and nodded. "My tea shops. There were many in the city who said I was a fool to offer a cup of tea at a price for which people could brew a whole pot themselves in their office."

"The secret to the success of your tea shops is their locations. You placed them where the new breed, the Chinese yuppies, work. Unlike their parents, they will pay a premium for a cup of tea, especially if it is presented to them as something special."

"And your idea is that we simply start selling coffee drinks along with tea." He shook his head. "We have the facilities, but there still is a question of taste."

"Let me give you the bottom line—the yuppies of Shanghai are aping Western culture. A coffee boom is sweeping America and Europe. Coffee has transpired from being a breakfast drink to being a fashion statement."

He was still completely expressionless. I felt like reaching over and grabbing his necktie and giving it a jerk. My patience was beginning to wane.

"On the plane over from the States, I met a professor of Chinese history who told me that I wouldn't be able to sell coffee to the Chinese until I was able to fit it into the culture. Last night I walked the streets of Shanghai. What I saw was a clash of cultures, East meeting West, East aping West while keeping its own identity.

"It won't be long before fast-food hamburgers are drawing money away from the fish stalls—and people who used to stand in line to buy tea drinks are going to be buying coffee drinks."

I picked up my bag. "*Your* coffee drinks."

37

❖

The session with Mr. Feng wasted me. I was worn-out from not just expending nervous energy but worrying about what he thought. His inscrutable features were unreadable. I didn't know if I'd made any points at all. His expression never changed. Now I knew what "poker-faced" meant.

He thanked me for coming, gave me a gift of rare jasmine tea and a delicate old teacup.

Everything but an agreement to buy my coffee.

His response to my question of whether he would venture into the coffee business with Café de Oro was to mutter, "We'll see; we'll see."

My tail wasn't there when I came out of the warehouse. Either the police had lost interest in me or being followed had been a figment of my imagination. The fact that I wasn't being followed also changed my plans to cut and run.

I decided not to hit the hotel at a run and race for the airport. If I wasn't being followed by the police, there was no longer any rush to leave. And desperation had set in. I had foolishly set my hopes on Mr. Feng, I suppose because he spoke English and his chain of tea shops was perfect for coffee sales. For sure, I needed to see the other businessmen on the list, all of whom would be more difficult because none of them spoke English or had ready-made outlets for my product.

My room phone was ringing when I came through the door. I answered it.

"It's me," Josh said. "Listen, don't talk—"

"What do you mean—"

"The police are coming!"

"What?"

"You have to get rid of the stuff."

"What stuff?"

"There's a bag of dope, maybe two, in with your coffee samples; it's hidden somewhere in the suitcase."

"What?"

"Get the dope and flush it down the toilet, tear up the bags it came in, too, and flush them down. Listen to me—be careful: Don't sniff the stuff; don't breathe it in when you dump it; don't even get it on your hands or clothes. Cover your nose and mouth with a towel when you dump it in the toilet. *Don't breathe any of it in.*"

"What is going on? How do you know—"

"Do it; hurry."

He hung up.

I gaped at the phone, my mind blown. I dropped the phone and spun around. I had to get rid of the—

Somebody shouted in Chinese outside my door.

Then it was crashed open.

Oh my God!

38

❖

Seated at a small table in a police interrogation room, I stared across at a man who was preoccupied with papers in front of him. My hands were in my lap, twined tightly together. When I put them on the table they shook.

My mind screamed, *This can't be happening to me!*

I had been seized in my room by police officers with guns. In a matter of seconds I was out of the room, handcuffed, and in a police car.

No one had said anything to me in English or Chinese.

The man at the table was the Joey Chin look-alike who I had spotted following me. Another man entered the room and spoke to the seated officer.

After he left, the man seated across from me said in English, "The penalty for bringing narcotics into the People's Republic of China is death."

I was terrified and ready to cry, but now a calmness had settled over me. It wasn't that I was no longer scared. But now my life had taken another bizarre twist, a surrealistic, dreamlike quality.

Here I was in a police station in Shanghai with a Chinese police officer telling me I was facing the death penalty.

This can't be happening to me.

"That's really funny," I said.

He reared back a little, frowning at me. "Did you say . . . funny?"

"Humorous, ha-ha, funny."

"A penalty of death is a joke to you?"

"Oh, no, no, no, I wasn't talking about what you said; that's serious. I was thinking about Seattle and Shanghai. A Chinese criminal almost killed me in Seattle; now a Chinese police officer says I may be killed here in Shanghai. They both start with an *S,* Seattle and Shanghai," I babbled, my mind in a state of calm hysteria.

He just stared at me. I had managed to make him speechless.

I rubbed my forehead. "I'm sorry; you probably think I'm a nutcase, a crazy. It's just that everything's gone to hell in my life the last few weeks. Everything was normal and now it's all insane."

"Is that why you smuggle drugs? Because you need money?"

He slipped it into the conversation casually. But the words carried a lethal charge—an affirmative answer would qualify me for the death penalty.

"I know nothing about drugs."

My mind wasn't functioning on all cylinders and the whole situation jangled my nerves, but I wasn't ready to confess to something I didn't do. In fact, I wasn't ready to admit to anything but my name and address, something like the name, rank, and serial numbers POWs limited themselves to when they were being questioned.

A friend who was constantly calling the police on her husband—and vice versa—told me that the best way to deal with a cop was *deny, deny, deny.* "Otherwise they twist everything you say."

So that was the only tactic my stunned brain could manage. It would be particularly easy in this case because I knew nothing.

"What about the drugs found in your room?"

"I have not brought any narcotics into your country. If anything was found in my room, I did not put it there or know it was there."

"It will go better for you if you just tell me the truth. Someone asked you to bring drugs here to Shanghai. Who was that?"

"I brought no drugs. If you found anything, someone hid it in my luggage."

He shook his head. "We know you brought the drugs in. It will go easier on you if you tell me where they are. If we have to find where you hid them, we will seek the maximum penalty."

The implication that they hadn't found any drugs dawned on me. It meant one of two things: Either they didn't realize that I had given a bellman the suitcase containing my samples . . . or Lily had already gotten the drugs out of the suitcase.

In any case, they hadn't found the drugs. If they really existed. For all I knew, this was all some sort of hustle by the cops; maybe they were—

No, Lily had used me to smuggle contraband into the country. It all fit too well.

"I don't know what you are talking about. I came to Shanghai to sell coffee, not narcotics."

As he went on and on about my need to cooperate, I gave him the same essential reply—I knew nothing about narcotics.

"You came to Shanghai in the company of a woman who calls herself Lily Soong."

"I flew in on the same plane, if that's what you mean. She came here for her own reasons; I came here to sell coffee."

"She is the one who was smuggling the narcotics—is that correct?"

"I know nothing about Lily Soong and smuggling. If she was smuggling anything, it was without my knowledge. I want to contact the American consulate."

I deliberately avoided the opportunity to put the blame on Lily. The problem with telling the police that the drugs belonged to Lily was that showing any knowledge at all would implicate me. I was between a rock and a hard place. I couldn't even put the blame on the guilty without proving to the police that I knew she was smuggling drugs into the country—and I had helped her, even inadvertently, by putting them in my luggage.

It went on and on, he asking me to tell him where the narcotics were—or to at least confirm that I knew of their existence—and me denying any knowledge and asking for the American consulate.

My head was splitting, my stomach volcanic, my throat raw and dry, after what seemed like hours of the monotone questions-accusations and my monotone replies.

They had taken my watch and jewelry, but I still had the clothes I was arrested in when they took me to a cell. It had a single bed and a hole in the floor that passed for a toilet. The "sink" was a faucet that came out of the wall and flowed into the hole in the floor, the same hole used as a toilet. It wasn't part of a cell block, but a single cell by itself.

I was sick from fright, but I maintained my own version of being poker-faced.

I was given a bowl of spicy fish and rice soup. I couldn't stomach food, but I forced myself to sip the juice. It burned my raw throat.

I lay on the mat on the cot and turned to the wall. Certain that I was being watched by hidden video cameras, I kept my face hidden as I sobbed.

39

❖

"You are being released," my monotoned tormentor told me.

He showed up at my cell in the morning and escorted me to a counter where a woman gave me back my personal possessions.

"You must leave Shanghai within twenty-four hours."

"I'll be on the next plane. Just give me a ride to the airport." *The plane can be going to hell for all I care,* I wanted to say.

"Colombia is a lawless country and you are a lawless person."

I smothered a reply that would prove his point.

"To return to China will subject you to arrest and prosecution."

"I guarantee you won't see me again. I've had enough Chinese hospitality to last a lifetime."

A limo was waiting outside. The window rolled down and Lily stuck her smiling face out. "We will give you a ride."

I returned her smile. "You bitch, I'd rather drink Drano than ride with you."

An evil-looking man in a black suit stepped away from the wall of a building. He had his hand in his pocket. He wasn't clutching his comb. He nodded at the limo. I took the hint and got in.

Lily and her boyfriend were the only other occupants in the passenger area. He rattled off something to me in quick-fire

Chinese. I didn't understand a word of it, but the fact he was pissed at me came across clearly.

"Where is our stuff?" Lily asked.

"Your stuff?"

She smiled. "My boyfriend is not patient. We need to know what you did with the package."

"I didn't do anything with it."

"You must have hid it—if the police had found it, you would still be in jail. And so would I."

"I didn't hide anything; I don't know what you're talking about."

The boyfriend pulled a gun and shoved it in my face.

"No!" Lily yelled at him.

He put away the gun. He struck me as a loose cannon that could go off again at any moment.

She patted his face. "I love him, but he's crazy."

"How nice for both of you. Maybe you can enjoy a murder-suicide someday together. Would you mind dropping me off at my hotel so I can get my things and head for the airport? I just spent the night in jail and almost got the death penalty because of you."

"What did you tell the police?"

"The truth. It was easy; I don't know anything."

"There was a package in your suitcase, one of the bags of coffee beans, but it wasn't coffee inside."

I shook my head and smiled sweetly. "I don't know anything about a package, other than the ones that have coffee in them. If there had been something there, the police would have found it. And you and Bugsy would be the ones facing the death penalty."

Bugsy got my drift. He went for his gun again and Lily was all over him.

She said to me, "Because you are my friend, I am trying to keep him from killing you. But I will not be able to hold him back much longer; he's very excitable. We need the package. The police don't have it or they wouldn't have released you. I bribed a maid to enter your room to get the package, but your suitcase was gone. What did you do with it?"

"It was stolen."

"*What?*"

The lie just popped out. But it fitted nicely. If I told her I'd left the suitcase with the bellmen and she got caught grabbing it, I'd be back in the Shanghai jail in a flash.

Lily locked eyes with me. "Listen to me. If we don't give him the drugs, he will go into a rage and kill both of us."

I was ready to break out crying. I smothered it and spoke in a firm tone. "Lily, use your head; you know I don't have the drugs. If I did, the police would have them and I'd still be in jail."

Her boyfriend didn't catch my drift. He pulled out his gun. Lily threw herself on him, shouting something. I heard the bang, a loud explosion, and she jerked back.

The driver slammed on the brakes and the three of us were flung forward. We crashed into something; I saw another car beside us. My door suddenly swung open and a man with a gun fired into the passenger area. The other door jerked open and more shots were fired.

It all happened so fast. My hearing was stunned, my nose filled with the acrid stench of gunpowder.

I was pulled out of the passenger area by gunmen and shoved into another limo.

Mr. Feng smiled and nodded. "So good of you to join us, Miss Novak."

40

❖

Another man was seated in the limo's rear passenger area, an older Chinese man about Mr. Feng's age, thinner and dressed as conservatively. The tea merchant said the man's name was Mr. Chow.

The limo flowed smoothly in Shanghai traffic.

Mr. Feng listened on his car phone for a moment. He hung up and gave me a small, polite smile.

"So many questions you must have. And no doubt a low opinion of our city." He waved his forefinger at me. "But don't judge a city of millions by the few."

I nodded. Or at least my head bobbed on my shoulders. My mind was numb.

"The lover of the woman you call Lily worked for Mr. Chow. But he recently decided that he wanted to work for himself."

I looked at the blood on my clothes.

Mr. Feng said, "Yes, his blood. He no longer works for anyone."

"Lily . . . ?"

"She has a small wound, mostly burn from her lover's pistol going off. Did he try to kill her?"

"He tried to kill me; she stopped him."

Mr. Feng rattled off something in Chinese to Mr. Chow, I assume a report about Lily.

I spoke slowly. "Will you explain what is going on?"

Mr. Feng sighed. "I am ashamed of my countrymen, ashamed for my whole country. But as I say, there are just a few bad people among so many good."

I nodded at Mr. Chow. "Who is this gentleman?"

"As I said, he is—was—the boss of the man who was killed."

I nodded. "Triad?"

"I have heard that word used."

"Is he the Master of the Mountain?"

Mr. Feng giggled and spoke in Chinese to Mr. Chow, who joined him in the mirth.

"As the hotel concierge told you, we know nothing about triads or Master of the Mountain."

Which meant that they knew plenty. Mr. Chow was a chip off the same block as Lily's Hong Kong "uncle." I wouldn't doubt that they were brothers.

"The concierge told you about my conversation?"

"She is Mr. Chow's niece."

I sighed. "Wonderful. Now, am I going to be murdered?"

"Should you be?" He giggled again and spoke to Chow. Both men had a good laugh.

"There's a suitcase everyone is looking for—"

Mr. Feng shook his head. "There is no such suitcase."

"But I—"

He shook his head some more. I got the hint through my dull brain. There was no such suitcase—anymore. The concierge must have taken care of it. That's why the police never found it.

I gave them a dopey smile. "Well, this has been a wonderful trip. I came to Shanghai to make my fortune. Instead, I have been arrested, spent the night in jail, narrowly escaped being murdered—and the death penalty—and now . . ."

"Now you will return to your own country and ensure that your coffee shipments start coming to me."

"Mr. Feng, do you mean that? You'll buy my coffee?"

"After I spoke to you last night, I asked my son what he

thinks of coffee. He was very excited. He will be in charge of it." He grinned, with pride. "He is a Shanghai yuppie."

I could see there was another loose end. Most pieces fitted nicely: Mr. Feng and Mr. Chow, whoever he was, knew from the concierge niece that I had been arrested and the police were searching for drugs. They would also know from her I had checked my bag.

Mr. Chow was obviously head of some sort of gang, triad, or whatever they called it. And knew from the concierge niece that I had contacted Mr. Feng.

But how did Mr. Feng fit into a scenario in which people were being gunned down on a street in Shanghai?

"Are you triad?" I asked him.

"No." He smiled and gave me a little bow of his head. "I am tong. Much older than triad."

He gave another one of his little giggle-laughs.

"Old dogs have much more bite than young ones."

MEDELLÍN

DEPARTMENT OF STATE
U.S. CONSULAR INFORMATION SHEET
REPUBLIC OF COLOMBIA

Criminals sometimes use the drug "scopolamine" to incapacitate tourists in order to rob them.

The drug is administered in drinks (in bars), through cigarettes and gum (in taxis), and in powder form (tourists are approached by someone asking directions, with the drug concealed in a piece of paper, and the perpetrator blows the powder into the victim's face).

The drug renders the person disoriented and can cause prolonged unconsciousness and serious medical problems.

Because it blocks memory and causes submissive behavior, the drug has been used as a date-rape drug and by prostitutes to rob their clients.

Scopolamine's effect on the central nervous system also makes it useful as "truth serum," by means of which uncooperative persons may be forced to answer questions. Because of its side effects, it cannot be used in the United States.

The form of scopolamine used as a street drug is called *burundanga*. It is a favored method of assault by Colombian criminals. Smuggled into the United States, it has been characterized by the DEA as the most dangerous drug to surface in decades.

41

❖

How do I get back to the plantation without getting murdered?

That was the question running through my mind and shivering up my spine as I boarded a plane in Shanghai that would take me to Hong Kong. I intentionally hadn't booked passage beyond the British colony for two reasons—I hadn't made up my mind what route I would take, and I didn't want to leave bread crumbs in advance for anyone to follow.

From Hong Kong, the first available transatlantic flight went to Lima, Peru. Colombia was in South America and I was sure Peru was somewhere there, too. I never claimed to be good with geography. After confirming the fact that Peru was in South America, I bought a ticket for Lima.

When I arrived in Lima, I bought a ticket for Quito, the capital of Ecuador, which is also conveniently located in South America. From a large map in the terminal, Quito looked like a convenient stepping-stone to Colombia. In Quito, I hesitated. There were flights to Bogotá, Medellín, and Cali.

Hmmm. Cali. Two things immediately struck me about Cali. It was almost as notorious as Medellín for its own drug cartel—and it *wasn't* Medellín or Bogotá. I feared finding a reception committee of thugs hired by Cesar or Escobar if I stepped off a plane in Medellín, where I might be expected—and murdered.

I bought a ticket for Cali. From the Cali airport I took a taxi into town and had the driver stop at a package wrap-and-ship store that advertised fax service. I sent three faxes, then caught another taxi to the train station. I purchased a ticket on a train bound for Medellín and points north. I didn't get off the train in Medellín—I stayed aboard and got off in the small town that Cesar had waited for me to arrive at but didn't.

I hired a taxi at the station to take me to the plantation. I sat back in the taxi for the hour drive and thought about my plans.

When I arrived at the plantation after nearly three days of travel, I was tired, but in one piece. The house and yard were strangely quiet as I got out of the taxi. Stepping inside the cool living room, I immediately felt at home.

I stopped by the stairway and smiled and shook my head at the portrait of Carlos. "You have no idea of what I've been through," I told his painted figure.

Juana came out of a room on the second level, stopped at the top of the stairs, and stared down at me as if she'd seen a ghost.

"I'm home."

She crossed herself and muttered a prayer.

42

❖

We had lemonade at the kitchen table, as we did the first time we met. She gave me a tearful hug when she came down the stairs.

"I was worried when we didn't hear from you. Cesar heard that you had been arrested in Shanghai."

"Where is he?"

"He went to Medellín on business, for the plantation. He will not be back until late tonight."

"Are you sure he's not meeting with Pablo Escobar?"

Juana appeared ready to cry. "One does not make an appointment to meet with Don Pablo; it might be a police trap. He comes to you or has you picked up without warning and brought to him. The motor on one of the machines broke; Cesar went to get a replacement."

"I'm sorry; I'm paranoid about everything."

"I don't blame you. You must not stay here; it's not safe. You should return to your home in Seattle."

"I can't go back. I made a deal for our coffee, at premium prices, all the coffee that the plantation and the *colonos* can produce. We can operate at a profit, a good one; we just have to provide green beans on time. There isn't any reason why we shouldn't be able to do it."

"There is a reason and it's that this is Colombia, not a civilized country. You can't ship coffee to China if you are dead. For some reason, Don Pablo has taken an interest in the work of the two chemists. He must believe that they will succeed in creating a decaffeinated coffee plant. If he wants the plantation, he will take it. Cesar claims that Don Pablo will pay if he takes the plantation, but sometimes he pays with bullets."

I stared at her, wondering if she could be so naïve as to believe they were really working on a new type of coffee plant—and decided that she was. She had spent her entire life in a rural area, far from the machinations of the world. It was time she knew the truth, for her own safety, if nothing else.

"Juana, they're not working on a coffee plant."

She wrung a dish towel with her hands. "I feared that. Cesar said they were, but I wondered if he was lying to me."

"He was—and is. I don't know exactly what they're making, something to do with cocaine probably, processing it or something, I'm not sure. But it's not coffee beans. Whatever it is, some of it was hidden in the coffee samples I took to China; it got me arrested."

Juana's features were dark and sad. "This is all so different from when Carlos was here; he would not have let these things happen. There were always problems, even in those days, toward the end of his life, money problems, illness, but criminals were not part of our lives." Juana stared down at the table. "I'm sorry, Nash. You do not deserve the terrible things that have happened to you. You do not deserve to come here and claim your inheritance and find that there are criminals threatening your life."

I squeezed her hand. "Juana, I need to know the truth about things, about Carlos, my mother, my inheritance, about you and Cesar. How did you first come to the plantation?"

"I was born here; my father was a *colono*. I came to the casa when I was fourteen. My aunt was the housekeeper for Carlos and his wife, Maria. I was brought in to help care for the house and Maria." Juana smiled and shook her head. "Maria was very beautiful, but fragile. A weak heart, something perhaps that they repair today but was a death sentence a couple decades ago. Carlos loved her very much. I was seventeen when

Maria died. And I was hopelessly in love with Carlos from the first moment I saw him.

"Of course, he did not know of my love for him, not for many years. I was just a young girl who idolized him, as did all the women who knew him. Some men love *things;* others love women. A woman recognizes that in a man; she can sense where a man's heart truly is."

"Wasn't he devoted to the plantation?"

"Yes, but Carlos loved the plantation not as a physical possession, but a living environment that included all the people in it. He never saw the plantation in terms of the money and power it could bring him. He believed running the plantation was a duty assigned to him by God, to preserve the land for the people who were dependent on it."

"You and Carlos became lovers?"

"A day came when he saw me as a woman rather than just a young girl helping around the house, but that was years after Maria died. The light went out in him when she died. He went into a deep mourning, hardly spoke, just worked. When it was too dark to work, he sat on the veranda and thought about her. They had no children to soften the loss."

She sighed. "And before he would notice me, another woman entered his life. Three or four years after Maria died, a young *norteamericana* woman came to the plantation to speak with Carlos."

"My mother."

"*Sí*, your mother. She was very pretty . . . but more than that, she had a love for life. She was inquisitive about everything, asked many questions, laughed a great deal. And she was very outspoken. Within minutes of meeting Carlos, she was accusing him of being an old-fashioned dictator who kept hundreds of *colonos* in slavery. He stared at her for a moment in complete amazement. I thought for a moment he was going to order her off the plantation. But he broke out laughing."

"That was my mother; she said what she thought, even if she was completely wrong."

"If a man had insulted him as your mother did, he would have struck him, but your mother was a woman and he was very gallant. And she was not just any woman, but one who immediately lightened his heart and made his eyes smile. It was the first time I had seen him laugh since Maria died."

"So they became lovers."

Juana stared down at the table. "Yes, your mother stole the heart of the man I loved."

"I'm sorry."

"No, it's nothing to be sorry about; it is just life. And Carlos was not ready to notice me; I was just part of the furniture of the house."

She stood up. "Just a moment." She left the room and returned a moment later with an envelope. She opened the envelope and sorted through pictures. "Here."

She handed me a picture. It showed my mother sitting on the hood of the Nash. She was laughing, her head thrown back. My emotions swelled. She was beautiful, full of life. I missed her so much.

"That day they went for a picnic; I packed their lunch. They did not return until the next morning."

I now knew for certain why my name was Nash. I had been conceived in that car. A backseat conception. In a heat of almost adolescent passion by them. It wasn't something I could share with Juana, but I felt a sense of pride at that, too.

"But she wasn't willing to spend her life on the plantation," I told Juana.

"No, she wasn't. She had too much . . ."

I helped her as she searched for the word. "Energy; she was constantly on the move."

"Yes, energy; she never stood still. To Carlos, the plantation was his whole world. To your mother, it was a prison."

"She returned home, pregnant with me. Did she ever see Carlos again?"

Juana shook her head. "No. She left; he mourned his loss again, but devoted himself to work to forget."

"How did he find out about me? Did my mother contact him?"

"No, for whatever reason, and I didn't know your mother well enough to judge her, she chose not to tell him that she had had his child."

"My mother didn't need a reason; she acted on her emotions, regardless of the consequences. She was extremely independent, self-reliant. She probably never told him because she would think he'd interpret the news as a request for money."

"But she let her daughter grow up without knowing who her father was. A mother should not do that, no matter how she felt about the man," she said.

"My mother was wrong. But she did what she thought was right. It's hard for me to go back and judge her; she's gone and can't defend herself. I wish she had told me about my father, but it didn't happen—and she was a good mother. She just wasn't a perfect person."

Juana handed me another picture.

I gawked at it, a picture of me, coming down the steps outside a building at college. It wasn't a posed shot.

"I must have been a freshman or sophomore. This picture must have been taken without me knowing it. I don't remember it, at all."

"Carlos had it taken."

"My mother told him I was in college?"

She shook her head. "He learned about you by chance. One of the Peace Corps volunteers who had worked with your mother twenty years before returned for a visit. He had kept in contact with your mother and mentioned to Carlos that she had a nineteen-year-old daughter. I don't know if the man guessed that it was Carlos's child and was dropping a hint, or if it just came out during small talk, but it caused Carlos to wonder.

"He hired a detective in Santa Barbara, where you and your mother lived at the time. The man discovered your birth date, which confirmed that you were probably Carlos's child. And the detective took a picture that confirmed it. Anyone who knew Carlos could see some of him in your features."

"By this time you were Carlos's lover?"

"Yes, we became lovers, many years before, soon after your mother returned to her own country."

"Why didn't he contact me?"

"He wasn't sure what to do. The detective reported that your mother lived with a man. Carlos thought that you had been raised to believe the man was your father. If that was the case, it would harm—"

I shook my head. "No, my mother had many men in her life; she changed them like seasonal clothing."

"He didn't know and he feared upsetting your life. We talked about contacting you. One of the reasons he didn't was because of my feelings. I was jealous once again of your mother. That she had borne Carlos a child opened the wounds I had felt twenty years before."

"But you also had Carlos's child."

"Yes, Cesar is his son. But I thought he was Carlos's only child."

"How did I end up as his sole heir? Cesar was disinherited, wasn't he?"

"Carlos had always intended to leave you something; not the plantation, that was to go to his son, but he had valuable jewelry that had been in his family for generations, and it was to be yours. He ultimately had to sell the jewelry to keep the plantation running, but he would have left you something else of value."

"Why did I end up with the plantation?"

"Toward the end, when Carlos was ill and the plantation was suffering from the drop in coffee prices, Cesar played an active role in running it. It brought father and son into conflict. Cesar is a good businessman, in some ways, I think he is better at business than Carlos was, but to Carlos, the plantation and the *colonos* were a family, not just a business enterprise.

"During an argument, Cesar told Carlos that when Carlos died, he would sell the plantation to one of the big coffee growers that would remove the canopy of trees and drive out the *colonos*."

"Turn it into a mechanized sun farm. That would have ripped out Carlos's heart."

"Yes, I think it quickened him to his grave. I don't know if Cesar really meant it; sometimes he talks with more machismo than good sense. He really is a kind person. But he said it, the worst thing Carlos could have heard, especially when he was so sick. But Carlos was not a man who would permit someone to kick him—he had a good heart, but was a fighter.

"He hired a detective again, found out you were a success at business and even ran a coffee business. I can't tell you how that excited him. And you called the business Café de Oro."

She squeezed my arm. "Nash, he cried when he heard that, from both joy and guilt."

"I got the name from my mother—"

"It didn't matter; to Carlos it came from God, a miracle. We talked again about contacting you and he decided that he would do it. But he was in pain for some time before he died. Time was short when he made his decision to leave you the plantation."

"Did he disinherit you, too?"

"No. When I had his son, Carlos set up a trust fund for me so that no matter what happened, I would have an income."

"But he disinherited your son."

"I encouraged him to make you his sole heir."

"That's incredible. Why?"

She was near tears. "You must understand, I was Carlos's woman—and I was a *colono*. I had spent my entire life on the plantation. To permit my son to destroy it, and the lives of so many people, would have been a great crime. It is not all Cesar's fault; it is my fault, too. I loved Carlos more than he loved me. Carlos remained loyal to me as the mother of his son, but he never married me. He never loved me with the passion with which he loved Maria or your mother. But it was enough for me just to be his woman, even if he never made me his wife. In your country, it is not as great a matter to a child that his parents were not married. Here, it is.

"Cesar was raised with the stigma of being a *bastardo*. I think that is why he so resented Carlos, why he has never loved the plantation. Carlos never accepted him in the way that he wanted, by marrying his mother. And it's why, in the end, he taunted Carlos that he would destroy it. He knew Carlos loved the plantation over everything else. Like your mother, Carlos was a great person, but he was not perfect."

"I wish . . . I wish Carlos had contacted me. I would have liked to have met him."

Tears formed in Juana's eyes. "By the time he was ready to meet you, it was too late. He was very sick, thin and pale. He did not want you to see him in that condition."

"What are you doing here?"

I nearly jumped out of my chair. Juana was as startled as I was. Josh had entered the kitchen without us noticing him.

43

❖

"Are you fuckin' crazy? You weren't supposed to come back here."

I got up so fast, my chair went over backward. "You have no right to talk to me that way."

"Like hell I don't; I risked my life warning you in Shanghai. You should have gone back home."

"Please, don't yell at her," Juana said.

"It's okay." I gave her a kiss on the cheek. "Everything's going to be all right. I need to talk to Josh alone. I'll be back in a little while."

He went out the door first and I flew by him. I wanted him out of her hearing. When we were a safe distance, I jumped on him.

"I appreciate your call, but why didn't you warn me *before* I was arrested and nearly murdered."

"I told you before you went, go back home—"

"*I can't go home!* You don't know—"

"I do know what happened in Seattle, and so does everyone else in Colombia, including Cesar and Escobar. But that's been cleared up. You're not a suspect."

"What do you mean, I'm not a suspect? How do you know?"

"I have my sources; so do they; they've been keeping tabs on things. A security camera at a bank ATM near your store picked up Jorge passing money to the arsonist before the guy went in and blew himself up."

"Cesar arranged to blow up my place in Seattle, with me along with it."

He shook his head. "I don't think so."

"He got Escobar to do his dirty work for him."

"No, I think he told Escobar that Carlos had left you the property and Escobar arranged it himself. Escobar doesn't do anyone's dirty work for them; he murders solely for his own profit."

"So why didn't he just have me killed when I arrived here?"

He shrugged. "Who knows? No one can figure out Escobar. Maybe he decided he didn't need any more bad American press. Maybe he liked the idea of you and Cesar at each other's throats. Maybe—"

"There are thousands of coffee farms; why doesn't Escobar get another one?"

"These are questions the oracle at Delphi couldn't have answered. I think Cesar was stupid enough to contact someone close to Escobar for financial help when the bank started breathing down his neck. Hell, maybe Escobar owns the damn bank that carries the note on the plantation; he has a piece of almost everything in the region that makes a profit. Regardless of how it happened, once Escobar decided he had a need for the plantation, Cesar had to cooperate or kiss his ass goodbye. Making a deal with Escobar is worse than dealing with the devil. The devil only wants your soul; Escobar takes your ass, too."

"I think Cesar is up to his eyeballs in drugs. Lily Soong was involved and he was involved with her."

"That came later. Escobar sent him to meet with the triad in Shanghai. He met up with Lily there."

"So Cesar *is* involved."

"He got drafted. Escobar makes the kinds of offers that are hard to refuse—if you want to keep on breathing. Don't forget Juana. If Cesar stepped out of line, he would come home and find Juana raped and chopped into pieces. I told you, don't keep making the mistake of thinking in civilized terms. Even the Mafia doesn't do the stuff Escobar does."

"How does a gem smuggler know so much about Escobar and his business? What are you, his local spy? Is that what you do, keep him informed of what's going on at the plantation?"

"Look, go home. Get married—if you can find someone dumb enough to marry you."

"Go to hell. I have a contract for a million pounds of coffee and it's just a start. I'm not going anywhere. Pablo Escobar can take his dirty business somewhere else. He's not going to run me off my own plantation."

"Are you completely nuts? You're not talking about a sane person. Escobar's a ruthless murderer; he kills cops and presidents; he'd swat you like a fly on a window."

"Maybe I'm not as stupid as you think I am. There's one thing that Pablo Escobar can't take, and that's the heat. The police and army in this country are hunting for him, along with our DEA, and looking under every rock they can find. Before I came back, I told them where to look next."

"What'd you mean?"

"I was bluffing last time when I said a friend would notify the world if something happened to me. Now I've sent a fax to the minister of justice and the American ambassador in Bogotá, and to the DEA in Washington, telling them that Escobar is trying to take over my plantation."

"Holy Mother of God." He pounded his fists on his forehead. "Tell me you didn't do that, you really didn't—"

"He isn't going to show up around here because everybody in the world will be looking for him here."

He shook his head, wide-eyed, awed, terrified. "You're not stupid; you're completely mentally deranged. You need to be institutionalized—you're going to get us all killed."

I stepped up and jabbed my finger against his chest. "I want you off my property or the next fax will be to those emerald mine owners you've been stealing from. I don't know what your game is, but as far as I'm concerned, you know too much to be innocent."

He headed for his Jeep. "I'm leaving, all right, to see if

there's anything I can do to head off a total disaster." He got behind the wheel and shouted at me, "I'll be back in an hour or two; you better be ready to go. I'm taking you to the airport; you're flying home."

His tires kicked dirt as he gave the Jeep the gas.

Juana was on the veranda. "Nash, what he said about Don Pablo, is he going to kill us all?"

I took a deep breath to calm my nerves. "Escobar is a mad dog. The only way to deal with him is with a bigger gun than he has. I don't have a gun, but the government and my country's DEA people do. There has to be easier prey than us if we have police and army around waiting for him."

"But what about his chemists, whatever work they're doing for him?"

"I've already thought of that. I'm going to tell them to leave."

"Will they listen to you?"

"They will if I put a fire under them."

I asked her to go back inside the house and start dinner. It would give her something to do while I started a fire. Literally.

44

❖

Five-gallon gas cans were stored behind the toolshed near the main house. I pulled the Nash out of the garage and stopped to put a can into the trunk.

It was a short drive to the huts where the Chinese and Colombian chemists conducted whatever alchemy skullduggery they were up to. No one was outside when I drove up. The metal front door was closed and the generator outside was running.

I took the can out of the trunk and was pouring gas around the base of the wood hut when Dr. Soong came out. He must have heard my car drive up.

He stared at me and said something in very bad Spanish, but I caught the gist of it—he wanted to know what I was doing.

"Burning down the place," I said, in English. "I'm burning out you crooked bastards so you get off my property."

I don't think he understood me, but he got the idea when he saw the match in my hand.

He ran, yelling for Sanchez.

I tossed the match and ran for the Nash. The two chemists came outside and stood and screamed nonsense at me.

I gave them the proverbial finger as I drove off. Not very la-
dylike, but I can't describe the enjoyment I got out of giving it.

The wooden hut burned nicely and I was confident that the
fire wouldn't spread far, hopefully just to the nearby huts. It
had rained in the wee hours, and the coffee trees and canopy
were too damp to burn. Or so I hoped.

Of course, with my luck, I would destroy the heart of the
coffee region and find myself on the country's Most Wanted
List.

45

❖

I stood on the veranda with Juana, watching the smoke from the distant huts slowly fade, when Josh returned in his Jeep. He came into the yard at high speed, another car, a decade-old Oldsmobile, behind him. A Colombian was driving the Olds.

Josh was grim. He stopped in front of us and got out of the Jeep, slamming the door behind him.

I stared at him with contempt. "I ordered you off the property."

"I'm out trying to put out fires and you're starting them with gas. Why didn't you just send Escobar an invitation to your bonfire? Juana, pack your bag. You, too," he said to me. "You have five minutes."

"I'm not—"

"I'm taking Juana to someplace safe; Jose is taking you to the airport at Medellín."

"It is that bad?" Juana asked.

"Worse. I've sent another man to warn the foremen to make sure they and the workers stay away from the plantation."

Josh was so cold and grim, my confidence suddenly evaporated. I stared at him, unsure of what to do.

He spoke quietly, calmly. "Nash, you don't realize what you've done. You haven't just put yourself into danger. What do you think Escobar's men will do when they come here? They'll kill everyone in sight. Everybody knows that, except you. The only way these people can avoid being murdered is if you disappear."

"Cesar will be in danger," Juana said.

"I got a message to him; he's on his way back. I've arranged for him to meet me rather than returning here. We have to figure out how to pacify Escobar."

I didn't know what to say. It never occurred to me that Escobar might send killers to murder workers and their families. I felt like a rubber doll that had been deflated, all my courage and confidence gone.

My God, what have I done?

"Get packed."

Trying to keep my voice level, I said, "I haven't unpacked."

I got my bag and slowly walked to the Olds. Josh and Jose were waiting.

I paused in front of Josh with my head hung down. "I really made a mess of things, didn't I?"

"The hopelessly insane aren't responsible for their actions." He gave me a big hug.

I started crying. Damn it, I didn't want to, but I realized all my bravado did was bring hell down on the plantation.

"I'm sorry, I'm so stupid."

He held me at arm's length. "Just get out of Dodge before sunset. I'll try to soothe things over with El Beneficiador. Who knows? Maybe the police or his enemies will get him before he gets even."

I hugged him, holding on tight until he pushed me back. "You have to go. And, please, go along with the program for once in your life. When you're safely out of the country, let me know how to contact you."

I kissed him. "You know, if you weren't a common criminal, I could grow to love you."

"I am not a *common* criminal."

I WASN'T IN any mood for small talk on the way to Medellín. Josh made me wear a bandana and pair of sunglasses. I thought it made me look like an American woman hiding her identity from Colombian killers, but after screwing up *everything,* I wasn't in any position to object.

I spoke little to Jose as we drove. He appeared a bit nervous. I didn't blame him—so was I.

I got out in front of the airline terminal and had started toward the doors when a man approached me with a partially unfolded map.

"Senorita, my eyes are too old; can you assist me?"

As I turned to him, he stuck the map in my face and blew on it, sending a fine powder at me. I stepped back in surprise, gasping, my eyes burning. Strong hands grabbed my arms and I was propelled into a black SUV waiting at the curb.

I wanted to say something, to scream, struggle, but thoughts swirled in my head like a tornado.

JOSE SLOWED DOWN and watched in his rearview mirror as Nash was hustled into the SUV.

"Dios mio!"

He crossed himself and hit the gas pedal.

46

❖

Jorge rubbed the scar on his neck as he sat in the backseat of the SUV and stared at Nash beside him. The old wound itched during times of excitement and stress.

Nash was dazed and submissive. Almost in a catatonic state, her body appeared awake but her eyes and face blank. She had inhaled enough of the drug to capture her mind—a little more and she would have lapsed into a deep sleep.

Jorge hated her. She had humiliated him, causing Escobar and other members of the cartel to laugh at the way she had easily slipped away. But this time she wasn't going to slip away. And he would get his revenge. He would kill her when Don Pablo was through with her.

He placed a mobile phone call to Escobar, a quick call in which no names were used. "Bueno," good, was all he said before he hung up.

He didn't know how much "boo" she had inhaled but knew it didn't take a lot for it to take effect. Boo was the cartel's name for burundanga. He'd never inhaled the stuff himself, but he'd been told it was tasteless and odorless. It was produced by trees that could be cultivated but grew wild around Bogotá. Mothers warned their children not to play under the *bor-*

rachero tree, the drunken tree. The pollen was said to conjure up strange dreams.

Processed in a laboratory, as the two chemists had been doing at the Café de Oro plantation, the drug scopolamine could be drawn from it. Scopolamine had medical uses as a motion sickness drug and in the past was used as an anesthesia. But its use to the cartel was in its resale value as a street drug. Because it caused unconsciousness, submissive behavior, and amnesia, it was used by Colombian criminals to gain control of victims. Drinks could be doped, the powder blown in one's face and even put into food and cigarettes. Once victims became pliable, they were robbed, raped, or kidnapped, whatever evil the crook had in mind.

The drug made one so compliant, it was used by intelligence and police agencies as a truth serum. And because it also created complete amnesia while a person was under its influence, it was used as a date-rape drug and by prostitutes to rob johns. Whores had been known to smear it on their breasts for men to lick.

Boo not only made people submissive; it removed inhibitions, even sexual ones. Women put under its control were gang-raped without resistance and even placed in prostitution.

As it was a potent drug, a tiny amount went a long way. Strapped for money, Escobar's cartel saw it as a new cash crop, with a huge infusion of money from the Far East, where it would become the newest toy in the robbery—and blackmail—of tourists.

A man in the front passenger seat turned and asked Jorge, "What do you think? Did she get a big enough dose of it to stay quiet for hours?"

"There's one way to find out, isn't there?"

Jorge unzipped his pants and pulled out his penis. It was already throbbing and inflating. He had been thinking about what he planned to do once he had her.

He pulled Nash's head down to his lap.

47

❖

Josh sat in his Jeep and drank beer as he listened to the sound of the approaching vehicle. He was parked in front of a hut he used occasionally when he wanted to disappear and get a good night's sleep and not have to worry about any enemies paying him a nocturnal visit. The hut had felt warm and claustrophobic, so he sat in the topless Jeep instead as he pondered his next move.

From the squeal of a vehicle's new brakes going too fast over the narrow, rutted dirt road he knew Cesar's Toyota Land Cruiser was approaching. Just in case Cesar wasn't the only one in the SUV, Josh kept his hand on the trigger of an Uzi he had covered on his lap under a folded poncholike *ruana*.

When he saw that Cesar was alone, Josh took his hand off the trigger and put it back on the beer he was drinking.

Cesar flew out of the car, leaving the motor running and the driver's door open. He stalked up to Josh, fists clenched, features dark.

"That bitch will get us all killed. She better not—"

"Pablo has her."

That stopped him. "How do you know?"

"Jose saw her kidnapped at the airport."

He stared at Josh. "She's dead, for sure."

"Not yet."

"Then she'll wish she was." Cesar stared at Josh. "You like her, don't you?"

"Yeah, I like her. And she's your sister; don't forget that."

Cesar struggled with the statement, as if it were an accusation rather than a fact. "She brought it down on herself, on all of us."

"The fuckin' system in this country brought it down on her and everyone else. And you're part of it."

"I didn't know; I thought they'd just cause her some trouble in Seattle, get her to sell cheap to me. It's my place; I was born here; I worked here my whole life; that bastard didn't have the right to give it to her; I earned it."

"So you sicced Escobar on her."

"Not deliberately. In return for Jorge getting her to sell, I said I'd cut him in for a piece of the sun farm I planned to put in. Next thing I knew, he brought Pablo around and the bastard staked a claim on the plantation in order to produce boo for the Asian gangs. He even made me go to Shanghai, almost got me killed." He wiped sweat off his face. "I killed a man; did you know that? I killed a Chinese in Shanghai."

Josh shook his head.

"A triad killer was sent to kill me as a message to Pablo to work with them and not with the gang he was dealing with. Lily diverted the guy with her naked cunt and I killed him. I puked all over him afterwards. I was so scared, I nearly wet my pants."

He stared at Josh again. "What have they done with Nash?"

"They took her from the airport to a plane on a dirt runway about thirty miles from Medellín, one of the fields Escobar has graded to use for a pickup or delivery before he moves the rendezvous spot somewhere else. The plane headed for the Amazon."

The vast Amazon Basin of South America covered over two million square miles. The jungle-choked world was almost uninhabited, little explored, giving it the status of one of the last frontiers of the unknown on the planet.

The Colombian region was so sparsely populated, less than

seventy thousand people lived in an area the size of France. Because the jungle was so dense and impenetrable, a Stone Age culture of indigenous people, "Indians," managed to survive in a world where scientists were sending spaceships to explore other planets.

There were no Colombian roads connecting the few small towns and settlements in the jungle region—access was by plane from Bogotá or by boat up the Amazon River from Brazil and Peru.

The region's very remoteness and inaccessibility made it a perfect place for the drug cartels to conduct business.

Cesar shook his head. "It's not my fault; she brought it on herself."

Josh ignored the comment and stepped into the doorway of the hut. He picked up a carry-on bag he'd already packed. He hid the Uzi under a board and strapped a 9mm Beretta above his right ankle and a snub-nosed .38 revolver above the left ankle.

"You're an American cop," Cesar said, using the American slang term for a police officer. "Bandidos carry their guns in front so everyone can see them; only cops hide them. What are you? DEA? CIA?"

"It's too complicated to explain right now. Get your mother and get out of the country. She's at her sister's. It's the only way to protect her."

"What good would that do? We'd have to come home sometime. Besides, when Escobar wants you dead, he doesn't care where you are, he'll send his *sicarii* anywhere in the world."

"El Beneficiador may be busy taking care of his own life at the moment. The authorities know he's in Medellín's Los Olivos district. The combined task forces have the area surrounded. Sooner or later they'll flush him out. He's flaunted himself too often in Medellín."

"He's been trapped before. I'm not leaving. This is my home, my country, some fucking bandido isn't going to run me out. My mother will be all right until they get Escobar or I can straighten it out with him."

Josh boarded his Jeep.

"Where are you going?"

"Where do you think?" He started the motor.

"You're going after her, aren't you? They'll kill you, too."

"Maybe, but I'll die like a man, not a cowardly asshole who lets thugs beat and rape his sister."

He hit the gas and the Jeep leaped forward.

"Wait!"

Cesar grabbed onto the side of the Jeep as if he thought he could stop it himself. Josh stopped and stared at him with contempt.

"I'm going with you."

"You'd just be a liability."

"I can use a gun; I'm a crack shot, better than you when we practiced together."

"It's not just shooting—"

"You can handle the rest of it; I'll be there when you need me. I told you, I killed a man; I'm not a virgin. Besides, you don't have a choice, not unless you kill me. Either I come with you or I call Jorge and tell him you're on your way."

Josh hesitated, mulling it over. "Why do you want to go?"

"You would never understand; you Americans don't think like us. Regardless of how I feel about Nash, she's family. I'm not going to let those *bastardos* destroy my family honor. It's all I have left and it's already been tarnished by my stupidity."

Josh knew he was telling the truth. Colombia was a land where the blood feud had been refined to a science. And vengeance was taken to revenge a relative even if the person wasn't on the favorite relatives list. It was all part of the skewed honor and machismo that drove so much of the violence in the country.

Josh drove Cesar to the plantation casa so he could grab a change of clothes and his gun.

Leaving the plantation, Josh said, "The plane filed a flight plan for Bogotá, but it never went there. It started for the capital, then veered south and headed in the direction of Leticia."

"That's bad."

Leticia was a small river town on the Amazon where the borders of Colombia, Brazil, and Peru meet. It was surrounded for hundreds of miles in each direction by dense jungle; no highways went there. The only way Colombians reached their southernmost outpost was by air.

Cesar's reaction was due to the small town's reputation. In an almost lawless country dominated by brutal drug cartels, warring leftist guerrilla armies, and right-wing paramilitary murder squads, Leticia had a Wild-Wild-West atmosphere, "Dodge City" Colombian style. Its isolated position, surrounded by impenetrable jungle where three countries met—and none seriously patrolled because it was almost impossible—made the town a natural as a crossroad for drug smuggling and gunrunning.

Coca paste, brought in from other countries, was processed into "white gold," cocaine powder, in jungle plants by the Colombian drug cartels, while planes and riverboats brought weapons purchased in Eastern Europe to supply the warring political factions.

Cesar said, "There must be police in Leticia who can stop them, the army; she's an American—"

"Even if they were willing to step in, which is doubtful, they wouldn't find her. Besides, the plane won't land in Leticia, not with her on board. The cartels have airstrips deep in the jungle. When they kidnap people, they can keep them there indefinitely without fear of discovery."

"And bury them there. I thought we were going to go bust her out of a house somewhere around Medellín. How are we going to locate her in the damn jungle? We'll need a small army just to find her, and gunship choppers—"

"We have to do it ourselves. No one gives a damn about a headstrong American woman who got herself into trouble. Right now everything's focused on bringing down Escobar."

"They won't help at all?"

"I've got a contact, an old friend who feeds the operations guys information obtained from satellites, tracking devices, and reports from informers and observers. She'll give me everything she can about the plane. But no one is going to pull planes and troops off a showdown with Escobar to scour the jungle for Nash."

"What's your plan?"

"I know a pilot who will fly us into Leticia. He's expensive, but the only other choice is to go through Medellín and Bogotá, and we wouldn't make it there until tomorrow."

They stared at each other for a long moment.

Finally, Josh said, "It's going to be dangerous. These people are stone killers. You can't hesitate to shoot one of them. They'd kill you with no more thought than squashing a bug."

"I don't care," Cesar said. "Remember, she's my sister. It's about blood. And honor."

BLOOD AND
HONOR

In Colombia, stories of family tragedies and the vengeance they spawn have a name: "culebras" (snakes). The Colombian novelist Fernando Vallejo once wrote that *culebras* are "outstanding debts. As you will understand, in the absence of the law that is always being rewritten, Colombia is a snake house. Here, people drag behind them feuds sealed generations ago: passed from fathers to sons, from sons to grandsons: and the brothers fall and fall."

Sometimes it seems as if every alliance of every feud in Colombia begins with the killing or kidnapping of a family member.

—ROBIN KIRK,
MORE TERRIBLE THAN DEATH

48

❖

The small plane carrying Nash, Jorge, one of his cohorts, the pilot, and a load of ether and other chemicals used to process cocaine touched down on a short, narrow runway scratched out of the jungle in southern Colombia. The strip was a mile from the river and less than two hundred yards from the plant where the chemicals were processed.

The region was little populated, but the cartel had no problem getting help. As soon as a processing plant was assembled, Indians who had subsisted on fishing from a dugout, a canoe made from carving out the guts of a log, suddenly found short-term employment with high pay. The employment was short-term because eventually the police, army, or other raiding drug traffickers soon brought the processing at that location to an end. But within weeks, another plant was being assembled at another location hidden by the ubiquitous jungle. The jungle was illimitable and so was the greed of the narco-traffickers.

Donkey carts met the plane to haul the chemicals. Jorge and his *compañero* Benito commandeered one of the donkey carts. The two of them carried Nash out of the plane.

She began mumbling incoherently and struggled as they grappled with her. Jorge put a cloth to her face that had boo on it and she quickly became docile. The workers who had come to haul the chemicals turned their heads away to avoid staring at the helpless woman.

Once they had her lying in the cart, they loaded water and supplies into it. Jorge led the donkey with Benito following behind. They didn't follow the carts carrying the chemicals to the processing plant but veered off, heading directly to the river and then alongside it. A small path had been chopped out of the jungle to accommodate the cart.

Jorge and his partner had brought kidnap victims to the location in the past. Kidnapping ranked close to murder as a dark activity in Colombia. No place in the world compared in the number of people kidnapped, nor did any have a greater percentage of seized victims killed after the ransom was paid.

The narrow path hacked out of the foliage led to a palm-thatched-roof shack on stilts within shouting distance of the river. During high-water times in the rainy season, only a boat could reach the shack. It had belonged to an Indian family that etched a bare existence from fishing and gathering liquid rubber from the trees that grew wild in the area. They had willingly taken a thousand pesos to abandon their shack, building another one five miles downstream.

Jorge and Benito carried Nash up the platform of logs that had been tied together to create steps to the veranda in front of the one-room shack. Carrying her inside, they placed her on a wood cot with a dirty mattress.

The only other furniture in the room was a three-legged table made from local wood. The table leaned over because one of the legs was ready to fall off. Cooking was done outside.

After depositing her, the two men went back outside. Their "sleeping quarters" were mosquito-netted hammocks hanging on the veranda. Other than to get inside when it rained, there was little reason to be inside the shack.

Two dirt mounds, about a foot high, that looked like big anthills stood in back of the building. About forty feet apart, they were a *tejo* court, for the traditional Colombian game similar to horseshoes, but a game with a bang. In each of the mounds was a metal pipe that came up to the top. The tops of the pipes were loaded with a small amount of gunpowder charge called *mecha*. Most towns had *tejo* courts.

Players took turns throwing a smooth, round chunk of metal or stone at the loaded pipe. When it hit exactly right, the impact caused the gunpowder to go off with a bang like a big firecracker. It was a traditional man's game—bets were placed; egos were put on the line.

In this case, the winner would have first rights with the unconscious woman in the shack.

49

❖

The pilot of the plane Josh hired had a particular interest in Leticia. "There's a doctor there I know, one of the few in the town, that wants to go into business with me. I fly him once in a while to Cartagena, where he picks up medical supplies.

"He wants me to fly in people for adventure tours. After I bring them down to Leticia, he'd have a small riverboat take them along the Amazon. Says there are foreigners dropping in on Leticia all the time, not just the drug crowd, but adventurous young Canadians and Australians who come down to check out the Amazon. There's even a national park near Leticia, but it doesn't get many visitors. Hell, there are more animals in the park than people in the entire Amazonas."

Amazonas was the name of the vast, little-populated tropical area for which Leticia was the government center.

They all knew why the national park didn't get many visitors—the region had a reputation for drug running and gun-running. The two main "industries" in the jungle were smuggling items to avoid custom duties and smuggling in coca paste for processing. Growing high-grade coca plants for processing was also becoming a local business—the cartels had developed a coca plant that could be grown in the jungle and was almost as good as the plants gown in Bolivia and Peru.

"Why not tourists?" the pilot asked. "The Brazilians conduct tours. Their riverboats with tourists even come to Leticia. You have all the resources God gives us in the Amazonas. The area is larger than most countries and it's almost uninhabited."

From the air, the jungle was an endless green carpet that stretched forever at all views from the plane. It looked flat from the air, but Josh had read that some sun-loving trees, called emergents, grew two hundred feet high, about the height of a twenty-story building, with much of the jungle a hundred feet deep.

Not only were there few humans; there were animals, monkeys and sloths, that spent their entire lives in the trees, never touching the jungle floor, and others so deep in the foliage that they never saw sunlight.

"It's not quite uninhabited," Josh said. "There are plenty of bushmasters and fer-de-lance," naming two of the world's most poisonous snakes, "not to mention those big crocodile things you call caimans, mosquito swarms carrying fever, spiders as big as hats—"

"That's the adventurous part," the pilot said.

Josh said, "Why don't you and the doctor just stick to drugs? That's why you fly him to Cartagena, isn't it, to pick up medicines smuggled in, so he can resell them in Leticia for a thousand percent profit?"

"We all have to make a living." He shrugged.

Josh knew exactly how the pilot had made his living—until recently. Cesar was wrong, Josh was neither DEA, CIA, FBI, army, navy, nor Coast Guard, the U.S. government agencies operating in and around Colombia as part of the joint U.S.-Colombian war on drugs. He was a member of a multinational group recruited from the top echelon of police and military intelligence in the world who operated independently in the country, but whose job was to point the way for the other agencies.

He had not lied to Nash when he told her he had an engineering background and had come to Colombia to work in the oil industry. But he left out the fact he had been recruited by the DEA after a close friend had been killed by drug traffickers. Josh hadn't been inducted into the DEA proper but the splinter group that used lookouts like him who could rub shoulders with the cocaine barons but keep enough distance so as not to raise suspicions.

The pilot of the plane taking them to Leticia had also been recruited after he was caught flying chemicals into the jungle for the Medellín cartel. He no longer flew clandestine missions for the cartel, using a truthful excuse that he had police watching him, but he had eyes and ears and learned a great deal just being around the airports and drinking with other pilots. He relayed what he heard in return for avoiding a jail sentence.

"Some of these people kill for their living," Josh said. "What do you know about the airfields around Leticia?"

Josh wasn't asking about the airport they were bound for but the illegal runways that were scratched out of the jungle.

"Everybody knows the cartel has moved into the Amazonas, that they're using the cover of the jungle to manufacture cocaine. It brings money into Leticia, but there's always the devil to pay when you make a deal with criminals." He grinned, as one who had dealt profitably with the devil. "You'll see American dollars used more in the town than pesos.

"Besides the ones who are spending big money, the doctor says he gets Indians in every day, mostly from around Puerto Nariño, a settlement about a hundred kilometers upriver from Leticia, their hands swollen double in size from the chemicals used in processing cocaine in the jungle factories.

"What do they get for poisoning their bodies with harsh chemicals? They are paid so little for the unhealthy work, it makes little difference in their lives. They drink more beer and buy more two-dollar whores, but they get old fast and die in agony. It's a curse."

"You didn't answer my question," Josh said. "What have you heard about the airstrips?"

"There's an airstrip near Puerto Nariño, nothing more than a clearing in the jungle, but it gets so much traffic the locals jokingly call it Nariño International Airport. Every few months, the army puts on a big show of enforcing the drug laws. They blow up an airstrip and publicize it as if they had made a major blow against the cocaine desperadoes, but these airstrips are just scratches in the jungle. You get rid of one and they hire the Indians to clear another." He shook his head and grinned. "The doctor told me that drug trafficking is like a cancer that has metastasized. You can find it and treat it, but it always seems to pop up somewhere else."

Josh knew the pilot was being evasive about giving information about the cartel, perhaps due to Cesar's presence. But it was true that airstrips had short-term use.

Josh got the name of the doctor from the pilot. The doctor's daily contact with laborers from the jungle factories would make him an invaluable source of current information. He probably heard more about the logistics and operation of the cartels' drug manufacturing from his patients than undercover narcs heard from paid informers.

The pilot was getting uptight, so Josh changed the subject to the stories of the "rubber terror" in the old days. In the early 1900s the Amazonas went through another type of boom, only instead of cocaine the "cash crop" was gummy white latex.

With the advent of the automobile and bicycles, the demand for rubber became phenomenal. The Amazon Basin region of Brazil and Colombia produced most of the rubber in the world at the time. The area was lawless and impossible to govern. Men made their own law, with "rubber barons" staking out enormous claims, often thousands of square miles, as their "rubber plantation." They employed small armies to enforce their claims and rounded up thousands of Indians as slave laborers.

The Atrocities was a period of black history in a country and region that already had many marks against it. The plantation owners' thugs would come into Indian villages and rape and murder if there was any resistance. Women were captured and held in "breeding farms," raped to provide future labor for the owners.

It all came crashing down by an act of theft.

Josh said, "Some guy working for Britain's India Office smuggled out seeds for rubber trees. They used them to grow plants at the royal botanical gardens and then shipped the plants to Sri Lanka and Singapore. Now it's the Asians who produce almost all of the rubber in the world."

"It's justice, isn't it."

The comment came from Cesar.

He added, "Labor in the Amazonas is probably cheaper than in Asia. But when you enslave and work your people to death, you end up losing your seed corn."

50

❖

The Leticia airport terminal was composed of just one building. It was no cooler inside than the suffocating heat that met them as they climbed out of the plane. The difference between the comfortable humidity of the mountainous coffee country in the Medellín region and the tropical jungle of Leticia was striking—tropical heat was a sauna. Warm, sunny, humid, and most often oppressively hot, with occasional—and sometimes torrential—thunderstorms.

Josh would have preferred to have landed on a jungle airstrip rather than at the very public airport, but it would have taken more time and planning to make the arrangements than he had to spare.

Inside the terminal, a man wearing a beer-and-babes T-shirt and faded jeans approached them. At first Josh thought they were going to be hit up for a hotel or taxi, but the man flashed a badge.

"Welcome to Leticia, senors. Did you have a good flight?"

Josh knew the man could have cared less if they had crashed and burned. "Yeah, good flight," he said.

"Your identification, *por favor.*"

The man took their IDs and carefully noted their names and other information on a well-thumbed pad.

In the States, Josh would have asked why he was being questioned, but no one else ever accused the Colombian government of being a zealous protector of liberty.

"What is the reason for your visit to our city?"

"Adventure tours," Josh said immediately. "We're starting a Colombian company to provide tours of the Amazonas to Americans, Europeans, Canadians, and Australians."

Josh liked the tour angle. It gave them great freedom to ask questions. It would even be natural to ask about places the tours should avoid because they were cartel territory. Now he tensed as he wondered how the Colombian cop would react to the story. And whether Cesar had looked surprised. They hadn't discussed a cover story.

The man looked intently at Josh for a moment, then pursed his lips and nodded his head, grinning. "*Excelente!* We get Germans, Australians, and Canadians already, but few of them. Not many Americans at all, a few druggies with melted brains who come down to find cheap cocaine. Mostly the foreigners come up the river from Brazil on a boat and only stay here a night. Tourists should stay longer; we have jungles and rivers filled with monkeys, jaguars, caimans, pink dolphins, and green parrots. An animal kingdom, no? Like Mickey Mouse at Disneyland, only our animals eat people."

He howled with laughter and Josh joined him, wishing Cesar would stop looking so nervous. They had started to move around the man when he put his arm out to block them.

"Something for the policemen's fund, senors."

Something for the "fund" meant a bribe, also known in some Latin American countries as *mordida,* "the bite."

Less twenty dollars, Josh and Cesar left the terminal.

Cesar said, "I'm glad he was with the police and not a lookout the cartels hired to keep track of visitors."

"You've forgotten you're still in Colombia. He probably works for the police *and* the cartels."

51

❖

As a rusty, battered VW van hauled them along mostly dirt roads into and through town, Josh thought, *Dodge City, Tombstone, Abilene—none of the gold-and-cattle boomtowns of the American Wild West had anything over Leticia for having a rough, frontier-outpost look.*

One big difference between the jungle outpost and the Wild West, besides the climate, was that instead of women wearing bonnets and bustles, some of them wore camouflage-colored battle fatigues and had butch haircuts—trademarks of one paramilitary revolutionary group or another. Others had a more feminine look—the kind that meant sex for sale.

Josh told the driver to take them around town first so he could get his bearings. There were supposed to be about fifteen thousand souls in the town, but from the looks of the place, the census taker was counting a lot of people who had already given up the ghost and taken up residence at the cemetery.

None of the men Josh saw on the streets carried guns openly, but they let the gun butts show or had telltale bulges under their clothes. A notch up from just packing heat, they looked tough enough to use it.

The paramilitary and drug cartel types reminded Josh of

something a dog trainer had once told him about guard dogs: Guard dog trainers look for big dogs that are instinctively territorial wherever they're at. Josh decided that must be what cocaine barons and jungle fighters looked for in their soldiers.

Most appeared mean-streets tough, even the women, junkyard Rottweilers and pit bull mixes that had been alternately kicked and thrown a piece of meat until they'd bite anyone that came near except the one that fed them.

But the real truth about the members of the various revolutionary groups was that they almost always came from desperately poor backgrounds and not all of them had left their families and joined voluntarily. Some had been "inducted" by fear or force and grown used to the life of a soldier, with no other life to go back to. Some had joined after family or friends were brutally murdered by the side they now opposed.

Josh also noted there wasn't much in the way of wheeled vehicles in the town, not like you'd expect for a place with thousands of people. He saw some "vintage" VWs, battered pickups, mopeds, scooters, and many bikes.

Other than cantinas, glorified bars that passed for "casinos," and whorehouses, most of the town didn't look flush from cocaine trafficking, but drug money usually didn't filter down much to the locals. Houses were mostly wood, some brick, most with tin roofs, a few with tile, some with a coat of cream-covered paint or stucco-looking stuff, not unlike the creamy color of some sidewalks and walls.

Some businesses were in buildings, but most of the vendors were at the numerous stalls in the marketplaces where fish, vegetables, and odds and ends passed hands.

Though it was still early on a hot afternoon as they drove by, Josh could see that the bars, bordellos, and "casinos" were already doing a thriving business. The gambling joints were small and appeared dingy. For sure, they wouldn't scare Las Vegas or Monte Carlo with competition.

As Josh and Cesar went by visual advertising that had all its sins covered—booze, whores, and cards—Cesar told the driver to stop.

"Let me out," Cesar said. "I need to do some reconnoitering."

Josh was glad to get rid of him. He didn't dislike Cesar. He actually liked him, even felt sorry for him. Having had a problem living up to his own father's expectations, Josh tended to blame Cesar's father for Cesar's attitude about the plantation. But Cesar wasn't good when there was a crisis. He was too emotional, drawn between having the macho courage expected of him and the reality in Colombia where a guy's machismo comes from the barrel of a gun.

Josh knew Cesar's "reconnoitering" would be limited to matters of the flesh. He had his own scouting to do.

ENTERING THE BAR, Cesar paused to enjoy the coolness and let his eyes adjust to the dark interior.

Two young women at the bar, Brazilian girls with toasted complexions, low-cut blouses, and short-shorts that let everything but modesty hang out, eyed him. Both girls were at an age when they should be finishing school and thinking about marriage, but neither probably had been in a classroom in four years.

The girls gave each other a knowing look. He smelled like money.

They took turns, an "up" system with johns, and the girl who was up approached him.

"Will you buy me a drink, senor?"

Her Spanish was heavily accented with Portuguese. In Brazil, the enormous country next door, the town of Tabatinga was literally joined at the hip with Leticia, which was across its border—and the border was just down the street.

Brazilian women were considered the most beautiful, or maybe they were just the most available, but it was these girls who came from Tabatinga on their bikes and mopeds that were the whores of the town.

"Tell your friend I want her, too."

"Her, too?"

"I'm going to fuck both of you."

JOSH WENT INTO a working-class bar, ordered a beer, and retreated to a dark corner. It was the third saloon he'd been in that night. He stayed back, pretended to be preoccupied with his own problems, and listened quietly.

Besides the usual talk of wives that nagged and fish that got away, he heard stories about jungle processing plants and locals who struck it rich one way or another dealing with the narcos.

When he heard a whispered conversation about a *"norteamericana,"* he waited outside until the speaker, a mestizo, left the bar an hour later. Pretending to know him, Josh grabbed the man and hustled him into an alley.

Shoving a gun under the man's chin, he said, "Tell me about the *norteamericana.*"

"I know nothing—"

Josh kicked him in the nuts. "Where is she?"

"I don't—"

He shot him in the knee. The sound was a dull thump instead of a sharp report because the pistol had a silencer.

The man screamed and Josh shoved the hot barrel in his mouth.

"Next one is in your mouth."

Over the next thirty seconds he got not an address but coordinates—upriver eight kilometers past Puerto Nariño, on the Colombian side—the other riverbank was Peru. At a place where three shacks were on stilts, an island formed in the middle of the river. On the right was an opening into a bay; he should head due east to three shacks in a grove of banana and rubber trees. The shacks appeared abandoned but were not. The cocaine processing plant was two kilometers, a little over a mile, north of the shacks. The airstrip was a kilometer farther north of that.

When Josh got everything he could out of the man, he hit him with the pistol butt until the man was unconscious. Josh knew he should have killed him, that if the man came to his senses before Josh reached where Nash was held, he could warn the drug traffickers holding her. A true professional would have killed the man, but Josh wasn't a cold-blooded murderer. Josh just hoped he gave the man enough of a concussion to keep him out or in a daze for the next twenty-four hours.

That night, as Josh lay on a hammock cloaked by mosquito netting—having abandoned the "hotel" room as too hot and claustrophobic—he listened to the sounds of the night in Leticia. Gunshots—probably just someone celebrating something by firing wildly into the air—and the folk sound of *corridos prohibos,* "forbidden" rhythms, competed with each other. The country ballad–type music was about the narco or guerrilla life. A guitarist was playing a tribute to Pablo Escobar, El Beneficiador, the man who sold white dreams to rich Americans and built housing and parks for the poor.

The part about killing hundreds of human beings who got in his way—not to mention the thousands of lives he ruined—was left out of the lyrics.

Later that night, with Cesar still gone, after the bars and whorehouses closed, a different sound made its way to him . . . the subdued strains of a *flauta,* an Indian flute.

People say that the flute sound of the Indios is a sad one, but Josh had always found it more eerie. Tonight it was uncanny, almost supernatural, as if the flutist knew why Josh was in Leticia—and what his fate would be.

52

❖

Early the next morning, while Cesar was still asleep, Josh left the hotel and followed the road down to where it terminated at the port. The waterfront was already a busy place, with fishermen rowing in their catch to offer it for sale and every variety of food and fruit being offered by people whose "store" was a tarp on the ground.

Josh asked around until he found a boat carrying cargo to Puerto Nariño, the Indian settlement upriver. He booked passage for himself and Cesar with the captain of the two-man crew.

Next, Josh bought a small flat-bottom boat with an outboard motor mounted at the stern to be hauled behind the riverboat. Using the outboard to get to the Indian settlement would have taken too long, turning a half-day trip into a couple days of fighting the current.

He was loading the small boat with water and supplies when Cesar arrived.

Cesar had a hangover and bad temper. He had awoken to find a message pinned to his shirt asking him to meet Josh at the dock.

Josh indicated the riverboat being loaded with cargo. "It's

carrying supplies to Puerto Nariño, about sixty miles up the river. It'll pull our boat behind it."

"Your little boat doesn't look like much of an armada to attack a cartel camp with."

"It's just to get us there. We have to attack the camp with our bare hands."

He wasn't in any mood to pacify Cesar. Josh was once again wondering if he should leave him behind. Cesar vacillated too much for him, sometimes talking tough, sometimes running scared, all the time a victim of emotions that pulled him this way and that way. Josh wasn't sure whether Cesar would be up to a hit-kill-and-run plan when the time came.

The cargo boat they boarded looked like a river mate of the *African Queen,* little more than a dry-rotted, unpainted barge with a small railing and a pointed bow. Cargo stacked on the deck—cans of kerosene and crates of canned goods—was tied down with rough hemp lines.

The boat was slow, chugging along, groaning arthritically as it fought the current.

Out of earshot of the two-man crew, Cesar asked, "Why did you choose this boat? We could have hired something faster and gotten there in half the time."

"This boat goes up and down the river every day; no one notices it. It's not the sort of thing drug runners or drug enforcement agents would ride in."

"Do you want to tell me what's going on?"

Josh considered throwing him overboard. Instead he took a swig of beer before he answered. "We're rescuing your sister, remember?"

"How do you know where they have her? Has someone told you?"

"Yeah."

"Who?"

"Escobar's thugs."

"You're not making sense; why would they tell you?"

"They don't know they told me. All right, relax, I'll give you an education in drug trafficking. You know that the best coca is grown in Peru and Bolivia, about the same altitudes that

Colombians grown coffee. The coca plants are grown best at several thousand feet on the east side of the Andes, nourished by warm, wet air rising from the Amazon rain forest. The coca farmers haul the leaves to a central location where they're turned into coca paste."

"I know; they put them in barrels and fill the barrels with kerosene."

"Kerosene, sulfuric acid, some other stuff. They end up with gray gook in the bottom of the barrels. That's the coca paste."

"We put that in cigarettes and smoke it."

"Right, freebasing, but you can't put it up your nose, not even if it's dried and turned into powder. That's where cocaine barons like Escobar and the other cartel kingpins come in. They buy the paste from Bolivia and Peru, smuggle it into Colombia, and process it in jungle plants, mostly in the north near the Panamanian border and south in the Amazonas. They go where there is less heat from the police or where they can hire guerrillas for protection."

"I know all this; I was born in this country, remember?"

"You know what you read in the newspapers, but I'm going to tell you something that you don't read. In the plants, the paste gets processed again, with more kerosene and sulfuric acid, alcohol, acetone, ether, and other stuff that people wouldn't drink or eat but don't seem to have any problem snorting and smoking.

"Now, here's the critical part. In order to process the cocaine at the cartel plant, some of those chemicals have to be imported. The most important one is *ether.*"

"Okay, ether, what does that have to do with finding Nash?"

"Someone involved in the war on drugs once cleverly figured out that if you follow the chemicals, they will lead you to the plants."

He finally had Cesar's attention.

"Ether is the critical chemical because there are only a couple countries where enough of it is manufactured to supply the cartels' needs. The DEA has been putting tracking devices in barrels of the stuff, a radio signal that is picked up by satellites. That plane that took off from Medellín didn't just have Nash in it; it had containers of ether to deliver to a plant down here. And one of the containers has a tracking device in it."

"And that's why you're carrying a satellite phone? You can get the tracking information?"

"I get the tracking information by calling the friend I told you about. She gets it from the satellite tracking it."

"The container's been tracked to Puerto Nariño?"

"It's been tracked to Lago Tarapoto, the big lake near the settlement. The exact location is about fifteen miles from Nariño."

"That would be heavy jungle. How detailed is the tracking?"

"It pins the location down closer to yards than miles. The plant is a few hundred feet from the lake, far enough in so it can't be seen from a boat going along the lake, but close enough so supplies brought in by river don't have to be hauled far."

"So when will the army and police hit the place to rescue Nash?"

"I told you before, they're not going to rescue Nash. We are."

"But if they know where—"

Josh shook his head. "The Colombian police and army have an almost one hundred percent track record of getting hostages killed. These jungle factories are multimillion-dollar concerns; the cartels have spies out. They'll know a raid's coming down before the choppers lift off. Even if they don't get advance word, standing orders are to drop everything and flee into the jungle. They kill witnesses on their way out the door."

"How are we going to take on so many? There must be dozens of men at the plant."

These were questions Cesar should have asked yesterday, Josh thought. Apparently he was getting nervous coming face-to-face with the reality of shooting it out with cartel gunmen.

"There are, but they don't typically keep hostages at the plant. They hold them far enough away so they're not seen by workers and so no one gets sympathetic and tries to help a hostage escape. I've been told there are a couple huts about a mile from the plant itself. Satellite photos show little activity at the huts, no foot traffic going back and forth. Those huts are our target. If Nash is at the plant, she'll be in one of them."

"What do you mean, 'if'? You said they tracked her there."

"I said they tracked the plane there. Sometimes they throw passengers out over the jungle."

It wasn't a pleasant thought.

The boat captain took a break for a cigarette, a beer, and small talk. Josh was reasonably certain that the captain hadn't bought his story about scouting out adventure tours. He had spiced up the story by asking questions about the smuggling that goes along the river from Peru into Colombia, letting the captain know that he was interested in pre-Colombian artifacts. The idea of sneaking antiquities out of Peru and to Europe or the States via Leticia worked much better with the riverboat captain than the tour story.

"There are few government gunboats on the river, not Peruvian or Colombian. Downriver, the Brazilians have more." He described how and who had to be paid to make sure a boat carrying contraband wasn't stopped and searched.

Smuggling wasn't considered criminal by the captain, any more than Americans who fudge a bit on their income tax "expenses" thought of it as committing a crime. It was just a way of life.

53

❖

Josh and Cesar spent the night sleeping under mosquito netting on hammocks after a dinner of chicken and rice and warm beer. The little "hotel" at Puerto Nariño had three rooms—and no competition to rent them. The floors were woven mats rather than wood. There was no running water in the rooms. Two outhouses were posted in the backyard. Bottled water was sold in the lobby—which was also the living room of the owner's house—but after seeing gunk gathered on the bottom of the bottles, Josh decided to stay with beer and their own supply of water.

The beer was good to replenish body fluids and rinse out the mouth. The wonderful thing about beer in third-world countries, where bad milk could kill you and bad water makes you wish you were dead, was that it was almost universally safe to drink.

Since the rooms were hot and stuffy, they retreated to hammocks with mosquito netting hanging outside. Small black monkeys with light-colored faces hopped around and leered at and heckled them. A black spider the size of a large hand scurried on the ground by them. Cesar threw a beer bottle at it—he missed and only raised the excitement level of the monkeys.

Josh had used the same cover story that had been their calling card since flying into the Amazon Basin: They were scouting out sites for adventure tours for Canadians and Australians with money and courage.

He got the same dull-eyed stare from the hotel man that he got from the riverboat captain. Neither man believed the story, but neither cared.

Josh guessed that either or both men would report their presence on the river to a cartel representative, probably with something akin to CB radio. He decided that Cesar was probably an asset in that regard. He was going to pieces emotionally, drinking too much, showing too much temper, the closer they were getting. It wasn't the sort of behavior that one would expect from drug enforcement cops or high-profile drug traffickers who might plan to poach on the cartel's jungle enterprises. Josh hoped the report sent to the narcos would not tag them as cops or competitors.

The fact that they were not heavily armed and didn't appear to have communications equipment also took them out of the serious threat category. With a little luck, and some laziness on the part of the cartel's watchers, they might get close enough to find Nash before they were tracked down and neutralized. And a bit of laziness was to be expected in a place where it was oppressively hot almost all of the time.

The next morning they rented a small canoe called a *peque-peque* to haul behind the flat-bottom boat. Josh had to leave a deposit big enough to pay for the canoe when he told the owner that he didn't want a guide along.

They bought blankets and enough provisions for a three-day trip upriver.

When they got the outboard going on the larger boat, they cast off and headed upriver. It would take an hour or two to find the place where an opening led into a lake, or bay, formed by river water. When the small global positioning device Josh was carrying told them they were close to where Nash was held, they would stop the motor of the flat-bottom boat. The dugout would not only be quieter; it would get them in closer.

The Nariño settlement was at the junction where the mouth

of the Rio Loretoyaca, an inlet to the vast Rio Amazonas, and a leg of Lago Tarapoto all came together. As they motored up the river, the scenery was no different from what they'd seen for hours on the large riverboat that brought them to Puerto Nariño—trees, trees, and more trees, some with their trunks in water, all of which at some time of the year would be in water. Occasionally they saw a single house or wood huts with thatched roofs. A few more permanent ones had tin roofs. There was an occasional clearing where corn grew or a few scrawny cattle grazed.

They passed a "cattle pen" flowing downstream, a flat barge made of hardwood logs and a railing. Another railing went down the middle of the square barge, creating two pens. Palm thatch protected the cattle from the hot sun.

In one area, they saw rubber trees leaking latex from old and new cuts. Someone would make a few dollars gathering the latex and molding it over a fire into a ball that could be sold to a rubber merchant in Leticia. Today's rubber baron was a man who dealt in buckets of latex, not shiploads.·

Once they passed a small boat carrying a fisherman, exchanging waves and shouted greetings.

The vastness and desolation was almost unimaginable to Josh. It was the most isolated place he could remember experiencing. For hundreds of miles there was nothing but rain forest—trees, trees, and more trees, although at times the vines and brush camouflaged the trunks.

The strangest creatures in the waters of the vast waterways were dolphins, river mammals that were related to whales. Unlike the more familiar-looking bottle-nosed dolphins of *Flipper* and his pals at Sea World and in movies, these dolphins had long beaks and rounded foreheads.

The males, who were bigger, grew up to be eight feet long and weighed 350 pounds, Cesar said. Information he remembered from his school days, when he had to learn about the flora and fauna of his country.

The creatures ranged in color from dark gray to bright pink. The pink ones were unusual, more like big wrinkled sturgeons. He'd heard that the dolphins used a sonarlike system to navigate, not needing eyes because the water of the river was so dark and muddy, but he didn't know if that was true.

The captain had told them that the eyes of the dolphins were considered an aphrodisiac by the indigenous peoples, that if the eye was dried, grated, and sprinkled into a woman's food, it would put her into a sexual frenzy. He swore to the tale as gospel, but it smacked of urban legend to Josh.

"I remember a dolphin story told to me when I was a child," Cesar said. "It's a tale like the Sirens that sang songs and lured men to their destruction, and Lorelei, the bitch who lured fishermen onto the rocks of the Rhine. I was told the pink dolphins transform into beautiful women and lure men to their dwellings at the bottom of the river."

The long-snouted creatures were definitely strange, Josh thought. They made eerie sounds when they broke the surface to breathe, blowing steamy air from their blowholes before going back under. According to the captain, the pink ones were incredibly dexterous, bending and turning like they were made of rubber as they swam through the sometimes flora-crowded waters.

Talking about the dolphins seemed to lighten Cesar up a little. When a big dragonfly landed on the boat, he said, "Some people call them snake doctors, because they think that they nurse sick snakes back to health."

Josh knew a different version. "The story my grandmother told me was that they are the devil's darning needles, that they sew up the ears, eyes, and mouth of a sleeping child who's been bad."

When they had passed a water channel that flowed away from the river and into the dense, primordial world of Amazon jungle, the captain told them, "The river people believe that canals are made at night by a giant water snake. It's so big, it can swallow a large canoe of people with one gulp. That's why you never see them on the river at night; they're afraid of the snake."

The river was alive with plants, not just on the shoreline but formed into islands that sometimes floated downstream or appeared to take root in a particular spot until stormy high water broke them loose.

When they reached the lake, Josh took a battery-operated GPS and used it to compare their position to the satellite coordinates supplied by the transmitter in the ether container.

Twenty minutes later, they beached the boat along the riverbank, hidden by bushes, and started trekking across the damp floor of the rain forest.

54

❖

I stared up at the ceiling. Bare logs held up palm thatch. A spider sat in a web between log rafters. A big and hairy thing, it was the size of a fist. I was sure the spider was staring back at me, blinking its large round eyes.

Even though spiders scared me, I tried not to kill them. When I was small, a friend had pushed me into a large spiderweb. I panicked and clawed at the webbing. After that, I always had a fear of spiders. My mother told me that killing a spider inside a house was bad luck, so I would always grab a glass and piece of paper and trap the spiders to release them outside.

The thought of trapping the spider in the rafters was not urgent to me. Some time ago, I realized I was in a hut, on a cot, alone. Opening my eyes, falling back into a deep sleep, awakening again . . . I don't know how many times or how long I had been in that cycle of in-and-out. Heat, oppressive humidity, bore down on me and soon it came to me that I was no longer in coffee country. What had Ramon told me? One of the climate zones of the country was tropical jungle.

Other than the fact I was in a thatched-roof hut somewhere that was hot and humid, I didn't know where I was. For a while there I didn't know who I was. Thoughts had come and gone.

For a long time I thought I was nailed to the cot, because I couldn't move. I was able to move now, had raised my arms and legs, but still had not tried sitting up. Keeping my eyelids open had been a chore that I accomplished turning my head.

The sedatives that my neighbor in Seattle gave me had never affected me like this, but I had that same feeling of separation of mind and body that the prescription drug gave me.

The room was empty and almost unfurnished—only the cot and a rough wooden table made from raw forest wood. Little light made it into the shack—the windows didn't have glass but were covered by crude wood shutters that let in a little light along with mosquitoes and flies.

Moving my hands down my body, I felt bare, sweaty flesh. *I was naked.* I tried to sit up, but my brain exploded. I grabbed my head and pressed to keep it together. An image flashed in my mind—the man at the airport with the map, he had blown something in my face. Strong hands. I remembered that, too. It was after he'd blown something in my face that I had been grabbed.

Josh had warned me that I could be kidnapped or murdered and I hadn't listened. *They take their victims to remote places where they won't be found.*

Drugged. Kidnapped. Taken from the airport to a jungle. Why? Why not just kill me? They needed me for something, maybe nothing more than signing papers giving them the plantation, and then they would kill me.

My heart beat faster. Despite an adrenaline rush, my body was stiff, slow to move. My head ached and pounded. I slowly stretched, creating a tingling sensation as blood flowed into my extremities. I became aware of pain between my legs.

Light came in from a split in the wall, falling across my legs. Blood was on the inside of my thighs. I hurt and burned. I gasped aloud as I realized what had happened, what had been done to me when I was unconscious.

A storm of feelings—fear, anger, disgust—gripped me.

They had kidnapped and raped me.

Fuckin' bastards. Animals. Did they think it was macho? To violate an unconscious woman?

Rage gripped me, anger fed by hate and repulsion that turned into fury. The sons of bitches.

I sat up and got my feet onto the floor, slowly urging myself to rise but going back down as my head swirled. *No! I have to keep moving.* I forced myself back up again, uneasy on weak knees, but so damn angry that I wouldn't let myself lie back down and drift into the analgesic black void again.

My clothes were in a pile on the floor. Using the bed for support, I put on my panties and pants and slipover shirt. My bra was across the room and I left it there. I slipped on my sandals and got to my feet again.

My footsteps made creaking noises—I treaded lightly, creeping to a shuttered window to the right of the door. The shutters were spread enough apart for me to see between them.

I noticed a man asleep in a hammock, covered by mosquito netting, on a small veranda just outside the window. I couldn't expressly place him, but he looked like one of the men who could have been with Pablo Escobar and Scar when they came to the plantation. I was reasonably certain he had been with the group.

No one else was in sight, but I only had a small field of vision through the shutter. I didn't want to risk waking the man by opening the shutters. I crept to the window on the other side of the door and peered through the openings. About a hundred feet away, a man stood fishing at a riverbank. His back was to me. As he twisted to cast out the line, I got a good look at him. Scar. That came as no surprise. The bastard had been dogging my heels since Seattle.

He wore a gun belt and had a gun in the holster.

The man in the hammock let out a snore that turned into a rumbling sound as he turned a little.

I froze in place and waited for the steady rhythm of his snores to resume. He had a gun, too, a pistol in a holster hanging on a peg that supported the veranda. Little more than the butt was visible of the pistol. It looked like the butt of a revolver.

I stared at the holstered gun, trying to recall what I had learned about guns in a self-defense course during college. The class had included two trips to a firing range, but it had hardly qualified me to use a gun, much less shoot someone with it. And I had to get my hands on it first.

To grab the gun, I had to get out the door and around the hammock. The question was, once I had it in my hands, could I use it? I knew I could shoot the sons of bitches; that wasn't even an issue. My life or theirs. If we were going to take turns dying, these two animals could go first. But my concern was whether I could handle the gun. From the look of the butt, it appeared to be a revolver, a gun with six bullets in a revolving chamber. That was the type of gun recommended by my instructor for home protection because it was idiot proof—all you did was point and pull the trigger.

I remembered the instructor telling me that until recently revolvers had been the almost universal weapons for police because semi-automatic pistols could jam. However, as criminals used more firepower, cops went to the semi-automatics despite the jamming problems.

Point and pull the trigger.

Without thinking, without reasoning or planning, I burst out the door of the shack. I stumbled on the rough flooring of the veranda, knocking against the man in the hammock.

He jerked awake with a start, yelled, and twisted, throwing himself out of the hammock.

I grabbed at the gun in the holster—*a strap held it in.* I hadn't thought about the piece of leather that kept the gun from slipping out of the holster.

The man had flipped out of the hammock and hit the flooring. Still prone, he grabbed at my ankle, getting a hand around it. I screamed and clutched at the gun. Instead of the gun slipping out, the holster pulled off the knob of wood.

He jerked my leg out from under me. I tipped over backward. The veranda didn't have a railing. I flew off it, hitting the ground with a breath-snapping thump. A shock went through my body as I hit, but the ground had a soft, moist mat of grass covering it and the landing was softer than hitting hard dirt.

I was still clutching the holstered gun as the man above got to his feet. He let out a roar as he leaped down at me feet-first.

I twisted and rolled to the right as he hit the ground with both feet. He stumbled forward, off balance as the soft ground gave way underfoot.

As I jerked the butt, the gun came out of the holster and he turned to me, throwing a kick at the gun in my hand. I dropped my gun hand down and pulled the trigger as his foot came over me. The gun went off with a deafening explosion and flipped out of my hand.

The man attacking me flew backward, clutching his groin and screaming. He started to scream again, but it stopped in his throat. He shook, convulsing, both his legs and arms twitching and shaking as if his nerves were on fire. He suddenly collapsed back, still as death. The bullet had caught him from underneath and driven up as if he had been impaled by the piece of lead.

The pounding of feet came from the river's edge. I scrambled for the gun that had flown out of my hand. I got it by the butt and turned, clutching it in both hands as Scar charged at me. His gun, a semi-automatic, was out, pointed at me. He pulled the trigger. *It jammed*—jungle humidity almost thick enough to swim in was no good for the complicated firing mechanism.

I was still on my back, clutching the revolver in both hands, supporting it between my legs, and he was only ten feet away. I almost squealed with delight as I pulled the trigger.

I missed.

Sonofabitch!

He wasn't there when the bullet got there. He ducked down and was running for trees, trying to unjam his pistol as he ran.

I ran the other way.

55

❖

Josh and Cesar were in the boat with the outboard motor, hauling the dugout, when the shooting began.

"Not far away," Josh said.

"Someone hunting?"

"Maybe, but that sounded more like a handgun than a rifle."

"Should we turn back?" Cesar was jittery.

Josh didn't answer him but turned off the outboard and gave Cesar one of the paddles, taking the other for himself. "We can't afford to let anyone know we're coming; start rowing."

They rowed for five minutes before they saw bushes moving near the riverbank. No more shots were heard. They stared at the location where they'd seen the bushes moving. They didn't know if it was an animal or a person and couldn't move in any closer with the larger boat. Landfall was an area that was almost as much river as it was solid ground. Something short of what the locals called *pantano*, a swampy marsh or bog, full of mud and brown water oozing through the mat of swamp grass, the area was still soggy and muddy. Narrow channels appeared clear of enough vegetation for the dugout.

Josh saw a flash of white moving through the bushes. He stood up in the boat and impulsively shouted, "Nash!"

"You saw her?" Cesar started up, rocking the boat, and they both went back down.

"I saw something." He yelled again. "Nash!"

She answered him back.

They still hadn't gotten a good view of her, just a movement in the brush. Josh directed the boat toward the movement.

"It might be too muddy for her to make it to the water," Josh said. "I'm going for her." He climbed out of the larger boat and into the dugout, casting off to row into where he'd spotted the bushes moving.

As he rowed, he yelled her name and she yelled back, giving him a clue of her location.

He was almost to the bank when a scream and the sound of a shot came from the bushes. He started to call her name and stopped, not wanting to have her give away her location if someone was chasing her. He heard a splash and a moment later saw her in the muddy water. He rowed toward her as she swam. A shot came from another point along the bank. The bullet struck the wood dugout.

He saw the man with the gun well enough to realize it was Escobar's thug, Jorge, the man Nash called Scar.

Josh reached for his gun and realized with a shock that he'd left it in the boat with Cesar.

Scar fired again and the bullet hit the water by the dugout. Pistols weren't as good as a rifle at this distance, but it didn't take much thinking to realize he had a whole clip of ammo with which to get it right.

Josh heard the sound of the outboard revving and turned, thinking that Cesar was making his escape. But Cesar didn't turn the boat toward the river; he steered it straight across the water to where Scar was standing on the embankment.

Speeding across the water, Cesar set the auto-control on the outboard so the engine kept going at full speed when he let go of the throttle. He stood up in the flat-bottom boat and held his semi-automatic in both hands, crouching and firing wildly in the unsteady boat.

Scar turned and returned his fire. To Josh it was a scene out of a western movie—two gunmen with blazing guns firing at each other.

Cesar flew off the boat as if a big hand had smacked him. He hit the water as the boat sped for the embankment.

Scar turned back in the direction of where Josh was rowing to reach Nash in the water.

The cartel gunman stood perfectly still for a moment, then slowly crumbled, dropping to his knees and falling facedown.

Josh hauled Nash into the boat. Not waiting for her to get her breath, he continued rowing, turning the boat and heading for where Cesar had gone into the water.

Nash stared up at him, drenched. Her voice trembled as she said, "Glad to see you. What took you so long?"

"Thank me later."

"Cesar's hit; he's in the water. We've got to get him before the piranhas or caimans do."

They found him floating facedown and pulled him into the dugout. He had taken a bullet in his chest.

56

❖

I sat in a flat-bottom boat powered by a small outboard as Josh sped it across a bay toward the river. The dugout was too small, too slow, and too hard to row. Josh had rowed us to the larger boat and gotten us aboard. He had tried to slip Cesar's body back into the water because he was hard to handle, but I stopped him.

"He's my brother," I said.

We hadn't gone far when we first heard the roar of helicopter motors. A moment later, olive-drab gunships—armored military choppers—flew over us heading toward the processing plant.

"Delta Force and Colombian commandos," Josh said. "They'll take out the cocaine processing plant."

He had explained something to me about global positioning in the war on drugs, but none of it had penetrated. I was too overwhelmed with just being alive. And the loss of Cesar.

Cesar's head was nestled in my lap. He would never know the love I felt for him; he was the only brother I'd ever have. And he had died for me.

Josh used a satellite phone to communicate with someone. It

didn't surprise me that Josh had something to do with the war on drugs. He was full of surprises.

"Are you all right?" he said.

I didn't say anything, just nodded and stared at the brown water moving by. My adrenaline surge was gone; my heart had stopped pumping frantically. I felt cold and knew I was slipping into shock.

"Thank you," I told him.

I lay back, still clinging on to my dead brother's body. And closed my eyes.

Terrible things had happened to me. In a strange sort of way, I felt cleansed . . . but not by the muddy river water.

Deep in my heart, I'd always believed in biblical justice, an eye for an eye. Many times when I'd heard of some atrocity committed by some murderous bastard, my thought had been that I hoped they got their just dues . . . slowly and painfully.

Not very enlightened of me, nor even very nice, but they say you feel different about muggers . . . after you've been mugged.

57

❖

Back at the plantation, the place bristled with plainclothes U.S. agents and Colombian police. I had burned the lab that had produced the drug with the street name of boo, but the police were carefully sifting among the ashes and fire-and-smoke-blackened equipment to reconstruct how the two chemists had manufactured it.

Pablo Escobar, the richest, deadliest criminal mastermind who ever lived, was dead.

The conclusion to the hunt-and-kill drama came when U.S. intelligence forces tracked Pablo's voice on a mobile phone call to Los Olivos, the barrio of Medellín, where he was king. A battle ensued and Colombian forces killed the billionaire cocaine baron. Although the official story was that Pablo had died in the gun battle, photographs later revealed that he had been executed by a shot to the head.

Considering the number of murder squads—official and unofficial—gunning for Pablo, giving up the ghost execution style was the most likely way he would go.

The police had recovered my purse but not my carry-on. I had a new traveling bag now, packed and ready to go. I was leaving the country, with Josh. Returning to Seattle on my part,

I guess to try to pick up where I had left off—like the police in the boo lab, I needed to sift through the burnt bridges I'd left behind to see what the future held.

I had insisted upon coming back to the plantation. And I insisted that Cesar's body be brought back for burial. His mother was there waiting for him. His father was there, too. Up on the hill.

I couldn't leave without standing beside Juana as she buried her son. My brother. Juana chose what I considered to be the most appropriate spot—on the hill, overlooking the plantation, next to his father.

Looking back on my discussions with Cesar, I firmly believed that he truly loved the plantation and the business of growing coffee. He had taken some wrong turns, had some rotten tricks played on him by life, and he had reacted in the only way he knew how. In the end, all he had left was his courage and honor, and both shined brightly.

The morning after the funeral, I grabbed my new carry-on and got it as far as the veranda. I left it there to return to the hill. I had to talk to my father and brother alone before I left. I had to let Carlos know that he should really be proud of his son. And I needed some advice from the two of them.

Atop the hill, I put fresh flowers on each of their graves.

"Well, guys, another fine mess I find myself in. I have to go home."

Suddenly I was crying.

I was wiping away tears when Josh found me.

"You okay?"

I nodded and blew my nose.

"They're waiting for us," he said.

"I'm not going."

He didn't say anything for a moment, just looked at me, kind of nodding his head, as if I'd said something like *Do you think it'll rain?* or *I like catsup on my potatoes.*

"I'm not going," I repeated.

"You're not going."

"Not going."

He nodded some more. "They're down below, cops and soldiers, armed for a war, ready to take us to the airport."

"I just had a family conference. I've been asked to stay."

"What are you talking about?"

I nodded behind me at the two graves. "I'm staying to run the plantation. With Cesar gone, there's no one to run it. If I go, it'll be lost; it's not something I can run from thousands of miles away. I promised my father I'd stay and run it, that I'd carry on his tradition of producing the finest coffee in the world. It's going to remain chemical free and shade-grown."

"Nash, you can't stay; this is Colombia—"

"I know, I keep thinking civilized and this isn't a civilized country. But I can and will stay. They destroyed my dream in Seattle; it's been cleared up, I can return, but it would never be the same. I'm not going to let Pablo Escobar destroy another one of my dreams.

"I have a deal to sell my coffee in Shanghai. Once I get established there, I'll have the money to specialty-brand it in the States and Europe. When that happens, I'll keep adding acreage, partnering up with other shade growers—Josh, if you keep shaking your head like that, it's going to fall off."

"You're completely insane. You can't stay here."

"Yes, I can. Like you always said, it's a beautiful country filled with wonderful people; you just have to avoid the snakes that have human heads. I want to fulfill my father's dream, and my mother's, too. Don't forget she was a Peace Corps volunteer right here on Café de Oro. I know she would be angry if I turned my back and let the big growers kill the coffee plantation canopies that birds thrive on."

"You can't—"

"I can and I will—and so can you. You told me that you're not really a cop, that you got into the business of spying on drug traffickers because they killed a friend of yours. What you told me about cutting and running from marriage and college in the States, that was all true, wasn't it?"

"It was true."

"Well, maybe it's time you stop and take a stand."

"I can't stay here; word will get out that I'm a drug agent."

"You can quit. Escobar is dead. Whoever takes over isn't going to want to fight his old battles. In a few days, you'll be old history. Besides, I need you; I can use someone clever who knows all about the import-and-export side of the business. As a former smuggler, you're perfect for the job."

I wasn't going to let the man whom I wanted to spend the rest of my life with slip away.

"You're not sane. You talk to dead people."

I put my arms around him. "It's okay; they won't tell anybody."

Historical Note

No criminal in history cast as large a shadow as Pablo Escobar. Many mafia chiefs no doubt counted their personal for-
tunes by the millions—none was a billionaire like Escobar.
And while a tough guy like Al Capone could shake things up
in Chicago, Escobar took on a nation of nearly forty million
people, a country with almost unparalleled experience itself
with violence.

Three American presidents—Reagan, Bush, and Clinton—
considered Pablo Escobar *a threat to United States security.*

Pablo made the mistake of getting so rich and powerful, he
threatened to overpower the Colombian government and send
a shock wave through world politics.

Colombian leaders tried to handle the situation themselves. The idea of having U.S. police and military forces on
Colombian soil was repulsive to the proud Colombians, but
when the Colombian president realized that the situation had
spun out of control, he made a call for help. By that time,
Pablo had been behind the assassination of three of five candidates for president of Colombia in 1989, had instigated a
siege of the supreme court building in the capital in which

nearly a hundred people died, including eleven supreme court justices, and had blown an airliner out of the sky with 130 people on board, including Americans. While others carried out many of the black deeds, he was there with money and advice.

Along with these world headline–grabbing events, the murders of government officials, police officers (several hundred in the Medellín area alone), journalists, judges, and politicians became almost daily affairs.

At one point, Pablo "graciously" had a prison built at a small town near Medellín and put himself in it as a deal with the government. He would serve a short term and be cleansed of his crimes. Before he entered the jail, he had hundreds of people in and about the town killed—literally, anyone who could in any way be a threat to him.

The "prison" was a comfortable suite in which he had full communications equipment and assistance in running his billion-dollar cocaine business, while enjoying himself with visits from female friends and prostitutes.

His decision to walk out of the jail (which was "surrounded" by a brigade of Colombian troops) and challenge the Colombian government for power was to be a fatal one.

After the U.S. found out Pablo and his pals were in the market for Stinger missiles and a submarine, the unofficial policy went from assisting the Colombians to being actively involved in a hunt-and-kill mission for him.

The NSA, FBI, CIA, DEA, the intelligence agencies of all the military establishments—army, navy, air force—became involved in an effort to feed information to the Colombians battling Pablo. And the intelligence information was supplemented by Delta Force commandos who could get on the ground and in the shooting when necessary.

Colombia was not a country in which politics and police hunts were handled with moderation. The massive U.S. military/police/intelligence establishment soon discovered that they were not only helping legitimate Colombian forces but inadvertently in league with the death squad Los Pepes, the group that claimed to be composed of victims' and survivors' families. Besides the unofficial death squad, the Search Bloc, the official team pursuing Pablo, conducted its own style of summary executions.

Unable to get their hands on Pablo himself, the death squads went after his family, lawyers, bankers, and drug-trafficking *compañeros*. The idea was to isolate Pablo. When this was combined with a strategy to keep him constantly on the run, using high-tech U.S. intelligence surveillance to direct commando units, it was inevitable that something had to give.

What gave at first were the forces lined up against him—as his pals were murdered, he'd kidnap people and have them tortured and murdered.

There was really nothing to admire about Pablo. Rather than admiration, the fascination is more akin to what we experience at seeing a deadly snake at our feet.

The reason that he rose so high as a criminal was only because he was more vicious than anyone else around him. He was said to be soft-spoken, intelligent, and even well-read. But he also had a total lack of conscience and the ability to order murder. To paraphrase Nash, he ordered murder as easily as the rest of us order pizzas.

To call Pablo the world's biggest criminal doesn't do him complete justice. When a criminal rules a large area by force and violence and threatens the security of a nation of nearly forty million, he has transcended merely being labeled a criminal.

Pablo Escobar was in essence an old-fashioned warlord, a brutal commander of troops who staked out a territory and ruled it as king.

Pablo's ultimate downfall was a criminal mind-set that the late great author Malcolm Braly, a man who spent much of his early life in prison, called the "delusions of invulnerability."

How many times do we hear about a criminal who made an enormous amount of money in a criminal scheme but rather than retiring well-heeled kept at it over and over until he ended up behind bars or dead?

Fortunately for those of us who have a conscience, delusions of invulnerability is a disease most criminals suffer from.

The most tragic thing about the career of Pablo Escobar was greed—not his personal greed; that was only to be expected. It was the greed of Colombia's military and political leaders that permitted him to succeed. Colombia is a country of nearly forty million people and has a significant military force. Escobar kept up a reign of terror for over a decade because so many of the nation's leaders were taking his *plata*.

The world of priceless art is a playground for billionaires—a rarified atmosphere even more privileged and ruthless than owning a champion race horse or a sports team. Money and ego have turned the quest for art into a deadly business in which the superrich battle to possess the rarest and most beautiful objets d'art on Earth.

HAROLD ROBBINS'

The LOOTERS

BY
JUNIUS PODRUG

A September 2007 Forge Hardcover

PROPHETIC

"When Peregrine Pollen suggested that Harold Robbins might be tempted to set one of his sagas of power, sex, and money at Sotheby's, Peter Wilson [Chairman of Sotheby's] was enthralled.

'Tell him we'll give complete facilities,' he said, 'and all his expenses paid.'

Wilson's flash side was fascinated by the opulent vulgarity of *The Carpetbaggers*."

Sotheby's: Bidding for Class, by Robert Lacey

Oh, how the mighty have fallen. I railed against the depressing thought but it punched back. I had had it all, but now I was on the run from killers and the police, stuck in traffic as the Jersey-bound lanes of the George Washington Bridge turned into a parking lot. My gutless rental car was boxed in between a tanker truck that blew lung-blackening smoke back at me, a dangerously shaky, overloaded car carrier on one side and a Bekins moving van on the other. Another behemoth was behind me, but all I could make out was a grill the size of a wall with a silver bulldog glaring down.

Before I maneuvered out from behind the Bekins van, I saw that it had a California license plate. Jesus . . . what I would give to be able to crawl into the back of that van and snuggle between mattresses as it headed for the West Coast—or anywhere but here.

Behind me was Manhattan, my penthouse with a park view and a lifestyle I might never see again. A thirtysomething woman with ambition and drive, I had ten good career years out of grad school with a master's in art history. Avoiding the safety net of academia, I had jumped with both feet into the cutthroat world where the superrich pay tens of millions for "priceless" art and antiquities.

What a wake-up call that was about human nature for a girl from backwater Ohio. That writer who said the rich were different didn't go far enough—the superrich were way different, far out. They lived in a rarified atmosphere of privilege, but often bored and eager for stimulation. And for reinforcement of their own accomplishments. It's hard to keep your ego swollen when you've never had to do anything but eat, breathe, shit, and sleep.

Buying something that no one else could possess was a way for them to flex muscles. The rarer, the more desirable. That turned the world of art into a playground—and battleground—for billionaires, an atmosphere even more ruthless than owning a champion race horse or a sports team. Money and ego have turned the quest for art into a ruthless business in which the superrich battled to possess the rarest and most beautiful objets d'art on Earth. Prices paid were stratospheric. The hundred- million-dollar mark for a painting by an artist most people would not recognize the name of had long since been surpassed.

When billionaire greed and egos collide, anything goes, at any price. And where mere money won't do the job, drugs, sex, and murder are used.

Yes, I saw some things a woman shouldn't see. Maybe I even did a few things a woman shouldn't do. Hard lessons. The Greeks thought highly of the concept of *pathos-mathos*—gaining wisdom through suffering. I wish to hell I'd gained insights with a little less damage to my life. If I only knew then what I knew now . . .

I sighed and melted down a little more in the seat. I was tired, beat, soul-weary. *Madison, you really know how to enjoy yourself.*

Madison Dupre. That's my name. My friends call me Maddy. But right now I had some openings on my list of friends.

LOST IN THOUGHT, gazing blankly as traffic moved, I got a blast from the bulldog truck's horn behind me and almost jumped out of the seat. I pressed the gas, sending the cheap little import surging a few dozen feet before I had to hit the brakes again to keep from rear-ending the tanker truck in front of me. Tight-jawed, I dropped my chin to my chest and told myself to stay calm. The grating horn had scorched my frayed nerves and made my heart pound like a jackhammer.

I was usually a calm person but I hated traffic, hated big trucks, and hated to be stuck in traffic with big trucks, breathing in their stinking fumes . . . when I desperately had to flee the city. My life was on the line and I was getting more agitated as the traffic slugged along.

I checked my rearview mirror as that monster rig closed in again until I could see only the massive front grille. If I was in my expensive sports car, I would have flipped him the bird despite constant reminders to myself not to antagonize anyone because road rage created roadkill. *Deal with it.* But being hemmed in gave me the sick feeling in my stomach that I was in a prison cell. I had already briefly experienced a jail cell at the federal detention center and that was enough for a lifetime.

I turned on the radio to hear traffic reports on the threes.

"Forty-five-minute delay for the GW out to Jersey."

I banged my hands on the steering wheel. I already knew it—hell, I was stuck in it, but hearing it made it worse. It took away hope.

Okay, think positive. Forty-five minutes wasn't so bad. It could be worse. The bridge could be closed even longer for an accident, bridge maintenance, someone being murdered . . .

The sick feeling in my stomach started again. They wouldn't try anything in front of hundreds of witnesses. I was sure of that. But not that sure. Only one thing was for certain: If they were behind me, they were stuck, too.

Get a hold of yourself, girl. My nerves were on edge, and crawling in this stop-and-go traffic didn't help the situation; it just fueled my frustration and paranoia.

I thought about my predicament as I sat in the stalled traffic. My life was in ruins, the police were looking for me, and on the seat beside me was something "priceless" that someone wanted very badly, enough to kill for it. And here I was stuck in traffic on the world's busiest bridge.

I had left my $85,000 XK Jaguar parked in a monthly garage, my $10,000-a-month penthouse, my designer wardrobe, and everything else I'd worked for back in the city to run from imminent danger. I hadn't taken my Jag because I figured I'd be less noticeable in a rental car. They probably also knew where the car was garaged. At least that was my theory.

The traffic started moving. I started to zip out of my lane and in front of the moving van, but my economy rental car didn't have enough horses. Another car zipped into the coveted space.

My mind went back to my problems. How could have I gotten myself in such a mess? I was basically an honest person, never involved in any trouble before. Now I'd gotten myself into trouble with a capital *T*. I had made a deal with the devil and he was coming to collect when I had only wanted to right a wrong.

Naïve, that's what I'd been. I thought ten years of big city and bright lights had made me as tough as the crowd I ran with, but the small town in me came percolating out when I saw greed that couldn't be satisfied with less than murder.

Another opportunity to change lanes arose and I pressed hard on the gas pedal. My Jag would have compressed me back into the seat with g-force but this car had the surge of a tortoise. The brakes of the car carrier made a horrible rusty squeal as the big rig rattled and shuddered to a stop behind me. At least the driver didn't lay on the horn.

I rolled down the window a few inches and stuck my hand out to wave "thanks for letting me in." When I checked my side-view mirror I saw his hand come out with his prominent third finger extended in my direction.

I didn't seem to be able to please anyone.

OFF THE GW bridge and on my way through Newark, I was exhausted and tired of traffic and trucks. I needed to get off the road for a while, get some rest, clear my head, and figure a way out of the mess. Only early evening, but I was too mentally drained to keep the car going.

A motel sign in the distance advertised "easy access" and

"cheap hourly rates." Hourly rates? Perfect. It didn't take much imagination to figure out what that meant. Nobody would think to look for me at an "adult" motel.

The motel was close to the freeway exit. It looked pretty much like what could be expected from the neon sign—two stories of tacky pink caked on like too much powder on a whore.

I took one look at the place and shook my head. *Oh, yes, how the mighty have fallen. . . .*

I was beginning to sound like a broken record even to myself.

Walking into the lobby confirmed that the motel was a sleazy dive for paid quickies, but I thought that a place that accommodated prostitutes and rented porn movies wouldn't be the kind of place to look for someone who lived in the Museum Mile area with a view of Central Park.

After I paid for the room, ignoring the lecherous look from the clerk and the hint that I should "tip him" if I planned to use my room for "business purposes," I walked past a condom machine, up the wood steps, and down the outside corridor to my room. I had the last room on the end, the one closest to the freeway. No surprise that the room reeked of cigarettes and store-bought sex. Both were popular vices.

I had asked for a second-floor room, as I always did after reading that it was a safer bet than a ground-floor motel room for a woman traveling alone. After I double-locked the door and wedged a chair under the door handle, I checked the big front sliding glass window. Unlatched, of course. I locked it.

The bedspread smelled as if it hadn't had sex washed off in a while, so I took it off and put my long coat on top of the bed sheets to lie on it. The sheets were the one thing in the room that got periodically washed, but I still didn't plan to use them; they rented the room by the hour, but that didn't mean they changed the bed sheets by the hour.

For a long time I half-sat, half-lay on the bed and stared up at brown water stains on the cottage cheese ceiling, thinking how capricious life was. One minute everything in your life is fine and the next minute you're roadkill. Life just wasn't fair sometimes. Bad things are supposed to happen to bad people, not good people. And I was not a bad person. At least, not *that* bad.

I closed my eyes but couldn't fall asleep—I had company. The sounds of their real and faked lust came through the common wall: the excited grunts of a john and the false cries of a whore. Naturally, the walls were paper thin.

The sound effects got more intense and their bed rocked against the wall with a frantic rhythm: *Grunt-bang-moan . . . grunt-bang-moan.* The woman's moans sounded as sincere as a sermon in a whorehouse.

Please God, make them climax. I resisted the impulse to pound on the wall and yell to the woman, *Goddamnit, fake your orgasm and get it over with.*

My body was shaking but it wasn't due to the vibration from the trucks that rumbled by or my neighbors' frenetic fury. Fear and disgust made me tremble. I had really screwed up my life . . . or, more accurately, someone else had screwed it up for me. I had just been a willing victim.

Flickering flashes from the tacky neon motel sign in the parking lot passed through the dirty window and dusty sheers to give life to the mask on the dresser across the room.

As I stared at the mask I sensed it was staring back. The golden death mask of a Babylonian queen from three thousand years ago, it was a valuable museum piece—over $50 million valuable.

After the greatest warrior-queen of antiquity died, the mask was prepared by taking a mold of the queen's face. Over the centuries, it had gained repute as a harbinger of misfortune to the possessor. Strangely, that drove up its value.

People attached value to evil: The Hope Diamond rests in the Smithsonian not only for its size, but because of the bad luck—and death—it brought to its possessors. Hell, Hollywood made a cottage industry out of revenging mummies after archeologist Howard Carter broke into King Tut's tomb in the 1920s and eleven people connected with the project had died of unnatural causes within a period of five years.

The vibrant mask staring at me from the dresser also carried a legacy of murder and lust across the millenniums. I had grown to hate it.

I wasn't sure how long I gazed at the cursed mask before I finally closed my eyes. But my sleep was interrupted by a nightmare.

I dreamed I was asleep on an iron cot in the corner of a large room that had cold, bare, gray concrete walls. My cell phone started to ring, and I fumbled around on the cot trying to find the little phone in the layers of brown Army blankets. A man suddenly appeared beside me in the darkness. I didn't recognize him.

He bent down and said in a whisper, "You shouldn't be in here alone."

The irritating cell phone kept ringing. Why couldn't I find it?

Finally, my brain registered that my cell phone was actually ringing in the room. I sat up. Coming out of a deep sleep with a sense of dread, I looked around for the stranger, but I was alone. The dream seemed so real.

I got up and checked the door and the window.

My cell phone started ringing again. I followed the sound to my handbag on the table. As I fumbled with the handbag, the phone fell on the floor and bounced under the bed. I got down on my hand and knees in the dark to retrieve it. By the time I got the phone in hand and flipped it open, the ringing had stopped and the face plate registered 1 MISSED CALL.

I hesitated to check my voice mail, wondering if it was a trick to trace my location. Curiosity got the better of me. I went ahead and accessed it. The message was simple. A man's voice said, "Maddy, it's me. I'll catch you later."

I recognized the voice. It raised the short hairs on my soul.

I hit the repeat key to listen to it again—and again.

I couldn't understand how he had called me.

He was dead.